A CLAWS AND FANGS COLLECTION

INTERNATIONAL BESTSELLING AUTHOR

SARAH SPADE

Cover by Francesca of Merry Book Round

CLAWS AND FANGS BOOK FOUR

# HINT OF HER BLOOD

SARAH SPADE

INTERNATIONAL BESTSELLING AUTHOR

CLAWS AND FANGS BOOK FOUR

SARAH SPADE

INTERNATIONAL BESTSELLING AUTHOR

Cover by JoY Design Studio

# FOREWORD

Thank you for checking out *Hint of Her Blood*!

It might be the fourth book in the **Claws and Fangs** series, but it can also stand as an entry point to this universe since it features a new couple than the previous books. Aleks was an important part of Gem's story, but Elizabeth only made her first appearance in book three, *Forever Mates*.

Now it's her turn to take over as narrator, but if you haven't read the first three books, you can start here and go back to see what happened between Gem and Ryker. Gem's story begins with *Never His Mate*, or you can buy/borrow *Never Say Never*, a collection that features all three books with Gem as the narrator.

As a side note, there are a few passages in this book where the characters are speaking in another language. For example, Aleks speaks Polish, Dominic some French, and Roman is Russian. Because this story is told in Elizabeth's POV, there aren't many translations given in the text, though—like previous times

Aleks speaks Polish—you can get more insight into this character if you look up what it means :)

Also, in this book, I made a conscious stylistic choice not to use the Russian alphabet for when Roman speaks in his native language during his dialogue. This way the reader can get a better idea of what Elizabeth heard. Just in case you wonder later on in the book, I wanted to put a small note right up front.

Enjoy, and I'm so excited to introduce you to the inner workings of Elizabeth and her Luna-touched wolf!

*xoxo,*
*Sarah*

# CHAPTER 1
# DING DONG, THE WOLF IS GONE

The Western Pack is no more.

Its Alpha is gone, the blond bastard running to plot and plan and fight another day. The Wolf District is quickly becoming an abandoned territory as all of my former packmates follow his lead; some chasing at his heels, others running as far and as fast in the opposite direction as they can. Before long it won't be safe for a lone wolf to linger on this suddenly unclaimed land, but that realization doesn't do anything to change my mind.

I'm not leaving until I find my treasured cards.

Two years ago, when I first arrived on his territory, Jack Walker decided that I wouldn't need them anymore. In the district, the Alpha provided for all of his packmates. We had food and shelter, plus a barter system for goods. The cards might've been my only way to earn human money while I was a lone wolf, but none of his shifters used currency. And if his insistence that I turn the only possession I held dear over to him was a red flag wagging in front of me and my wolf, I ignored it because I had been so desperate just to belong to another pack.

Even if the previous two times had ended in disaster, I held out hope that the third time would be the charm.

Oh, Luna, was I wrong about *that*.

The Wicked Wolf took my cards because he could. Because he expected obedience, that no one would ever deny him anything. He took my cards because he wanted to make it harder for me to leave, and even when I accepted that I never could, he kept them if only to remind me just how much power he held over me.

He was the Alpha, and I... I was *other*. I didn't fit anywhere in the pack's hierarchy, and he never let me forget it. I lived only due to his insistence that I would one day take him as my mate. Even when I found the nerve to refuse him, he declared that my special skills belonged to him alone. If he couldn't have me as a chosen mate, then he'd have me as his pet.

For two years, I was just that—until a couple of days ago. Until the Wicked Wolf lost his first ever Alpha challenge and, as a result, lost control of his pack.

I'm free. After so long spent locked in his gilded cage, I can start all over again without the threat of his rough hands, his demands, and his lecherous leer hanging over my head. Maybe, this time, I'll find a pack where they won't discover what I can never quite conceal from other shifters. Or maybe I'll go back to living as a lone wolf, hiding my supe status as I try to exist alongside humans.

I've done it before. I can do it again.

I just need my cards first.

The district is eerily empty. It's only been a little more than forty-eight hours since the Alpha abandoned his territory and already it seems as if the entire pack has disappeared. My ears strain, searching for a hint of another soul as I jog along the wooded border of the main square. Nothing. I'm not that surprised. Gemma and her mate—Henry Wolfson's only pup—left at sun-up this morning. Without the two alphas' presence, the lesser dominant shifters wouldn't stick around.

I should be gone, too. It's not safe here for me—and not just because of my rank in the pack. Gem and Ryker left, taking another pair of Mountainside packmates with them, but that was all.

Which meant that *he* might be long gone, or he could still be somewhere near.

Giving my head a clearing shake, I pour on the speed. As my jog becomes a sprint, I know it's not just my memories of Walker I'm trying to outrun. If the last two years of being his pet weren't bad enough, this last week alone has been awful and all because of *him*.

Just get the cards, Elizabeth, I tell myself. If they're still in the district, if the Alpha hasn't already gotten rid of them, there's only one place that they'll be. And though I swore to myself that I'd never willingly enter his cabin again, I have to. In the human world, I'll need money. Simple as that. I'll need food and a roof over my head and to get as far away from California as I can. A lone wolf rarely settles down, and though there are other ways I can make a few bucks, I learned a long time ago that my best bet is tarot.

Thanks to my eerie silver gaze and my Luna-given instincts, I don't have to be a true cartomancer. A diviner. *Fortune-teller*. With my weathered tarot cards in hand and a haunted expression, human customers have never doubted my readings. As long as I haven't lost my touch these last couple of years, I'll be able to survive on my own until I figure out what comes next.

Claws crossed.

Now, I don't know what I'm expecting when I make it to the Alpha's cabin. After packing up everything I plan on taking with me when I go, I waited until sundown to make the play for my cards. You'd have to be an idiot—or really, really desperate—to run around an unclaimed shifter territory after dark. Not only is it a magnet to ferals and other scavengers, but it's almost like putting out a welcome mat for the most dangerous kind of supes.

*Vampires.*

Despite what pop culture says, our ancient enemy isn't weakened by daylight. With the right amount of sunblock, vampires can walk in the sun. But at night... at night is when they're at their strongest.

And it's already well-past sunset.

Make it quick. In and out.

I can do this.

As I slow my run to a quickened walk, I take a deep breath, sampling the scents on the slight breeze. The moon is only beginning to wane again after being full a few nights ago, and she sheds enough light that my shifter's eyes can see everything. For the moment, at least, I'm alone.

Thank the Luna.

With a bit of a hitch in my breath, I head right for the back door to the Alpha's cabin; even knowing that the Wicked Wolf is gone can't keep me from avoiding the front. The knob turns easily under my hand. Of course. No one in the district ever locked their doors, and with his power and his reputation, the Alpha wouldn't think twice about leaving an entrance to his cabin open. Why, when anyone and everyone who dared come inside without an invitation would end up another victim in the pit, fighting for their lives?

I don't bother with turning on the light. It would just be a beacon to my presence if anyone else is still around. Besides, there are windows enough that my goddess is guiding me almost as much as my wolf.

I'm doing as well as can be expected. It's not as easy as I hoped, walking around this cabin again... my skin was already crawling even before I entered in through the back door. My poor wolf was whining at me to stay away the whole time I was running, to heed the layers and layers of warnings in the territorial markings that surrounded the towering structure, retreating deep inside of me as I pushed past them.

She doesn't understand why I'm so attached to a particular set of tarot cards. And I know that I could "read" palms as easily as my cards, but that's not the point. I've carried that deck with me for more than a decade, ever since I left my home pack when I was barely eighteen, and I'll regret it if I don't at least *try* to find them.

Gulping back my discomfort, I close my eyes. Two years is a long time for a scent to cling to a worn deck of cards, but I'm not just searching for a hint of my scent. I don't own much—I haven't since I left my home pack—but anything that I've imprinted on doesn't just carry my scent on it. Courtesy of my "gift", it bears the mark of the Luna.

My eyes spring open. It's faint, but it's there. Somewhere above my head, I can sense her power.

Without even a second thought, I go after it. Though my hackles are up, my wolf reminding me that I shouldn't be here in the Alpha's cabin, I ignore my growing unease as I go. It's so different from the single-floor, two-room cabin I've called mine up until recently, and I can't help but peer around me as I look for the stairs.

The only time I've ever been inside his cabin before now was about a week after I stumbled onto the hidden territory. I'd known him as Jack Walker, Alpha of the Western Pack, then; it wasn't until much later that I realized he was the infamous Wicked Wolf of the West. Forever on the run, I'd needed community. Safety. Security. He'd offered all that and more when he said I could stay in the Wolf District instead of being kicked back out—or worse, I discovered later. Still naively trusting that an Alpha who ruled over hundreds of devoted packmates meant that he was *good*, I jumped at the chance.

Silly, Elizabeth. I should've known better by then that anything that seemed too good to be true often was.

When I agreed to join the pack, he told me to come to his cabin. That he had details he wanted to discuss with me.

He invited me into a spartan kitchen. I thought it was because the Alpha had no need to cook. Nope. Unfortunately, I was wrong about that, too; when it came to Jack Walker, I was wrong about a lot. In a reversal of how true packs work, he demanded that his packmates tend to *him*, cooking every meal for the Alpha while he lorded over his table in the district square.

Food has always had a special meaning to us shifters. So what if he hadn't prepared it himself? He told me to sit at his table, giving me food to eat. I knew then that I was in big, big trouble. That night was the first time he proposed a partnership. I didn't have a mate. His fated mate was bonded to another male. Why shouldn't we choose each other?

I stammered and stumbled and thought of any excuse to

keep from accepting the meal—and his unexpected proposal. I hadn't known then that he was well aware that my unusual eyes meant I was Luna-touched; I'd only seen it as the most powerful wolf in the pack wanted to bond with me. It was much easier to refuse his offer once he admitted he knew the truth, but though he eventually conceded that I wouldn't be his mate, being his pet... it wasn't any better.

At least I didn't have to join him in his cabin. Like with any pack, the Alpha's cabin was reserved for his mate. Jack Walker made lovers of nearly every female in the pack, but always in their home. In fact, I think I might be one of only a few who ever set paw inside of the cabin at all.

It's not just the kitchen that is empty. His whole cabin is like that. Probably because he thought of every home in the district as an extension of his, staying with his lover of the hour before finding another to satisfy his substantial appetites.

We're shifters. We fight and we fuck, and the Wicked Wolf did more of both than any male I've ever met. Even if I wanted a mate, I never could've tamed him. He would've been the death of me.

Honestly, he still might be.

Our laws are clear: an Alpha that loses a challenge is no Alpha. Without a pack to lead, Walker's vicious wolf will be looking for a way to regain control, to continue his cause. How much do you want to bet he'll be looking for a Luna-touched female to conceal his scent to do so? To threaten his enemies with the one thing we all hold dear?

He'll be coming for me. I failed him when he needed me the most, and if I've learned anything about Walker these last two years, he's going to make me pay for it.

Gritting my teeth, trying to ignore just how creepy his empty cabin is, I follow the trace of the Luna up the stairs and down the hall. I'm not surprised when I ease open the door and see the giant bed taking up much of the space. It reeks of the Alpha's musk, but no one else. Just like I thought, he kept all of the females he took out of his cabin.

That makes this a little easier. Against his dark scent, the brightness of the Luna is like a true beacon.

Next to the bed, there's a tall obsidian nightstand that gleams despite the shadows in his room. If they're anywhere, my cards are in there.

On the wall, hanging over the nightstand, I see a massive framed picture. I can't tell if it's a painting or a blown-up photo—or what it's of, actually, since the picture has been slashed to the point it's nearly in tatters. Though my wolf is spurring me to get this over with, I can't stop myself from grabbing the largest piece of torn canvas.

It's a painting, I discover. Of a pretty brunette with golden eyes and a kind smile. And though I've never met her before, I know exactly who this must be: Janelle Booker, the Wicked Wolf's fated mate who rejected him in favor of another Alpha before she was forever bonded to him.

That was twenty-five years ago. Now, Walker is no romantic. He's ruthless and cruel, and if he has a painting of his former mate on the wall of his bedroom, it's only because he gets a kick out of slashing it with his claws.

That's the kind of male I have to avoid. I dodged the bullet of being forced into a mating with him, but I'd be a fool if I thought he'd let me go.

With my abilities, he never will. And if my instincts are right, he's not the only one...

Another shake. Rougher than the one before if only because

I'm running out of time. I've been in here too long, and I don't even have my cards yet.

The nightstand has two drawers. I tug on the first one, gagging when my shifter's sight picks up on the distinct white pieces inside of it.

It's a drawerful of teeth.

No. Not teeth.

Fangs. *Vampire* fangs.

As I stare down at them in surprise mingled with horror, I can't help but think back to the strange conversation I had with the former Alpha's daughter yesterday. Before Gem left the district, she tried to convince me to follow her and her Alpha mate back East.

Yeah, *no*. I tried that once before. It hadn't worked.

She didn't push when I refused. As if sensing how skittish my wolf is these days, she gave me her phone number after explaining that she had a couple of options for me. I could join the Mountainside Pack in Accalia, or even stay at her personally owned townhouse in the nearby city of Muncie.

For some reason, she seemed very interested in getting me to agree to visit her in the Fang City. And not just her, either.

*Him*.

Still reeling over how I broke my promise to her, my first instinct had been to thank her, but immediately pass on her offer. She was still determined, though, and as I made my escape, she had called after me, mentioning *his* name.

Aleksander. The fierce yet beautiful vampire that I still can't get out of my head.

She'd said, "If Aleks offers you his fang—"

"His *what*?" It had come out as a squeal. I couldn't help it.

She grinned. "You'll see. *When* he does, do me a favor? Make him explain, but then take it." With a glimmer in her golden eyes, Gem had promised, "You won't regret it."

I'd had no idea what to say to that, so I didn't say anything. I couldn't understand why she thought Aleks—Walker's captive, and Gem's good friend from back East—would give me a fang of all things, but now that I'm looking at a drawer full of them...

I grab a handful, shoving them into the front pocket of my jeans. After closing the drawer, I yank on the second. A sigh of relief escapes when I see the familiar design of the wooden box I've always kept my cards in. Then, because I don't trust the Wicked Wolf at all, I slide it open, double-checking that it isn't empty.

Thank the Luna, it's not. Quickly, I jam the box in my back pocket. It's a tight fit, but I manage.

That done, I slam the second drawer closed before dashing from the room. I've gotten what I came here for—plus more—and now it's time to get my packed bag and get out of the district before it's too late.

With my cards in my pocket, I'm more reckless than I should be. I'm careful while tiptoeing back downstairs, just in case anyone followed me into the Alpha's cabin, but once I'm outside again, I exhale softly.

"Elizabeth?"

I choke on my next inhale.

My mistake. I didn't pay attention to my surroundings as I slipped out of the back again, or even use my nose to see if anyone was lurking nearby.

A dark-haired male moves out of the trees, loping toward the cabin before I can shift or bolt.

It's Brendan. A delta wolf, and one of Walker's soldiers. What is he doing here?

"Elizabeth... I didn't know you were still in the district. I thought everyone was gone."

"So did I," I murmur, trying to calm my suddenly racing heart. To another shifter, it must sound like a beating drum.

It'll also sound like *weakness*.

He doesn't say anything about me stepping out of the cabin, even though it's obvious that that's where I just came from.

Instead, he gives me a boyish grin that doesn't do much to help my nerves as he stares down at me in a way that has my wolf on her guard.

"I'm glad you haven't yet—and I'm glad I saw you tonight when I was getting ready to head out. I mean, I know it's not fate, not really, but it sure seems like it. Don't you think?"

What does that mean, I wonder before answering him with a non-committal, "Oh?"

"Well, yeah. The Luna as my witness, I've been working toward approaching you for a while. It just never seemed like the right time because of your pack status. Now, if I don't, I'll never get another chance and that just doesn't sit right with my wolf."

Uh-oh. I think I know where this is going.

*Great*.

To make it worse, Brendan says his showing up at the cabin isn't fate. To my suspicious wolf, that just means that he arranged this meeting. Did he stalk me across the district? Why in the Luna's name would he do that? I think I've said maybe three words to Brendan in the two years I've been in the Wolf District, but the look he's giving me...

I keep my expression friendly even as I fight the urge to turn tail and run. "Talk to me? About what?"

His golden eyes darken just a touch. Lust is a sudden slick

coating the night air. Even before he begins to explain, I know my earlier suspicions were correct.

That doesn't stop Brendan. Taking a few steps closer to me, careful as if he can tell that my wolf is different, is *other*, and can be either skittish or brutal... he approaches like I'm a wounded wolf caught in a trap.

In so many ways, I *am*.

"You were always so protected by the Alpha," he says softly, "and when he didn't claim you as his, I thought maybe... maybe you were free to be claimed by another. Willing, too. I was hoping to tell you that my wolf was interested in yours, but then there was Theo..." Lifting his hand, he runs his fingers through his shaggy, dark brown hair. His claws leave track marks in the thick strands. "Well, after what happened with him, he's out of the running. But maybe... maybe I could be. In it, I mean. 'Cause I know we have to go. If you want, maybe we could head out together."

His voice is gentled. Soothing. The lust, though? It's as dark as the look in his eyes.

Why do I get the idea that, if I say no, he'll follow behind me anyway?

This is just my luck. Is this why he's still hanging around the district even though it seems like everyone else is already gone? Using my wolf's instinct, I guess he seems earnest enough, like he really means it. Like he really wants me to choose him.

And while I have to admit that my wolf assures me that he's no danger to either of us, I never would've guessed he had any interest in me. I have no idea where any of this is coming from, especially after what happened the last couple of days.

A couple years younger than my twenty-nine, Brendan was born and raised to serve his Alpha. Since coming of age at eighteen, he's been a loyal soldier to the Wicked Wolf's cause. He would never make a move on me if he thought I had his Alpha's eye.

And Theo...

I don't know if you'd call it a blessing or a curse, but my "gift" doesn't just allow me to break bonds. It also gives me an insight when one might be possible. Not all mates are fated, and if a chosen pairing has potential, I can feel it like a chilled whisper on the back of my neck.

I've known of Theodore Michaels for almost as long as I've been in the Wolf District. He was the odd alpha who was submissive enough to serve another devotedly, a position that saved his hide as Beta after Beta failed the Alpha of the Western Pack. He survived, rising to the highest ranks within the pack. Whenever Walker was between Betas, he used Theo as his errand boy, so I got to know him pretty well since he was often the one sent to drag me in front of the Alpha whenever he had need of me.

While Brendan's interest is undeniably genuine, Theo barely seemed to notice I was a female. I'd thought it was because I made the Wicked Wolf believe that I *couldn't* have a bond with another male, so why would any wolf in his inner circle pay any attention to me as more than his pet?

In fact, never once did Theo turn his fake smile and calculating eyes on me—until a couple of months ago when the rumors of Ruby Walker still being alive began to wind their way through the Western Pack and, suddenly, I could be of use to him.

Ruby Walker... only that isn't her name anymore, is it?

Gemma Swann. The female alpha who threatened to gut me if I did anything to the bond she had with her beloved mate.

The same Gem who forgave me when her father ordered me to do just that, if only because I hadn't been able to.

Gem and Ryker's bond is both fated and unbreakable. The Luna blessed them, and not even my touch could break them apart. Still, I had to try because the Alpha commanded me to, and it was impossible to refuse him.

She threatened to gut me, but the Wicked Wolf? He would've done way worse.

Theo wanted Gem. He never wanted *me;* like the Alpha, he just wanted what I could do for him. If I used my ability to break her bond with Ryker, then Theo could attempt to claim her for himself. But too eager to make her his, he couldn't wait. He challenged Ryker Wolfson, and he lost.

Then Gem challenged her father. He lost, too, though she showed mercy at the end. Theo is dead while Jack Walker lives on.

I already have him to worry about. Brendan's proposal is a complication that I don't need.

And that's not all...

His scent reaches me before I see him. Brendan's considerable bulk shielded him from my sight, but once I pick up on that icy, chilly aura, I shift to the side, looking past the shifter to spy the vampire in the not-too-far distance.

How long has he been there? Where did he come from?

And, most importantly, what is he doing here?

I should've expected this. When he didn't leave with Gem and her packmates, I told myself it was because he fled as soon as she freed him from the cage that the Alpha had thrown him in. Why would a captive vampire want to stick around any longer than he had to? I had thought he might already be on the trail of the Wicked Wolf, looking for his revenge.

But he isn't. He's here, towering in the distance, watching me so closely, I can't stifle my shiver.

I slip my shaky hand with its trembling fingers into my pocket, searching for the fangs. Squeezing them against my palm, I pray to the Luna that they give me some level of protection against the hungry look in the vampire's blood-red gaze.

There isn't much I know about the bloodthirsty supernaturals, but even I understand that the red eyes are a warning sign. Vampires, as a race, all have light eyes—until their thirst takes over and their irises turn red.

And unless he's had a meal since Gemma ran the Alpha off two days ago, he has to be very, very thirsty.

If I'm being honest, though, fear of his bite isn't what has me staring back at him, unable to look away. Taking in his beautiful form isn't, either, though Luna knows he's gorgeous even after a week of captivity.

The moon shines down, illuminating his sculpted features. His hair is tousled in soft-looking caramel-colored curls, the tips of his fangs peeking over his lush bottom lip. Strangely enough, his hands are clenched into tight fists at his side while his expensive-looking shirt is still riddled with bullet holes.

He's not only gorgeous. He's awe-inspiring.

And he's supposed to be *mine*.

Brendan falls away; he's still standing in front of me, but it's like he doesn't exist at all. At that moment, it's just me and a vampire who looks at me like he knows me—and who I instinctively recognize in return.

*Yours*, whispers the Luna.

*Mine*, I agree—

No. *No*.

Never.

I'm a wolf shifter. He's a bloodsucker. I'm damaged goods, and he... well, according to Gem, he has his own baggage, doesn't he?

Like the fact that the Alpha of my pack had him captured, shot repeatedly, caged, then forced to fight for his life.

Is that what he's doing here now? Vampires don't worship the Luna like shifters do. Even if I recognize who he's supposed to be to me, there's no guarantee that he feels the same. For all I know, he's been haunting the district, attacking any of us who stayed behind before targeting our former Alpha.

The murderous look he shoots Brendan makes me suspect I'm not too far off base with that thought.

Swallowing roughly, I tear my gaze away from him. Mumbling some excuse to Brendan, I purposely turn my back on both males. My wolf yips, telling me that I should go to *him*. When I refuse, she goes silent.

It's better this way, I tell her. If he really thought of us as his mate, he would be moving toward us instead of gliding away again.

Which he is.

I reach out with my senses, subtly sniffing the air. An electric pulse courses through my body, fading as his presence does. His lingering scent hangs on the breeze, but it's only a tease.

When I look behind me again, he's gone. Brendan, too, but I barely notice his absence.

Oh, no. Just like my wolf, I'm only concerned with the vampire, but he's gone.

And if I'm lucky, I'll never see him again.

# CHAPTER 2
# SNOWY DAYS IN THE FANG CITY

## FIVE MONTHS LATER

Does it ever stop snowing in Muncie?

Letting the curtain slip from my fingers, I sigh.

My bedroom overlooks the back of the townhouse. I've learned that, depending on the wind, snow piles up faster out there. Considering there have been more wintry days than not since I moved here, there was a good four or five inches already out back. After today's storm? There are probably another three more.

I'm quickly becoming sick of it—and it's only February 3rd. Yesterday was Groundhog Day. The furry little rodent supposedly didn't see his shadow so that means that we should have an early spring.

I really freaking hope so.

I'm a West Coast female. As a shifter, my fur coat is a part of me. The winter chill doesn't affect me the same way it does the humans, but I'm used to living in California. It was nice to see snow at first, but if I never did again, that would be perfectly fine, too.

It's been snowing since early morning. I keep hoping it will stop since, for the first time in days, I actually have plans to leave the townhouse.

It hasn't.

*Ugh*.

Out of habit, I cross the bedroom and pick up my tarot deck, absently shuffling the familiar worn cards. Since I arrived in the Fang City two weeks ago, I haven't had to use them. As a welcome gift, Gem stocked the refrigerator and cabinets with food, telling me she was paying me back for the food she ate from my kitchen during her stay in the Wolf District so that I wouldn't feel a certain way about the younger female trying to feed me. As if I would. If I was already accepting shelter from her, I'd only be spiting myself—and my wolf—if I refused the food.

I don't know how many strings she pulled so that I could live among the vampires. Plenty, I'm sure. A Fang City is supposed to be as tight-knit and protective of a community as a shifter pack, only for vampires instead. As a shifter—the vampire race's ancient supe enemy—I decided not to risk provoking them. Just in case, I've been choosing to stay inside of my own personal territory whenever I could.

It's the first time in forever that I've actually had a permanent address. I'm going to enjoy it for as long as it lasts.

For five months, I traveled all across the country, never settling in one place for long in case the Wicked Wolf sniffed me out. I haven't been able to forget how he threatened to go to the Alpha collective about me. If I betrayed him, if I ever tried to leave his pack, he would tell them that I was an abomination. He promised I'd be put down, and even though Gem tried to convince me that they would understand I'm not to blame for my abilities, I've always made other supes uneasy.

I hate to see what vampires would do if they realized what I was, and what I'm capable of. And if I used that as an excuse to reject Gemma's offer of a place to stay over and over again since our time together in the Wolf District, I'd rather cling to that than the real reason I stayed away from the East Coast for so long.

By December, though, I... I just couldn't do it anymore. It was harder to find tourists who wanted a street performer to read tarot cards for them during the holidays, and the overwhelming loneliness that settled over me while I was on the run became unbearable.

My wolf wanted her mate, and I wanted to pretend I never discovered that Aleksander Filan was fated to be mine.

I celebrated Christmas in a roach-infested motel, the only type I could afford. By January, I was spending more and more time in my fur when the last of my money ran out. Then, one day, I swore I picked up something on a whisper of a breeze. A scent that made my wolf keen and my heart sing. Looking back, I'm sure it was an olfactory hallucination, but I'd lost all will to fight my other half sometime around the middle of January.

I called Gem, and I accepted her offer. Within days, she gave me the okay. I moved into the townhouse that Ryker Wolfson gave her as a mating gift two weeks ago with a single duffel bag stuffed with my belongings, a pocketful of vampire fangs, my tarot deck, and a determination that I wouldn't track down my mate.

I didn't have to.

He found *me*.

Of all supes, vampires have a distinctive scent. It's a mixture between meat and the icy chill of death, but it's not… unpleasant. Maybe it's because, deep down, I'm a predator, it doesn't really bother me. Of course, because of the way shifters are wired, scenting a vampire is enough to put our backs up. You sniff a vampire, you know that there's a threat.

When I scent Aleks, I'm in even more trouble.

That night outside of the Alpha's cabin in the Wolf District was the last time I've seen him. But, the morning after I moved into the townhouse, I started noticing something on the sidewalk out front. Thanks to the snow, it's impossible to hide every and all tracks, and no matter if it's slushy, crusty, or freshly fallen powder, when I wake up in the morning, there's a pair of footprints positioned perfectly before my door, as if someone has stood guard like a sentinel over me as I slept.

At first, I refused to believe it. But that's the thing when it comes to being a shifter. The footprints make it easy to tell that someone's been there, but I don't need them. His scent lingers, so I know exactly who watches me.

It's the same scent that I still want to believe I imagined in a dry forest in Arizona.

Aleks.

He knows I'm a shifter. My nose might not be as strong as some others, but I'd have to be completely stuffed up to miss the way his scent hovers inside of my own territorial markers.

He's a vampire. From what I understand, his own keen senses would have noticed that my markers are so very different than Gem's were. Even if he doesn't know it's *me* living here, it's sure as hell not Gem.

So the footprints? I decided a week ago that they were deliberate. They have to be. Though he's never made it a point to meet me face to face, he's stopped by my townhouse every night since I arrived, and he wants me to *know* that.

Too bad I have no idea what to make of his intentions. If he was a wolf, I'd understand, but he's a vampire. For all I know, it could be a threat.

I tried to be suave. Casual. Anytime I spoke to Gem, I made it seem like an afterthought before I inevitably mentioned Aleks. It was almost as if I was incapable of forgetting about him, and considering their history, she was the only one I could talk to about him.

I learned that he wasn't just an unlucky vampire who got caught along the edge of the district. He was her former roommate, one of her closest friends, and he was in California because Ryker asked him to keep Gem safe while she was matching wits with the Wicked Wolf. When cornered, he could be a vicious killer, but he spoke six languages fluently, wore a pair of glasses when he read his favored thrillers in paperback form, and was one of the most respected vampires in all of Muncie.

And, five months after I first laid eyes on him, the Luna is still whispering insistently that he's my mate—though he's made no move to let me know that he feels any kind of pull toward me in return.

The only way I could deal with knowing he was watching me was by convincing myself that it was a security thing. A member of the Cadre, of course he'd want to make sure that the unfamiliar shifter in their territory wasn't a threat to anyone else.

Especially since he knows I came from the Western Pack. It might be disbanded now, but its reputation is still alive and kicking. For all I know, Aleks thinks I'm just as sadistic as the Wicked Wolf.

Of course he's keeping a careful eye on me.

Right?

This afternoon is no different. Though the snow covers his tracks from last night, I can still make out the vague dips where the new snow piled up on the old snow before filling in the center of his footprint.

His scent is faded, but undeniable. Feeling silly but unable to stop myself, I breathe in deep as I pass his stationed spot after I head out into the lingering flurries. The only way to get to the downtown area where I can find Charlie's is by walking right by it. Besides, I don't want him to think that he's the reason why I rarely leave the townhouse.

At least, not the *only* reason...

I'd known for a while that this was something I would have to do. I might not be able to use my tarot cards to make money, but Gem did me another favor by contacting the vampire owner of the supe bar where she worked for a year before moving permanently to Accalia, the mountain settlement where her pack lives. Charlie was always looking for new help, and he got along great with Gem. All I needed to do was go down to the bar tonight when he was actually there, talk to him about the job, and hopefully I won't have to worry about how I'm going to support myself in Muncie any longer.

I've been worried for days now. My meager savings is long gone, and though I don't need much, I'm pretty sure stealing is frowned upon in the Fang City.

I need a job.

As I scurry, careful not to slip on the slick snow since I didn't have any boots to put on, I bow my head against the wind; the cold doesn't bother me, but the snow stinging my eyes is freaking annoying. On the plus side, I do have a coat and a scarf on to help me hide out among the humans. My hood is pulled over my hair, tugged as low as possible to cover the way my silver eyes seem to reflect the snowflakes.

Last thing I need is a human to notice and start staring. They're everywhere in the Fang City. Obviously. I mean, vampires have got to eat, don't they?

I don't bother hiding from them, though. No matter what, they—like all other supes—can sense there is something different about me. Not just that I'm a shifter, either, but *other*.

Case in point? A towering vampire who is walking out of Charlie's just as I'm approaching the bar.

It has the owner's name stenciled on the window, so I know I've found the right place, but I was too busy looking at it to notice that the glass door was being pulled open, a vampire stalking out into the snow.

We don't quite touch, though that has more to do with his reflexes than mine.

Even beneath the white sky, I see his eyes flash, going from an almost icy blue to a deep red. Ducking my head even further, shielding my odd silver gaze, I tamp down my own innate scent. While I wouldn't say being Luna-touched has a ton of perks—the Luna pops into my head like an unwelcome conscience at the weirdest of times, and having the power to snap mate bonds makes me an outcast among my kind—being able to conceal my scent is one of them.

He does a double-take, shaking his head, then continues walking down the street.

I slip inside, grateful that I made it to the bar without any real incident.

Shaking the snow off, I pull my hood down, glancing around. Gem told me that Charlie rarely spent time out on the floor so I should look for a human bartender named Hailey instead. She would smell like a mixture of blood, vampire, and vanilla, but if the overwhelming scents surrounding the bar were too much, I should look for a vampire bite on a pretty brunette.

Her description is spot-on. Almost immediately the dark-haired human female standing behind the counter—wearing a half-healed vampire bite on her throat like a badge of honor—looks up, almost as if she was expecting me.

She comes rushing out from behind the bar. "Hi there. I'm Hailey. You must be Elizabeth."

As she grabs my hand, I stiffen. I'm not used to other people touching me. My packmates would never dare, and the customers I often did tarot readings for always kept their distance.

But she's friendly enough, and I don't want to give off a bad first impression if she's going to be my co-worker so I don't say anything as she tells me that Charlie is already waiting for me in their storeroom behind the bar.

Hailey leads me there, pointing out the door I need to take, then returns to talking to one of the customers at the bar.

Praying to the Luna that this goes well, I let myself in.

Most vampires appear ageless, but Charlie is one of those odd ones who turned late in life and must've stubbornly kept their grump. There's no other way to explain it. He's got a thick middle, a deep scowl, and eyes that are a muted brown. I don't get the feeling that the scowl is for me. Charlie is just one of those people who looks pissed off at the world no matter what.

I offer him a wave. "Hi. I'm Elizabeth."

"Come on in."

I try not to be too nervous as I walk into the cramped room. A massive fridge stands across from me, a desk in one corner, and shelves full of all kinds of supplies take up two of the four walls.

Gem assured me that this is just a formality. She vouched for me with her old boss and her co-workers, and so long as I didn't screw this up too badly, the job is mine.

There are two folding chairs set up in the middle of the space. Charlie is sitting in one. He points to the other.

I sit down.

"So, Gem tells me that you're a friend of hers."

Huh. I guess I am. "Yes."

"And you need a job."

"Yes," I say again. That one is way more emphatic.

"Okay. Let's talk about what I expect from my employees. I'll ask you a couple of questions to make sure you're a good fit. Then we'll go from there. What do you think?"

I swallow back my nerves. "Sounds good."

"Great."

For the next ten minutes Charlie does just that. It's very informal, and I see exactly what Gem meant when she said that I didn't have to be nervous. He might be the owner, but he's not the type to micromanage. He wants a team that knows what they're doing and doesn't cause any problems for him.

In the middle of his explaining exactly what hours he's looking to fill, his nostrils flare a split second before there's a rap at the door.

He doesn't even have to ask who it is. He just calls out, "Come in, Tony."

A human male pokes his head in. "Hey, boss. You busy?"

The vampire's gaze flickers over to me. "I'm in the middle of an interview. Got someone to take over Gem's spot. Why? What is it?"

"One of the Cadre wants to speak with you."

"Who?"

"Zakharov's right-hand man."

Charlie doesn't even hesitate. "Tell him I'll be right out."

Now, I'm not too well-versed in vampire politics. All I know is that the Cadre controls Muncie. They're in charge of keeping the peace—and, for the most part, the secret of supernaturals—and they protect everyone who lives in the Fang City. Made up of the most powerful vampires in Muncie, they uphold the laws and protect the citizens from any outside threats.

The main way they do this is through patrols. Most vampires and humans have a free pass to come and go from the city, but non-vampire supes like me aren't allowed at all. For twenty-four hours a day, the Cadre employs dedicated vampires who do constant perimeter checks, making sure that no threats breach the borders.

The vampires all respect those who are part of the Cadre. If one of their number is here to talk to Charlie, that definitely trumps my interview with him.

After telling me to sit tight, that he'll be right back, he heads back out into the bar.

I sit anxiously on the edge of my seat as I wait for him to return, grateful that this is just a formality.

# CHAPTER 3
# SUMMONED BY ROMAN

Some formality.

Charlie finishes the "interview" about five minutes after he finally comes back into the backroom. I don't even know why he bothers. There are no more questions, just half-hearted excuses why he doesn't think I'm a good fit for the bar. Cheeks flaming from the rejection, I just nod along, barely listening as he stands up from his chair.

Automatically, I rise. He tells me that he'll keep me in mind, and if another position opens up, I'll be the first to call. Since I know he's only saying that because he can sense my raging disappointment, I pull a gracious smile to my face, then thank him for his time.

As I walk out of the backroom, my head is already spinning as I try to figure out what I'm going to do next.

I can't perform tarot readings in the city. My whole act relies on unwitting humans who have no idea that supes really exist. Half of my customers are sure I'm a fraud, while the other half believe I have a real gift; either way, they're entertained and I'm paid. The ones who think I'm a fraud... they're pretty spot-on. I'm not a fortune-teller. I'm a shifter who uses her wolf to pick up on little things about the customer I'm reading. A racing heart, a nervous chuckle, how a scent changes... if I can't read the cards for real, at least I can read body language. After all these years, I can spin any card to give the customer the experience they're after.

No one would buy that here. At best, they'd figure out I was some kind of supe. In our world there are plenty of different types of supes, though the main ones are shifters and vampires. Claws and fangs. My silver eyes and concealed scent might cover me for a bit, but it's obvious I'm not a bloodsucker; if I'm not a vampire, with my power level, it doesn't take a genius to figure out that I must be a shifter. And the number one rule I agreed to when I moved into Muncie was hiding what I was so I don't inadvertently start another war between our peoples.

They happen. Claws and Fangs wars... over the thousands of years that we have considered each other enemies, brutal skirmishes were inevitable. The last great war happened over two hundred years ago, but with my luck? I'll draw the attention of the wrong vampire and start another one.

No, thanks.

As I slink out from behind the bar, I'm reminded once again that I really shouldn't be here. It had seemed like such a good idea at the time, finally having a place that I could settle down for a while as I decided whether or not to join Gem in the Mountainside Pack. I thought I could deal with being near enough to my mate without acknowledging him. So far, so good on that front.

It's the other vampires that are giving me a problem.

There aren't that many Fang Cities in the States. Because vampires have such a long history with Europe, most of their kind settled there centuries ago and never left. Some of those that did became the equivalent of a lone wolf. As rogues, they hunted on their own, but rarely made it long before the bloodlust took over and the most powerful of vampires had to clean up after them.

But for the vampires who wanted community, who wanted a place where blood was just another transaction, the Fang Cities were born. Each territory is ruled by members of the Cadre, with a single leader that's like their Alpha. Because they're basically food for the vampires, humans are welcome; supes are an open secret in a city like Muncie, but the humans in the know all keep the truth of their vampire rulers from outsiders. The Cadre protects every soul inside their borders, and they're very choosy about who they let inside.

As far as I know, I'm the only non-vampire supe in all of Muncie; definitely the only shifter. I took Gem's place when she passed her townhouse over to me, but that doesn't mean that the vampires who realize my wolfish secret are happy I'm here.

Working with humans—whether they know about supes or not—would only be a disaster. After talking at length with Gem about the city, I got the idea that very few vampires would be willing to hire me. She only got the job behind the bar because Aleksander vouched for her, getting Charlie to agree to give her a chance.

She did the same for me, but it obviously didn't work.

And despite the fact that the Luna insists that Aleks is meant to be mine, it's not like I can ask him for help. With me pretending he doesn't exist, and him stopping by my home but never formally letting me know he's aware of my presence...

I don't even know for sure if he remembers me. He could just be curious about the female who moved into Gem's townhouse. Just because I recognize him as mine doesn't mean he feels the same.

Especially since he spent the last year in love with Gemma...

I huff out a breath. As if I couldn't feel any worse about losing out on the job at Charlie's, that intrusive thought just has to pop into my head.

*Again.*

Whenever I think about how my mate might be in love with another shifter, my stomach goes tight, my throat raw. It took weeks into our friendship before I admitted to Gem that I felt a pull toward Aleks, and she's spent the months after that assuring me that she never reciprocated his feelings. That he told her following what happened in California that he was over her. It still bothers me, even if I wish it wouldn't.

For now, I can't worry about Aleks. If I can't find work, I'll be out of Muncie before this awkward dance we're doing around one another ends with us eventually coming face to face with each other.

Will I still be able to reject him then?

Adjusting my scarf as I prepare to head back out into the snow, I push Aleks out of my head. It's harder than I'd like since my next breath brings his innate scent into my lungs, almost as if he had been here. My wolf is quiet. If he *was,* he's not now, and maybe that's what's best for the both of us.

Okay. I struck out at Charlie's. Fine. It happens. I should call Gem now. Maybe she has an idea what I can do for a backup.

With that thought in mind, I make a bee-line for the front door. As I do, the male customer—vampire, my wolf warns me—

that was chatting with Hailey near the far side of the bar suddenly breaks away from her, heading straight for me.

I'm only aware of him because my wolf subconsciously watches out for vampires whenever I'm walking around in Muncie.

Slipping my hands in my pocket, my fingers stroke the fangs I have in there. They're still the ones I stole from the Alpha's nightstand, and I treat them like a good luck talisman when I'm forced to be around vampires.

Remembering her warning about Aleks offering me one of his, I asked Gem once why Walker would've had a drawer full of them. She couldn't tell me, though she did mention that, in some Fang Cities, carrying one gave you a measure of protection.

Since then, I've had at least three in my pocket at all times.

Just as I'm pushing against the glass door, eager to get the hell out of the bar, he calls out my name.

I freeze.

Please, oh please, let there be another Elizabeth in here...

Before I know it, he's right behind me. "Excusez moi. You are Elizabeth Howell, yes?"

My heart sinks.

I glance over my shoulder at him. Like all vampires, his skin is flawless, his features inhumanly divine. His blond hair is styled precisely in one of those two hundred dollar haircuts. His suit probably cost more than all my wardrobe combined.

"Uh. Yeah. That's me."

"Bon. My name is Dominic Le Croix. I've been sent to retrieve you."

What? "I... I don't know what you mean."

"I work for the Cadre. Roman wants to see you. I'm to bring you to him right now."

Did I think today couldn't get any worse? "Roman?" I repeat. "You don't mean Roman—"

"Zakharov, yes."

I might be a shifter, but even I know who *that* is.

And I'm utterly screwed if he's sent one of his patrollers after me.

Now, Gem has wanted me to join her pack since we met when she came to confront the Wicked Wolf, her birth father. Mountainside is aptly named. The shifters turned the sides and the top of a mountain into a protected community called Accalia. But I… I just wasn't ready to join a pack again. I was a lone wolf for eight years. The only two times that I allowed myself to believe I could go back to pack living were disasters. Kyle fooled me, and Walker captured me.

After two years in the Wolf District, I looked forward to being free again. But without any family, any money, any roots… it sucked. Sucked even more once I learned who my fated mate was meant to be.

I guess it was inevitable that I'd end up in Muncie. I gave it a good shot, but I couldn't stay away.

When I accepted her offer to stay in the townhouse, she gave me a crash course in living inside of a Fang City. Apart from making sure I understood that most—though not all—vampires hate shifters instinctively, the biggest thing she impressed upon me was never to get on the wrong side of Roman Zakharov.

He's basically the vampire's Alpha. What he says goes, and I'm only allowed to live within Muncie's borders because he agreed.

And now he wants to see me?

That can't be good.

I'VE NEVER BEEN TO THE CENTER OF MUNCIE BEFORE AND FOR good reason, too. The Cadre—the vampire-run government in charge of the bloodsuckers, their donors, and the humans who have no idea what goes bump in the night around them—controls every element of the bordered settlement, but it is headquartered in the exact middle of the city.

Their towering headquarters is named, aptly enough, the Cadre building. Very simple. Very self-explanatory. From the outside, there's no way to tell that it's effectively the most important structure in the Fang City with one exception: every single window on the twenty-five-story building is blacked out.

Perfect for vampires.

Dominic offered to drive me over, but I suggested we walk. The two miles between Charlie's and the Cadre building is nothing to a shifter and, like most of my kind, I get a little anxious inside of enclosed spaces. To my wolf, they're too close to being cages.

Cars are out. Trains, too. Buses.

Luckily, Muncie is an urban city similar to Manhattan. It has a great public transport system, but for us supes, walking is not only normal, it's almost expected. Any Cadre member on patrol does it on foot; with stamina and speed almost as impressive as a shifter's, most vampires don't bother with driving when they could be faster without a car.

Dominic agreed to walk, though I get the idea it wasn't his first choice. It takes until we've made it to the heart of Muncie before I figure out why.

The center is full of vampires, and they all sense something different about me. Among humans, I can do a pretty good job of hiding. Walking up to the building? I *can't*.

Smart, Elizabeth. Really smart.

To outrun their murmurs and their stares, I increase my pace, Dominic easily matching it. I let him overtake me as he leads me into the front lobby of the building.

Soft music is playing. Over the noticeable scent of *vampire* that clings to everything in the room, there's a hint of fresh linen being pumped through the vents. Directly in front of us, there's a huge counter that couples as a rounded desk for the stunning vampire sitting behind it.

Her eyes widen when she spots me, but Dominic nods to her. That must mean something because she doesn't say a word as he guides me down the hall that leads past her desk.

"The elevator's this way," he tells me.

My wolf backs up, shaking her head as she whines. I know how she feels. An elevator is just like a car. If I can avoid it, I don't want to go in there.

"Are there any stairs?"

Dominic gives me a curious look. "Roman's office is on the twenty-first floor."

And?

He nods. "Of course. Let me show you."

Together, we take the stairs. The higher we climb, the more I notice a very powerful, very old aura crackling like electricity against my skin. If I wasn't already nervous as hell to meet Roman, that does it.

I knew he was the leader. Now I know why.

Once we exit out on the twenty-first floor, Dominic gestures at a closed door. "He's expecting you."

"You're not coming in with me?"

I don't know why I asked that. He told me he was sent to retrieve me and he did. But... I really don't want to go in there by myself.

Dominic shakes his head. "Not yet. I have something to take care of first, but I'm sure I'll be seeing you soon. Before I go, though..." He holds out his hand, palm up. "The fangs, please."

When I stare at him blankly, he gives my right pocket an impatient nod. "They're in there. I don't know where you got them from or why you have them, but you don't want to offend Roman. In Muncie, you earn a fang. They're gifts. The ones you have are worthless."

Oh my Luna. He knows about the fangs I stole from Walker.

My blush returns as I hurriedly jam my hand in my pocket. Grabbing the three I have stowed in there, I shove them at Dominic. "I'm sorry. I... I didn't know."

"You're not the first to misunderstand how we do things here. It'll be fine. And you don't have to be afraid of Roman. Just don't lie to him, and don't offend him, and everything is going to be okay."

That's easy for him to say. He's not going in there.

I nod. "Thanks."

Then, before I lose my nerve, I grab the doorknob, give it a turn, and push it open.

The force of Roman's aura nearly knocks me over, it's that strong. It takes a second for me to recover, and when I do?

I'm nearly bowled over again by his appearance.

I'd heard whispers of his name even before I came to live in Muncie. I don't know what I thought he looked like, but I'm definitely not prepared for the male sitting behind his wide, oak desk.

Like most vampires who were fair-skinned before they were

turned, his skin is iridescently pale. His hair might've been blond once, but there are so many silver strands poking through his short mane, it nearly sparkles beneath his special vampire-friendly fluorescent lights. He has it parted precisely on the left, the longer hanks of hair swooped over to the right, covering one of his eyes.

The other? It's so pale, it's nearly colorless. I can see the whites of that single eye, his pitch-black pupil, and then... *nothing*.

And they say my silver eyes are creepy. Next time I hear that, I'll have to remember that it can always be worse.

He could be twenty. He could be thirty. He has that ageless sort of classic face that screams *innocence*, though his powerful aura puts him at a couple of hundred years old at least.

And he's looking at me as if he's seen a ghost.

"Julia." He rises from behind the desk, rubbing his chin as the single eye I can see seems to glitter. Then, almost under his breath, he adds, "Ne mozhet byt'."

His voice is gruffer than I expect from his striking looks, though maybe I just think that because of his notable accent. If I'm not mistaken, it's Russian, which makes sense. With the name of Zakharov, I figured he was probably one of the Eastern Europe vampires.

I have no idea what he just said except for maybe the first word. Though I get the idea he was talking about me, I glance over my shoulder, looking for the Julia he mentioned.

There's no one there.

When he clears his throat, my head swivels forward again. His flawless features are rearranged into a careful mask. The faint expression of surprise when he saw me is gone. In fact, he looks more like how I imagined the immortal leader of a Cadre would.

Hard.

Strong.

Judging.

My wolf goes down on her belly, prepared to bare her throat in submission to Roman. I don't blame her. His aura is as icy cold as every other vampire I've met, but his is... it's different. Like it's so powerful, a single touch would freeze me so completely, I'd burn.

Alpha, I think again. He has fangs, no pulse, and he drinks blood—but, make no mistake, Roman is as much an Alpha as the Wicked Wolf of the West.

As I can't help but stare at him, he nods at me as if he's found something inside of me that's worth his time. Then, after sitting back down, he presses a button on the old-fashioned office phone perched on the corner of his desk. A red light blinks.

"Yes, Roman?"

"Leigh. Tell Dominic I'm ready for him and Felicity, won't you?"

"Right away."

"Thank you."

He releases the button, folding his hands in front of him. "I'm glad you were available to meet with me, Elizabeth. I've been meaning to do this for some time, but I've finally found the perfect opportunity."

"Um. Okay."

I have so many questions. How did he know that I was going to meet Charlie this afternoon? It's Sunday, just before dark, and though it stopped snowing earlier, it's still a mess outside.

And what does he want me for? If Gem got his permission to give me her old townhouse for the time being, he knew where to find me. Sending Dominic to Charlie's could've been coincidental, but I doubt it. For some reason, he didn't want to have one of his vampires approach me on my territory.

Makes sense. I might not be an alpha, but I guard anything I consider mine as ruthlessly as any other shifter.

But because I'm *not* an alpha, I don't dare ask Roman any of those questions. I just stand in the middle of the office, unsure if I'm supposed to sit down in one of the empty chairs placed in front of his desk. He doesn't invite me to, and I'm not too keen on getting even closer to the powerful vampire.

Yeah... I'm just going to stay right here while we wait for the vampires he called for to appear.

It's not a long wait. Less than five minutes later, the door swings in. Dominic holds it open for a vampire female. Felicity, I assume, who, like every other vampire I've met, looks like she belongs on a runway. She has wavy brown hair that hits her shoulders, a body I'd kill for, and light violet eyes that have me wondering if they're contacts.

She's a vampire. I doubt it.

She enters the office, bowing her head in respect as she greets Roman. Dominic follows her, and while I can sense the bond tying them together, he keeps his distance.

That's interesting.

"Elizabeth," Roman says, calling my attention back to him. "What can you tell me about these two? About their connection?"

It's a test. Obviously. Somehow he knows exactly what makes me different than every other shifter I've ever known—and I don't just mean the color of my eyes.

"Um. Sure. These two are bonded together." Then, on a guess, I add, "But they don't want to be anymore."

Felicity's head shoots over to me, the surprise doing nothing to make her any less stunning. "That's right. How did you know that?"

"She's been blessed by the shifter goddess," Roman announces, and it's my turn to look over at the head vampire of Muncie in surprise.

Okay. Now how did he know *that*?

He nods at me. "Yes. I know all about your gift, Elizabeth. I've been hoping to see how it works for myself. When Dominic came to me to ask if I'd consider his bonding to Felicity effectively broken, I remembered what I heard about you. I thought you could try to make their separation more permanent."

"I can. I mean, it doesn't always work." Gem was proof of that. "But as long as one of the two bonded mates wants their bond to break, it should."

"What if both of us do?" asks Felicity.

"It was an arranged betrothal," Dominic explains. "She's not my beloved and I'm not hers. I found mine, but I can't claim her fully while I'm still tied to Felicity. It wouldn't be fair to either of them. And Felicity..."

She shakes her head royally. "I'd like the chance to find my own mate. My beloved or one I choose to bond with myself, I'm not picky. I care for Dominic, but I don't love him. We both deserve to be with one that we *do* love."

In that case, it should be easy to break them apart, and I tell them that.

Roman gestures for me to go ahead.

Taking a deep breath, viscerally aware that I'm surrounded by three vampires, I place one hand on Dominic; after our walk to the Cadre building, I'm more comfortable touching him than Felicity. It only takes me touching one half of a bond and I know whether it's unbreakable.

And theirs isn't. Just like that, it's severed in half.

Felicity sighs in relief. Dominic clutches his heart, a determined expression already twisting his classically handsome face.

"It is done?" Roman asks.

Both of the vampires nod.

"Then you're free to go. Elizabeth, I would ask that you stay. But, first... Dominic? I assume you'll be requesting some time off?"

"Uh— yes, sir. If that's fine with you."

"Of course. Congratulations on your new beloved."

"Thank you, Roman." The male vampire turns on me, pure gratitude written all over his face. "And thank you, too, Elizabeth."

Isn't that a first? A supe *thanking* me for breaking their bond? "You're welcome."

With another reverential bow toward their leader, Felicity and Dominic leave his office, each one of them much happier than they were when they entered.

As soon as the door closes behind them again, Roman turns his stare back on me before saying the last thing I expect from the leader of the Cadre:

"I want to hire you."

# CHAPTER 4
# ELIZABETH'S NEW JOB

I blink. I'd been halfway convinced that he was going to boot me from Muncie after my display of power. "Hire me? For what? To break bonds?"

"When necessary, yes. To sense them as well, since I know that's also part of your blessing. But, more than that, I'd like to make sure that you don't use that ability against my people."

"So you're going to pay me *not* to use my 'gift'?"

"Mm. In a way."

There's got to be a catch. Being paid to act like I'm not a Luna-touched female? That's the freaking dream.

"Anything else?"

"Since you mention it," Roman begins, even as I want to say: *I knew it*, "I have another offer for you."

"Okay."

"I'm sure you know that vampires prefer the night. Me? I'm old enough that I rarely sleep, but that's not the case for all of us. Our doors are open twenty-four hours a day for every citizen of Muncie. But because I can't hire just anyone to serve as a receptionist for me, I tend to struggle to find a vampire who will willingly take the dayshift. Did you see the vampire at the lobby desk?"

I nod.

"That's Leigh. She's doing the daylight hours temporarily as a favor to her mate. Eventually, she'll either take over at night or take on a patrol. You're a shifter. You're diurnal. I think you'd be perfect for the job."

And I'll be close enough that he can keep his eye on me. A shifter who can snap even a vampire's blood bond even though he acts as if he doesn't want me to? I'm just as valuable to Roman as I was to the Wicked Wolf.

On the plus side, I don't sense even a hint of interest coming from the cool vampire. Sure, he doesn't have a bond of his own, but my instincts tell me that, unlike the Alpha, he isn't going to try to convince me to join with him permanently.

Nope. He just wants to hire me.

And I need money way more than I need a mate.

"It won't be a difficult job. Answer calls, keep my schedule, do my filing. Keep out any unwanted visitors. Hardly taxing, and I'll pay you well for your time." Steepling his fingers, Roman leans back in his chair. "What do you think?"

I think that I would be an idiot to refuse.

I'm used to those in authority wanting to warp my "gift" for themselves. Even before I developed the ability to break bonds —when my gift became my "gift", or sometimes *curse*—my Alpha used the way I could dampen scents to his advantage. I was happy to let him because it meant I was serving the pack. I was useful.

Needed.

If the vampire wants to hire me as a receptionist while really keeping an eye on me and my Luna-touched wolf, that's fine with me. I woke up this morning looking for a job. Charlie's was a bust, but this might just be a better fit for me after all.

"When can I start?"

---

THE SECOND I EXIT THE CADRE'S BUILDING, I PULL MY PHONE out of my pocket. There hadn't been time when Dominic told me that Roman wanted to see me, but since I don't have my first shift until tomorrow morning, I can call Gem now.

And after what went down in Roman's office, I really need to.

It takes her a couple of rings before she answers. When she does, she squeals through the phone, "You got the job!"

"That bartending gig? Uh, no. I actually didn't."

"What?" Her excitement for me turns into a straight demand. "Why the hell not?"

Good question. "I don't know, but it's okay. I got *a* job."

"You did? That's great! I'm happy for you, Elizabeth. So... where are you working? What are you doing?"

"Thanks. As for what my new job is... that's actually part of the reason why I'm calling." Over the phone, it's so much easier to go against my wolf's instincts when it comes to the female alpha. I probably wouldn't dare ask her in person, but with miles between us, I manage to spit out, "Did you tell anyone in Muncie about my abilities? My... 'gift'?"

*My curse?*

She doesn't hesitate to answer. "Yeah. Remember? I said I might need to use that to convince Roman to let you stay. You said that was okay. Why?"

She's right. I did give her permission. From how she described Roman, he made every decision with the safety of his people in mind. But he wasn't heartless. Gem thought telling him that I was on the run from the Wicked Wolf of the West would be enough, but if he decided he didn't want my trouble following me into the city, my abilities were supposed to be her trump card.

I guess she had to use it.

"No reason. Just wanted to make sure that it didn't get any further than the leader of the Cadre."

"And let my sperm donor figure out that you settled down at the foot of Accalia? No fucking way. We still don't have any idea where he's hiding out, but if he learns that you're on the East Coast and we're practically neighbors, you know he won't be able to resist making a move. And, as much as I hate to admit it, even Ryker agrees that we're better off gunning for him instead of letting him attack us again."

She isn't wrong.

Just then, the same old familiar guilt starts to claw away at my insides. I'm not just risking my safety by settling down in one place, I'm also risking Gem's—and everyone who lives in Muncie.

Including my fated mate.

"Thanks for that. I just wanted to check. But, uh, I… I have to go now. I'll call you later. Okay?"

As an alpha, her senses are incredibly keen. Just like how I can resist her dominance, she can't catch my scent through the phone, but she doesn't need to. She immediately can tell that something is off by the tone of my voice.

"Is everything alright?"

"Uh. Yeah. Of course."

Gem's senses are keen, and I've always been a terrible liar.

"In that case, we should celebrate. Come to dinner. Here, in Accalia. I'd come down to Muncie, but... yeah. It's probably better if you come up here."

Where the phone won't make it difficult for her to use her dominance against me. I can't blame her for her tactics, either.

After all, she *is* an alpha.

"I start my new job tomorrow," I tell her. "Once I know what my schedule is, I'll make time to visit."

"You better. Or else I'm going to hunt you down and drag you up here so we can really chat."

I know Gemma well enough by now to tell that she's mostly teasing. Tell that to my submissive wolf. Even through the phone, she reacts to Gem's threat.

"I will. Promise."

---

THE NEXT MORNING, I WAKE UP EARLY, READY TO START MY new job.

Roman has me working at the front desk in the Cadre building's lobby from ten in the morning until six in the evening, Monday through Friday. If he needs me for any other reason, he has my phone number, making it clear that I'm expected to answer any call.

He doesn't give me his. I didn't expect him to.

My phone is basically a burner I bought for cheap right before I decided to visit Muncie. For now, I only have one number stored: Gem's. It rarely rings, so I'll know immediately if the call is coming from Roman. I'm fine with that.

Starting work as a receptionist?

That's a little more nerve-wracking.

I show up a good fifteen minutes early, lingering in the lobby when I see that two unfamiliar vampires are sitting behind the desk. They must be third shift; I'm considered first. I think about introducing myself before quietly moving to one corner of the lobby, waiting until the minutes pass and it's ten o'clock.

At two minutes before, a pair of female vampires glide into the lobby together. The one on the left is Black, her dark vampiric skin gleaming beneath the lights. She has her black hair styled in box braids that fall down her back; her light eyes are the closest to gold I've seen on a vampire.

I recognize her. She's Leigh, the vampire who was sitting behind the desk yesterday afternoon.

The one on the right is about an inch taller than her companion, with bright red hair, shockingly white skin, and a spattering of freckles over her nose. Her eyes are closer to green, though still with the tell-tale lightness that marks her as a vampire.

They're holding hands as they enter, and before they go their separate ways, they kiss.

Obviously. Even from my hidden corner, I could sense the solid bond stretching between them.

While the redhead disappears down the hall, Leigh unerringly tracks me down, a smile highlighting just how beautiful she is.

"Hello. I'm Leigh," she says, introducing herself even though I already knew that. "In case you're curious, the gorgeous redhead going up to check in with Roman? That's my beloved. Tamera. And you're—"

"I'm Elizabeth."

"I thought so." She scrunches her nose, then gives me an

apologetic expression when she realizes what she had done. “Sorry, but I also thought you were supposed to be a wolf. Roman told me I’d be showing you what I do, but I definitely remember him telling me that you’re a shifter.”

“I am. Does that bother you?”

“Me? Nah. Maybe if I caught you when I was thirsty...” At the look on my face, she laughs, then quickly says, “I’m just kidding.”

I’m pretty sure she’s not.

Glancing over her shoulder, she sees the two other vampires getting up from their seats. “Looks like it’s time to switch shifts. Come on. Let me show you what I do when I first arrive.”

And that’s the end of us discussing that I’m a shifter. Seems as if, now that Roman’s hired me, I’m Cadre. In a Fang City, that’s all that matters.

The job, I decide, is kind of basic even if there’s a lot to learn; makes sense, since Roman didn’t hire me for my secretarial skills. Leigh is kind and patient with me. She’s also friendlier than I expected any vampire to be, and before long I start to feel a little more comfortable sitting next to her as she shows me how to work the computer and answer phones.

Then, when the mail delivery comes, she even shows me how to go through it.

It arrives in a massive cart since we’re responsible for all of the mail in the whole of the Cadre building. As the daytime receptionists, this is one of our main jobs. I don’t mind. It’s something to keep me busy.

Until I reach inside the mail bin and feel a jolt of electricity when I brush against one particular package.

Leigh was sorting mail on a folding table she set out for just that purpose. “You alright?”

I nod even as I drag that package out from under all of the others. As soon as it's free from the pile, an enticing scent wafts up from the cardboard box.

My first instinct is that it smells of *hope*. My wolf—who's been dozing as soon as she realized that Leigh is no threat to us—perks her head up, snout snuffling as she takes the scent into her as well.

What the—

It's addressed to *me*.

Looking over my shoulder, Leigh notices it the same time as I do. Her nostrils flare, picking up the same scent as I did. I don't know what it smells like to her, but she's quicker than I am.

She obviously recognizes it, too.

"A package from Aleksander Filan? And it's addressed to you?"

"It looks that way," I say weakly.

Because that *is* Aleks's scent. And instead of pinpointing it immediately, my first reaction was to think of hope.

Yeah... that can't be good.

Leigh's expression turns curious. "You know him? He's pretty high up in the Cadre. I thought you just started today?"

"I did." I'm still staring at the cardboard box. Giving my head a clearing shake, I add, "And I don't know him. Not really. I mean, I've heard of him, but I've never met him."

Every last part of that is true. I just kind of, sort of neglect to mention that my goddess won't give up on the idea that the mysterious vampire is my fated mate.

And now he's sent me a package.

I open the box at Leigh's urging, just as curious as she is.

It's... a box of teabags?

Why would Aleks send me teabags?

I don't know. There's no doubt that it's meant for me—Elizabeth Howell is definitely printed on the label—but I… I don't understand.

As far as I know, he has no clue who I am.

And now he's sent me *tea*?

Leigh uses the pen in her hand to point at the package I'm still holding. "That's the good stuff, too."

"Is it?" I ask vaguely, setting it down, pushing it away from me. "I wouldn't know. I don't drink tea."

"Really? Then why did Aleksander send you some to the Cadre building?"

That is a very good question. Too bad I have no idea how I'm supposed to get an answer to it.

So I shrug, and hope that's the end of it—and it is if only because, suddenly, the phone rings.

Leigh answers it and, after a quick exchange, she says, "Roman would like to speak to you."

When I reach for the phone, she shakes her head before dropping the office phone back into its cradle. "I forgot you're new here. When Roman wants to talk to you, he means in person. He wants you to go up to his office."

Okay, then.

---

It's like déjà vu. Me, standing in the middle of Roman's office. The powerful vampire giving me a searching look while I wonder what part of me he's scrutinizing now.

After a few minutes when I contemplate throwing myself out

of the freaking window, he nods, then gestures for me to take a seat.

Taking a twenty-one-story nosedive seems pretty tempting when the alternative is sitting with barely a few feet separating me from the leader of the Cadre. But I do because, as big of a coward as I am, I'm a wolf. The drive to survive is almost as undeniable as the one to mate.

Then again, I have made it five months rejecting *that* urge...

I sit, folding my hands primly in my lap. Hey. It's the only way to hide how much they're shaking.

"How are you liking your work so far?"

"It's going well," I tell him honestly. "Leigh has been very helpful."

"Good to hear that. So you'll be staying on then?"

I hadn't realized today was a trial. Trying to calm my racing heart, I say, "I'd like to. If you'll let me."

"I think that will be for the best," Roman agrees. "But now that you're part of the Cadre, I'm as responsible for you as any of my people. Here. I want you to have this."

His hand is folded in a fist. When he gestures for me to come closer and offer him mine, I do. He opens his fingers, dropping a golden chain into my waiting palm.

Attached to the center of the chain is a bright, white vampire fang.

I marvel down at it. It absolutely hums with power. "What is this?"

"Dominic told me about the fangs you carried here yesterday. My people won't respect any that weren't freely given. But this one? They will."

"How is this any different than the ones I collected from my old pack?" I wonder, peeking up at him again, making sure he knows that that was exactly where I got those other fangs from.

Roman curls his lip, showing off an even white smile—and a missing fang.

Oh, boy. That explains the power I felt. "This is yours."

"You work for me, Elizabeth. This is a symbol of protection. No more, no less. But I do insist that you wear it while you live within my borders."

*Make him explain*... that's what Gem told me, but she meant Aleks.

I think she'd understand why I'm too terrified to ask the leader of the Cadre why he's giving me one of his fangs.

"Wear it over your heart. I've hung it on a golden chain since I know silver bothers shifters as much as it does my kind. No vampire should give you any trouble within the city if you do."

You know what? Maybe this is one of the benefits he mentioned when he offered me the job.

Protection and a paycheck? I'll take it.

Something tells me that I don't have a choice, either.

"Thank you."

"Don't thank me, Elizabeth. Never forget, I only do what's best for my city. For my city, and for those loyal to me. Be one of them, and you have nothing to fear. But betray me?"

Roman's strange eyes flash in warning.

I gulp.

He nods. "Then I trust we understand each other."

More than he ever knows. "Yes."

"Good."

# CHAPTER 5
# GEM'S GIFT AND A BLAST FROM THE PAST

When Gem pulls open the door to the cabin she shares with her mate up in Accalia, the first thing she does is give the fang necklace I'm wearing a side-eye. Gesturing for me to step inside, she closes the door, then spins on me.

She points. "That's not Aleks's."

I don't even ask how she can tell the difference. Alphas... they're wired differently than most shifters. Their senses are more keen, including their eyes and their noses, and they sense things the rest of us don't. Lies, for example. Bad intentions. In order to be the lead protector for a pack, they need those skills. It doesn't surprise me at all that she can look at one fang and know it's not the same as another.

"No. It's not. And before you ask, I did make it a point to find out what it means when a vampire offers an unmated female one of his fangs. That's not the case here. He told me it's not a proposal, but for protection instead."

"He?"

"Yeah. Roman."

Gem's eyebrows shoot sky-high. "Roman? Roman Zakharov?"

"Yeah. I work for him now. Three days so far, and it's been going great."

"Hang on... you *what?*"

The way her voice went all high like that... my wolf is suddenly contemplating a quick retreat. "I told you I got a job—"

"Yeah," she says, cutting me off. "It was supposed to be at Charlie's. I thought you were gonna work behind the bar like I used to until you told me he didn't hire you. And now the cagey bastard is ignoring my calls."

"I'm sorry." What else can I say?

"Don't worry about it. I'll get to the bottom of it eventually. But you working for Zakharov? Let's go sit down in the living room. I think I'm going to want to be sitting down to hear this one."

Gem leads me away from the promise of a quick escape, bringing me to a living room full of alpha pheromones. My wolf hesitates in the doorway, yipping when she realizes that Ryker Wolfson is sitting in one of the armchairs, a map sprawled across his lap. He has a red marker clutched in his right hand, jotting notes on the paper as he consults something on his phone.

Sidling around me, Gem says, "You don't have to worry about him. Ryker's all bark, no bite."

As if to prove that he's not as absorbed in his work as it appears, Ryker lifts his head, snapping his teeth at us.

I jump, and Gem rolls her eyes. "Ignore him. He's just pissy that he can't have my undivided attention today. As if I can ever compete with that damn map of his."

"Love you, too, sweetheart," Ryker calls out, already adding another note to the map's corner.

He means it. I'm pretty sure that, even without my "gift", I would be able to tell just how much he cares for Gem. It's in the way he angles his body in the seat, always keeping her centered, and in the way he sneaks peeks at her as she shoots him her middle finger before bounding over to take a seat on the couch. That's pure affection mingled with outright lust when he takes her flipping the bird literally.

My cheeks heat up as his dark gold eyes turn molten. He's probably already imagining it, and I'm the only thing keeping his fantasies from being acted out.

"I can always come back another night," I offer. "If I'm interrupting anything."

Gem pats the open seat next to her on the couch. "You're not interrupting anything. We had plans first, and I'll make it up to him later." The pheromones in the room thicken so quickly, I know exactly how she'll be doing just that. "Forget him, Elizabeth. I want to hear all about you and Roman."

Ryker's head jerks up. "What was that?"

"There is no me and Roman," I say quickly. "He's my boss. That's all. Remember how I asked if you told him that I was Luna-touched? That I could break bonds?"

"You said I could. I needed some reason why you'd prefer living with vamps instead of up here with us, and telling him about you being Luna-touched did the trick."

"I know. But that's exactly it. He asked me to prove it, and when I did, he wants to make sure that I only use it at his request. He gave me a job as his secretary, but we both know that it's my 'gift' that makes me valuable to him."

"It also makes you a security risk," Gem points out. "If other supes know about it, they might come after you in Muncie."

I nod. That's also very true.

Though I know all three of us are thinking it, no one mentions Wicked Wolf Walker. He kept me close for two years because of what I could do. Odds of him coming back for me are pretty high. Unlike Gem, I would never challenge him, and we all know it.

"You want a guard? Take one of mine. I have *three*."

"That's okay." I pat Roman's fang. "This is enough for me, I think."

"No. Please. I mean it." If I didn't know any better, I'd think Gem was pleading with me. "Take at least one. What about Jace? He's cute."

Ryker growls low in his chest.

"Something wrong?" she tosses behind her easily to her mate.

"I'll say. Please don't make me challenge my Beta again, sweetheart. We finally got a new one. It would be a shame to put Jace down just because you think he's cute."

I almost choke on my laugh. I can't help it. It's such... such an *Alpha* thing to say, that any awkward tension in the room slips away with Ryker's threat.

"You've got nothing to worry about, Ryker." Gem grins before blowing a kiss over at him. "Jace is cute. You, my mate, are fucking sexy as hell."

Ryker is slightly mollified by that. "Better. But stop trying to get rid of your guards. Duke is an exception. You know the other three won't give up on you."

"Yeah, yeah." Turning her back to him again, missing the way his eyes follow her every move, she leans into me. "Speaking of mates... how are things with Aleks?"

I exhale. As much as I wanted to see Gem, to talk to another shifter female... I just can't talk to her about Aleks. Mainly because there's nothing really I can say about him, but also because of their history.

For a year, Aleks courted her, trying to convince her to be his mate. He gave her his necklace, only it wasn't just for protection; he had claimed her as his intended. She never really gave his pursuit any thought since she's always known that Ryker Wolfson was meant to be her mate, but Aleks tried to get her to change her mind all the way up until the week of her Luna Ceremony, when Ryker and Gem finalized their mate bond.

She told me all of this when I finally agreed to stay in her townhouse in Muncie. She wanted to be honest so she wasn't going to hide her past with Aleks. She was his roommate, nothing more, but in case it got out, she was letting me know before I ran into Aleks again.

At first, I thought she was mentioning Aleks because she knew he lived there, and that he would want revenge for how the Wicked Wolf treated him in the district. Before long, I realized that she sensed that I felt something toward the vampire.

When she asked, I told her I had no idea what she was talking about, and she called me out on it. I thought it was because I'm a crappy liar. Nope. Like I can sense bonds, she can sense lies.

So I folded. I told her that the Luna said that Aleks was meant to be mine.

Luckily, she promised she wouldn't interfere. If I wanted to stay away from Aleks, that was fine. And since the most the vampire did was pace outside of the townhouse, I left it at that.

Hey. I can take a hint. If he feels anything toward me, he's pretending he can't. I'm perfectly okay with it.

See? I really am such an awful liar. I can't even lie to myself.

"How's Aleks? Same as before," I tell her. "I saw him the other day, but he didn't even seem to notice me."

It was so quick. Though I pretended not to notice at the time, no denying he was walking out of the bar right as I was walking out of the back room following the disastrous interview. I was flagged down by Dominic, and by the time I followed him onto the street, Aleks was already long gone.

"He will," she says firmly. "You might not want him to, but he will sooner or later. But that's okay. I got something for you for when he does."

"You... you do?"

"Yup." Gem jumps up, holding her hands out. "Don't move. I'll go get it for you."

"Um. Okay."

I knew she was inhumanly fast. Even fast for a shifter, too. After the dinner where she discovered that Walker regarded me as his pet, when he was bragging about my "gift", she turned on me. One minute we were walking into my cabin, the next she had her claws centimeters from my throat. I never even saw her move.

Now, she dashes from the room. Ryker's dark gold eyes are drawn to her ass as she goes. He gives his head a shake, almost like he'd been in a trance, then glances over at me and shrugs, his unabashed smile turning the stoic Alpha into a ruggedly handsome male.

My heart skips a beat. No wonder Gem was willing to hold onto her mate with both paws. If I had a male who looked at me like he does Gem, I'd never want to let him go, either.

She's back in a flash, holding something out to me.

"Here you go."

It's a book. Flipping it over so that I can see the title, I give her a quizzical look. "A Polish dictionary?"

"Polish to English," she corrects. "Trust me. You're going to need it."

If she says so.

---

ROMAN'S FANG KEEPS ME PROTECTED IN THE FANG CITY. Ryker and Gem have given me permission to visit pack territory. Theoretically, I should be in no danger on my way back from my visit to the Mountainside Pack.

In between Accalia and Muncie, there's a dirt road that's about twenty feet wide. It's a road that leads into the mountains, as well as out of the vampire's territory; the next city over is straight-up human, just past the River Run Pack's wooded land. It's considered the official border between two powerful supe communities, a kind of no man's land.

Fittingly, that's where the female shifter is waiting for me.

It's my fault, too. I've grown so used to being able to walk around without looking over my shoulder since I arrived in Muncie that I never thought twice about leaving it. I forgot that Roman's fang is just a weird fashion choice outside of the Cadre-run city, or that I have a massive target on my back.

It's been seven years since I met her last. Peyton Slate, the former mate to the Beta of the Oak Valley Pack.

I can't believe this is happening—though I probably shouldn't be surprised. She'd promised revenge on me like so many others, and now that I'm free again, she didn't waste that much time coming after me.

Damn it. I let my guard down. My wolf is up inside of my

chest, her ears folded back against her skull. I can feel my eyes darken from silver to black, a mixture of fear and disgust.

She's not only wearing her scent on her skin.

He's here. I don't know where, his scent apart from the way it mingles with hers is faint, but it's near.

*Walker.*

Peyton, I can handle. She's a delta, so not much more powerful than me, and her broken bond is a weakness I can exploit if I have to. But Peyton *and* the Wicked Wolf?

I'm fucking doomed.

With a nasty look on her face, Peyton runs her claws through the length of her pitch-black hair. It's styled in loose curls that frame her face, highlighting the cruel twist to her mouth, her patrician nose, and her eyes.

Her eyes...

They used to be a bright shifter gold. Since the last time I've seen her, they've *changed*. Like the malice tucked in her smile, they're darker. Angrier. More of a burnt yellow than gold, they promise retribution.

Her lips curve.

My stomach plummets. "What are you doing here?" There's no doubt in my mind that she was waiting for me in particular. "What do you want from me, Peyton?"

"Isn't it obvious? You took my mate from me. It's only fair I take yours from you."

---

UP UNTIL I WAS EIGHTEEN, THERE WERE ONLY TWO CLUES that I, like the rest of my mother's line, had been touched by the

Luna: my silver eyes, and how I didn't quite fit into our pack because I was *other*.

Just because I was out of the hierarchy, though, that didn't mean I was an outcast. Far from it. My mother was revered for her connection to our goddess, and my fellow packmates treated me the same way. Around puberty, I developed the ability to cover my scent and those who were around me. It was a huge advantage when it came to hunting, and I truly considered it to be a gift.

And then, a couple of weeks after I came of age, I accidentally touched my Alpha's mate.

Their bond broke instantly.

I hadn't known I could do that. The weeks leading up to that birthday, I had started to sense the bonds in my packmates. I could tell how they were related to each other, who was a fated match, and who was chosen. The nuances came later—sensing the promise of a bond, or when one was shaky—but I had no idea that a simple brush of my hand could snap a mate bond in half.

There had to be doubt. One of them had to have been looking for a way out, unhappy in their mating. Of course, I didn't know that at the time.

All I knew was that I destroyed my Alpha.

He'd protected me and my family from anyone outside of our pack learning the truth of our line, and how did I repay him? By separating him from his fated mate forever. The Luna refused to bless their mating a second time.

And it was all my fault.

I ran. With nothing except the clothes on my back, I ran.

Those early days, I was little more than a scavenger. I never went fully feral, though it was close. I'm not exactly proud to say that I did whatever I could to survive. After abandoning my pack, I shied away from shifters; turning to other supes for help never occurred to me. I fell in with the humans, tucking my wolf down deep as I tried desperately to pass among them.

I stole. I slept with males if I got some food or money out of it. When I stumbled upon unclaimed land, I spent days in my fur, always being run off by either other lone wolves or real predatory animals who sensed the two-legged side of me.

And then, a few months into my new life, I stumbled upon a traveling carnival.

I'd learned it was better to hide among humans, especially those who had no idea that supes existed. Explaining away my silver eyes as colored contacts, they didn't have the nose or the instinct to know I was different; those who intuitively sensed my wolf gave me a wide berth. At the carnival, I was looking for the safety of the crowd and the chance to steal some food, and that was all.

I found something better.

A beautiful human female with eyes as deep blue as the sea was sitting in a simple stall, a deck of weathered yet intricately illustrated tarot cards set in front of her. Over her head, there was a sign. It had the stereotypical crystal ball painted on it, and it read:

***Madame Zoe***
***Palm readings $5***
***Tarot readings $10***

She picked me out of the crowd. When I murmured that I had no money to pay for any kind of reading, she pulled a single card for me for free.

*Wheel of Fortune.*

With a secretive smile, she pulled another.

*The Moon.*

It was nighttime. The carnival was bright with neons and spotlights, my wolf laying her head on her paw to avoid the sights and the sounds. The air smelled of fried foods and the musty stink when too many humans were together, and still I sensed something... intoxicating about the fortune-teller.

Crooking her finger, she beckoned me closer. Then, without a word, she reached below her table, grabbing a wooden box. Her voice had a thick accent I couldn't quite place, when she said, "For you. Use them well."

She gave me my deck of tarot cards that night, as well as a change in my fortune.

Just like her cards said.

From that moment on, I did exactly as she said. Instead of frequenting carnivals, I set up a lopsided tray table on city street corners, telling fortunes until it became second nature. I never earned enough to be considered comfortable, and life as a lone wolf meant I could never settle down for long, but it was better than it used to be.

Then, four years later, I met a shifter in the city I was living in and, for the first time, I didn't run. Then, when Kyle Ridgewood tracked me down despite me hiding my scent, I thought: *This is it.*

This could be *fate.*

I couldn't have been more wrong.

I was twenty-two, my wolf aching for some sense of community; love and touch, too. I'd been alone for so long, and when I first looked into his golden eyes, I felt the echo of a bond reaching toward me.

Back then, I didn't understand my curse as much as I do now. I didn't know the difference between a possible bond and one that had been finalized. I just saw a handsome male, felt a bond brush against me, and fell head over heels.

I fell into his bed, too. For weeks, I acted as if I was Kyle's mate; he even told me I was a member of the Oak Valley Pack—his pack—even though I never left the city. I ate his food, cooked him meals, and mated him any time I had the chance. He had been visiting the city I was living in for pack business that fateful day, and though he came back to see me every weekend after that, I loved the idea of eventually moving to stay with him in Oak Valley.

He promised to bring me back to live with him in the protected woods of his pack eventually, giving me a place where I could finally belong. All I needed to do was be patient while he explained to his Alpha that he wanted to choose a lone wolf—and a recent packmate—for his.

I'm not like Gem. I can't tell instinctively when someone is lying to me. I could guess, but I wouldn't know for sure until presented with the proof.

Like, oh, his furious mate showing up on my doorstep, ready to challenge me for the right to call Kyle hers.

Because *surprise*. Kyle neglected to mention over the months we were together that he already had a bonded mate. Peyton was actually his *fated* mate, and his Alpha pushed him to claim her even though he was reckless and wild and didn't want to settle down. Most bonded shifters are incredibly loyal to their mates once they take them; as Kyle and the Wicked Wolf prove, though, it's not *all* shifters. Though he was Peyton's in name, he mated available females whenever he wanted to.

And then he set his eyes on me, and I inadvertently gave him two things he desired desperately: his freedom from an unwanted bond and a willing pussy with no real strings attached. The first time I slept with him, I broke the thread tying him to Peyton. It never occurred to me that he was already taken. Sure, he had a white scar on his shoulder, but he explained it away as a shifter tattoo and not a mating mark.

So what if I knew that mating marks were white and shifter tattoos were more a silvery gray? I wanted so badly to be loved that I overlooked all the warning signs—until Peyton showed up, ready and willing to claw my guts out for getting between her and Kyle.

I managed to avoid that by siccing the furious female on her former mate. Kyle was lying in my bed, sated and drowsy after another round of vigorous mating when she unexpectedly appeared. My scent on his skin had Peyton nearly frothing at the mouth. As she charged into the room, I grabbed my deck of cards, my purse, and the spare pair of flip-flops I kept by the door, and I was gone. He lied to me, making me promises he couldn't keep. Bitter at his betrayal, me and my wolf both agreed he deserved whatever his spurned mate was going to dish out.

Only Peyton didn't do anything too terrible. I'd heard rumors that, for a while, she tried to pretend she still had a mate bond with Kyle after she dragged him back to pack territory. When that didn't work, she fled the Oak Valley Pack on her own, leaving Kyle free to be the manwhore that he was.

Now, seven years later, she's found me. But, unlike then, she's not threatening to gut me.

No. She just wants to take my fated mate.

You know what? Go right ahead, Peyton.

Aleks isn't mine. He'll never be mine, either.

"You're wasting your time," I tell her. "I don't have a mate."

It's the truth. So why does my wolf bare her teeth when Peyton's lips curve in a wicked smile?

"That so?"

"Yeah."

Peyton snorts. "You were a shit liar back then, too, Howell. Telling me you had no idea that Kyle was mine. Now you expect me to believe that you don't know that you're someone's intended?"

"I don't care what you believe," I say, bravado filling my voice. "If you want to blame anyone, blame him. Blame Kyle. He courted me. He initiated mating with me. He touched me. Your bond broke because he never wanted it."

"You're still trying to lie. Do it again and I'll go for your vocal cords, you silver-eyed freak."

I'm not a liar when it comes to this. I'm *not*.

"Stop this, Peyton."

"No. You think you're so much better than me because of the Luna. You're not. And I look forward to fucking your mate whenever I want." Lifting up her hand, Peyton flexes her fingers, showing off her sharpened claws. "Carving up his back. Marking him again and again until his flesh is nothing but bloody pulp. Maybe then you'll know that some things are sacred." She scoffs. "Maybe then you'll understand what you took from me."

A male who preferred getting his dick wet over being loyal to his fated mate. That's what I took from her, but if Peyton is still holding a grudge after seven years, there's nothing I can say now that will change her mind.

I'm not always a liar, but I'm definitely not a fighter. Not really. I never have been. But before the Luna's touch changed my life, I was a maternal she-wolf. I adored watching over the pups, and even if they weren't mine, they were pack. I'm not a fighter, but I would go feral to protect them.

When Peyton threatens Aleks, it doesn't matter that I've spent weeks—*months*—rejecting what the Luna tells me constantly. He's mine, even if I can't have him. I won't let her hurt him, especially before I can figure out what he thinks of me.

My silver eyes shift to black as my claws lengthen, matching Peyton's. "No. You won't."

"Who's gonna stop me, freak?"

"I am."

"Go right ahead," dares Peyton. "Give me your best shot."

Our gazes are locked. This is a challenge, in more ways than one. The stakes are higher than they were when she stepped out of the trees marking the boundary of the dirt road, and I know that if our wolves start fighting, only one of us will walk away.

And that's when a voice calls out to me.

"Elizabeth? Is that you?"

# CHAPTER 6
# ALEKSANDER FILAN

If I look over my shoulder, I'll break the stare with Peyton. Unacceptable. She'll take it as me losing our little challenge, and I can't have that.

Luckily, I don't need to look behind me to know who has just joined us.

*Dominic.*

I exhale in relief. *Saved by the vampire.*

I would've fought Peyton if I had to. I'm just super glad that I don't.

"This isn't over," she sneers, the first one to look away as her dark yellow eyes lock on something over my shoulder. "I have plans for you. One way or another, you'll pay for what you did to me. To us. Your precious parasites might've saved you tonight, but don't get used to it."

Then, with a snap of her human teeth, she shifts. A sleek grey wolf takes the place of the black-haired female. Growling low, her ears flat against her skull, Peyton's wolf kicks some snow up at me before loping away just as Dominic approaches me from behind.

Together, we watch the wolf disappear into the distance.

"Friend of yours?" he asks.

Not even a little. "She's a shifter," I tell him needlessly. The pile of torn clothes by my feet, plus the wolf prints hightailing it down the stretch of dirt road are a couple of big, honking clues what type of female Peyton is.

Dominic frowns. "You didn't invite her into the city, did you? I know Roman has approved your stay, and the Mountainside Alpha's mate can still visit, but that's it. No other shifters."

I shake my head. "No. Actually, I was just telling her she had to go."

"You should probably head home, too. We patrol the borders for a reason. It's not always safe out here."

He doesn't know the half of it. If Dominic hadn't come over to check up on me, I don't know what Peyton would've done—or me, for that matter.

One thing for sure: I wouldn't have liked it.

Satisfied that he got his point across, Dominic says, "Allez. Come on. I'll walk with you back a bit."

When he goes to take my elbow to steer me past the border that leads into Muncie, I move out of his reach. It's an instinctive gesture; I don't let anyone touch me if I can avoid it. I haven't accidentally severed a bond since Kyle. I've learned control. Learned how to use my curse instead of it using me. However, with Peyton's taunts and threats echoing in my ears, I can't be too careful.

I just removed an unwanted blood bonding from Dominic. I can already sense that a new one has taken its place. As shaky as I am right now, a simple brush against my skin might snap it.

"It's okay," I say, lying through my teeth. I'm not always a liar, but sometimes I *am*. "I'm okay. I wouldn't want to keep you from your patrol."

He frowns as if he can tell I'm completely full of it. "Does Roman know you left the city? I don't think he would approve."

My hand lifts to my chest, patting the fang nestled there. Peyton had thrown the fang a look of disgust, but in Muncie, it's basically my golden ticket. The fact that it's Roman Zakharov's token is supposed to be special, but I don't ever want his vampires to get the wrong idea. He was very clear: he traded his fang and his protection to have control of my abilities. That doesn't mean he can tell me what to do, right?

"I'm off duty. Roman can't tell me what to do when I'm off the clock."

"You've not been in the city long enough, cher. When you live in Muncie a little longer, you'll understand that the Cadre... and especially Roman... tells us all what to do. And we do it."

He pats me on the shoulder. I feel the hum of a secure bond through my shirt.

"Don't worry. You'll get used to it."

Honestly? I'm a low-ranked shifter. Following an established authority is kind of hard-wired into me and my wolf. It'll be easy to fall in line if I have to so that's not really what's weighing on me right now.

Fact is, Dominic's perfect timing saved me from a fight I'm not so sure I could've won. A regular delta female... I could take down one of those easily.

But a broken shifter with a jagged bond?

I don't think so.

Worse, Peyton will be back. I'm sure of it.

And I still haven't said two words to Aleksander Filan since I've been in Muncie.

---

ONCE I MADE IT BACK TO THE TOWNHOUSE, I CALLED GEM and let her know about my run-in with Peyton. I hesitate over whether or not I should tell her I sensed her father before deciding that she deserved to know.

It's okay. I recovered the hearing in my right ear about twenty minutes after her furious curse nearly blew out my eardrum, and at least she's on her guard now, too. Her overprotective mate is probably going to give her a hard time whenever she leaves their cabin for a while, but I couldn't *not* tell her after everything she's done for me so far.

The next morning, I walk to work, a little less confident than I was the day before. I have Roman's fang, and Gem assured me that the Cadre's constant patrols should keep Peyton and Walker out. When I doubt that, I remember how Dominic popped up so suddenly. With as many patrollers as Roman employs, odds are if he hadn't, someone else would've.

No one bothers me the entire walk from the townhouse to the Cadre building in the center of the city. Taking that as a good sign, I walk into the lobby, shrug off the coat I wear to blend in with the humans in Muncie, and fold it up.

Leigh is already sitting behind the counter. She's talking to a tall, leggy blonde whose forearms are resting on the countertop. I murmur a quick 'good morning' to her as I stow my coat and my purse on one of the shelves below our shared desk.

As I do, I hear someone click their tongue. Glancing up, I see it's the blonde. With her flawless features, her pale eyes, and her vaguely judgmental expression, I pin her as another vampire.

"Oh," she says. "Who is this? Let me guess. It's Aleksander's new puppy."

I freeze, like a deer in headlights.

What does she know?

Better questions: *how* does she know?

"Gretchen. Be nice."

"What? You're the one who told me about the box of teabags and—"

With a casual gesture that's somehow still incredibly obvious, Leigh brushes her hands over her impressive chest.

Gretchen immediately looks at mine.

"Oh."

"Uh-huh."

Her skin is already alabaster, but she goes impossibly paler. Like, so pale I can almost see through her. Muttering something under her breath, she gives me an incredibly fake smile. "Let's forget what I just said, okay? Hello. I'm Gretchen, and you are?"

...so incredibly impressed that me wearing Roman's fang just knocked the mean girl out of her.

"Elizabeth."

Her gaze looks me up and down. "She's not as mangy as the last one, is she, Leigh? I suppose, if Roman was gonna mark one, she'll do."

Okay. Maybe not *all* of the mean girl.

Next to me, Leigh looks like she wants to get up and slap some duct tape over Gretchen's mouth.

Huh. I now understand why Gem calls the trio of Gretchen, Tamera, and Leigh the Nightmare Trio; she'd groaned when I admitted that I worked with Leigh, and met Tamera. I thought

Gem was being kind of catty since Tamera seems friendly enough and Leigh's been good to me so far, but now that I've met their ringleader?

I get it. I do.

She's not all that malicious, though. I don't know. Maybe it's because I spent the last ten years mainly living among humans, but if that's the worst that Gretchen is going to dish out? I can take it.

I smile at her, and hers wavers. "I'm glad to meet you. I've heard so much about you already."

"All good things, I expect."

"The best."

Gretchen fluffs her hair. "As it should be. Leigh loves me."

"I do," Leigh mutters on a sigh, as if she can't believe that she does. "Almost as much as my beloved. And I love it when you stop by, Gretch, but is there anything you need? Because I've got a lot of training to do with Elizabeth and—"

"I hope you're not being a distraction, Gretchen. If you're bored, perhaps you'd like to join Tamera and Leigh in the Cadre."

*Aleks*.

As his lightly accented voice washes over us, Gretchen spins around, moving just enough that I can't miss him.

My breath catches in my throat. He was standing right behind Gretchen, and her vampire aura covered him until he announced his presence like that.

Suddenly, it's all I can do not to notice that *he's right there*. Even though the counter is between us, this is the closest I've been to him since that night in the Wolf District.

He's just as beautiful as I remember. More, really, when you factor in his fresh haircut, his clean-shaven cheeks, and a perfectly fitted sweater that doesn't have a single bullet hole in it.

My heart skips a beat. I'm pretty sure every supe in the building noticed, too.

"Join the Cadre? Actually spend my days working when I can be sleeping? No, thanks, Aleksander," Gretchen tells him, hurriedly stepping further away from the counter. I have half a mind to beg her to stay. "I was just saying hello to Leigh before I turned in. I've done that, now I'll be on my way."

She's gone in an instant, leaving me torn between gaping after her—or gawking at the male who's moved directly in front of me.

Leigh looks as surprised to see him as I do. "Aleksander. How can we help you?"

He's staring at me—but not just *me*. Unless I'm imagining it, his pale eyes are locked on my chest. As if he can see right through my shirt, I know he's sensing Roman's fang hanging around my neck just like Gretchen had. He doesn't seem to react to it one way or another, and I'm not sure how to feel about that.

But—and, again, unless I'm imagining it—he does seem to be waiting for me to acknowledge him. If that's so, he's going to be waiting a long, long time.

Aleks takes a breath, about to speak.

I tense. It's instinctive.

What if he says something to me? Would he mention the box of teabags? Worse, will he say anything about California?

What about *bonds*?

Before I start to work myself up to a panic, I remind myself that I've never been officially introduced to him. I cling to that as my trembling hands shuffle through the pile of papers in front of me. Looking down at the pages, my eyes are unseeing as I strain to hear their pleasant conversation over the pounding of my heart.

Get it under control, Elizabeth.

The male vampire might just think I'm nervous because of him—and he wouldn't be wrong—but my co-worker would know for sure that something's up. I've worked alongside her for a few days so far and, until now, I've never been so close to losing my shit.

I blame the gorgeous vampire drumming his short yet neat nails against the top of the counter. I don't know. It's like we had an unspoken agreement to pretend the other didn't exist. He stalked me from outside of the townhouse, and I acted like I had no idea that he was standing there, looking up at my window, before disappearing into the shadows of the night and the softly fallen snow.

It's worked so far. Since I joined Leigh as one of Roman's secretaries, I thought that it would continue that way, the inexplicable box of teabags notwithstanding.

Guess not.

He opens his mouth. I try not to make it obvious that I'm listening, only relaxing when he says in his lightly accented and cultured voice, "I'm here to see Roman."

Leigh clicks on her mouse, pulling something up on her computer. "You're not on his schedule."

"No. But he'll see me."

Aleks must have some kind of pull around here. The first thing I was taught during training was that no one—absolutely *no one*—was allowed past the lobby if they weren't on Roman's schedule.

But, instead of telling Aleks that, Leigh types something,

then nods. "Okay. It's right—"

"Yes. Thank you, Leigh. I know the way."

He strides down the hall, heading straight for the elevator. I can sense Leigh watching me closely, curiosity written all over her lovely face. When she starts to speak, I quickly cut her off, asking her a question about something written on the page I'm holding.

Thankfully, she doesn't push me on the subject of Aleks. Returning to her role of trainer, she answers my question, then gestures for me to scoot closer so that she can show me how to view Roman's schedule on the computer.

I've barely learned how to open the program on my own when the reception desk's phone begins to buzz.

I'm not even a little surprised when Leigh reminds me again that the red light means it's coming from inside the Cadre building. Like Roman's office maybe?

She picks it up and, after a quick exchange, sets the receiver back down again.

With a slightly sympathetic expression, she turns to me. "Roman wants to see you."

Crap. From the moment Aleks disappeared behind the elevator's closed doors, I was afraid of something like that happening. Call it intuition—or my wolfish instinct—but I couldn't help but think that Fate decided I was taking my sweet time in regarding Aleks as my fated mate. If I wasn't going to go to him, maybe it was time my mate came to me.

Rising up from my seat, I just hope that he's already made a quick retreat himself by the time I climb all the stairs up to Roman's office.

He hasn't.

Like the first time I met him, Roman is seated behind his desk. To his right, as far from the entrance as he can get, Aleks is watching with an unblinking gaze as I ease the door in, then slowly step into the opulent office.

I can feel the weight of his stare on me. Pretending I don't, I focus solely on my boss.

"You wanted to see me?"

"Ah, Elizabeth, yes." He waves at the pair of leather chairs across from his desk. "Please. Take a seat."

With Aleks leaning oh so casually against the far wall, I don't feel comfortable being the only one of us two sitting down. But what can I do?

I take the seat.

He gestures in Aleks's direction. "This is Aleksander Filan. He's one of my trusted patrollers. I hope you find that you can trust him as well."

He's supposed to be my mate. If I can't trust him, I have even bigger problems than I thought.

Roman doesn't know that, though. Neither does Aleks, I'm willing to bet. As far as they're aware, this is a simple introduction.

With a shy nod, purposely avoiding meeting his gaze, I say, "Hello."

Aleks nods. It's brisk and quick and almost standoffish.

My wolf whines inside of my chest. Lifting my hand, I rub between my boobs, trying to settle her.

Roman follows the motion. For a second, I pause, misunderstanding his intent expression. A second later, I realize that he isn't watching my hand but, instead, his fang.

"You've kept it on. Good."

Of course I did. He told me I had to.

Thinking about how the blonde vampire reacted when she saw it, I murmur, "Thanks. It's worked so far."

"I'm glad. But that's exactly why I've called this meeting today. Forgive me, but I was... distracted when I gave it to you."

Oh. Reaching behind me to unclasp it, I ask, "Do you want it back?"

"No, no. Of course not. It's just... Aleks here has reminded me that a fang from a Cadre leader is different from others," Roman says. "It's a mark of favor. Of protection. Those who follow me—or those who fear me—will respect it. But"—his near colorless eyes are strikingly rimmed with red—"there are those in my city who won't. And they'll make you pay for wearing it."

So, in other words, I'm in the same situation I was in while I was still living in the Wolf District. He's marked me as his pet, and now there's a target on my back. Because of my tiny association with Roman, vampires will be gunning for my blood, just like Gem suspected.

Damn it! I took the fang so that this exact situation *wouldn't* happen.

And, okay. I'm still trying to deal with Peyton's unexpected appearance last night. With her threat hanging over my head, I already knew my time in the Fang City would be cut short. If she found me, it was only a matter of time before the Alpha did. The fact that she was near enough to him recently to wear his scent on her skin—which usually only happens after a mating—means that I'm already beginning to look over my shoulder again for that handsome face and those deceptively golden eyes.

It's not fair. I came to Muncie because I hoped it would finally be safe for me to settle down instead of going from human town to human town. Living among bloodsuckers wasn't my first choice, but I thought I could hide in plain sight. No shifter could enter the town without Roman knowing, so I should've been safe from my kind of supe at least.

And now I have to worry about vampires gunning for my blood?

It's still a better risk, I realize. I'd rather be bitten a hundred times over by a vampire than get mixed up with Jack Walker.

And I know that the Wicked Wolf will be coming for me eventually. If not me, then Gem, but she's up on Accalia with Ryker and her personal guard watching over her.

In Muncie, I've just got me.

Can vampires read minds? I have no idea, but when Roman frowns over at me, I'd bet anything I had that he knows exactly what I'm thinking about right at this moment.

Then he says, "And you have enemies of your own," and I'm sure of it.

Yup. He knows.

"I guess Dominic told you about last night." When he doesn't deny it, but just waits with an expectant expression, I try to explain. "I didn't invite her here. The shifter he saw me talking to. And you're right. I guess she is an enemy." Walker, too, but I keep that to myself. If Aleks wants to act like he doesn't know me, or where we could've possibly met before this, I'm not going to be the one to mention the shifter who forced him to participate in a fight to the death. "But I learned my lesson. She ambushed me when I left Muncie to visit Gemma Swann in Accalia. I won't do that again."

Out of the corner of my eye, I watch for Aleks's reaction when I mention Gem. I don't know why I'm torturing myself, but it's like... I don't know. Like I have to see if he *will* react.

He does. I doubt I would've noticed if I wasn't looking for it, but his eyes flash brighter than the light fixtures hanging over our heads at just the mention of her name.

He doesn't say anything, though. He just keeps as quiet as ever as Roman continues addressing me.

"I understand. But, in Muncie, you'll still need someone to watch over you when I can't. You see, I rarely leave this building. I run the whole city from the Cadre's headquarters, and while my fang will keep you safe from most, there are still dangers, even here."

Now, I know that Gem was joking when she offered to give me one of her personal guard. With Roman's solemn tone, though, I'm beginning to second-guess my knee-jerk reaction to refuse even if she was kidding. Her guards—a trio of delta wolves, even though Jace was recently promoted to Pack Beta—are loyal to her and her alone, but maybe there's a packmate who wouldn't mind doing a little freelance guard duty for a Luna-touched female.

I open my mouth, prepared to ask Roman if he would open Muncie's border to a second shifter. It's the best idea I have other than packing up and going on the run again, but I barely get the first syllable out before I'm cut off.

"I will."

It's Aleks. No longer leaning against the wall, he's straight-backed and assured as he moves to stand opposite Roman's desk.

"Aleksander?"

"Me, Roman. I will guard Elizabeth."

*What?*

# CHAPTER 7
# THE IMPORTANCE OF WHITE BORSCHT

Five months. I managed to avoid actually talking to my fated mate for five months.

Even after he showed up outside of my new home, watching me, leaving his scent behind... I could still pretend like I didn't know who he was. The teabags? For all I knew, it was a welcome gift automatically sent to anyone joining the Cadre. Gem made a point to tell me that he was as almost high up as Roman himself.

Now?

Now I can't.

"You don't have to do that."

"Yes, I do." His features are soft, pretty, but his jaw is so sharp, I bet I could cut a sheet of paper with it. "A threat to one of us is a threat to all. We can't put the city at risk."

Of course. Of freaking course that's the only reason he's volunteering. Not because of me. Not because he senses the same thing that the Luna insists: that we're fated mates. No.

He's only agreeing to watch my back because of his duty to Muncie.

I pat the necklace. Addressing Roman, I ask, "Will this keep me safe while I'm within the borders?"

"From most, yes."

"And the patrol will keep any other shifters out?"

Aleks answers this time, brow slightly creased as if he knows where I'm going with this—and he doesn't like it. "They will."

"So then I don't need anyone watching over me. I appreciate the gesture," I say to Roman, "but I'm a she-wolf." And I'm so very tired of running. I've put roots down here, and I'm going to stay until I can't anymore. "To treat me as any less is kind of insulting."

"Roman, give me leave. Give me permission. Tell her that I'll be her guard."

"Aleksander." It's a warning tone I haven't heard from Roman yet. "Perhaps we should have this conversation after Elizabeth goes back to the lobby."

Aleks shakes his head so emphatically, his curls nearly bounce. "Not while she's in danger. Someone must keep her safe. It has to be me."

"Why?"

I want to echo Roman's simply stated question.

*Why?*

As if he heard my thoughts this time, Aleks turns to me. Just like me, he'd been avoiding looking straight at me while we've been up here, but no longer. He peers directly into my eyes, pinning me into place with his gaze.

"Why? Because you're my beloved."

I blink, momentarily stunned. It breaks the stare, but even

when my eyes shutter closed, the insistent expression on his face seems seared on the back of my eyelids.

I've known exactly who Aleksander Filan was to me all along, even when I was pretending I didn't. From the moment our eyes met when he was thrown in the pit and I was still at the Alpha's heel, the Luna told me that he was mine. I'd had dreams of a gorgeous male with pale green eyes before I ever saw him. When I did, it was like my dreams brought to life—only impossibly more beautiful.

However, the tug I felt toward him was so powerful, I could never be sure that he felt anything in return. It was one of the only times my "gift" failed *me.* Eventually, I convinced myself that he didn't. I had my reasons for staying away, but I've never heard of an able-bodied supe male purposely avoiding their fated mate—and for a vampire, their "beloved" counts—unless they were rejecting the bond.

What's worse? My fated mate not recognizing me as his, or rejecting me instead? I clung to the first option because the second was soul-crushing.

And now, after five months, he's finally admitting what I would've never known for sure?

He's my fated mate—and I'm *his*?

Roman rises up from behind his desk. Switching from English to Russian, he says in an ominous tone, "Ona ne Julia, moy brat."

Julia again. Who is Julia?

I don't know, but Aleks surely does.

His eyes turn blood-red. "I know she's not Julia, Roman. Julia's been dead for two centuries."

She has? Two centuries... Gem said Aleks was more than two

centuries old himself. Who is she—more importantly, who is the mysterious Julia to Aleks?

"You can't bring her back," Roman says, his voice softer than before. More soothing.

Aleks jerks his head, a rough nod. "I know that as well. But Elizabeth is here now, and she's in trouble. She might be wearing your fang, but we both know that's not enough. I will watch over her as well."

"Oh? You will?"

"No," I say, answering Roman before Aleks can. "He won't." Ignoring the determined look Aleks is shooting my way, I face the Cadre leader. "Is it okay if I go back downstairs now? I'm only scheduled until six and I want to finish some of the training work Leigh gave me."

"Elizabeth—"

"Of course," Roman says, speaking over Aleks. "Go on."

"*Roman*."

"Stay behind with me, Aleksander. We have more to discuss."

Disappointment mingled with fury seethes off of Aleks. But, like the rest of the vampires in Muncie that I've met so far, he obeys Roman the same way that a pack does its Alpha.

I just hope Roman keeps him occupied until after my shift's over.

---

WHEN I FIRST FEEL THE SUDDEN CHILL CREEPING IN, goosebumps popping up along my arms, I think it's because it's snowing again. Big, fat, white flakes are falling heavily from the night's sky. We're looking at another few inches by morning, and as much as I'm sick of the stuff, I can't deny that it doesn't look pretty as it coats the sidewalk, the grass, and the roads.

In fact, I drift over to the front window to get a better look —and that's when I realize that it might be cold out, but that wasn't what I was reacting to.

Aleks is standing outside of the townhouse again.

He hasn't been there long. In fact, judging by the prints left in the snow, he must have just arrived when I got up to take a peek.

There's no time to duck and pretend I didn't see him. The second I moved the curtain, his head turned to see me silhouetted against the light. In one hand, he's holding a brown paper bag. He lifts the other, a friendly wave.

Unsure what else to do, I wave back.

As if that's all the permission he needs, Aleks bows his head, walking into the snow, striding purposely up my walkway.

I back away from the window, biting the claw on my right thumb.

The doorbell sounds.

I can't ignore it, can I?

Glancing down, I check to make sure I'm presentable. I've only been home for about an hour and a half. I kicked off my shoes as soon as I got in, but I'm still wearing my work clothes. My hair is piled high on top of my head in a messy bun. I wiped the make-up off of my face a couple of minutes ago, and had plopped down to watch some mindless tv before dinner in order to forget all about today's events.

*You're my beloved...*

You know what? Fine. Let's see if he likes at-home Elizabeth because if I'm his fated mate, so is she.

Almost as if I'm daring him to change his mind about his

unexpected declaration, I shuffle over to the front door. Then, after taking a steadying breath so I don't look as nervous as I suddenly feel, I pull the door in.

"Aleks... um. Hi. What are you doing here?"

He holds up the bag. "My patrol starts at ten. I had some time so I thought I'd bring you dinner."

Oof. Good thing I'm leaning against the side of the door because the earnest way he says that? I need the support. I'd left him fuming in Roman's office, and his response is to bring me dinner?

"You didn't have to do that."

"Maybe before you knew that you were my beloved. But you know now, Elizabeth. And if I want to prove to you that you should accept me as your mate, this is one way to do it. A good mate provides, yes?"

"Uh. I guess."

"So you'll take it?"

Can I really say no?

I've never willingly accepted food from a male before. To do so while living in a pack has repercussions. But Aleks isn't trying to feed me the way a shifter male would. He's just trying to convince me that he meant what he said in Roman's office today.

Honestly, I don't know *what* to say.

A part of me wants to tell Aleks that he's meant to be mine. That the Luna has been telling me for more than five months now that he's my fated mate. But I can't. He's made a big leap, claiming me as his beloved. If I tell him that my wolf recognizes him the same way he recognizes me... it'll be settled. I'll be a vampire's mate.

And I'm not ready for that.

But I can't say no, so I nod. "Yeah. Why not?"

"Where do you eat?"

This is so bizarre. And yet...

"Usually on a tray table in front of the television."

"In the living room?"

I nod.

"Tak. I've been here before. I know the way."

And, just like that, Aleks marches into the townhouse. He knocks the snow from his shoes, shaking the flakes from his water-dark curls, and comes inside without so much an invitation.

Guess pop culture got *that* wrong.

I chase after him, unsure what I'm supposed to do now. When I opened the door, I hadn't expected him to actually come inside, and now I have a vampire in my private space.

Even worse? My wolf is pleased to share it with her mate.

Aleks pulls the tray table away from the couch, gesturing for me to sit down. A little bit dazed at how quickly I lost control of this situation, I do. He places the tray table in front of me again, placing his brown paper bag on top of it.

Reaching in, he takes out a plastic container of some kind of soup. It's white with hunks of sausage and egg floating in it. He pops the lid, then sets it in front of me. The spoon comes next. He places that next to the container.

"It should still be warm. If not, tell me and I'll fix that for you."

I'm not getting out of eating this right now, am I?

He waits on bated breath as I scoop up some of the stew, then lift the spoon to my lips. When I swallow, he shudders out an exhale. "How does it taste?"

*Sour and tangy, yet delicious*. "It's good. What is it?"

"Bialy barszcz. In English, white borscht." He gives me a

crooked grin that makes him that much more stunning—and a little more relatable. "I made it myself."

If he was a shifter, this would be courting behavior. Good thing he's not.

"Go on. Eat. It's hearty for this type of weather. Tea, too. I could make some if you'd like." He pauses for a moment before oh so causally asking, "Did you get my package?"

I was wondering if he was going to bring up the box he sent me. At least, now, I know why he felt compelled to send it.

"I did, thank you. I appreciated it. The soup, too. That was very... thoughtful of you."

"Consider it making amends for today. I could've broached the topic of your being my beloved a little more tactfully. I wasn't avoiding you, Elizabeth," he says, and once again I wonder about his mind-reading skills. "I was hoping to ease you into knowing who we are to each other but I no longer have the luxury for that."

I hurriedly spoon a chunk of sausage into my mouth, taking my time to chew it. Sorry, Aleks. Can't talk. Mouth full.

He smiles again, before moving so that he's standing next to the far side of my couch. Hiking up his trousers, he sits down. Not once does he take his eyes off of me, almost as if he's getting pleasure out of watching me eat his food.

He should. It's pretty yummy.

As I make quick work of the meal, his gaze finally begins to wander over the room. I know he said he's been here before—when Gem lived at the townhouse, I'm sure—so he seems interested in how I've made it my own space. Too bad there isn't much to see. I came here with very little, and most of the changes I did make were upstairs in my bedroom.

Not that Aleks is going to see that anytime soon.

When he notices the wooden box that I have sitting on the side table next to the couch, he asks, "Are those your cards?"

"My cards?"

"Your fortune-telling cards. I've seen you with them before."

*How*? I never used them in Muncie. They're specifically for when I'm fleecing human tourists. So how the hell does Aleks know about them?

With an openly suspicious glance at him, I nod slowly. "My tarot cards. Yes."

"Would you read me?"

*Huh*?

"Me? I mean, I'm not an actual fortune-teller. I just faked it for the humans to get money, that's all."

"Entertainment, then?"

"I guess you could say so."

"Okay." Aleks settles deeper into the couch. He props one ankle over his knees, his arms stretched along the back. "I wouldn't mind being entertained."

Yup. Totally out of control.

I have to make this work for me. But how?

Ah. I think I have an idea...

"Let's make a deal. When I do a reading for a client, I pull three cards. I'll do the same for you, but I want you to answer three questions for me first. What do you think?"

His eyes glimmer with open interest. "I think you have a deal. I'm through hiding. To you, I'll be an open book. Ask me anything."

My first question is easy. I don't even have to think about it before I'm asking, "Am I really yours?"

I've known for five months that Aleks was my fated mate. Longer, really. For years, I dreamed of a gorgeous male with his carelessly tousled curls and a pair of seafoam green eyes that I could drown in. He was so otherworldly beautiful, I knew he could only be a product of my lonely imagination. He couldn't be real.

But he was.

When I saw him being forced into the pit, I could barely believe it. I *knew* him even before I ever learned his name.

My question is easy. So, it seems, is his answer.

"Yes."

Because I don't want to give anything away with my expression, I busy myself with opening the wooden box I keep my tarot cards in. Lifting them out, I give the deck a cursory shuffle.

It takes a couple of seconds before I have my next question.

"Do vampires form bonds like shifters do?"

"They can, and they do. Like your kind, we can choose our beloved, but Fate also has her say. You see, blood tells."

"What does that mean?"

"I don't have a beast inside of me or," he adds with a pointed nod at me, "a goddess guiding me, but a vampire has a second sense about these things. We can look at a prospective mate and know that they're meant for us and us alone. With a single taste, though, it's undeniable. And it would only strengthen any existing tie the more we drink. By the way, that should be your second question, but I'm enjoying this game. You still have two more."

I ignore his slight tease as I focus on the way he said *we*. As he spoke, I noticed that his fangs grew longer. Sharper. Almost as if he's getting ready to do just that. Suddenly, I realize that we're not just talking about the differences between our kinds of supes anymore.

I keep a wary eye on the points of his fangs as I ask, "Do you want to bite me?"

From the sudden hunger in his gaze, I can tell that he's dying to. "Yes."

"Oh."

"Don't be afraid of me, Elizabeth. I won't unless you invite me to."

So it's like being invited into my bedroom then? *Never*.

And yet—

"Would it hurt? Being bitten, I mean."

"Vampires can give pleasure or pain with their bite. As my beloved, I would never see you in pain. So no." He gestures at the cards with his chin. "And that's your three. Now it's my turn."

With a shrug, I pull three cards for him.

Oh, come *on*.

"Like I said, I'm really just a fraud. When I read the cards, they don't mean anything."

Gathering up the cards together, I stack them on the bottom of the deck, eager to change the subject. Even though that's true, it's too much of a coincidence that the three cards I pulled for Aleks are actually pretty fitting: The Moon, the Lovers, and Death. I couldn't have picked a better set of three if I cheated.

Aleks leans forward. He shifts, lowering both of his shoes to the floor as he turns to me. "Are you sure about that?"

I drop the cards back into the box. "Can I ask you one more question?"

"You can."

"Who is Julia?"

Aleks sits up from his slouch. The companionable air that

had settled around us as we played the question game disappears immediately.

"No one you need to worry about."

*He's lying*, murmurs the Luna. *In this, he hides from you*.

Roman never explained who she was. When I mentioned her name to Gem during our dinner the other day, she said that Julia was a female that Aleks once loved before hurriedly adding that it wasn't her story to tell. I'd have to ask Aleks if I wanted to know more.

And Aleks, I'm absolutely convinced now, never will.

Of course not.

What am I doing? Why am I playing this game with him? He says he's an open book, but at the first sign that I've asked him a question he doesn't want to answer, he shuts down.

And maybe I did the same thing when it comes to the cards.

Still.

I never thought I'd have a mate of my own. Living in fear that a single touch would break any bond I made with another, I long ago gave up on the hope that there might be someone who loved me so irrevocably that they never doubted that we belonged together forever.

And Aleks won't be able to do that, either. I'm sure of it.

Getting up, ignoring my wolf's keening whine, I cross the living room. Grabbing the doorknob, I give it such a hard turn, I nearly snap it off.

"You should be getting ready for your patrol."

"I still have another hour."

He's really going to make me kick him out, isn't he?

"I'm tired. I think you should go."

"But—"

"Good night, Aleksander."

"Elizabeth, your *eyes*..."

That's right. You're not the only one who can change their eye color when you're experiencing strong emotions. Only I'm not feeling bloodlust like he does when his eyes go from green to red.

For me, my eyes change from silver to black when I can't control myself.

And, as I've just discovered, when it comes to Aleks, I don't think I'll ever be able to.

---

AN HOUR LATER, I'M STILL STRUGGLING TO COME TO TERMS with what a difference a day can make. Yesterday, I was sure he had no idea who I was. Early this evening, I learned he thought of me as his beloved. And now? Now I'm sure that he's set into motion his pursuit of me—right when I've accepted that I can never have him.

That's not all, either. Aleks never mentioned how the rest of his discussion with Roman went, but considering he felt comfortable enough to bring me dinner? I'm thinking that he convinced my boss to give him the okay to watch over me.

Well... if that's the case? I might as well give him something to watch.

I need to get out of the townhouse. I need to run. Because I'm so close to both my wolf and the Luna, I don't have to shift as often as more powerful wolves do, but if I go too long in my skin, I get antsy. After the meeting with Roman and Aleks? I have this urge to run until my pads are bloody and my wolf collapses on her belly.

As soon as I'm sure Aleks has left, I trade my outfit for a

simple shift dress. My shoes are slip-ons, and I go without a purse. At this hour, I don't have any intention to go anywhere but the only patch of dense forest and greenery in all of Muncie; even in winter, the evergreens provide cover. It's the closest to wild land as I can get while living in an urban city, and it's the sole place I feel free to let my wolf loose.

It's one of Roman's rules. If I want to stay in Muncie, I needed to keep any unsuspecting humans from finding out that shifters—and, by extension, *vampires*—exist. That means no shifting in front of anyone else, no walking around on the streets while I was still in my fur, and no running unless I'm concealed in the trees.

I'm probably pushing my luck. My wolf will leave actual prints that won't be too easy to explain, but right now? I don't care. If Roman is pissed, I'll deal with it later.

I just need to *run*.

Once I'm about thirty feet past the border of the trees, I take a deep breath. It smells like snow and frozen earth and that's about all. No one else is within scenting distance. Quickly shucking my dress, I fold it neatly. I tuck my discarded shoes beneath it.

When all I'm wearing is a sliver of the moon and Roman's fang, I reach inside of myself, giving control over to my wolf. Where dark-haired, silver-eyed Elizabeth was standing seconds ago, there's now an arctic white wolf with similar eyes that glimmer beneath the moonlight.

I wasn't sure if the chain would transform with me. Jewelry has a tendency to—like rings and earrings—while clothes don't. Shaking my wolfish head, I can see that the chain is gone, but it's not broken on the crusted snow beneath my paws. It's still on the two-legged form waiting inside for the run to be over.

The quaint breeze ruffles my fur. My ears twitch when it whispers through the branches on some of the empty trees. Rearing back, I pounce, chuffing when my paws land in a pile of powder and it puffs up, tickling my snout.

When I'm presenting as a human, everything is made up of shades of grey. As a wolf? Things are black and white. Aleks is my mate. The wintry weather is fun. The park has some tiny prey I can chase.

My wolf wants to run.

So I do.

# CHAPTER 8
# NOT YOURS

I run for a couple of hours, reveling in the sensation of being in my fur. I make laps, careful to stay inside the wooded land. At one point, I think I hear someone approaching, but instead of playing a stalking game with them, I head downwind, then put some distance between us.

Before long, though, my stomach starts to growl. In the winter, most prey is hibernating. The mice I chased would be nothing but a mouthful for my wolf and I didn't bother. After expending so much energy, I needed more than that, and Aleks's borscht is a distant memory by now.

Making my way through the words, I pad back toward where I left my pile of clothes. Resting on my haunches, I shift, then push myself off of the ground before bending over and grabbing my dress.

I'm just yanking it over my head when I sense that I'm not alone anymore.

Fresh out of a shift, my senses are a little hazy. Everything is much keener when I'm a wolf which means that my nose seems duller, my vision less acute. After a couple of minutes, I'll adjust, but when the vampiric scent and powerful aura brushes up against my back, I'm not so sure I *have* a few minutes before I have to face him.

Still, I call his name as I slip my bare feet into my shoes. "Aleksander—"

*Not yours,* murmurs the Luna.

What?

Of course it's Aleks. What other vampire would have tracked me down to the edge of the woods?

I don't know why I thought I knew better than the Luna. Spinning around, the skirt of my dress flaring around me, I expect to find Aleks watching me, just like he told Roman he would.

But my goddess, as ever, was right. It's not Aleks.

At least I understand why the aura seemed as powerful as his. It's because I'm not looking at one vampire.

There are *two* standing a few feet away, watching me with intent expressions.

The one on the right is about a head shorter than his companion. He has black hair that falls to his chin, pale blue eyes, and a pointed nose. The vampire on the left is taller. Bald. I don't know what his eyes normally look like but, as he runs his gaze over me, they're already the tell-tale red of bloodlust.

He's also sneering at me in a way that has my claws unsheathing.

Roman's fang is tucked beneath my dress. I want to show it to them, to let them know that they shouldn't be looking at me like that—like I'm prey—but I stop when I realize that my claws are out. That's a sure sign that I'm a wolf shifter, something I'm suddenly eager to conceal.

I will them back. With my wolf so freshly in control, it's hard to banish them, but I try.

I need to show them the fang. Before I get the chance, though, the shorter of the two nudges the other vampire in the side.

"What do you think, Hector. Is that her?"

Hector—the bald, sneering vampire—gives me a look of disgust. "Don't you scent Zakharov on her? Of course it is."

"She's a shifter? She doesn't seem like one of the dogs." His nostrils flare. "Doesn't smell like one, either. You're right. I only get Zakharov."

I smell like Roman? Must be because of the fang I'm wearing.

But if they know that Roman offered me his protection, why aren't they backing off?

Unless... unless they're some of the vampires that Roman warned me about earlier tonight.

Uh oh.

"Don't you remember, Anton?" Hector says, his low voice a rumble. "That's what the other one said. What makes this one so dangerous. You don't know that she's a shifter until it's too late."

Anton's curious look turns cautious. "Hurry. Let's do what we came here for."

I brace myself. If these two come any closer, I'm either going to use my claws against them or, if I can shift fast enough, my wolf's fangs. I have no clue what they came after me for, but I'm not going to let them get away with it.

And then Hector strokes his clean-shaven chin, his eyes still blood-red. "I have a better idea."

"We're supposed to bring her to the border, make the trade. Those are the orders. That's why we're here."

"I know. But that was before I realized what this means. Sure, we could give a dog to another. Or... and hear me out... this is Zakharov's new female. It will weaken him to throw her back to the wolves. But if we kill her, leaving her drained body outside of his precious headquarters..."

Anton's blue eyes light up. "It'll destroy him."

"Exactly."

Oh my Luna. For a second, I was so stuck when they mentioned something about dogs—a vampire's derogatory name for wolf shifters—that I didn't really understand the rest of what Hector said. When I do, though?

I'm *stunned*.

They're... they're talking about draining me. Killing me. Leaving me for Roman to find. And I'm the fucking idiot who's still standing here, listening to these two bloodsuckers plot my fate without doing anything to stop them. I could be attacking. I could be running away. I could be doing anything—but I'm not.

What the hell is wrong with me?

My eyes turn black. Neither one of these vampires have a bond with another, or even the promise of one. I can't use that against them, but do they know that?

"Back off," I tell them, my voice vibrating with the power I've drawn from the Luna herself. It's more effective against another shifter—it isn't often that I use the Luna against them, but I have the ability to control them if I choose to—but even vampires can sense that I'm not just another supe when I get like this. "Leave me or else I'll—"

"Elizabeth."

*Yours*, says the Luna, my borrowed power returning to her as quickly as it came.

*Aleks*.

I nearly sag with relief. Nearly, since my instincts warn against giving these two vampires something to use against me. If they know that I have any kind of tie to Aleks, this could get uglier than it's about to.

"Evening, Aleksander."

If he notices the cold way I'm addressing him, he doesn't act like it. Then again, considering how we left things back in Roman's office—not to mention me kicking him out of the townhouse—he probably is expecting a less than happy welcome from me.

"Are you done with your run?"

Even as I nod, I can't help but think: Huh. So he *was* watching. At least long enough to know what I spent the last few hours doing.

Did he watch me shift? See me naked?

Do I *want* him to have seen me naked?

What took him so long to realize I was in trouble—

"Enough!"

While Anton had taken a few steps' retreat when Aleks strode over to where we were, Hector refused to back down. Now, looking even bigger than before, his fangs lengthening past his bottom lip, he turns a murderous gaze on Aleks.

"Filan. Leave us. This has nothing to do with you."

"Oh?" He sounds pleasant, but the hard look in his eyes tells us all that he's anything but. If I didn't believe to the depths of my soul that, despite not knowing him at all, he'd never hurt me... I would've bolted at that single syllable. "It doesn't?"

"No."

Aleks *tsks*. "That's where you're wrong, Hector. This has everything to do with me."

"You've been loyal to Zakharov for too long."

"Maybe. But your rebellion... it won't work. Monroe has already lost his head. So has Stefan. You all seek out death, so eager to join Marcel. When will you learn that Roman *is* the Cadre?"

"Roman is a male like the rest of us. See if he can stay so heartless and cold when we present his drained female to him."

Up until then, Aleks kept the conversation loose. Casual.

Not anymore.

"She's not his," he retorts with enough emotion that I suck in a breath.

The shorter vampire—Anton—glances from Aleks to me. He must be smarter than his pal because understanding flares in his blood-red eyes.

"She wears his fang—"

"She's not Roman's, Hector. She's *mine*."

My heart leaps into my throat.

The bald vampire's face twists in an expression so fierce, I fight the urge to cling to Aleks's back. Meanwhile, Anton must really know which way the wind is blowing because, while his buddy's attention is on Aleks, he disappears into the trees.

"Two blows with one kill," Hector says, bouncing on the balls of his feet, preparing to launch himself at me. "A message to Roman and his most devoted servant then."

In the blink of an eye, Aleks moves from five feet away from us to directly in front of me. "You have to get through me first."

*"Gladly."*

"Stay back, Elizabeth," he commands right before he intercepts Hector.

He doesn't have to tell me twice. I scurry backward, looking for cover, as the two males collide.

Vampires don't feed off of each other. When Hector bares his fangs, he has every intention of going for Aleks's throat if only to tear it out. At the same time, Aleks hammers him with blows, pushing him away from me, while jabbing his fangs in every part of Hector's flesh he can find.

I watched Aleks fight once before this. It was a massacre. I didn't know if all vampires had the same skill, but now that I'm watching the two of them, I notice that Aleks is a much more effective killer.

Hector figures that out about the same time that I do. Realizing that he won't win a clean fight, he reaches behind him, pulling a weapon out from somewhere.

The moon reflects against the blade. I know immediately that it's made of silver, a metal known to weaken supes.

In a shifter challenge, no one uses weapons. Our claws and our fangs and our beasts are all we need. It's just not done. Even Christian only wielded a gun after a challenge, never before.

I can't let him use it.

Cupping my hands around my mouth, I shout out, "Knife!"

Later, I still won't be sure if I made a mistake. Because Aleks? When he hears my voice, he immediately glances over at me. That split second of him focusing on me instead of the fight is all Hector needs. He buries the knife in Aleks's side.

I scream.

Aleks *roars*.

With the knife buried to the hilt inside of him, Aleks whips his head around. He shoots out both of his hands, reaching for

Hector's neck. You would never know the silver affected him since, with impressive strength, he tugs Hector by the throat up to his fangs, biting a huge chunk out of the vampire. Hector gurgles on his own blood, flailing, while Aleks tightens his grip on Hector's neck.

The next thing I know, his head is in Aleks's grip, his body crumpling to the frozen earth. Aleks punts it with his expensive dress shoe before rolling Hector's head like it's a freaking bowling ball.

As I gape at him, he drops to his knees. With a grunt, he yanks the knife out of his side, flinging it far, far away from him.

I rush over to him. He's covered in blood, his eyes in full bloodlust mode, his fangs extended longer than I've ever seen on any vampire. But when I throw myself to the dirt in front of him, he lifts a shaky hand, wiping his face with the back of the other as if trying to make himself more presentable.

I could give a shit. "Aleks? Aleks! Are you okay?"

"Yes." He closes his eyes, taking a few seconds to gain some control. When he opens them again, they're light green rimmed with red. "I wish you hadn't seen that."

I'm not. Shifters respect strength; Aleks is strong. They understand being challenged and having to fight to the death. Aleks did both multiple times now.

I just... I wish I hadn't distracted him long enough for Hector to attempt to gut him with that knife this time.

"I'm fine," I tell him honestly. Some of the blood spray stained my dress, but apart from that? I'm perfectly fine. "But you... he got you with the knife. I know you'll heal eventually, but how bad is it?"

Aleks immediately clamps his hand over the bloody wound in his side. "Not bad at all."

Good to know. Aleks is a shit liar, too.

"Please. Let me see."

He hesitates, but eventually lowers his hand again.

"Oh." I gulp. "Yeah. That's bad."

Bad? He's probably lost more blood than a vampire can afford to, and it's still oozing out.

"Nothing that a few feedings won't cure, księżyca. Don't fret for me."

*Kher-zhitza.*

Okay, then.

I have no idea what that means, but if he wants to call me that, that's fine. I mean, if it wasn't for Aleks, Hector would've gone for my throat. I'm nowhere near as strong as Aleks. I wouldn't have survived. He can call me whatever the hell he wants.

I owe him my life.

*Repay him. Feed your mate.*

*Give him your blood.*

When I recoil at the Luna's suggestion, Aleks glances away. "I should be going. I must inform Roman about this."

Aleks is already pale, but beneath the moonlight, he's lost any of the color he already had. And he wants to go make a report to his boss?

Maybe the Luna *is* right. I think... I think he needs to feed.

I gulp, then scoot closer to him. "Wait. Aleks... before you go, have some of my blood."

He goes motionless.

I nod. Hours ago, I swore I'd never let him bite me. How quick things change... "I've got plenty, and you need some. Take mine."

His gaze slides over to me, searching my face. "Are you sure?"

"You wouldn't have gotten hurt if it wasn't for me," I point out. "It's the least I can do. And you told me it wouldn't hurt."

He wants to do it. I don't know how I know for sure, but Aleks wants a taste of my blood more than he wants anything else at this moment.

Still, he resists. "I can find another donor. It doesn't have to be you."

"You fed me tonight," I remind him. "Let me return the favor."

Aleks frowns. "For reasons I'm sure you understand, I fed you, yes. I didn't do it because I expected you to reciprocate."

Right. Because I'm supposed to be his beloved.

And he's supposed to be my mate.

"Will you heal faster if you have some now?" When he doesn't answer, I can't keep myself from prodding. "Will you? You can't protect Muncie if you're half-drained."

*He can't protect you*, the Luna adds. *Remind him.*

Following my goddess's lead, I echo, "You can't protect me."

That does it. Slowly climbing to his feet, Aleks stumbles, then straightens. Once he's steady, he offers me his hand, helping me up until I'm positioned directly in front of him.

Hoping that I'm doing this right, I tilt my head, baring my throat to him.

He moves into me. His hands land on my shoulders, his eyes completely red again as he forces back a shudder.

"Will it... will it hurt?" I whisper. He already told me it wouldn't, but I'm a coward. Those fangs of his look even sharper this close. I have to make sure.

With the points of his fangs mere millimeters from my neck, the chill of Aleks's breath cools my overheated skin as he vows, "I'll never hurt you, księżyca."

And then, before I can ask him what he keeps calling me, Aleks plunges them into my skin.

He's true to his word. After a slight pinch, I feel nothing except the strange sensation of something pulling on my neck. It's vaguely uncomfortable at first, and I find myself hoping that he'll be done soon, when, out of nowhere, heat starts pooling low in my belly.

It... it feels *good*.

As he sucks, I melt against him. The pleasure rises, and after a few more seconds, I moan.

He groans in answer, increasing the pace of his suction.

All too soon, though, he stops. Releasing his fangs with a gentle *pop*, I'm panting as I realize that I started grinding my pussy against him. My skirt rode up slightly, though not enough that Aleks is able to see that I'm panty-free right now.

My vampire? He's hard as a rock, his erection a thick bulge that I was rubbing against while he was biting me.

I shouldn't be embarrassed, but I am. He's my fated mate, and I'm dry-humping him after offering my blood to heal his wound. What the hell is wrong with me?

I start to back away from him—but he doesn't let me.

His eyes a rich blazing red, fangs impossibly longer, he grips my shoulders, holding me steady.

In a flash, I suddenly remember what he said before. How he would know for sure if I was truly his beloved—his vampire mate—as soon as he tasted my blood.

And I just served myself up on a silver platter for him.

From the way he's holding onto me so tightly, he's about to head back for seconds. As he crouches slightly, putting us on the same level that his dick is only separated from my pussy by a few layers of clothes on his part, I wonder if we're about to go one step further as mates.

Will I let him?

Better question: can he stop me from initiating?

But he doesn't do either of those things, and I don't know what to think. No biting. No fucking. Instead—with his fangs still fully extended, and his eyes an unholy red—he goes to *kiss* me.

With his mouth full of my blood, and his erection grinding against me, Aleks wants to kiss me for the first time.

I can deal with the blood. I've tasted far worse. But with the Luna's voice in my head and my wolf keening for her mate, I know it won't stop there. Not tonight. Two seconds ago, I wondered if he was about to unzip his pants, throw up my skirt, and shove himself inside of me. I would've let him, too. If I don't get away from him now, I still would.

So a kiss?

I *can't*.

Aleks leans into me. I turn my head just as his lips brush my cheek. They're warm, I notice; his breath, too. Drinking from me has turned him from the undead to a warm-blooded male.

When I avoid his kiss, Aleks immediately reacts like one. You would've thought I slapped him across the face instead of simply turning away.

Aleks lets go, shoving himself away from me before coming back, like we're two magnets that can't help but be pulled together.

He reaches for me, fisting his hands before we touch as he says in a rasp of a voice, "You deny me. You deny *us*?"

His chest is heaving, his cheeks hollowed as he breathes in deep.

That should've been my first warning. Vampires are one of the undead. None of their kind needs to breathe. But he's heaving, and like before, I'm the idiot who forgets when she's supposed to get the hell away from a threat.

Then again, my mate is never supposed to be a threat...

His hand lashes out. Crooked fingers grab my chain. A brutal twist has the links breaking in two as Aleks snatches Roman's fang from me.

"You're mine, Julia—"

Julia?

Julia.

Again!

My wolf lets out a pained yip, like she's been kicked in the side. I gasp, swallowing the sound before my two-legged form can utter it.

Aleks pulls back, horrified. Even if I wanted to pretend that he hadn't just said that, his reaction makes it impossible. I don't even know if he's more upset by his slip-up or the way he just ripped Roman's fang from my neck, but it doesn't matter.

I have had *enough*.

"Julia might be," I snap at him, clamping my hand over the marks he left on my neck. They'll be gone by morning—I'll make sure of that—but I already regret my reckless offer since the vampire *doesn't even know my name.* "But I'm not her, whoever she is. My name is *Elizabeth*."

I kick off my shoes. My dress? It's tatters as I fall back, letting my wolf take over again, shifting shapes in the blink of an eye.

Aleks shouts after me, but it sounds like so much noise as I tear off through the woods. Right then, I could care less that I'm breaking all of Roman's rules. After the way *three* of his vampires have treated me tonight, I think I should get a pass.

Especially since Aleks immediately starts chasing after me.

Good luck.

He might be fast, but nothing can catch up to a wounded shifter trying to outrun rejection.

Once again, turns out that I'm wrong.

*Julia...*

I guess he can't call me whatever he wants after all.

# CHAPTER 9
# JULIA ZŁOTY'S TWIN

I didn't realize how much I'd grown to rely on Roman's fang—and his protection—until I don't have it anymore.

Luckily, my ability to shield my scent whenever I want to gives me a little wiggle room to work with. Any vampire I met would be able to tell that I'm some kind of supe, but as long as I'm in my skin, they can't be sure that I'm a shifter. No reason to ask Roman for another one.

He'll know. Of course he will. But I'm not going to be the one who brings it to his attention. If he wants to know where the fang went, he can ask Aleks. Last I know, he had it clenched tightly in his fist, leaving me to run the rest of the way to my townhouse without it.

It was probably for the best. Roman was right. The fang had put an even bigger target on my back. Those two vampires came after me for a reason, but the lead one—Hector, the one Aleks killed—had changed his mind when he realized that I had Roman's fang on.

Let Aleks deal with that. At least he's proven that he can destroy his fellow vampires as easily as taking down a shifter.

He was ruthless, yet beautiful, showing no mercy as he savagely ripped Hector's throat open with his fangs. When he fought Jasper, the shifter back in the district, he'd been just as fierce. Beneath his pretty face and his noble nature, he's a cold-hearted killer.

And there's no way that should turn me on as much as it does.

Hey. I'm a shifter. Being attracted to strength—knowing that he would be a provider *and* a protector—is kind of part of the deal.

Then there's just how good it felt to have his fangs in my neck, warm lips sucking intently, pulling the blood from my veins as I was able to provide something for him.

Until he, you know, called me by another female's name.

I had hoped he might give me some time to lick my wounds. I should've known better. A supe is a supe, after all, and males courting their mates just don't know when to stop.

Midway through my next shift, right before my lunch hour, he enters the lobby of the Cadre building.

He tries to catch my eye, but I was prepared. One good thing about him being a powerful vamp? His aura is unmistakable, and so is his scent. Now that I know to look for it, I can catch his approach from a few blocks away so that, when he strides inside of the lobby, my nose is already buried in a mound of paperwork.

Sorry, Aleks. Too busy to say hi.

You understand.

Does that stop him? An overbearing vampire who has finally decided that I'm his?

Not even a little.

He has a plastic bag in his hand. "I brought you lunch."

I can't help it. I glance up at him. "Excuse me?"

"I noticed that you usually bring some from home, but when you don't, you prefer eating at the deli down the street. I got you a ham and turkey sandwich. Cheese, no lettuce."

My exact order.

Did I need the reminder that he's been my shadow for weeks? Nope. Will I read too much into the seemingly friendly gesture? Aleks is a supe, so hell fucking yes.

"Thank you."

"Will you eat it, księżyca?"

"We'll see. Like you said, I usually pack my own lunch. Maybe Leigh wants it."

Leigh is a vampire. She takes lunch, but it's never where I see her. So, yeah… I don't think she wants my sandwich.

He exhales, his aura going arctic.

Uh-oh. I think I touched a nerve.

There's something about Aleks. Maybe it's because he's my fated mate, I don't know. Because, while his dominance and power level are attractive to me, I don't feel the need to submit to him; at least, not the way I would the Alpha. He's strong, but I can stand on my own two feet around him without the fear of being bulldozed.

"Is there another reason why you're here? Can I help you with something?"

Leigh—who had been watching the exchange with an interested eye—cuts in. "He arranged for a meeting with Roman. He's waiting for you, Aleksander."

Aleks gives me one last searching look before nodding. "Let him know I'm on my way up."

"Of course." She makes the call as Aleks reluctantly heads

toward the elevator. Once he's gone and she's hung up the phone again, she scoots her chair closer to me. "Okay, Elizabeth. Spill."

I should've expected this. Anyone who thinks that a shifter pack is full of gossips has obviously never met vampires.

"It's nothing." At her disbelieving look, I flush. "He's gotten the idea in his head that I'm his beloved."

Leigh's eyes widen. "Are you?"

Am I?

I shrug. "I don't know. It's... it's complicated."

"Trust me. I know all about complicated. When I first met Tamera, I thought I was straight. Had no idea I was bisexual until we met and I felt a pull toward her that I couldn't deny. But while 'complicated' is never easy, it can work out in the end. Look at us. We've been mated for sixty years and we're even looking for our third."

"Your *third*? What, like a third mate?"

She laughs. "Don't worry. I think you're pretty, but we already have our intended in mind."

My cheeks are immediately on fire. "No. I didn't think you were hitting on me. I just... shifters only get one fated mate. We can choose to take a different one if we want, but once the bond is made, it's for life." Or until my "gift" breaks it. "I guess I thought it was the same for vampires."

"Ah. I get it. Yeah, vampires are a little different than that. We share our blood to make our bonds. We can't feed off of each other... we can only get sustenance from shifters or humans... but the blood exchange builds bonds. You're right. Once we have one, we can't break it, but we can make as many as we want as long as it's consensual."

So that's why Aleks is convinced I'm his beloved? And why he courted Gem the same way? Because, as a vampire, he could've loved his Julia, somehow lost her, then moved on to try to develop a bond with another.

Oh. I… I don't know what to think about that. Having been born and raised knowing that I'll only be lucky enough to have *one* mate, discovering that my fated mate could have many.

That's definitely something to think about—and I still am about a half an hour later when Aleks steps off of the elevator and approaches the lobby desk again.

I glance up from the papers in front of me when I sense his aura heading toward me. I'm looking to see if he's going to stride right through the lobby's door, but he doesn't.

He moves toward the desk, stopping right in front of me.

"Elizabeth?"

"Yes?"

"May I speak to you?"

I hesitate for a moment, struggling to come up with a plausible reason to refuse. When I can't, I nod. "I guess."

"If you're worried about your work, I already asked Roman for permission."

"Oh?" I try to keep my expression calm. Unaffected. Useless when I'm surrounded by other supes, but at least I *try*. "Was that before or after you apologized to him for yanking his fang off of my neck?"

His eyes flash. "I don't apologize," he says, "but I… I explained the situation to him. He understands."

I'm glad he does. "In that case, I think I should go back to work—"

"I don't apologize," he says again, "and I can count the times I have between two hands. But, for you, księżyca, I offer one. I'm sorry about last night."

If it's as rare as he claims, I should just accept it—but I can't.

Not while I don't know what exactly he thinks he's apologizing for.

Was it taking Roman's fang and leaving me defenseless to the other supes in Muncie? Was it getting pissed when I decided not to kiss him? Or, I don't know, was it calling me another female's name?

"What part of it?"

"Excuse me?"

"What part are you sorry for?"

Aleks's gaze flickers past me. Out of the corner of my eye, I can see that Leigh is watching us with rapt attention, not even bothering to hide it.

Clearing his throat, he gestures with his head toward the entrance. "Perhaps we can have this discussion in private."

Of course. Why wouldn't he want to do that?

I follow Aleks as he guides me through the doors, leading me a few feet away from the entrance. When he turns to face me again, his gaze is immediately drawn to my neck.

"Don't get any ideas," I huff. "I'm off the menu."

He nods. "I understand. And I should probably apologize for that, too, but... I'd be lying if I said I was sorry that I tasted you. For a hint of your blood, Elizabeth, I'd risk your wrath and more."

The idea that he wants to bite me again should not be as sexy as it is. It takes everything I have not to offer my neck in submission. It feels right to do so, but I just manage to resist the urge.

"If you won't apologize about that," I say after a few moments of tension, "then what are you apologizing for?"

"For not explaining myself before now." Reaching into his pocket, Aleks pulls out a chain. I choke on a gasp, assuming it's the same sort of chain as the one Roman gave me, but it's not. Instead of a fang hanging off of it, it's a metal pendant.

No. A locket.

Using his thumbnail, Aleks flicks it open.

Inside the locket, there's a picture.

"Who is this?" I breathe out.

Because it isn't me. It looks like me, so much so that I can't believe what I'm seeing, but it's *not* me.

*I know she's not Julia, Roman...*

Don't let it be her. Don't let it be the female that everyone keeps mentioning—

"Julia Złoty."

Of course it is.

So many of our features match. Her wide forehead. The slope of her nose. Her plump mouth. The shape of her jaw. Even the color of her hair.

It's a portrait, an old-fashioned painting, but it could easily be a picture of me—except for her eyes. They're not silver. They're a bright, gleaming golden shade.

Vampires don't have eyes that color. Neither do humans.

"She was a wolf shifter?"

"Julia was an alpha." Aleks's nod is jerky and short as he snaps the locket shut. "She was also my beloved before her death two centuries ago."

I want to say that it's just like I thought, just like I guessed even thought I never spoke my suspicions out loud, but it's not.

It's so much worse.

His former beloved isn't just another shifter. She isn't even just a rare alpha, considered by my kind to be the Luna reborn like Gemma.

His Julia is my twin, and now I can't shake the feeling that

I'm simply her replacement.

"Thank you for showing me that." I mean it, too. After what Leigh said, I'd started to think that maybe—*maybe*—there was a chance for us. Now that I've learned the truth about Julia? There's no fucking way. "If you'll excuse me, though, I really do have to go back to work."

I'm just reaching the door to the lobby when Aleks calls after me.

"You must know that Roman is only keeping you close because you're valuable to him."

I don't turn around. I just shoot back, "At least I'm valuable to someone," before leaving him out on the corner by himself.

As I take my seat, Leigh doesn't ask me what happened with Aleks. She just takes one look at my face, then announces, "You need a distraction."

"I need to work," I mumble. That's all the distraction I need.

"No. Really. Listen, me and Tamera are going to Mea Culpa after sundown tonight. Gretchen, too. It's a vamp club, but you're one of us now. Cadre. You should come with."

"I don't know..."

"Come on, Elizabeth. You said it yourself. Your situation with Aleksander is complicated. Why not have one night where it isn't?"

You know what? She has a point.

"Will they let me in?" This is Muncie. A Fang City. It's a pretty valid concern. "With me being a shifter, I mean."

Her eyes sparkle. "If you're with us? Trust me, girl. Not only will they let you in, you won't have to buy your own drinks all night."

Considering it's a vampire club, I probably won't partake, but it's the thought that counts.

"Okay. I'll go."

---

GEM CALLS THE THREE FEMALE VAMPIRES THE NIGHTMARE Trio. If she finds out that I've actually become *friends* with them, I'm sure I'll hear an earful from her. Just because Gretchen, Leigh, and Tamera thought they could feed off of her when she first drove out of Accalia and into Muncie, she's harbored a grudge.

And, okay. That's a pretty good reason. But they've always been nice to me. Even Gretchen, who, despite her comments, has never actually been that malicious to me whenever she stops by to flirt with Leigh.

I meet them about a block out of Mea Culpa, anxiously tugging on the hem of my dress. It took a couple of blocks before I grew used to the wobble of my high heels, and I'm glad tonight isn't as windy as it has been. For the first time in ages, I took care with my hair and my make-up, and I would've hated for the wintry weather to ruin it.

They're already waiting for me, each one more of a knock-out than the last. I made a good choice, getting as dressed up as I did, because the three of them are so inhumanly stunning that they look like they belong in a photoshopped ad straight out of a high-class magazine.

Not only that, but their cheeks are flushed. Clearly, the three gorgeous vampires have already had their dinner.

As I walk over to them, I'm treated to a once-over by each of them. Holding my breath, I wait to see if they think I look good enough to join them inside of the club.

After how much I spent on this slinky dress, I hope so.

Roman, I've learned, is a very generous boss. When he hired me, he made it clear that he was keeping me close because of my ability. Sticking me in the lobby with Leigh had been a good way to explain what I was doing there, and I'm becoming a pretty decent receptionist. Make no mistake, though. When he had an envelope full of cash waiting for me this morning as payment for my first week, it wasn't my typing skills or my phone-answering that had him giving me as much as he had.

Am I complaining? Not even a little. I'll break as many bonds as he wants me to—so long as the bonded mates *want* to be separated from each other like Dominic and Felicity did.

Look at me. Elizabeth Howell, vampire divorce expert extra-ordinaire.

Hey. It's a much better gig than snapping bonds at the Wicked Wolf's whim. Punishing those who pissed him off by taking their mate from them. And, sure, I can only do that if there are any doubts—any cracks at all in the bond—but when the Alpha was threatening you, it's not surprising how quickly some mates fold. It takes a forever bond like the one between Gemma Swann and Ryker Wolfson—not to mention their alpha natures—to withstand that.

Roman wants to keep me on retainer, reserving my skill for his use only. I'm okay with that, especially when I saw how much he was willing to pay for the privilege.

I'm not a fool; at least, not when it comes to money. I've eaten out of dumpsters, slept in sketchy motels, and sold fortunes for pennies. Easy come, easy go... Roman Zakharov might be a better master than Wicked Wolf Walker, but either he'll tire of me or he'll want something I can't give him. Everyone does eventually. I can't get used to having this much money.

Doesn't mean that I'm going to hoard it. I went looking for a job in the first place because I knew that I had some expenses. Foods. Toiletries.

Clothes.

When I moved into Muncie, I only had a few changes of clothing that I carried in my duffel bag. Some old t-shirts, two pairs of jeans, a simple shift dress, and a couple of sets of cheap panties and bras. Enough to keep me covered, but nothing fancy.

And then I got my first paycheck and decided I deserved a tiny upgrade to my wardrobe.

I didn't go overboard. The dress code for working under Roman is non-existent. I've seen Leigh dressed to the nines some days, while wearing jeans and a simple tee the next. It's the same with the other vampires that come and go in the building. So long as I'm decent, he doesn't care what I wear.

I got a few nicer sweaters, an extra pair of jeans, more luxurious undergarments—and a dress.

I didn't need it. There was no reason to buy it. But when I saw the sleeveless, fitted golden dress… I couldn't help myself. I tried it on, stunned at how well it molded to my curves. It barely covers my boobs, reaching to the middle of my thighs, but it looked so good on me, I couldn't stop myself from buying it. Plus the color… like how red is the color of vampires, gold belongs to the shifters. This dress was made for me, and it was the only thing I owned that was appropriate for a night out.

"You look hot," Gretchen says approvingly. "You'll fit right in at Mea Culpa."

"Um. Thanks."

"Don't mention it. Just stay close, and prepare to have the best night of your life. When you're with us, it's always a given."

# CHAPTER 10
# OUT ON THE TOWN WITHOUT A FANG

Despite Gretchen's boasting, I'm a little nervous as I follow the trio into the club. I keep expecting the bouncer to figure out I'm a shifter and tell me that I'm not allowed inside, but it seems like being buffered by three vampire females is all I need.

Mea Culpa is a supe club, no humans allowed. Of course, because I'm the only shifter in Muncie, I'm the only non-vampire inside. That catches a couple of curious club-goers' attention, but no one bothers me. It's like we all came here for a good time, and before long I begin to shed my nerves.

Until about an hour into our night out when, suddenly, I feel the familiar prickle of ice against the back of my neck.

Oh, no. Not now. Tell me Aleks isn't here *now*.

I turn behind me. And, yup. There he is. Standing on the edge of the dance floor where I'd been bopping along with Tamera and Leigh, Aleks is watching me with an unreadable expression.

One thing for sure? He isn't happy.

As our eyes meet across the floor, I immediately stop dancing. There's a hunger in his gaze that isn't as noticeable in the thin line of his lips. His eyes dip down to the low cut of my dress and his whole body goes tight. Then, before I can duck behind someone, he crosses his arms over his chest.

Oh, boy. I'm in trouble.

Tamera is the first one to notice that something is up. Following the direction of my stare, she frowns when she spies Aleks.

"What is he doing here? I thought Aleksander was on patrol tonight."

She glances over at Leigh.

Leigh nods. "Every night, from ten pm 'til six in the morning." Or, I think to myself, whenever he's not standing outside of my townhouse—or is that part of his patrol, too? "As far as I know, he's on schedule tonight. Roman didn't mention that someone else was taking his shift."

And he would know, too, since every part of protecting the Fang City's borders goes through Roman.

Tamera's puzzled look turns to one of understanding. "Ah. I don't think he's here to dance, my beloved. I think he's here for his wolf."

I think she's right.

Leigh brushes against me. "You want us to get you out of here? Tamera can distract him and I can cover you while you go."

That's a tempting idea, but I never get the chance. Before we can escape the crowd on the dance floor, Aleks is already making a beeline straight for me.

I might as well meet him halfway.

"Thanks for the offer," I mumble, "but I should probably handle this myself."

Leigh murmurs a quick *good luck* while she and Tamera slip away, probably in search of Gretchen.

Taking a deep breath, I bring a smile to my face as I meet Aleks. "Hi. Didn't expect to see you here."

"Me, neither. What are you doing at this club?"

"Um. Dancing?"

Aleks doesn't like that. A hint of a growl underlines his accented voice as he tells me, "It's for vampires, and you don't have your fang."

"You mean the one you stole from me? Gee, Aleks. I wonder why not."

Ah, Luna. Why am I mouthing off to him? He's a powerful vampire, I'm a cursed wolf, and I've spent too many years being taught over and over again not to talk back. When it comes to Aleks, though? I don't know... it's like it's the only time I *can* fight back because, no matter what, he won't hurt me.

He promised.

I shake my head, tossing my hair over my shoulder. "Besides, I think I'm okay. I might not have the fang on me, but I'm not here alone."

"I know. You were dancing with another male."

Wait— was I? I didn't even notice. I thought I was dancing in a group, alongside Leigh and her blood-bonded mate, with Gretchen off getting a shot of O-negative from the bar.

"That's not what I meant. I was invited out by Leigh and her friends. She said I'd be safe with them even without the fang."

Aleks doesn't have a response for that. Instead, his light green eyes suddenly threading with red, he says, "Tell the other ladies goodnight. I'm taking you home."

"What? Already? I... I want to stay."

That's a lie. I've never been much of a club girl even when I was younger, and the sights and scents inside of Mea Culpa have made my wolf uncomfortable from the moment I entered behind Gretchen. The amount of vampires has her growling under her breath, and I don't blame her. I'm the only one in the whole club with a pulse. Something like that would make anyone leery.

But I'm not about to admit that to Aleks. He might be my fated mate, but I don't want him to get the idea that he can order me around. I mean, I *like* it. Letting him take control... it flips a switch inside of me, making him even more attractive—as if that was even possible. There should still be some element of a partnership between mates. He can tell me what to do, and I should feel free to tell him to shove it.

Not tonight, it seems. All Aleks says is, "No. You don't," before he lifts his hand, waving over to where Tamera and Leigh are now. He catches the redhead's eye, nodding down at me. She returns the nod, leaning to whisper something in Leigh's ear. Leigh's soft hazel eyes widen, but before she can start toward me, Aleks has his arm around my shoulder, guiding me through the throng of dancers.

No one even looks twice. They definitely don't try to interfere.

I wait until we're back outside before I push his arm off of me. Satisfied that he whisked me out of the club, he allows it.

"What are you doing?" I demand.

"Keeping my beloved safe."

*Yours*, whispers the Luna.

I ignore her.

"I'm not your beloved."

"*Yet.*"

Oh my Luna... he's got to be kidding me.

"I think I liked you better when you were pretending you didn't know who I was."

Aleks frowns. "I had my reasons."

Right. Just like I had my reasons to go along with it. "Remember them," I suggest. "Then we can go back to how it was."

"What if I don't want to?"

His gentle whisper seems to echo all around me. I shiver.

"You're cold," he observes. "Did you bring a coat? I can go back inside and retrieve it for you."

I'd rather wear a hundred coats than admit that I was shivering because of what he said.

I shake my head, letting my curtain of hair fall forward, covering my cleavage. "It's okay. Since you dragged me out of the club, I might as well just go home anyway. I'll be okay until then."

He immediately starts shrugging off his jacket. "Wear mine."

So he'll have an excuse to see me again to get it back? I'll wear a hundred coats—just not his. "No, thanks."

Aleks freezes, but I think he can tell that he's pushed me far enough tonight. "Are you sure?"

"Yes."

"Very well. If you change your mind on the walk, let me know." He pulls his coat back on. "Lead the way, Elizabeth."

"Excuse me?"

"I'm coming with you."

What? "Aren't you supposed to be on patrol?"

"Tak. But I'm also the reason you don't have protection. I'll walk you home so that I know you're safe then head back out."

"I'll be fine." When Aleks's eyes flash in the streetlight, I cut him off before he can argue with me. "I made it nearly thirty years without a bodyguard. Made it a couple of weeks before I started working for Roman. I've always been able to take care of myself on my own. Don't worry about me."

"Muszę, mój Elizabeth." Then, in a low voice, he adds, "You shouldn't have *had* to. I should've found you well before this."

Maybe. And maybe if he had, I wouldn't feel the need to reject him in order to save myself from more trouble.

"Goodnight, Aleks."

I turn, already walking away. If I don't, he might say the right thing, get me to stay. And I can't.

I *can't*.

He calls after me anyway. "Elizabeth. Wait."

Don't turn around. Don't turn ar—

I look over my shoulder. "Yes—*oh*."

He's right behind me, closing the gap between us. Reaching up, Aleks snaps the fang out of his mouth with a cracking sound that sends another round of shivers coursing down my spine.

"Before you go, take this."

Holding up my hands, I back away from him. "I… I can't."

"If you're worried that it won't grow back—"

"It's not that." I already know it will. Roman's did within two days.

"Then what is it, księżyca?"

I really need to find out what that means. Gem wasn't kidding when she said I'd need a Polish to English dictionary. My idiot self left it on my nightstand. At least I started practicing on the language app I downloaded, but so far all I've learned is how to count to ten, that 'tak' means 'yes', and that Roman's Russian is totally different than Aleks's Polish.

"Roman gave me a fang to wear so that no one would bother me in Muncie. If I take yours, what would that mean?"

His eyes flash beneath the growing moonlight. "Ah. You've been talking to Gem."

I don't deny it. "She's told me a lot about you."

I could've meant anything by that. She lived with Aleks for more than a year before Ryker tracked her down and made his move, so there's plenty she could have shared.

Then Aleks frowns, and I know that *he* knows exactly what I'm talking about.

"I make no excuses for my pursuit of her. I spent two hundred years believing I'd never have a beloved to call my own after Julia was... gone, and when a female alpha appeared at the borders all those years later, I believed I found her. Of course, then I saw you, and I knew that it wasn't a female alpha I was waiting for, but"—he gestures with his hand toward my eyes—"one with the mark of the Luna."

So... he knows what the silver color of my eyes means, huh? Looks like I'm not the only one who's been talking to Gem.

"Did you love her?"

I can't believe that just popped out of my mouth. The second it does, though, I realize that I need to know. He obviously still loves his Julia, but what about Gem?

"I love her still, but not the way you think, księżyca."

I wait for Aleks to elaborate. When he doesn't, I ask simply, "Is that true?"

"Can't you tell?" When I shake my head, he says, "Gem could sense when someone was lying to her."

"I'm not Gem."

"No," Aleks agrees easily, "you're not. And you're not Julia, either. You're Elizabeth."

I nod at the fang nestled in his palm. "And you still want me to take that?"

"Tak. Because you're *my* Elizabeth."

I want so badly to believe that he *is* telling the truth.

But I can't. Not yet. Not while I can't shake the belief that, when he looks at me, he sees someone I'm not. That I can never be.

My lips part. At first, it's a sigh, then it's the beginning of another rejection—but I don't get that far.

Moving into me, Aleks cups my nape, tilting my head back.

Our eyes lock.

At this moment, I know that he could easily take my mouth if he wanted to. I couldn't stop him. Deep down, I know I wouldn't even if I could.

He waits, searching for permission.

Parting my lips further, I give it to him.

It's been years since I've been kissed. I avoided any and all male attention in the district pretty well. No one wanted to go up against the Alpha, and even someone like Brendan, who showed interest, never shows it for long. I guard myself carefully when I'm playing at being a human, so that never worked. Before that, I was so scarred after what happened with Kyle and Peyton, I couldn't risk a repeat of starting an affair with the wrong male.

Aleks is wrong for me in so many ways. I need a mate who will put me first, who will help heal a decade's worth of loneliness. With the vampire, I know I'll never get past being his second—or even his *third*—choice. He's pursuing me now because he believes I'm his beloved, his fated mate, and that I owe it to him to surrender.

As his lips brush gently against mine, the beginning of a kiss that turns probing, then demanding a heartbeat later, I try so hard not to. It'll only lead to heartache in the end, but... *Luna*... this male is the best kisser I've ever known.

He has his right hand cupping my neck. Folding his left hand into a fist, holding tightly to the fang, he rests it against the small of my back. He's holding me upright, leaving me to do just what I didn't want to.

I surrender to his claiming kiss.

His tongue slides against mine. I follow his lead, lapping at his, avoiding the point of his remaining fang. There's no lingering taste of blood in his mouth. It's fresh and it's clean and I clutch my hands against his chest, pulling him closer.

He doesn't need to breathe, but I do. Eventually breaking the kiss, Aleks bows his body over me, trailing his soft lips against the column of my neck. When his chin nuzzles the point where it meets my shoulder, I suddenly remember where I am—and who I'm with.

I stiffen.

He's not going to bite me again, is he?

Trailing a line with his only fang, he doesn't break the skin. "If you won't wear it close to your heart," he murmurs into my hair when he's done, "then at least place it in your pocket. It'll give you nearly as much protection as Roman's, and I need you to be safe. In time, I'll earn your neck again—and your heart."

Something tells me that Aleks isn't just talking about me wearing a golden chain around my neck, his fang hanging over my heart.

"Okay," I say breathlessly. Pulling away from him, putting as much space between us as my wolf will allow, I hold out my hand. "I'll take the fang."

He presses it against my palm.

Aleks's fingers are chilled. So, tell me, why am I burning up again from that one last touch?

---

It's times like these that I wonder why, when I go from skin to fur, my other half is a white wolf. If my animal truly represented what I was, I should be a giant fucking chicken.

I'm a coward. I hate it, but it is what it is. As soon as I left Aleks outside of Mea Culpa, I made a break for home. I didn't shift, though I did kick off my heels about a block into my journey back. I wasn't so desperate that I was going to call for a ride when, normally, the distance between the club and my home was nothing for me and my wolf, but I move a lot faster without the shoes. It was bad enough I was already slowed down by my dress. I couldn't walk the streets of Muncie naked without drawing attention, but hopefully none of the humans I met realized I was barefoot.

After that, I didn't leave the townhouse again. And if I sensed him out there? I kept my shades drawn so that I didn't tease my lonely wolf with glimpses of him.

On Monday, it was time to return to work. I had hoped that I could put my last conversation with Aleks behind me. That I could forget all about him.

Yeah... that lasted until I stepped outside my front door and discovered that someone had recovered my heels and propped them up neatly on the porch.

Someone.

*Right.*

It had to be Aleks. By Monday, his scent isn't as strong as it would've been Friday night, but I've become so much more sensitive to it lately. Is it because of his fang in my pocket? Maybe. Or because I fed him my blood. Either way, he's the one who saved my shoes which means he must have followed me home that night.

Keeping watch over me, just like he told Roman he would.

I don't know what to think about it. So I do what I always do: I don't. I pretend I don't notice, scurrying past them, making my way to the center of town all while hoping that I don't run into him.

From what I understand, Aleks is one of the vampires who gets his rest during the day. Because Muncie is a Fang City, the more powerful Cadre members devote their attention to the night. That's why Aleks's patrol runs from ten to six, and why he always seems to visit the townhouse while I'm sleeping.

It's another reason why I was always able to avoid him during the day—until he decided to start checking in on me at the Cadre building while I was working.

Claws crossed that he doesn't today.

# CHAPTER 11
# VAMPIRE'S BLOOD AND WOLF PISS

By Thursday, I've decided I'm not just a chicken. I'm also a *hypocrite*.

Aleks hasn't stopped by the Cadre building all week. I caught a hint of his scent lingering near the townhouse on Tuesday, but we've had a bit of an unseasonably warm spell. It hasn't snowed in days—and any slush and ice lingering has long since melted—so there was no way for me to check to see if he left any prints behind on my sidewalk.

It's like he disappeared. He called me his beloved, gave me his fang, and now he's gone.

*He's waiting for you to go to him*, the Luna whispers. *He doesn't know you long for the chase.*

How could he? He's a vampire. He doesn't know how to participate in the mating dance, not the way a shifter would, and it's driving me nuts that—despite rejecting him—my shifter side needs him to come after me to prove he's serious in his pursuit.

And Aleks? It seems like he's giving me my space. Either that, or he's decided I'm not worth the hassle.

I don't know what's worse, and by Thursday, I almost want to call Aleks just to hear his aristocratic voice.

I blame Gem. After my last visit to Accalia, I realized I didn't just leave with the dictionary. Oh, no. Somehow, she got her paws on my phone, entering Aleks's phone number into my meager list of contacts.

She even put the blood drop emoji, followed by the heart emoji next to his name, in case I knew a million other Aleks's and I needed to differentiate.

I had half a mind to erase it. If only to get rid of any temptation, my finger hovered over the delete button before I decided against it. After all, Aleks is a high-ranking member of the Cadre. It might not be a bad idea to have a way to contact him in an emergency.

Though Aleks might not be visiting the receptionist desk, that doesn't mean that no one has. Thursday evening, just before the end of my shift, Gretchen came by to flirt with Leigh again.

On the one hand, I finally discovered who Leigh and Tamera were hoping to make their third. On the other, the iridescent vampire seems to have decided to make me her pet project.

Emphasis on the *pet* part.

Gretchen leans against the counter, her blonde hair spilling over one shoulder as she glances down at me. "You're coming with us this weekend. We'll have a re-do of last Friday, and hope that Aleksander doesn't act like a spoilsport again."

If there's one thing I've learned since living among vampires —especially those who are part of the Cadre in one way or another—it's that they never *ask* for anything. They demand, and they expect to be obeyed as if it was their due.

"Maybe," I say, giving her a non-committal answer.

"What's the matter, wolfy? You had fun the other night with us fangers, right?"

Fun. I guess you could call all that unresolved sexual tension I dealt with later *fun*—if you were a sadist.

"Gretchen. Leave Elizabeth alone. She doesn't have to come if she doesn't want to."

Gretchen sniffs. "Is it because she traded Roman's fang for Aleksander's? A bit of a downgrade, power-wise, but I get it. He is much prettier than Roman."

"Oh my god, Gretchen." Leigh casts her eyes to the ceiling, nibbling nervously on her bottom lip. "You know that Roman probably heard that, right?"

Most likely. There are cameras in nearly every corner of the Cadre building. I can't decide if Roman is paranoid, or just very particular when it comes to security. I'm leaning toward a mix of options A and B. Any good leader does what it takes to keep his people safe, but even I think constant patrols and perimeter checks around Muncie's borders might be a tad bit overkill.

Do I think he watches what goes on in this building? Definitely. Does he have the mikes on? I doubt it, but that doesn't mean he can't flick the switch to listen in whenever he wants.

Gretchen's not wrong, though. Aleks is prettier than Roman—not that I'll ever admit that out loud where it could be used against me later on.

I don't even bother asking how she knows I have Aleks's fang. Just like how Leigh was the first to sense it when Roman's was gone, it had to be obvious that I had another one in my possession—and exactly what overprotective vampire would have been the one to give it to me.

Tossing her long blonde hair over her shoulder, Gretchen

says to Leigh, "So? You guys work for the Cadre. I don't. Besides, we all know that Roman rarely gives out one of his fangs while Aleks makes a habit of it. It doesn't mean anything—"

Leigh slaps the front of the counter with the flat of her hand. "Gretch!"

"What? Again, you know I'm right. Everyone in Muncie knows about his wolf fetish." With a royal look my way, she adds almost flippantly, "No offense."

The worst part? She actually means that. She's not trying to be rude. Gretchen just comes off that way.

Besides, she isn't wrong. When it comes to Aleks's wolf fetish, I'm more than aware of it. Just like how I've had more details about Gem's run-in with my new friends.

Over the last weekend, I checked in with her. I let her know that something was brewing down here in the Fang City, and she gave me a little more detail about the two vampires who ambushed me. Turns out that, while she lived in Muncie, she had more than a couple of altercations with vampires who were plotting against Roman. It was actually Ryker who killed Stefan when he targeted Gem, while Roman executed Monroe for selling his fang to Ryker's former Beta, Shane. The Wicked Wolf had been calling the shots back then; now that I've had some time to think about it, I'm terrified that he's doing the same thing now.

*Sure, we could give a dog to another…*

*It will weaken him to throw her back to the wolves…*

Because I figured I had no choice, I also told her about the two who came after me. Aleks handled Hector when he tried to lunge at me, fangs bared, but Anton is missing and could still be a threat. I might not be a member of the Mountainside Pack, but Gem has my personal loyalty. In case it didn't get back to her and Ryker already, I wanted her to know.

She thanked me, then—in pure alpha fashion—ordered me to bunker down in the townhouse where I was safe. She even offered to send me one of her guards again, but I gently refused.

Why bother when I have a vampire of my own watching over me?

I also let slip that I had visited Mea Culpa with Leigh, her mate, and the blonde vampire. Like I thought, she wasn't happy, though she was impressed that I made friends with them without any of the Nightmare Trio going for my throat first.

And I guess we are friends, as strange as that seems. If not friends, then *friendly,* but still. It's a start.

When six o'clock comes, Gretchen is still trying to convince me that I should give the club a second try. Promising her I'll think about it, I say goodbye to her and Leigh, grab my coat and my purse, then head on out.

February in Muncie means that it's already dark at six o'clock. I don't really mind. With Aleks's fang in my pocket, I feel comfortable walking around the city again. I can flash it if any vampire wants to give me trouble, and if it's a human? I might not be as strong as one of the higher ranked wolves, but even a Luna-touched shifter like me can handle a human no problem.

I have a couple of errands to run. They barely take a half an hour, and by quarter to seven I'm just strolling down the street that would lead me home.

There's about a two-block radius surrounding the townhouse that I consider my territory. When I reach it, it's almost instinctive. I breathe in deep, tasting scents, making sure that it's just as I left it when I headed off to work this morning.

Tonight, it isn't.

At first, I can't put my finger on it. Pausing on the corner, my wolf's hackles rising, I reach out with my senses. When I butt up against a territorial marking that isn't mine, my heart starts to pound.

My reaction is instantaneous. Without even realizing what I'm doing, I reach inside my bag, trembling fingers finding my phone. It takes two tries to select my contacts list.

Aleks starts with A. It's at the top of the list.

I call him, torn between the need to reinforce my territory and a decade's long habit of running away at the first sign of trouble.

*Your mate will know what to do.*

I really fucking hope so.

On the second ring, he answers. "Who is this? How did you get this number?"

He sounds so annoyed, I almost hang up. If it wasn't for the Luna's advice, I might have.

Instead, I whisper, "Gem gave it to me. I... I hope it's okay."

His attitude changes in a heartbeat.

"Księżyca? What's wrong?"

I don't know. How can I tell him when I'm not so sure? Especially after it's been a week since I spoke to him last, and now I'm calling him for help?

It seems right, though, like he's the only one I *could* go to for this.

"I... it's my house. Someone's here." No. The scent markers are old. "They were here. I think they're gone now." Another tentative sniff, reinforcing my first opinion. "Shifters," I tell him. "It's a wolf. I'm not sure who, but it's definitely a wolf."

"Did you tell Roman?"

It never even occurred to me to do that. "No. You're the first one I called."

"Wait for me," Aleks orders. "Don't go inside until I arrive."

I want to remind him that I'm a shifter, too. That I have no idea why I reached out to him when I'm more than capable of protecting my own territory.

He's used to alpha females. Julia. Gem. Neither one of them would take his dominance without a fight.

But that's the thing. I'm not an alpha. If it wasn't for my family's curse, I'd probably top out at a maternal delta—or, worse, a feral scavenger. I'm too selfish to be an omega, and too weak to be a beta.

There's only one thing I can do right now.

"Okay." Nodding to myself since he can't see me, I tell him, "I'll wait."

---

I DON'T KNOW WHERE HE CAME FROM. IT'S NOT EVEN SEVEN yet, so I doubt he started his overnight patrol, but wherever he was, I sense the approach of his powerful aura while I'm still working up the nerve to call Gem and let her know that someone sprayed around the outside of her old townhouse.

It's a territorial marking. Our animal instincts lead us to do it, though it's usually when the wolf's in control. At some point tonight, an oversized wolf was prowling the streets of Muncie in time to piss all over my porch before doing Luna only knows what.

If this isn't some kind of declaration, I don't know what is.

Thanks to my wolf, I sense Aleks before I see him. His aura is a gentle caress, warmer than the evening breeze; it carries the promise of snow in its chill. It's so strange that the undead vampire with the cold touch and the icy skin can have any kind of warmth. Of course, then I remember how hot his lips felt against mine when he kissed me and I guess it makes some sense.

His aura first, then his scent. Something about Aleks is unique. Each vampire has a similar base—the previously dead before rising again part—but his has a kind of unusual spice that belongs to only him. Fennel, maybe, or a very faint licorice aroma. You have to be in tune with him to notice it, and after all those nights he stood outside of my townhouse, it's ingrained in my memory.

Is that why the unknown shifter pissed outside of my house? To erase it?

I really hope not.

When Aleks appears in my line of vision, I stumble a few steps in his direction.

He races toward me, wrapping me up in his arms when he's near enough. I don't fight the embrace even though my first instinct is to push him away. Aleks might have finally decided that he's all in on me, but I still haven't.

Not yet, at least.

His body against mine is tight. Thrumming. As I pull back, I notice that his eyes are red in an instant.

"Aleks?"

"*Blood*."

I shiver. "What's that?"

"The street reeks of it. Freshly spilled." Pausing for a moment, he says in a deadly tone, "Vampire's blood."

I blink. "You're kidding."

He shakes his head.

I must've gone nose-blind in Muncie; either that, or I've been too complacent. The scent of blood is to be expected in a Fang City. The dark miasma that rubbed my fur the wrong way is what caught my attention, plus the wolfish notes mixed in with it.

And, you know. The piss. Can't forget about that.

"Did you go inside?"

"No. Not yet."

He eyes my front door before looking down at me again. "What are my chances of getting you to stay out here while I go and check it out?"

Smart vampire. Gem must've trained him well because that's definitely the sort of question one would ask a dominant female shifter.

"Honestly?" Despite how freaked out I am… "Zero."

This is my territory. I'm worried, but I'm also determined.

Aleks nods. Releasing me, he starts toward the door, but not before saying, "Stay close. I'll go first."

That works for me.

The door is unlocked. When Aleks notices that, he asks me if I left it that way. My answer is an emphatic *no*. Maybe in the Wolf District it was habit to leave doors open, but not in a Fang City. I lock up every time I leave, and something tells me that Aleks already knew that.

He pauses, fingers curled around the knob. "And you won't stay outside?" he double-checks.

"No."

He huffs, then pushes the door in.

The stench of spilled blood punches both of us. If it was bad on the street, it's a million times worse inside. Aleks immediately throws his arm up, as if he can shield me from it. I choke, then cough, trying to get past the worst of it.

Because, mingled with the blood, is a scent I know all too well.

*Wolf.*

And it's all coming from the second floor.

"Upstairs," I tell him.

He nods. "I know. I'm still going first."

"You do that. But I'll be right behind you."

He already thinks I'm some damsel in distress that needs to be saved—and maybe I am—but I'm not going to leave him to search the rest of the townhouse alone. If he's going up there, I'm going with him.

Even if I do keep a few steps behind him.

As soon as we reach the second floor, it's obvious where the source of the scent is coming from.

My bedroom.

To say that there's blood everywhere inside my personal space is an understatement. It's splashed on the wall, pooling in puddles on the floor, staining the quilt and the sheets on the bed a vivid scarlet. It's fresh, still shiny and wet, and it's so pungent that my wolf covers her snout with her paws. I do the same with my human hands and nose.

It doesn't help. The scent of blood covers everything—and I know exactly who it belongs to.

*Anton.*

His savaged body is thrown in one corner, but his head... someone has propped his head up on my pillow.

My *pillow*.

Next to it, there's a folded note.

While I zero in on that, Aleks goes right to Anton's head. Using his thumb, he peels back the vampire's lip.

Anton is missing his right fang.

"Cholera."

I had already unfolded the note when Aleks spat out the word. It's not the disease he means, but *damn* in Polish. Even if I didn't know the difference, the way he spits out the word makes it pretty obvious it's a curse.

Right then, I'm on the same page with him. I hadn't had the chance to read what's written on the paper yet, but the three W's scrawled at the bottom? I know exactly who it's from.

A dead vampire with a missing fang, and a note from the former Alpha of the Western Pack? You don't need to be a genius to put two and two together and get four.

Walker hates bloodsuckers, but he has no problem allying with them—or betraying them. And though it's not his wolfish scent that covers this room, hiding just beneath the reek of freshly spilled vampire blood, I have no doubt in my mind that this was done on his orders.

The note proves it.

While Aleks focuses on Anton's remains, I pick up the paper. It's splattered with blood, the words printed by hand in a rich black ink.

It says:

HE WAS SUPPPOSED TO BRING ME MY MATE.
HE FAILED, SO NOW I BRING YOU HIS HEAD.

UNTIL WE MEET AGAIN, ELIZABETH.

PS. TELL MY DAUGHTER I SAID HI.

*Elizabeth.* There goes any hope that this message—the broken door, the blood all over, *the vampire head in my bed*—was for Gem instead of me. *My mate...*

I'm not his mate. *My* mate is standing on the other side of the bed, glaring down at Anton's head, nostrils flaring almost imperceptibly as if tracing other scents. Anton's blood is the most prevalent, followed by the unknown shifter who slaughtered him. Then there's mine, and, of course, Gem's and Ryker's.

But that's not all. Centered on the note in my hand, there's a scent I hoped I'd never breathe into my lungs again.

Jack Walker's. It's all over the page. Even if he didn't sign it—three heavily lined W's for the Wicked Wolf of the West—I would know exactly who it's from by the dark scent alone.

Clenching the page with trembling fingers, I start to shake.

Oh, no. No, no, no. This can't be happening.

Aleks sneaks up behind me, moving soundlessly to my side. "What do you have there, Elizabeth?"

I jump, then stupidly shove the paper behind my back.

Right. Like that's going to stop Aleks from getting his hands on it if he really wants to know what I'm holding.

When he raises both of his eyebrows at me, I know his thoughts are along the same line as mine.

I sigh. "It's a note." A moment's pause. "From the Wicked Wolf."

"Jack Walker."

Aleks hates the Alpha. I knew that already. Why wouldn't he? But the expression of pure menace and loathing that shadows Aleks's beautiful face is a stark reminder that he can be as vicious with his enemies as he is careful with me.

I'm staring. I know I am. And I can't tell if I like this other side of Aleks—or if I want to bolt.

I think he can tell. Keeping his voice soft, he asks, "May I see it?"

"Uh. Yeah. Let me just..."

Pulling my phone out of my back pocket, I swipe up, opening the camera app. Centering the note so that I have the whole thing in the screen, I snap a picture, then hand it over to Aleks. I know that once he has it, I won't see it again, and the threat scrawled on the paper doesn't just affect me.

While Aleks scans the few lines on the paper, I'm already searching for her contact in my meager list.

"He calls you his mate."

"I'm not," I say firmly.

"What are you doing?"

"Calling Gem."

For a moment, Aleks looks like he's about to argue with me. Wiping his hands on his pants, he turns away from me. "You should do that. The Alpha will need to be informed."

Right. And, courtesy of the note at the bottom, so does his mate.

I select her name, purposely giving Aleks—and the vampire head—my back as I wait for her to answer.

"Hello?"

I shift my phone so that the receiver is at my mouth again. "Gem. Hi. It's Elizabeth."

"Hey." The suspicion lacing her tone when she answered immediately fades. "What's up?"

I immediately launch into the most basic explanation. About how someone broke into her apartment, making a huge disaster of her old home, before I read her the note in my hand and she understands exactly who was behind the breach.

When Gem goes eerily quiet, digesting everything I said, Aleks holds out his hand. He waits expectantly for the phone.

I give it to him.

Lifting it to his ear, he greets Gem with another Polish phrase. "Mały wilku."

"Aleks. I'm heading to the den right now to get Ryker. We can be at the townhouse in twenty."

His lips thin. I know there's no love lost between him and Gem's mate, but this is the first time I'm seeing it. "Better not. Anton might've been one of the rebels, but he was a vampire. This is a Cadre problem."

"What about Elizabeth?"

Good question, Gem. What about me?

"She will be protected."

"Oh. That's right. She has Zakharov's fang."

Not anymore, Gem. Of course, she doesn't know that, though, and he doesn't tell her otherwise.

I wonder why.

They talk for a few seconds more before Aleks ends the call. When he offers me my phone back, I accept it.

"I'm going to call Roman," he tells me, pulling out his own phone. "Let him know what we found. While I do, pack everything you're going to need. You can't stay here tonight."

*You will be protected*, the Luna whispers. It's exactly what Aleks said to Gem, but hearing it from my goddess has me frowning over at him.

"Where will I go?" Gem would welcome me. I know she would. "Accalia?"

"No."

Okay.

"Then where?"

With a look that dares me to defy him, Aleks says, "To my home. Now pack your bags, Elizabeth. You won't be coming back here for a while."

Then, before I do anything but blink up at him in surprise, Aleks walks out of the room.

I shake my head, just a touch stunned. And, if I'm being honest, a little turned on; the submissive wolf inside of me has always responded to a male more dominant than I am. Then, trying not to read too much into his command, I head over to my closet, yanking out the empty duffle bag I have stowed in there.

It's time to pack.

# CHAPTER 12
# IF ONLY FOR NOW

Aleks holds the door to his twelfth-floor apartment open for me.

"Thank you," I murmur.

"Nie ma za co."

*You're welcome.*

Look at that. I'm getting better at recognizing some phrases —and not just the curse words. Score one for the language app on my phone.

Holding the strap of my duffel bag to my chest, I walk into Aleks's apartment for the first time. The entrance leads directly into a stylishly decorated living room complete with a cream-colored settee, a glass-topped coffee table, and a huge screen television mounted on the wall. The kitchen is off to my right. Moving further in, I see the hall that will lead to the bathroom and the bedrooms, plus the wide glass sliding door that opens to the balcony outside.

I think it's beautiful. Exactly the sort of space I'd expect

Aleks to have, and I'd be giddy over finally seeing it if it wasn't for one teensy, tiny thing: it smells like Gem in here.

I thought I was prepared for that. I'm not.

She's been gone since last summer, but her scent still lingers. The only way I can get through this is by remembering what she said. They were roommates—platonic roommates. She had her own room, and Aleks had his.

Right now, I can't say for sure that I know what's going on between me and Aleks. Little more than a week ago, we were strangers. Since then, I've fed him my blood, kissed him, taken his fang, and now I'm staying with him because some sick shifter left a vampire's head in my bedroom.

I'm fucking exhausted. I'm beginning to think that I might have been better off grabbing my tarot cards and the cash Roman's given me already and getting the heck out of Dodge. Since that option is currently off the table, I'm going to bed. Maybe eat something. I always do my best thinking on a full stomach.

But, first, I'm putting this bag down. Aleks tried to convince me to let him carry it, but the stubborn side of me that rarely rears its head had refused. It's not heavy, not for a shifter, but I'd still feel better putting it down.

Following the scent trail, I start down the hall.

"Where are you going, Elizabeth?" he calls after me.

I point at the farthest door. "That one is Gem's room, right?"

He nods.

"I was going to put my bag in there, then figure out what to eat."

As bad as the scene in the townhouse was, I still have my appetite. When I was on the run—even when I was trapped in the district—I had to go hungry more often than not; either because I was low on funds, or because I didn't want to give any male the wrong idea. Now? I eat what I want, when I want, and I'm starving.

'That's fine. But don't put your bag in that room." Shifting on his heel, he points toward the first closed door at the beginning of the hall. "Put it in there."

"Whose room is that?" I ask, even though I'm pretty sure I already know.

I'm right.

"It's mine." His lips thin into a fine line as he meets me in the middle of the hall. "While you're here, you'll be sleeping in that room."

I will? "Aleks... maybe it's better that I take the couch then."

Tucking his finger under my chin, he tilts my head enough so that I'm forced to meet his steely gaze. His irises are still a gentle soft green, but I know that it won't take much for me to make them turn red.

"You won't wear my fang near your heart," he grates out, his accent growing more noticeable. "Won't you at least sleep in my bed?"

"Aleks, I—"

"You need your rest. I aim to make sure you get it. I'll sleep elsewhere."

"Where?"

"Excuse me?"

"Where are you going to sleep?"

If I'm in his bed, and he doesn't want to sleep next to me, would he use Gem's old bed instead?

The idea that he would bothers me more than it should. I have no right to be jealous, and yet there are two females I can't measure up to. One is dead, the other happily mated, and then there's me.

Maybe I *should* leave Muncie while I can...

"If you're not comfortable sharing," he says after a moment's pause, "I will take the couch."

It's not a matter of being comfortable. With the Luna only a week from being full, it's more that I'm afraid I'll lose control around him.

I have before. And, despite everything being so unsettled between us, I'm sure I will again.

"You don't have to make a decision now, though," he adds. Turning toward the kitchen he says, "You're hungry. I'll go make some dinner for you."

Alarm bells go off inside of my head at just how smoothly he offered to do so.

In shifter culture, making food for—or providing it to—a prospective mate has a very specific meaning. It means: *I will protect you, I will feed you, and you'll want for nothing if I'm around.* If I eat it, I'm basically saying *sure*.

"Point me to the kitchen. If you don't mind, I can fend for myself."

"You liked it when I cooked for you before."

I did, but that was before everything else happened. Before he so fiercely ripped Roman's necklace from my throat, replacing it with the one I have in my pocket right now. Before a similar fierceness replaced his usually gentlemanly facade tonight, giving me no choice but to follow him home.

He's acting too much like a possessive, bonded shifter for me to feel comfortable eating another of his meals when he doesn't know what it means to me and my wolf.

"Shouldn't you be on patrol?"

Aleks shakes his head. “Not tonight. When I called Roman, he passed my full-turn onto a quarter-turn patroller. Sonya is looking to rise within the Cadre. She’ll take the chance to prove herself to Roman, and I have the night to spend with my beloved.”

He sounds like he means it, too. Like having a few hours with me is all he wants.

I can’t take it anymore.

Because honestly? I kind of want that, too, and if it turns out that we were both fooling ourselves all along, I’m not sure I’ll survive his rejection. Even worse, I have the Alpha to worry about now.

*Until we meet again, Elizabeth.*

If the Wicked Wolf is regarding me as his, I’d hate to see what he does to Aleks when he finds out that the vampire he tortured truly is my fated mate.

The only way to keep him safe from the Wicked Wolf is by pushing him away from me, no matter how much it hurts.

I want him, but I still can’t have him—and he needs to know that.

“You don’t have to do that.”

He frowns. “What am I doing wrong, Elizabeth? How can I show you that I can be a good mate to you if you won’t let me?”

Wait... is that what he’s trying to do? That’s supposed to be a shifter thing, not a vampire courting ritual.

Then again, I *am* a shifter. And maybe Aleks is trying to appeal to me and my wolf by acting the way he would if he was the same.

Ah, Luna... we’re in the middle of the mating dance, aren’t we?

With the threat of the Alpha renewed, Peyton’s sudden reappearance after a seven-year absence, and the reminder of his first beloved still lurking in that back of mind, that is quite possibly the *last* thing I need right now.

"Aleks, I..."

I *what*?

"Gem told me that feeding you would show your wolf that I'm a good male. A good provider. You must be hungry. Let me feed you."

"Gem said that?"

He nods.

I bite back my scowl.

Next time I talk to her again, I'll have to ask her why she's giving Aleks tips to court me. I thought she was on *my* side.

I should say no. Accepting food from Aleks, knowing full well his intentions behind it now... I should say no.

But I don't.

Hefting up my duffel bag, I rest my hand on the doorknob to Aleks's room. "Okay. Let me put the bag down and I'll join you in the kitchen."

---

He cooked for me, but the manners instilled in me from puphood have me insisting on clearing the table and washing up. He joins me, insisting in turn that he be allowed to grab a dishcloth so that he can help. It isn't until we're done that I realize just how... *domestic* the scene was.

Aleks is in a much better mood after dinner. He obviously feels as if he's won one small battle in the war between us by getting me to eat his food. If you ask me, I came out ahead since

Aleks, for all that he doesn't eat human food regularly, is a pretty good cook.

He chats amicably about anything and everything—he tells me about the latest thriller he's reading before changing the subject to how the patrols around Muncie work—while I can't get past the fact that this is what life would be like if I ever bonded fully to Aleks.

I'm still dwelling on that when he asks if I'm ready to turn in for bed. Over dinner, I pointed out how ridiculous it would be for him to take the couch. I'm twenty-nine, he's... *older*. We're both mature adults. If we can't sleep in bed together without issue, there won't be any hope for me as his beloved.

Was it a manipulative move? At the time, I didn't think so. As Aleks strips down to his boxers, taking the left side of the bed, I begin to second-guess my intentions. I've already used the bathroom to brush my teeth, wash my face, and change into a t-shirt and sweatpants. It's what I usually wear to go to bed, but when he catches sight of me inching my way into the room, you would've thought I was wearing the finest lingerie.

He looks so... so *hungry*.

I can't get his expression out of my head. Even after he switches off the light, the two of us laying together in his king-sized bed, I still see it.

Turning on my side, giving Aleks my back, I begin to think that the couch might have been the better option after all.

In the quiet of the room, his voice seems to echo. "Elizabeth? Is everything okay?"

"Yeah. I'm just thinking."

That much, at least, is true.

"Thinking about what?"

"It's stupid."

He edges a little closer to me. His fingers reach out, caressing my hand. It's a reminder that, though it's dark, we're both supes. We don't need the light to see each other clearly. "I'm sure it isn't. Come, księżyca. Tell me."

"It's just... you didn't eat. I did, but you didn't have anything but tea."

"Ah." How can he make that single sound say so much? "You're worried about me? You want to take care of me, too? Is that it, my beloved?"

I want to tell him that he's way off base. That I'm not his beloved.

But those would be lies. And even if this ends up being one big mistake, it doesn't feel right lying to my mate.

"I..."

"Yes?"

Does he know what I *really* want to say? Something tells me that he does, that he's waiting for me to find a way to articulate it to him.

Oh, Luna. Why is this so embarrassing? Before Aleks, I had a good amount of lovers. Before the Luna's touch made me wary of touching others, I enjoyed many males so that I could learn all about pleasure before I met the one meant specifically for me. Kyle might have been the last, so I've had a seven-year-long dry spell, but you'd think I was a skittish virgin the way I can't tell Aleks what I want from him.

I want *him*. I might not be able to claim him, but I want to show him my appreciation for everything he's done for me lately. And, hey, if I get some pleasure out of it... it seems like a win-win to me.

I swallow, grateful for the darkness in his room as I blurt out, "You can bite me again. I mean, if you want. If you're hungry."

The silken sheets rustle as Aleks slides closer to me. The chill of his skin is a balm against my embarrassment; the erection poking into the small of my back is a sure sign that he has some idea what I'm thinking.

"Would it frighten you, mój księżyca, if I told you that being near you... you make me starved for you?"

The way his voice drops to a whisper like that? When I shiver, fear is the last thing I'm feeling.

"Not at all."

"What if I told you that I'd do anything for a taste?"

I gulp. His cock pushes against me, but I inch even closer to Aleks. "Then I'd tell you that you're free to do so."

"You mean it?"

"I'm not in the habit of saying things I don't mean."

I can just about hear Aleks's slow grin when he says, "That's good to know."

My back is to him. I can't see what he's doing, but I can sense him as he moves. The memory of the pleasure from just the other night has me getting wet already. Clenching my thighs together, I slide my head on the pillow giving him access to my neck.

Only... that's not where Aleks touches me.

To my shock, he pulls the blanket covering us off before resting his hand on my hip. With a gentle tug, he eases me onto my back. As I let out a small gasp, he slips his hand between my thighs. The push he gives them is a little firmer, forcing them apart.

Once he has, he climbs over my leg, settling his shoulders in the cradle of my body.

"What... what are you doing?" It comes out breathless. "Aleks?"

"You told me I could have a taste. Did you not?" His fingers hook in the waistband of my sweatpants. "Up," he orders. I immediately lift my ass off of the bed. He shimmies the sweatpants down, taking my panties with them. "Elizabeth?"

Is he talking to me? I'm too distracted watching the way he's scooted down the bed, giving him room to tug one leg of my pants off, then the next. Before I know it, I'm completely naked from the waist down, and Aleks is looking at my revealed pussy like he's just found heaven.

Returning to his position between my legs, he blows a stream of cool breath on the top of my mound. "I said, did you not, Elizabeth?"

Did I not *what*? "Huh?"

"I told you I was starved. Now, your blood is divine. I promise you that. But I've had teases of your true scent these last few days and, to put it mildly, they've driven me nearly mad. To have you in my bed? To scent you growing wet for me? I'm starved, księżyca. This"—he runs the tips of three fingers down my slick folds— "is all I want to eat tonight. May I?"

He's so close to pleading, I can hardly believe it. This god of a vampire begging to eat me out?

"What did I say before?" I ask him.

Another caress. "I recall something like 'you're free to do so'."

"And what else?"

"That you always say what you mean."

"Then what do you think?"

He doesn't answer me. At least, not with words.

Holding me open with two fingers, Aleks nips at my clit before using the flat of his tongue to swipe up the length of my whole pussy.

I wiggle. I can't help it. That one lick feels so damn good that I want to get closer to his mouth. My flesh is hot, and his cool vampiric mouth is fucking *amazing*.

With a gentle slap to my clit, Aleks admonishes me. "Don't move, Elizabeth. For once, I have you right where I want you. Can you do that? I'll make it worth your while."

The wicked promise in his voice makes me want to do anything he says. "I'll try."

"That's my female." Another lick with a little more pressure this time. When I don't move, he goes back. Before I know it, he's doing exactly what he promised. He's tasting me every which way he can, and, yes, he definitely makes it worth my while even though I can't keep from squirming for long.

When I whimper that I need something more, Aleks slips a finger inside of me, giving my muscles something to tighten around as he dedicates everything else he has to my clit. My hands fist the sheets before he takes a quick break to tell me that he wants me to touch him.

And I do. I caress his neck, holding him close to me. I remember being grateful that, as a vampire, he doesn't need to breathe, because I lose track of how long I ride his face. Eventually my fingers end up threaded through his curls. They're so soft, the texture has me clinging to him just as I begin to come.

As I finally start to wind down from my climax, Aleks lowers himself further down my trembling body until he's nuzzling my inner thigh. I'm glad. My clit is so sensitized right now, if he went back for another lick, I'd have to shove him away from my pussy. My thigh, though? I can handle the jolt of pleasure his cool tongue gives me as he laves my skin.

And that's when he bites me, sucking on my thigh, taking my blood into him.

It feels so fucking amazing that I'm tossed right into another orgasm, pressing the back of his head to my flesh as I give him whatever he needs from me.

If only for now...

---

THE NEXT MORNING, I WAKE UP WITH THE WEAK SUN streaming in through his blinds, one hell of a smile tugging my lips.

Ah, Luna. I haven't slept that well in *years*.

Waking up with an arm thrown over my waist? It's bliss, especially since it's connected to my gorgeous vampire.

He's still sleeping when I wake up. I take a few minutes to just drink in his beauty. He's absolutely stunning while at rest. He told me last night as he pulled me against him that his routine was to patrol all night—which I knew—and to get a few hours down when the sun was at its strongest—which I had suspected. I thought that meant that he was going to stay awake, but he murmured that he'd waited two hundred years to sleep with his beloved. Now that I was in his bed, he wasn't going to wait a single night more.

And though he seemed to enjoy himself, stroking me, tasting me, then *biting* me, when he told me that, I wondered if he meant that he wanted to finish the night with sex. Nope. When Aleks said sleep, he actually meant *sleep*. Sated by the two orgasms he gave me, I began to doze immediately. He could've done anything at all to me, and I would've let him.

Instead, with his rock-hard erection nestled between my ass cheeks, his arms wrapped around me, he spooned me until I fell asleep in the safety of his embrace.

He followed after me eventually, still sleeping when I pick up his arm, settling it down on a pillow after I slip out of the bed. My phone is in my purse. I'm not surprised that there's a missed call from Gem's phone number on the screen.

Before Aleks wakes up, I tap out a quick message, asking if there is any way we could meet up to talk. With Walker's latest threat still so fresh, I hate the idea of leaving Muncie—and I have no idea how I'd get my overprotective vampire to let me go without him—but I don't want to risk Gem, either. She was name-dropped in her birth father's note, and I'm not so sure she understands just how bad the situation in Muncie is.

Plus, I've got a thing or two I want to discuss when it comes to Aleks. With that in mind, I mention that I won't be free until after ten pm, leaving her to make of that what she will.

It's early. Not even seven in the morning when I send the message. I don't expect her to answer right away, but she does, and I let out a sigh of relief when she tells me that she'll meet me at Charlie's after Aleks's patrol starts.

Yeah. Gem understood my message all right.

Tossing my phone back into my purse, I climb into bed again. I don't know what tonight will bring, but if I can pretend that Aleks really is mine for a few hours more, I'm going to take them greedily.

# CHAPTER 13
# GEM'S UNSOLICITED ADVICE

Later that night, I'm sitting at the far end of the bar, nursing my ginger ale, when the door opens and I feel that familiar prickle against my back.

*Alpha.*

Her wolf's undeniable dominance hits me and my much more submissive wolf first, then the spicy cinnamon scent I know all too well; it overlays everything in the townhouse, and it still lingers in Aleks's apartment. I have to squelch the tiniest hint of jealousy that wells up inside of me, pulling my lips in a genuinely welcoming smile as I swivel on my stool.

I'm not the only one who's noticed her arrival. As the door swings closed behind Gemma, she's already waving at some of the patrons, offering greetings to others. Though she's slender and kind of short—she's a few inches shorter than me, at least—as she strides through the crowded floor of Charlie's, a path seems to clear for her like she's come kind of hulking wrestler heading for the ring.

Even the humans sense that there's something different about the pretty blonde. She pulled her long hair back in a high ponytail, the length of it swaying as she stalks purposely forward. Despite the February chill, she's wearing a short-sleeved t-shirt; it's black, like her jeans, and the dark color makes the gold-plated fang she wears pop. Shifters don't feel the cold the same way that vampires and humans do, so she seems perfectly comfortable in her spring wear—even as a few stray snowflakes cling to her pale hair.

Huh. It must be snowing again. It wasn't when I arrived at the bar, but I was so antsy and anxious that I showed up early. I came straight from work, purposely avoiding Aleks. By now, he's probably out on patrol. That gives me some time before I have to face him again.

I need advice. The only two people I even considered asking for it were Gem and Leigh. Leigh is happily mated, and Tamera is another vampire. Only knowing that she would inevitably tell Tamera—then Gretchen—about my confusion when it comes with being with *the* Aleksander Filan had me hesitating.

Gem is a shifter. True, her mate is another alpha, but she'd understand the mating dance much better than Leigh would. Plus, she knows Aleks extremely well, and meeting with her gave me an excuse to decline Gretchen's invite to join them at Mea Culpa tonight.

Then there's the undeniable fact that she also knows what it's like to be courted by him...

My grin wavers. Was this a bad idea? I really hope not.

Because here she is, and before I can think twice about this, she's plopping herself on the empty stool to my right. "Hey."

"Um. Hi. I—"

"Gem!"

Leaning back, looking down the length of the bar, she beams over at the pair of men waving at her. "Vin. Jimmy. Long time no see."

One of them is an older human. I'd put him at over sixty, with the grey hair and wrinkles bracketing his mouth and his eyes to prove it. He lifts his drink—a tentative sniff tells me it's whiskey—in Gem's direction.

The other man is a supe. Vampire. He looks like he's in his thirties, though his aura marks him as much older. He has slicked-back dark brown hair, pale grey eyes, and a lascivious smile as he greets Gem. A shot of chilled blood is set in front of him. Grabbing it from the countertop, he slips off of his stool, sidling down the bar until he's sitting on the other side of Gem.

"Off duty, Vin?"

"Nah," he says. "Just grabbing a drink before I head back out. What about you? If you're looking for Hailey, she's been out all week. Something about celebrating getting her fang and her man."

"I heard. Good for her. I wasn't sure Dominic would ever make it official, but I'm glad he did. Hailey deserves a Cadre vamp as her mate. But I'm not here for her." She bumps her shoulder against mine. "I'm meeting this one."

Easy touch is still difficult for me; with anyone except Aleks, that is. I tense as she hits me, bracing myself even as her carefree bump sends me listing a few inches to my left.

Gem might be small, but the alpha female packs a big punch.

As I re-seat myself, I focus on her mention of Dominic. If he's the same one I know—and I'm thinking so, since she called him a Cadre vamp—then Hailey must've been the female he wanted me to break his bond with Felicity for. Thinking back, I do remember him talking to her at the bar the night of my interview, but I never put two and two together until now.

Good for Dominic, then. He's been nothing but pleasant to me—gracious, too—and he's one of Aleks's friends. I'm glad he's happy with his new mate.

I just wish it could be that easy for Aleks and me...

The dark-haired vampire clears his throat. "Say, Gem. You gonna introduce us to your new friend?"

"Sure thing." She points at the vampire. "That's Vincent St. James. His buddy is Jimmy Fiorello"—she raises her voice—"who knows all about supes but is still sitting a couple of seats down like he thinks us shifters are gonna sniff his ass or something."

I nearly choke on Gem's obvious tease. It was so unexpected, especially when the older human jerks his chin in acknowledgement of her words. "That's got nothing to do with it. Was just finishing my drink, is all."

"Mm-hmm." Her eyes sparkle, and it's obvious that she misses them. "Anyway... guys, this is Elizabeth. She's like me."

"In more ways than one, I see," Vincent murmurs before taking a small sip of his blood.

What is that supposed to mean?

I don't know, and Gem ignores him as she adds, "She would've been behind the bar if Charlie didn't turn her down."

To my surprise, a bitter note finds its way to her tone. She wasn't happy when I told her that I didn't get the job, though she was mollified when I explained that I was working for Roman instead. It has all worked out in the end, but I guess she still harbors some annoyance that Charlie backed out of their deal.

I hadn't expected a reason why he didn't hire me. He interviewed me, and he passed. It happens. But Gem... she felt like he owed her one and it still obviously bothers her that he didn't have one.

Seems like nobody told Vincent that, though, since he takes another sip before telling her, "Yeah. I heard about that. Bad luck. Filan really didn't want Charlie to hire another shifter. I think you broke his heart, Gem."

Her good cheer from earlier dims a little further, a flush rising high on her cheeks. "Oh, stuff it, Vin."

He gives her a wistful look. "I tried. You kept on telling me no."

Reaching out, she shoves him, the vampire chuckling to himself as he moves on the stool.

Once again, I can't help but think that it must be nice to be able to touch someone as easily as that...

I shouldn't be jealous. For so many reasons, I shouldn't be jealous of Gem—but I am. She's strong. Powerful. Dominant. Her wolf doesn't cower like mine does. She's a fierce fighter, and a protective female. She wears an Alpha's marks on her skin, but she's kind, too. She's been looking out for me ever since we met in the district, and even if she has history with Aleks, she doesn't use that against me one way or another. She's a sweetheart.

But, most of all, I'm jealous because I think she *did* break Aleks's heart.

She's not his beloved. Julia was once, and I'm supposed to be now. Gem was never his beloved—but he wanted to be bonded to her anyway. When she rejected him, taking Ryker for her mate instead, Aleks didn't handle it well.

And I know I never would've met him if it wasn't for her. Aleks only showed up at the Wolf District because Ryker asked him to look out for Gem. Does that do anything to soothe this new burst of jealousy?

Not even a little.

Once she's recovered, she narrows her golden eyes on the vampire. "Hang on. What do you mean, Aleks didn't want Charlie to hire her? What the hell does he have to do with Elizabeth working the bar?"

The vampire's easy laugh ends abruptly. With an "oh shit" expression on his face, he shifts in his seat, reaching for his glass of chilled blood. Vincent drinks some more as a distraction, grimacing when he sees that Gem has locked her unblinking alpha stare on him.

He gulps. "I take it you didn't know that he's the reason Charlie said no."

Gem glances my way. I shake my head.

Her eyes go from vivid to molten. "Nope."

Honestly, I should've guessed. Maybe not right away—I didn't know Aleks all that well when this started—but since then? Yeah… I should've guessed. With the sway he has in town, the only one who would dare go against him when it comes to his beloved is Roman Zakharov.

Poor Charlie never had a chance.

Gem's obviously thinking along the same lines as me. She must be, because she actually lets it go. Something tells me that she won't for long—poor Aleks should expect a text in the future, and probably Charlie, too—but she doesn't give either of them shit for it right now.

Instead, she turns to look at me. Behind her, I see Vincent's shoulders sag in relief before he tosses back the last of his shot. Murmuring a quick goodbye, he hightails it out of the bar.

When I see Gem's determined expression, I almost want to follow him.

"I can't be here long. Ryker's spent the whole evening holding a joint council with our pack and Kendall's. He's the—"

"Alpha of the River Run Pack," I supply absently.

What can I say? When you're a lone wolf, you keep up to date on pack politics.

Gem gives me a strange look but doesn't comment. "Yeah. Anyway, he'll have my hide when he finds out I came down here without telling him, especially this late, but you made it sound urgent so... here I am. What's up?"

My insides twist with guilt. "I don't want to get you in trouble with your mate," I begin.

She waves me off. "It's fine. I like it when he spanks me." Shooting me a grin when my mouth drops open, she lays her hand on my stool, giving it a subtle shake. "Come on. You told me about my sperm donor's note. Aleks just said that Roman would get in touch with Ryker. He'll give me details when he gets them, but he's busy with Kendall. I need to know what's going on. Tell me. What happened?"

Her wolf is still in control despite the fact that Gem is in her skin. And while it wasn't quite a command—at least, not a deliberate one—I can't help but react as if it was.

Tell her?

Okay.

I tell her *everything*. Starting with the unfamiliar shifter's scent leading up to the townhouse and the slaughtered vampire he left for me to find along with Walker's note, all the way to how I ended up staying over with Aleks last night, I don't stop until I get to the point when I decided to call her and ask her to meet with me.

But not about the Alpha's delusional idea that I'll end up as his mate. That's my problem, and after how she challenged him and won, I doubt Walker will try attacking the Mountainside Pack until he's leading a pack as powerful as the Western Pack once was.

No. There's something else I want to talk to her about. I'm just waiting for the right moment to bring it up.

The whole time I'm telling her about last night, keeping my voice as low as possible so that I'm not overheard, Gem doesn't interrupt except to ask if I have a copy of Walker's note. Pausing only to send her a message with the picture I snapped of it before Aleks pocketed it for Roman, I continue talking while she nods, staring at the dark lines scrawled on the blood-stained paper.

"I'll have to let my mate know about this. No one's heard from Walker in months... Luna, we're still trying to figure out how he popped his head into town last week... but he's like a ghost. No one can find him. To have him do this? He's getting closer to making his next move."

And, unfortunately, it's against *me*.

"I know. And I would've told you last night. Only..."

"It's okay. I get it. I know how Aleks is, and his need to run everything through the Cadre. I'm actually surprised he's not here, acting in its interests as you tell me all about this."

"He's on patrol," I explain.

"Yup. Know all about his insane need to patrol at least eight hours each night, every night. I think he had like four nights off the whole time I lived with him. It won't be easy to get that workaholic to settle down."

I shrug.

I mean, who says I want to? Besides, I like that about him. It shows how protective of a male he is; he considers Muncie his territory and, like shifters, he's willing to do anything to protect it. But when I called him last night, in trouble and in need, he immediately ran to my side.

He protects me, too. Answering my call, coming when I'm in trouble, bringing me to his house... that's exactly how a bonded, possessive shifter acts.

Huh. Maybe it's not just a shifter thing, but a *supe* thing.

That's something to think about.

After sparing a glancing at the time flashing across her screen, Gem puts it back in her pocket. "You know... I've got a little more time if you need anything else from me."

"Oh. Um... I don't know."

"I mean it. Look, Ryker already had the whole pack looking for Walker before this, and a dead vamp is probably Roman's problem, but when it comes to Aleks... you want to talk to me about him some more?"

Do I? "Not really."

Gem laughs. "Appreciate the honesty."

Was that rude? It felt rude.

I sigh, then blurt out, "He moved me into his apartment. He *cooked* me *dinner*."

It's such a huge confession for me. But Gem? She's not even a little surprised by it.

She shrugs. "Made it longer than I did. I was living with Aleks within days. Took me months before I ate his food, though, and only because I made it clear we would take turns." A curious twist of her lips as she asks, "You in my old room?"

She'll know if I lie. It's an alpha thing. She'll ***know***.

"I slept in his bed last night."

Her eyes light up. "Did the two of you mate?"

"Gem!"

"What? It's a valid question. He's your fated mate. You're his beloved. The Luna's almost full. I still told myself I hated Ryker the first time we mated, but that didn't stop us."

*You're his beloved...*

So she believes that, too?

And maybe it's a valid question to her, and she obviously has no problem talking about her sex life with her alpha mate, but I'm a little uncomfortable discussing what went on between Aleks and me—especially with half of Charlie's as an audience.

I don't have to, though. With the tiniest flaring of her nostrils, she knows exactly how far we went last night.

Ah, Luna. Now I'm bushing.

Gem notices. "Hey. You like him?"

Do I? Yes. More than I should. When it comes to *lov*e, I'm a little less certain, but *like*?

I nod.

Gem pats me on my shoulder. "Thought so. Okay. Can I give you some unsolicited advice?"

I don't think there's any way I can stop her. "Sure."

"Listen to your wolf. Sometimes our people brains get in the middle of a good thing. Screw the brain. When it comes to your forever, it's your gut and your heart you want to pay attention to. If your wolf wants him, take him."

"I don't know."

"I'm not telling you to bond yourself to him right now. You couldn't tonight even if you wanted to. But... would it really hurt to give him a test drive?"

Oh my Luna. I don't think anyone is really paying us any attention right now. Doesn't matter. I feel like I'm about to die from embarrassment.

And Gem's still not done.

"If your two-legged half is giving you hang-ups, rely on your wolf. Maybe you need to get in touch with your wild side." With a wink, Gem lowers her voice so that I'm for sure the only one who can hear it when she murmurs, "There's a park not too far from here that I recommend."

The sad thing is I know exactly which one she means since it's where I almost jumped Aleks the first time I gave him my blood.

I grab my glass. There's still a mouthful of flat soda at the bottom. I hurriedly drink it, trying to cover up my sputtering.

"What?" Gem's suddenly so innocent, I finally understand how she was able to pass as an omega wolf for most of her life. "Was it something I said?"

"It's just..." The glass clinks against the countertop as I set it down. On a sigh, I admit, "I don't even know if he likes me back."

It's like I'm a fifteen-year-old virgin again. Even in a shifter pack, we all have those awkward years where we worry about who likes who, who will be the first to fuck, and what our future bonded mates will be like.

Now I'm drawn to a vampire, I haven't had sex since Kyle, and my mate...

I still want him. There. If I can't admit it out loud, I can at least admit it to myself. Fate has a way of pulling two souls who match together. Maybe Aleks needs a shifter female with dark hair, and I need a complicated male.

He's never shied away from considering me his. Even in the beginning, he allowed that there was a tie between us. He wants me to be *his*.

But it's true. I still have no idea if he likes me. Not my looks—so eerily similar to his Julia's—or my kind of supe—*everyone knows Aleksander has a wolf fetish*, scoffed Gretchen—but *me*.

Elizabeth Howell, a Luna-touched female who longs for her mate.

Gem cocks her head slightly. "Are you sure?" A devilish glint comes to her gaze as she adds, "Aleks hasn't done anything to make it obvious that he wants you? Not me, not some ghost of his past, but *you*?"

I think back. "He sent me a box of tea when I first got the job with Roman."

"Aleks does so love his tea. What else?"

"He also brought me my favorite sandwich for lunch."

Gem nods sagely. "Now that? That sounds like something a shifter would do to court his mate."

She's got a point.

He is a vampire, though. My instincts tell me to treat him like any other wolf during the mating dance, but while he's a supe, he's no shifter.

Hmm.

What about me? Aleks brought me food, *cooked* me food, when he doesn't need it. What can I do to reciprocate?

I fed him my blood twice now. The first time it had been an emergency. The second? I was so mindless with pleasure that I gave him permission without even realizing what I was doing.

There was an intimacy to the act that's undeniable, but a mating—despite the name—is more than just sex. It's caring for your partner. Protecting them. Taking care of them.

Feeding them...

Aleks eats human food out of habit, not necessity. I know he goes to donors like the rest of the vampires in Muncie, but his fridge is also full of bagged blood for when he feels like "eating in". If I bring him some back to the apartment, it'll be like him picking up a sandwich from the deli with me in mind.

Pursing my lips, I look up at Gem. "Do you think you can get Charlie to sell me one of his bags?"

She grins. "Yeah. I think so. Sit here. I'll be right back."

And then, visibly satisfied with herself, Gem disappears behind the bar.

# CHAPTER 14
# CAN'T GET ANY COLDER THAN DEAD

Ten minutes later—after Gem tracks down Charlie, then says her goodbyes to her old customers—I'm leaving the bar with a blonde shadow and a bag of chilled AB positive in my tote bag.

Even through the thick plastic and the canvas material, I can scent the rusty, tangy blood. You'd think it would bother me. When I first arrived in Muncie, it took me a few days to get used to the meaty, cold scent that clings to vampires, but blood? It often triggered my wolf's predatory instincts.

Not now. Not when I think of it as an early morning snack for Aleks.

Huh. Look at me. Getting all domestic over my new roommate.

As we step onto the street outside of Charlie's, I go still. My wolf whines, eager to rub flanks with Gem's, hiding behind the alpha's dominance. Taking a deep breath, I filter out the smells from the bar—booze, food, and BO—and the blood in my bag until all I'm left with is a forest-scented musk that undoubtedly belongs to a wolf.

My head jerks to my left. There, on the corner, is a boyish-looking male with sandy brown hair and soft golden eyes. His thumbs are hooked in his belt loops, his shirtsleeves rolled up to his elbows, leaving his forearms on display. He was watching the entrance like a hawk, already moving toward us before the door swings closed behind our backs.

It's not snowing anymore, but the ground is covered with a dusting. There's a bitter chill on the breeze. He should be wearing a coat. Even if his eyes and his scent didn't give him away, his outfit did—as well as his direct pursuit.

It's another shifter. A delta.

*Interesting.*

"Are you ready, Alpha?" he says. His voice is pleasant and a touch smooth. It's nice.

"Yup," answers Gem. "I probably pushed my luck staying this long, but it was worth it. I've got a lot to tell Ryker. Was everything okay out here?"

"Everything's fine."

"No sign of another wolf?"

His eyes flicker over to me. "Just this one."

It's a quick up and down, up and down before he moves a little closer. The first up and down I can understand; this is obviously one of Gem's "guards", and he's checking me out to make sure I'm not a threat to the Alpha of the Mountainside Pack's mate. The second one, though? Yeah. He was just *checking me out*.

Gem gestures at me. "This is Elizabeth. Ryker knows her. She's safe."

"Silver eyes? That's unique." His lips quirk in a flirtatious smile. "Hi. I'm Bobby."

Gem cuts in front of me. Then, planting her hand against his firm chest, pushes him a few steps back. "And she's unavailable. Down boy." Turning toward me, catching my surprised expression, she rolls her honey gold eyes. "Come on. We both know you have Aleks's fang in your pocket. If he catches Bobby's scent on you, I might lose another one of my guards the hard way."

The male shifter immediately takes another couple of steps away from us as I gape over at Gem.

I... I didn't tell her I had Aleks's fang. And, sure, Roman's isn't hanging off my neck anymore, but that could just mean I removed it. Vampires can sense the mark of one of their kind. Another shifter shouldn't be able to, even if they *are* an alpha.

Instead of asking her how she knows—I think my new roommate is conspiring with his former roomie more than I thought—I just wonder, "Whose side are you on?"

She won't tell me Aleks's secrets, and she's obviously been giving him hints on how to court me the way a shifter would. At the same time, she has no problem telling me to listen to my wolf while also making sure I had some insight into the vampire by passing along that Polish to English dictionary.

Is she helping me or Aleks? Ryker warned her to let Fate play out when he picked his head up from his map and realized the extent of Gem's meddling that night, but would I be walking out of Charlie's with a bag of blood if it wasn't for her?

Her impish grin is proof that she knows exactly what she's doing. "Both?"

I close my eyes and shake my head.

Yeah. That sounds about right.

---

I'm halfway back to Aleks's apartment building when the wind shifts and I suddenly go motionless.

I smell *wolf*.

Over the last few weeks, it seems I might've become nose-blind to all of the vampires that live in Muncie, but I haven't caught a hint of another shifter—excluding the unknown shifter who left Walker's mess for me to find—since I ran into a lone wolf during my last stint at that small town Christmas carnival. The female had lived a life similar to mine: pretending to be human, hiding out from our kind, while supporting herself any way she could. I closed up my table immediately, not wanting a pissing contest when she flared her golden eyes at me.

She had done a double-take when she noticed that my shifter eyes were silver, but that didn't stop her from unleashing her claws—or maybe that's why she did. Either way, I had to go.

But, somehow, my wolf has started to think of all of Muncie as hers, not just the townhouse. From the downtown area where Charlie's is, to Aleks's apartment, all the way to the center where Roman lords over the Cadre building... it's mine.

I'm the only wolf allowed inside of Muncie.

Walker's scent clung to the note that he left, but he wasn't the shifter who slaughtered Anton, leaving me for him to find. I still don't know who that was, but the scent that I pick up now?

I know this one.

*Peyton.*

She's not just lurking on the edge of Muncie's borders. She's found a way inside, and now she's taunting me.

Worse, she threatened to take Aleks from me. And, okay, I don't know exactly what's going on between us. My wolf won't let me forget that he's my fated mate—neither will the Luna—

and he seems determined to prove to me that I truly am his beloved.

But after last night? I feel closer to him than ever. With Gem's advice bouncing around my skull, I've finally started to think that there might just be a chance for me and him.

There won't be if Peyton decides to target him.

Aleks is out on patrol. If she's made it inside of Muncie, she could be going after my mate just like she swore she would. And with everything changing between me and Aleks so quickly, he has no idea that she threatened him—or that Peyton even exists.

Okay. Think, Elizabeth. What do I do now?

Gem's out. She's too far to ask for her or her guard's help. I could call her, but that would only waste time.

I can't tell Aleks now. Over dinner last night, I asked him where he was all those days where he seemed to have disappeared. Though I could tell that he didn't really want to let me know, he eventually confessed that he was expanding his patrol. Roman gave him the okay to go farther and further to keep Muncie safe. Anton's murder at the hands of a wolf had caught the head vampire's attention.

Aleks's, too. Only, he added in between nonchalant sips of his tea, he was determined to track down the Wicked Wolf wherever he could be. If he was gone, that was one less person who could come between the two of us.

He wanted to protect his beloved so that, this time, he got to keep her.

I didn't know what to say to that last night, and I'm just as speechless today. One thing for sure? If I called Aleks and told him I caught the scent of a shifter inside of Muncie, he'd drop whatever he was doing to go after her.

I'm almost positive that's what she wants, too.

Maybe I'm acting a little bit like a possessive, bonded shifter myself because, suddenly, I know exactly what to do.

*Stop her.*

Shoving past the humans walking along the sidewalk, I start with a quick-paced walk before turning it into a jog, then an outright sprint. Now that I have her scent and I'm on the pursuit, I won't let anything get in the way of me and my target.

I barely notice it when the sidewalk under my shoes becomes hard dirt. Just under Peyton's signature sweet scent, earthy notes hit me. Mud. Ice. Grass. Woods.

*Park.*

Even if we live in a city where we're surrounded by skyscrapers, automobiles, and way too many humans, shifters will always search out the wilderness. I did when I first arrived in Muncie; it became the place where I let my wolf run free. Looks like Peyton did, too.

And maybe it's a trap. Could be. I won't know until I track her down.

But now that I'm tucked among the trees?

I don't even bother kicking off my shoes. I just shift, letting my white wolf out as everything I was wearing—panties, socks, bra, shirt, jeans, and shoes—are obliterated with how badly she wanted to take over the hunt.

But whether I took a wrong turn or I got distracted during my shift, I'll never know. Peyton's scent fades as suddenly as I picked it up. I can't find her, but my need to protect my mate is too powerful to ignore.

I race through the woods, searching for... for something.

And that's when I hear Aleks.

"Elizabeth!"

I'm torn between two instincts: continuing to run after my

prey, or responding to my mate. With my wolf out, it's almost impossible to deny the growing bond stretching between me and Aleks.

My wolf stops short. She wants her mate, and now that she recognizes his aura reaching toward her, she plops her haunches in the old layer of snow.

If I leave it up to her, she'll roll over onto her back, exposing her belly to Aleks, begging him to love her.

I need more control than that. And the only way to get that is to put my human side in charge.

So I do.

Seconds later, I hear his shoes crackle over the old snow. My head was already staring in the direction from which he was coming because I was able to pinpoint the source of the aura.

Of course, that means that when Aleks appears past the trees, he gets a dead-on look at my skin.

He goes immovably still for a heartbeat before he recovers. "You're naked."

Too late do I realize that I made a huge mistake.

Nudity isn't a big deal in a shifter pack. It's only when sexual need comes into play that it's obvious just how open—just how *vulnerable*—I am when I'm in my skin. And last night? We were intimate for the first time so sexual need is definitely there. And though I know his vampire sight is as impressive as my wolf's, that he saw everything I had to offer from below the waist, he tasted me under the cover of darkness.

With the Luna bathing my skin, every inch of me is on display.

"I had to shift to run," I tell him, purposely avoiding the part where I destroyed my clothes, lost my bag, and was chasing after a threat. His fang was in my pocket, and I only hope the magic that let Roman's transform with me means that I'll find Aleks's again in the future otherwise I'll have to tell him the truth about what happened.

But that's later.

Now? Now I have something else on my mind.

He rubs his mouth with his hand. Still staring at me unblinkingly, he murmurs, "You're not cold?"

I'm not. Shifters run hot, and the look Aleks is giving me? It's burning me up.

"No. You?"

He has on an expensive-looking sweater that's perfectly fitted and a pair of black pants. Perfect for an upscale dinner in October, a little overdressed style-wise—and underdressed weather-wise—for an evening patrol in the second week of February.

"I'm a vampire. I'm already dead, aren't I? Can't get any colder than that."

True. Though we both know that, with blood taken straight from the vein, he'll warm up pretty quickly.

I blink, a thought coming to me. And maybe it's because I've always gotten a little turned on during a hunt, and I hadn't been able to slake the need to protect Aleks by chasing down Peyton, but the more he watches me with that stunned stare, the more aroused I'm growing.

He looks like he likes what he sees.

I desperately want him to.

Not only that. With his eyes beginning to develop that telltale red rim around his pale irises, I realize that I want *him*.

I don't even have to look up to know that the Luna isn't at her most powerful yet. I could enjoy him without worrying about claiming him since the only way a shifter can claim their mate is through the Luna Ceremony.

I'd have to get the Luna's blessing—while she was full—then mate him, and mark him. He'd have to mark me back, and then I'd have to willingly keep it.

Even if I wanted to tie myself to Aleks officially, I can't tonight. But if he's willing to take what we have one step further...

I'm ready.

To be fair, I wanted to last night. I denied it beforehand, but in the heat of the moment, when Aleks sank his fangs in me, I almost begged for him to use his cock instead.

As Aleks stares at me, I drop my gaze to his crotch. My vision is keen enough that I can see the notable bulge pushing up against his tailored slacks.

My body is ready to mate. So is Aleks's.

But is he?

I'm not a brave female. I'm not dominant. I have a tendency to obey, and my default is to run before I willingly put myself in a dangerous situation. I have to be backed into a corner to fight. When I became Walker's prisoner and his pet? His threat to out me to the Alpha collective—who, he assured me, would put me down as an abomination to our kind because of my family's "gifts"—was enough to keep me in my place. Not even after Gem arrived in California, promising to help me escape, did I ever think it might be possible.

Years ago, though, before I became even more of a lone wolf to protect myself, the only time I showed any backbone was when it came to mating.

That's why I was so frustrated last night. The old Elizabeth, seventeen and carefree, would've told Aleks exactly what she wanted.

I'm twenty-nine. I've spent ten years on my own, and the one time I gave in to the urge to take a male, it ruined my life.

*It won't be like that with him*, the Luna tells me. *He's yours*.

He is—and it's time I take him.

I move into Aleks. My wolf is snapping her teeth at me, telling me to hurry up. The Luna goes silent now that she can sense what I'm about to do.

His eyes follow every move I make. Every sway of my hip. Every bounce of my tits. If I want to seduce my vampire, I have to make it worth it, and I put as much effort into it as I can until I'm standing right in front of him.

Then, before I lose my nerve, I reach out and cup him.

# CHAPTER 15
# FOREVER HIS, OR JUST ONE NIGHT

He's so hard, I know I made the right choice. He needs relief, and I'm just the female to give it to him.

He shudders out my name. "Elizabeth…"

I loosen my hold on him, trading my palm for two fingers. I run them up and down his erection. "Is this okay?"

"It's more than okay."

"Good."

Aleks closes his eyes, throwing back his head as I add a little more pressure. I can't tell if he knows that he's doing it or not, but he begins to rock with the motion, showing me exactly where he wants to be touched.

I'm more than happy to oblige.

He lets me, though his eyes snap open again when my questing fingers find the button to his pants.

Reaching down, Aleks takes my hand in his. "I want you to," he says thickly, his accent suddenly more noticeable than it's ever been before, "but if you feel like you have to do this because of last night..."

That thought never crossed my mind.

Seduction, Elizabeth. Make him want this.

Make him want *you.*

I lower my fingers again, stroking him gently. "You're the one who said we don't reciprocate, right?"

He shifts his pelvis, giving me easier access to him. "I did."

"So why would you think that I'm doing this only because of the pleasure you gave me last night?"

Another stroke, higher up this time so I can reach for his zipper.

"I... I don't know."

Have I ever heard my vampire admit that? I don't think so, and if that doesn't make up my mind that we both need this, nothing will.

"I want you to know me, Aleks. The real me. Elizabeth. And Elizabeth can be very selfish when she wants to. I want you to feel good but"—I grab his zipper, tugging it gently down past the material of his boxers—"I want to feel even better. I ache. You have something that will make me feel better. Will you let me have it?"

I can only imagine what he's thinking. In the matter of a couple of days, I went from denying him, to seducing him out in the woods. But I mean every word I say, and he knows it.

Before I can reach inside of his boxers, searching for his cock, he lifts his hands, grabbing me by my arms.

"Elizabeth," he rasps out. "Look at me."

I do.

The only times I've ever seen Aleks looking so fierce were when he was about to fight for his life. And yet... I'm not afraid.

"Yes?"

"Are you my beloved?" he demands. "Do you accept me as yours?"

At this moment in time, when we're on the cusp of something great between us, I can.

"*Yes.*"

Aleks shutters his eyes, the fierce expression traded for a wicked look full of the promise of pleasure—and sin.

Just then, I almost tell him that he's my fated mate. The words rise up into my throat, perching themselves on the tip of my tongue.

But... I don't.

It would only be a complication if this doesn't work out. Until I can be sure that our bond is secure, that Aleks accepts me for *me*, I don't think I can tell him. He'll use Fate against me. If my blood assured him that I'm his vampire mate—which, well, obviously—and both my wolf and my goddess whisper the same when it comes to him, he won't stop until he's claimed me.

That's the thing. With my abilities... I've seen too many bad bondings. Mates who stayed together because they had to, not because they loved each other and couldn't imagine life without their partner.

Do I love Aleks? I... I don't know. At the very least, I'm halfway there, and it's definitely my human side that's hesitating.

Then again, it's also my human side that is dying to have some closeness with Aleks. A connection.

An intimacy.

I need him to want me, and when he shoves both his pants and his boxers down, freeing the most gorgeous cock I've ever seen in my life, I am undeniably convinced that he *does*.

Aleks kicks off his shoes, then hurriedly strips off his pants and his boxers. Then, with one practiced motion, he rips off his sweater so quickly that his muscles are still rippling before he drops it to the dirt.

He advances on me, the hunger in his eyes so stark, yet arousing. "You're mine. Forever."

I'm his.

For tonight.

Pulling my naked body into him, he hooks his arms under my bare thighs. Shifters are solid. I weigh a good one-sixty, easy, and he lifts me up as if I'm as light as a feather. He settles me just above his hips, encouraging me to wrap my legs around him as he digs his thumbs into my ass cheeks.

Using his strength, he bobs me up and down, spreading my wetness along his cock. It's already pointing skyward, ready to mate, but instead of him angling his hips to line our bodies up right, he teases me. My folds are slippery. As he bounces me easily, I rub against him, amazed at how strong my mate is—and how good his hard cock feels every time he bumps against my clit.

I'm achy. I feel so empty inside, but he seems to be enjoying himself, using my body as his plaything. For a few seconds, I wonder if he's planning on stroking himself off without ever getting inside of me. Which would be okay. The whole point of this is to make Aleks feel good—

Nope. I'm still a Luna-awful liar. I want Aleks to mate me more than I want my next breath and I whimper my need to him.

"I'm almost ready, księżyca," he says, and though he doesn't seem winded at all, his voice is hoarse. I realize then that it's taking all of Aleks's control not to just plunge inside of me.

I just don't know *why*.

"I need to feel you inside of me," I gasp out before pleading, "Make me feel as good as you did last night."

"That's my intention," he promises. "I know you're ready for me, but if I'm slick with your need, I won't hurt you as I take you. You were so tight last night... I never want to cause you pain."

That's right. In the middle of him tasting me last night, he slipped a finger inside of me. I might not be a virgin, but it has been seven years since I've been with a male. To make this mating as memorable as possible, he's doing a little foreplay while also reacting to my urgent need to skip most of it right now.

But I'm ready. I'm more than ready.

Bracing myself by clutching his shoulders with my claws, I try to take control. I appreciate his need to put me first, but I'm a shifter. I can take whatever he can give me.

And I want him *now*.

My claws cut right through his skin. Aleks's blood perfumes the air. I didn't mean to mark him, but I'd be lying if I said that the realization that I *did* doesn't drive me nearly mindless with lust.

I throw back my head and, though it comes out strangled because of my human-shaped vocal cords, I howl.

My marking his skin does something to Aleks, too. Gripping his cock by the base with one hand, he pushes my ass up with the other until he's able to position himself right at my entrance. I moan when I notice that the head of his cock is as chilled as his skin, but as he starts to push, it only feels *amazing*.

Slowly at first, he begins to feed me inch by inch while I'm panting at him to give me *more*. When he's halfway in, Aleks finally accepts that all I'm feeling is a mixture of pleasure and delicious fullness. I can take it and, with one last push, he gives it to me.

Aleks bottoms out inside of me. My skin sparks with electricity as I lift my hands up, shoving my fingers into his curls.

He doesn't need me to ride him. Pistoning his hips as he tightens his grip on my backside, Aleks begins to fuck me more savagely than any other male has ever before.

And I *love* it.

Another wolfish cry tears out of my throat. I'm not thinking about tomorrow. I'm not thinking about his past, or my future. Peyton is a distant memory, a problem I can deal with later.

Right now, it's just me and my vampire.

Arching my back as he thrusts in and out of me, I grab Aleks by his head, dragging his lips to my throat. I don't even realize I'm doing it until his cool lips brush against the side of my neck.

"If you want it," I tell him with more emotion than I should, "take it."

He doesn't hesitate. My skin pinches for a split second, lost in the pleasure of his touch, as he slides his fangs inside of me at the same time as he buries his cock all the way to the hilt again.

While he sucks, he keeps our groins pressed together. In this position, with me in his arms, every pull on my neck goes straight to my clit. By the time he's taken his fifth pull, my legs are shaking. At his sixth, I start to come around him.

He moans around my flesh, slowly dragging himself in and out again as he slows down on sucking my blood. He hasn't taken as much as he has before—it's nowhere near how much he needed after he got stabbed with the silver knife—but I'm already a little dazed.

Of course, that's probably because of the orgasm I just had.

I'm still pinned on his length as Aleks finally releases his fangs. Looking down at me, I see that his eyes are fully red but, for the first time, I understand it's not just because of bloodlust.

It's just straight-up lust.

Disentangling my fingers from his hair, I grab him by the shoulders again. I push up, then fall. Again. Up, then down. I start riding him because, though I already came once, he's still rock hard.

I need him to find his pleasure, too.

And that's when he lifts his hand. He's still holding my weight with his other—proving he's even stronger than I thought—but his right hand? He curves it around the nape of my neck, doing the same thing I just did to him.

He guides my head to the side of his neck.

"Bite me back, księżyca. Take my blood inside of you. Take *all* of me."

I'm not a vampire. The only time I ever drink blood is when my wolf is out and she goes hunting for prey.

But if this is what Aleks wants from me, I'll do it.

In my two-legged shape, my fangs are barely sharper than a regular human's. Tapping into my wolf, though, gives me the strength to bury them past all of the layers of skin until his tangy, meaty blood—warm after he took so much of mine—fills my mouth.

The second it does, Aleks releases my neck, splaying both of his hands against the small of my back. He bucks once, then twice, before he hisses right as he finally comes.

---

THE COLD DOESN'T BOTHER ME; IF IT DID, I COULD ALWAYS become a white wolf again, with a built-in fur coat. Coming down from mating with Aleks? I'm so incredibly hot, I'd probably melt the snow in a circle around me.

Tell that to my vampire lover. He's still inside of me, eager to keep the connection even though I'm sure he finished. After nuzzling my cheek, he leads us to the ground, sprawling out on the snow-trampled earth. He lays on his back so that he's the one lying in the snow, holding me against him as I'm on top of him.

I've never been more comfortable.

He presses a kiss to the top of my head. "Mm... księżyca. That was wonderful."

I'm glad he thought so. I thought he was pretty phenomenal himself.

Tracing an aimless pattern on his naked chest, I murmur, "I looked that up, you know."

"Oh?"

"You have no idea how many tries it took me to figure out how to spell it. I never even got close." And my Polish is laughable at best. Only when I finally tried mimicking Aleks's low accent into my translation app did I get a match that made any sense. "You call me 'moon', don't you?"

Fitting, I had thought. Because my only worth is my connection to the Luna.

He lifts his hand, running his thumb down the length of my cheek. "It's your eyes."

"Huh?"

"They gleam like silver, but they go dark, too. Full moon. New moon. It seemed like a perfect name for you."

Oh. That... that wasn't what I thought at all.

Then again, when it comes to Aleks, he usually surprises me in the best ways.

"I like it," I say at last. "Can't promise I'll ever be able to pronounce it right, but I like it."

"We'll have a lifetime for me to teach you Polish."

I should probably point out that the sex we just had wasn't a promise for anything past tonight. But he's so relaxed, and maybe I'm being selfish, but I like him this way. I don't want to take away his happiness when, odds are, it'll be short-lived regardless.

I know we can't stay out here much longer, even if I wouldn't mind. Any vampire who might want to investigate the wild sounds I made during mating would immediately turn around when they realized that Aleks was the one who brought out my wolf even while I was in my two-legged shape. Humans, though? Other wolves?

*Peyton?*

I don't want anyone to ruin this moment we have together. We might have forever, or only just this one night, but I want to treasure it for as long as it lasts.

So, though I know we can't stay here, I lay my head on Aleks's chest, amazed at how still he is except for those few rare breaths he takes.

Just a few more minutes, I tell myself. Then I'll get up and start to figure out what I'm going to do next. Peyton might be gone—I'm willing to bet she is—but that doesn't change the fact that she was here.

Or that I just had the best sex of my life with Aleksander in the middle of the woods, but now I'm naked and I'm really not supposed to walk around Muncie in my fur.

I get about ten peaceful minutes before I hear the buzz of a phone vibrating. It can't be mine. Unfortunately, I lost mine somewhere near the entrance of the woods when I dropped my purse right before I shifted.

Which means it must be Aleks's.

His discarded pants are within arms-length reach of him. Tugging them closer to him, he plucks his phone out of his pocket, lifting it to his eyes so that he can read the message.

The lazy, easy mood evaporates in a heartbeat. With a sigh, he sits up, using his arm against my back to ease me to a sitting position with him. His jaw tight, he reaches out, snagging his sweater next.

"Aleks?"

"It's Roman. He needs us to come to headquarters."

Damn it.

And, really, I shouldn't be surprised. From everything I learned about him, Aleks is a high-ranking member of the Cadre. He's like Roman's Beta, his second-in-command. Not only that, but he's supposed to be on patrol. I distracted him.

I just hope that Roman doesn't want him to check on reports of some kind of wild animal crying in the middle of the park or something.

Hang on—

"Did you say 'we'?"

"That's what the message says. That he needs to see me, and that I should bring you along since he wants to talk to you and we're already together."

There goes my hope that Roman expected Aleks to pick me up and bring me to the Cadre's headquarters with him. I have no clue how, but my boss knows that I'm with Aleks right now.

When I ask Aleks how, he just shrugs and says, "Roman knows everything."

That's about right. In a shifter pack, the Alpha knows everything that's going on, too.

Which means he probably has an inkling that we just mated in the middle of the woods.

Oh, I'm not looking forward to facing my boss right now at all.

Too bad I don't have a choice.

## CHAPTER 16
# THREE IN A MATING FOR TWO

We make a quick pit stop at the apartment before heading to meet Roman. It tacks on a few minutes to our journey, but even Aleks agrees it's essential.

I have no idea what the head vampire wants with me. Unlike Aleks, I'm off duty, so it must be important otherwise it could've waited until morning.

I'm not about to meet my boss wearing only Aleks's sweater, though. And we'll only be later if I have to stop and claw out the eyes of every person—supe and human—who gives him an appreciative once-over as he walks the streets of Muncie with his sculpted chest out for everyone to see.

Good thing that the park isn't that far from his apartment. His area of the downtown is heavily vampire, so they obviously know what we've been doing by scent alone. Our half-dressed state—not to mention the clumps of snow clinging to my hair—is just a big honking clue that we got frisky outdoors. One good thing about Aleks's reputation as a high-ranking vampire in a Fang City? No one will dare say a word to him about it.

Now, I could've shifted back to my fur, but as much as it bothers me to have others staring at Aleks, he preens knowing that I'm wearing his bite and his sweater and nothing else. He pulled his silk boxers and his slacks back on after tugging the sweater on over my head; luckily, it falls just past my butt, so most of my goods are covered. He offered me his boots, but I turned him down. I'm a shifter. I'm used to walking around barefoot.

Walking around without panties? Not so much.

Aleks keeps his arm looped around my shoulder, tucking me into his side. Even after we go inside, each of us putting on a new change of clothes more fitting to meet Roman in, he takes my hand as we head back out again. Since mating, it's like he can't stand to have a few seconds when we're not touching in some way.

And, surprisingly, I'm perfectly okay with that.

I don't think I really understood how touch-starved I was until Aleks. Doesn't matter that I've developed iron-clad control over my abilities. That I have to willingly attempt to break a bond for it to work. Old habits die hard and I spent more than a decade guarding every caress.

With my vampire, I want all of them.

At this hour, Destiny is sitting where I usually am. Cameron is sitting beside her, leaning back in Leigh's chair. Though our usual relationship consists of a quick hello/goodbye as our shifts overlap, both of them shoot Aleks and me wicked grins as we enter the lobby.

We might've changed our clothes, but the scent of sex lingers on our skin. Plus, when Aleks got changed, I noticed that his new sweater is cut low—which, wouldn't you know, leaves my messy, frantic bite marks on full display. Given his vampire healing abilities, it'll be gone in a few hours, but it's still there and my colleagues know exactly how a powerful vampire like Aleks got them.

Don't blush, Elizabeth. Blushing around a bunch of vampires is never a good idea, but I'm a fully mature female. I can have sex for the sake of pleasure. It doesn't mean anything.

And, if I keep telling myself that, maybe I might actually believe it.

---

I HAD HOPED THAT ROMAN WAS TOO NOBLE TO SAY ANYTHING to us. Reminding Aleks that Roman is also my boss, I took my hand back right before we entered his office.

I shouldn't have bothered.

Roman looks up from his desk, running his gaze over the two of us. With the smallest curve of his lips, he mutters, "Finally. My congratulations to the both of you."

Next to me, Aleks puffs his shoulders out in undeniable pride. "Thank you."

"You've been a loyal friend, Aleksander. As good as my brother. For two centuries, I had to watch you mourn your beloved. I'm so glad to see that you found her again."

I stiffen. Right. Because even the lead vampire of the Cadre looks at me and sees another female's face.

"You lost yours, too, Roman. In the same war that stole my Julia."

Oof. That hurts. Aleks calling Julia his... yeah. That one hurt a lot.

I work hard to pretend like it didn't, instead focusing on what Aleks just said. I knew that Julia was one of the first casualties of the last decades-long Claws and Fangs war between shifters and vampires. But Roman lost his mate then, too?

I didn't know.

"The difference is that I had Kira for the six centuries before it. We both knew what we were risking when we went to war. Death can be inevitable at times, even for one as deathless as we. But your Julia didn't deserve her end, just like you didn't deserve to lose her before you'd ever bonded her to you."

I… I didn't know that, either, and something tells me that Roman only added that last part out loud for my benefit. They were never bonded? I guess I just assumed that Aleks was chasing another female to take over his broken bond, but I never doubted that he'd claimed her before she died.

Aleks doesn't deny it. His shoulders go tight, an unreadable look flashing across his face, but he doesn't deny it.

Roman rises up from his desk. "Don't make the same mistake with Elizabeth," he says, every inch the command. "She's yours now. Protect her."

"Roman?"

"I kept her safe for you while you were being ridiculously noble and staying away. That all changed when you tore my fang from her throat, throwing it on my desk. I'm just glad you finally found your way to each other at last."

"You did that?" I murmur.

"Not my proudest moment," Aleks murmurs back. Then, to Roman, he says, "You planned this?"

"Me? No. Fate did. I just…" He purses his lips for a moment, the tips of his fangs peeking beneath his thin upper lip. "I just helped her along a bit."

"I... I don't know what to say."

Me, neither.

"Then say nothing." He turns his back on us, stalking toward the window. "I called you to headquarters to talk of other things."

"Yes."

He doesn't say anything in answer to Aleks, though. At least, not right away. And when he does? It's the last thing I expected to hear.

"War is coming." His hands folded behind his back, Roman looks out his window, casting his pale gaze over the Fang City.

"We'll increase patrols," Aleks answers immediately.

Roman glances over his shoulder. "Da. We must." A shadowed expression falls over his face as he turns away again. "I never thought I'd live to see it break out again. After Marcel..."

"None of us blame you for that. He wasn't fit to lead the Cadre."

"And I am?" Roman chuckles softly under his breath, trying to smooth over his last comment. "Ah. Forgive me. I've grown maudlin in my old age."

"You're only nine hundred, Roman."

"True. And you've little more than two centuries. So young compared to me. And you've been without your beloved nearly as long. I'm glad your wait is over." Under his breath, he mutters, "Mine is, too."

Aleks's normally flawless features crease as his brow furrows. "Roman?"

The head vampire shakes his head. "It's nothing. Just thinking." Clearing his throat, he moves away from the window. "As for Elizabeth... Dominic has asked for a short leave to honeymoon with his beloved. I'd like to reward Tamera by approving her request to make Leigh a temporary sunset spotter with her. When you leave, I'll have no one to sit in the lobby during the day, keeping out those I don't want to see. And you know how much I hate to be bothered most of the time."

It's a small tease, a tiny attempt at humor. Only...

"Who says I'm leaving?"

He turns, glancing at Aleks.

Aleks presses his lips together so tightly, there isn't a hint of his fangs peeking through.

Ah.

Who said that? I think I know.

"For as long as I'm welcome here, Muncie is my home," I say simply. "And this is my job. I don't plan on leaving anytime soon."

Roman bows his head. "Very well. You heard the lady, Aleksander."

He did. But he's not happy about it.

When Aleks opens his mouth, Roman cuts him off with a regal wave of his hand. "Now that that's settled, on to other things. Aleksander? I have a task for you."

Aleks swallows back his earlier retort. "Of course, Roman."

"There's been a report of a breach near the back side of our borders." Back side... by the mountains of Accalia? "It was called in by one of our people. None of my patrollers have seen anything out of the ordinary, but they're not the best. You are. Check on this for me?"

"I... yes. Right away."

This time, when Roman nods, he's almost distracted. Turning away from us, he braces his forearm against the window, staring out over Muncie again.

I glance up at Aleks. He's watching his leader with a curious look, though he shrugs it off when he realizes that *I'm* watching *him*. With a small smile and his head tilted toward the door, I understand.

We've been dismissed.

---

I DON'T KNOW IF IT'S BECAUSE OF OUR MEETING WITH ROMAN or not, but the atmosphere in Muncie seems so much more foreboding as we leave the headquarters together.

Neither one of us says anything until we reach the corner and I slip my hand out of Aleks's. He had taken it after we walked out of Roman's office, rubbing circles against my palm with his thumb as we took the elevator down together. I never told him that the enclosed space makes my wolf antsy—it's a shifter thing —but I didn't have to. Once again, I'm reminded how much history he has with other shifter females because he immediately tries to soothe my wolf the second the doors close behind us.

In the lobby, I purposely glanced away from Cameron and Destiny's curious looks. Aleks offered goodbyes on both of our behalves, then went silent.

Until I break contact with him, that is.

"Elizabeth? Where are you going?"

"Home. You're the patroller, Aleks. Not me. I'm just a secretary."

We both know I'm more than that but, smartly, he doesn't point that out.

Instead, a muscle ticking in his cheek, he asks, "Home? Do you mean mine? Or Gem's townhouse?"

It takes some effort to ignore the pang I feel when he reminds me that my choices are Gem's place or his. "I was going to go back to your apartment, but the townhouse is fine, too. Didn't you say you got someone to clean up the mess?"

"Tak. Of course. But you're still welcome to stay with me." Brushing the backs of my fingers with his, he murmurs, "I'd prefer it."

The jagged edges inside of me smooth over just a bit. "Okay. Then I'll go there."

"I'll escort you back."

No time. If Roman got a report that there was a breach, Aleks can't just worry about me. As a patroller, it's his duty to watch out for every soul who lives inside of the Fang City.

"Focus on securing the borders first. I'll be fine. Don't worry about me, Aleks."

That was probably the worst thing I could've said to him.

"I must. You are my beloved. You will always come first for me. Tonight only made that more clear."

He says it so simply. So matter-of-factly. Like I should know that already.

I wish I did.

Reaching out, Aleks snags my hand again. My wolf chuffs at me when I immediately yank it back.

"Elizabeth..."

"Don't *Elizabeth* me. Please." I can't say it was just sex, because it wasn't. Still, we didn't finalize a bond tonight... so why is he acting like we did? Like he's already my forever mate when I was only—as Gem suggested—"trying him out for a ride"? "Maybe this is my fault. I should've asked this before... but what are you expecting from me?"

"That's simple enough. Forever."

"Aleks—"

"You asked me, księżyca. I answered." That's true. I did. "But

I know you're still so young." Young? I'm pushing thirty! And, okay, Aleks has two centuries on me, but he's a vampire. To one of his kind, he's probably considered younger than I am! "I can wait a little longer for my forever. What's a year or two after two hundred?"

Oh, Luna. Two hundred years ago—when Julia died, and Aleks started the search for a chosen mate. He never found one until Gem, but he couldn't have her.

And now he wants me.

He says he'll wait. I'm not so sure he will.

Just in case, I say tentatively, "What about now? What do you expect for *now*?"

"You're my beloved. My mate. And I want everyone to know it."

That's the thing, though. I'm not. At least, not his *mate* mate. While there's no denying the sex we had, I didn't claim him as mine. Our bond isn't finalized. It *can't* be. Sure, I marked him with my teeth when I bit him, but the Luna isn't full. No full moon, no Luna Ceremony.

But wait— how does a vampire bond his beloved to him? I never asked, because I didn't want to be tempted, but after last night, then the park... maybe I should have.

No. *No.* With my ability, I'd know if he cemented the bond on his side. It's just the same as before, a fated tie that is strong, yet not quite unbreakable yet.

"How?"

Aleks dips his hand into his pocket. When he pulls it out again, the Luna reflects off of something hanging from his fist.

It's a golden chain. Even before he unfolds his fingers, I know exactly what is going to be laying against his palm.

"I had this made for you early this morning." The morning

after we were first intimate. Of course. "I was going to give it to you when I saw you next, but then—"

But then, the next time we met, I basically seduced him before he had the chance.

I know it's not the first fang he pushed on me. That sucker is in my pocket.

"Show me your mouth."

He does. It's the opposite fang from the one he gave me the night we were at Mea Culpa. That one's fully grown back in, but his left fang? It's missing.

And I have no idea how I didn't notice that until now. I guess I've been a little distracted, but *still*.

Even though I carry his fang with me, that's not enough for Aleks. He couldn't just ask me for the one he already gave me, either. Of course not. He snapped off another, turning it into a necklace, and now expects me to just put it on.

I... this is all happening too fast. It was one thing to sleep with him under the Luna; he's my mate, and I couldn't resist the way he looked at me. Staying over at his apartment? It just makes sense since the townhouse has been compromised. Keeping his fang in my pocket... in Muncie, with the target on my back, I need the protection.

But to wear it around my throat? I wore Roman's because it made me untouchable. I'm not his mate, but he claimed me as his own to keep my abilities close as much to keep me safe for Aleks's sake. I have no illusions about that; besides, I was perfectly okay with the situation. If Roman was going to use me, I was going to do the same. Add that to the hefty paycheck he gave me and the sense of belonging I got by working with the Cadre and I definitely made out.

Aleks is offering me his protection, but that's not all. I've been living among vampires long enough to know what a necklace like that really means. Add that to how insistent he was on hearing me say that I believed I was his beloved before we had sex and it's pretty freaking obvious.

If I put it on, I'm telling the whole supe world that I'm Aleksander Filan's intended mate. The bond might not be finalized just yet—on my side, we'd need the full moon, and I still refuse to ask how vampires complete theirs—but wearing his fang close to my heart? It's as good as saying that we will as soon as we get the chance.

I've known of Aleks for more than five months, but this... this *thing* we have going on between us? It hasn't even been a week and a half yet since he called me his beloved for the first time. And, sure, I grew up in a shifter pack where the Luna is revered, and Fate is our religion. Unclaimed matings like Jack Walker and his Janelle are an anomaly. When a shifter finds their fated mate, there usually isn't any hesitation. We trust that the Luna has picked the right mate for us.

And my goddess? She gave me a mysterious, sexy, possessive yet oh so caring vampire who looks at me and sees his past.

How can we have a future if I'm not sure whether he wants me for me, or because I'm his lost love's twin?

That's the problem right there. I've had to fight the pull toward Aleks ever since that night I caught him watching me outside of Walker's cabin. Then I spent months—*months*—traveling the country, doing everything I could to avoid him, before I inevitably ended up in Muncie.

I'm tired of running. I'm tired of my abilities being used against me.

Most of all, I'm tired of denying how I feel for Aleks.

Too bad jealousy and self-doubt are a bitch to shake. I want him, but if I ever heard him call me Julia again? If he looked in my silver eyes and he wished they were gold instead? Gem is his good friend, but he never called her his beloved. Would he give me his fang, but still carry Julia's portrait around in his pocket?

Would I always be a replacement?

If so, that would break me.

I want him, but until I can be a hundred percent sure that he wants *me* back, I really have to turn him down. No matter how proud I would be to wear Aleks's fang, to claim him as my intended in return... I don't think I can.

"Aleks—"

Intuitive as ever, he knows. Clenching the length of chain in his fist, hiding his fang, his pale green eyes seem to flash. "Is it because of what I am?"

What? He doesn't honestly think that I would reject him because of what kind of supe he is?

One glimpse at his face and I realize: yes, yes he does.

"No. Of course not."

Honestly, I've never minded the fact that he's a vampire. Because of what *I* am, I didn't have the luxury of developing a deep-seated prejudice like other shifters. I've had to blend in with humans, make allies of other supes. Julia herself proves it's not *that* uncommon for our races to mix. I mean, I tried bringing him blood back to the apartment!

"Then why? You feel something for me. I know you do. And you *are* my beloved. I've taken your blood. I've taken your body. You're mine, Elizabeth. I want everyone to know it."

I lower my eyes to the dirt. Seeing the emotion splayed across his beautiful face... I can't right now.

"If it's not because I'm a vampire, and you don't deny your

feelings for me, then what is it? You've denied us before. I've shown you I can be a good mate to you. Why deny us again?"

"I—"

He cups my chin with his hand. With a gentle tilt, he forces me to look at him. "Księżyca? What is it?"

"I… I want to." I *do*. "But what if—"

"There is no *what-if*," Aleks says decisively. "There is me and you—"

"And Julia," I mutter.

With a sigh, he pulls away from me. "Will she always be a ghost between us?"

"I don't know." It's an honest answer. "We've only known each other for such a short while, Aleks. And I care for you." I'm pretty much head over heels for him. "But I just…"

"What? Tell me."

"I just can't be sure that, when you look at me, you see me instead of her."

There. I said it. My biggest fear, and one of the reasons why I'm keeping some distance between us.

Not for much longer, though.

This time, when he swoops back in toward me, he braces my cheeks with both of his hands. He's trembling just enough for it to be noticeable, the chain nestled against his palm pressed against my skin as he keeps my head steady.

"I see you. Elizabeth Howell. Mój księżyca." Laying his forehead against mine, sharing breaths, he murmurs, "My beloved moon."

My heart rate kicks up. My pulse is pounding, blood thudding through my veins. It has to be a siren's call to my vampire. He doesn't respond to it, though. Gliding his hands from my cheeks down the hollow of my throat, his thumbs touching, he rests his fingers against my pulse points before slanting his mouth over mine.

I fall into his arms. Wrapping mine around his waist, for the moment at least, I let myself believe that I'm really his.

And a moment is all we get.

Out of nowhere, a fierce howl splits the air. It echoes, reverberating through the quiet night.

Aleks immediately pulls back, already in hunting mode. I'm not too far behind. Letting my wolf rise up inside of me, I push away from him, following the fading echo.

"That way." I don't quite recognize whose howl that is—and, if I do, I push down my suspicions—but I can tell where it came from.

He gives a jerking nod. "Yes." After stealing one more quick kiss, he squeezes my shoulder and starts to tear off in the direction I pointed in.

I'm right behind him.

I haven't taken five strides before he whirls on me, cupping my elbows "Elizabeth? What are you doing?"

Isn't it obvious? "I'm coming with you."

He'd shoved the chain into his pocket before he took off. Almost as if by magic, it's back in his hand.

"Only if you put the fang on."

*Really*? "Aleks—"

"It's stronger when it's near the heart. Take it off after if that's what you want, but please. Wear it for me."

I can tell what he *isn't* saying. The wolf could be part of the Mountainside Pack—or it could be one of our enemies.

How can I refuse?

Looping the fang around my neck, I fasten it as quickly as I can. My wolf is already up, head cocked, growling softly under her breath as she pads around inside of me. Her fur is bristling but, to my amazement, she seems to settle down slightly the moment his fang lands between my boobs.

"Good?"

Aleks nods. "Let's go."

# CHAPTER 17
# THE WICKED WOLF OF THE WEST

I haven't left Muncie since the night I visited Gem and her mate in Accalia. After how Peyton ambushed me, I decided to rely on the strength of Roman's reputation to keep me safe in the Fang City. Without a fang of her own, I didn't think she would ever dare cross the border into Muncie.

I still don't know if she did earlier today. No denying I caught traces of her on the wintry breeze. She was near enough for her innate scent to carry to me, but considering I didn't find any footprints—or even paw prints—as I chased after it, I have no proof. And then Aleks found me and... yeah. It wasn't the first time sex made me forget all about the idea of Peyton.

When Roman sent Aleks to check up on the breach, I wondered if it would be the wolf I sensed earlier; when I heard the howl, I was sure of it, and I couldn't just go home. I had to go with Aleks. All patrollers go on foot so I had a couple of miles' jog to worry if I'm going to find a familiar shifter at the end of this hunt.

Would it be Peyton? What about the Wicked Wolf? It's been barely more than twenty-four hours since he made the move on the townhouse Gem lent me, but even she's frustrated by the way he seems to have gone ghost for the months preceding his sudden reappearance. It doesn't matter that I'm not covering the Alpha's scent for him anymore. He can still hide which makes him infinitely more dangerous because none of us know *how* he is.

Then there's the fact that, to get inside the borders without it being considered a breach, he has to have a fang of his own to get in without being reported—and there hasn't been a report of another breach until tonight. Working for Roman, being the only shifter allowed to live in Muncie currently, I would've known.

During my first few weeks in the city, I'd already heard whispers of some kind of an uprising. While most vampires are content with Roman as their leader, not everyone likes his style. Some of the fanged supes have no problem working with shifters to get what they want.

And they want Roman dead.

I learned that when those two vampires—Hector and Anton—went after me. They wanted to hurt Roman, and they threw Aleks's loyalty to him in his face before my vampire defeated both of them.

Any one of those "rebels" would snap a fang, hand it off to a shifter, then sit back and watch as they made Roman's life difficult.

Like now.

I hope that this is all that is. That this is an easily thwarted attack on Muncie—on Roman—and not my past coming to bite me in the furry ass.

I manage to cling to that hope until we're about six blocks out from the edge of Muncie. When two well-known shifter scents—one sickly sweet like maple syrup, the other dark and bitter like burnt coffee—slam into me, I stumble.

Aleks is a few steps ahead of me. He's been leading the way, taking us on the quickest path with the least human obstacles. I thought he was entirely focused on the run. Should've known better. The second I stutter-step, he whirls around, grabbing my elbow so that I don't face-plant.

"Thanks." It comes out as a gasp.

"Are you alright?" Concern has red ringing his pale eyes. "What did you sense? The wolf?"

"Yeah. Two shifters." I hesitate for a heartbeat, before admitting, "The Wicked Wolf is one of them."

More of his irises begin to bleed red. Though he's careful no to mention his time in the district, Aleks has wanted to get revenge on Walker for how he made him his captive. Then the Alpha desecrated my sanctuary and only reinforced my vampire's hatred.

Did Roman know? When he got the report that there was a breach… did he know that it was Jack Walker out there? After our conversation earlier, I'm absolutely convinced that Roman treats life like a chessboard. He plans out every move ahead of time; the rest of us pawns just do what he expects. Like how he basically manipulated Aleks into treating me as his beloved. I can't blame him since I got a good job and a sweet wage out of it —not to mention Aleks's attention—but his sending Aleks to face off against Walker is just the sort of move I'd expect from Roman Zakharov.

"Any way I can get you to go back to the apartment while I take care of this?"

No, because that sickly sweet maple scent is equally recognizable. Peyton Slate is the other shifter waiting.

I shake my head.

Aleks huffs out one of his unnecessary breaths. "Thought so. Just—"

"I know, I know. Stay behind you."

"Ah, księżyca. You know me so well."

"Come on." I press my hand to the middle of his back, pushing just enough to get him to move. "We can't let them howl again."

I'm supposed to be the only shifter in Muncie. To be allowed to stay here, I had to keep that under wraps. No shifting where a human could see me, and definitely no howling. The Fang City might back up against a mountain, but there shouldn't be any real wolves so close to the urban center.

Supes are an open secret here, but we're still a secret. And one of the two wolves is willing to jeopardize that just to act as a lure.

No way they knew Aleks would be the one sent after them. We were too far from the border when the howl sounded for them to pick up our scent, but when the second howl—richer, deeper, *angrier*—rips through the night, I know they're guiding us right to them.

Damn it. A second howl. Are they impatient or...

Ah. Definitely impatient and eager to brawl. From the dark edge of his wolf's power, I can tell that the Alpha came here tonight for a reason, and he's not backing down until he gets what he wants.

My wolf is torn. She wants to run to safety, but she also can't leave Aleks.

*She's right. For good or for bad, he's our mate. We won't abandon him to the mercy of the Wicked Wolf.*

Jack Walker is standing a few feet past the unmarked border that separates Muncie from Accalia; predictably, he's on the Muncie side. His legs are braced against the slippery snow, arms folded over his brawny chest. Damn if he isn't as handsome as I remember, with his styled blond hair and honey gold eyes.

Bastard.

It would've been so much easier to get away from him if his outsides matched his black heart and rotten nature. By the time I realized he was twisted and evil, I was trapped in the district. I never wanted to see him again.

And there he is.

He's not the only one, either. Her scent is even more cloying this close, or maybe that's the lovesick, puppy-dog look on her face as she stands a couple of steps behind Walker, staring at his profile.

Peyton.

My claws unleash at the sight of her.

She's staring at Walker, but he only has eyes for me as I come to a sudden stop. Once Aleks realized I had, he falters, falling back to stand beside me.

The Alpha sniffs, gingerly at first, then more noticeably. His nostrils flare, a black look crossing his face as he pinpoints what's different about me. Now that he has a nose full of Aleks's scent, he can tell that it's covering my skin.

He has to know that we mated. Oh, boy. Considering he has this crazy idea that I would ever choose him after rejecting his proposals for two years straight, that can't be good.

Surprisingly, Walker goes on to ignore the vampire completely. I have no doubt in my mind that he is cataloging every tiny movement Aleks makes, but he acts as if he doesn't even notice he's there.

Good. The last thing I want is Walker paying any real attention to him.

"Ah. Elizabeth. I was beginning to think that if I had to wait for the parasites to roll out the welcome mat much longer, I'd just use this and take a stroll on inside."

Walker hooks his finger under the simple gold chain he has on, showing off the fang hanging there.

Well, that explains it. Just like I was afraid of, a Muncie vampire has betrayed the Cadre, working with their ancient enemy instead. Because, make no mistake, the Alpha isn't here to ally with Roman. If I know him as well as I think I do, he's here to take him down.

From the blast of chilled air coming off of him, my vampire's thinking the same thing.

"What..." It's a whisper. Only when Peyton tosses her hair over her shoulder, her expression as vicious as always when she's looking at me, do I find my voice. I'm scared of Walker, but not *her*. "What are you doing here?"

"I just told you. It's been nearly half a year and Luna knows I'm fucking tired of waiting. I've come here for two things. My loyal Beta is taking care of one." Beta? He still has one? "But for this..." Walker reaches down, not even discreetly adjusting himself. "I'll be taking my mate now."

My lips part as I gape in ill-disguised horror.

He can't mean me, right? Grabbing his erection, basically fucking me with his gaze while Peyton stands right behind him, Aleks at my side? Right?

*Wrong.*

Letting go of the fang, he crooks his finger at me. "Now,

Elizabeth."

"What?" screeches Peyton. "But Jack... you told me *I* was going to be your mate."

Wait a second... was that what Peyton meant when she confronted me that first night? When she said she was going to take my mate?

She meant *Walker*?

If so, she was way off base. She can have the Wicked Wolf if she wants him.

Just leave Aleks alone.

Walker's gaze slides to his right, a sneer twisting his face. "You? You were good for a couple of fucks. Desperate times call for desperate measures and all that. But my mate? Oh, no, no, no. If I can't have Janelle, I want Elizabeth. No more fucking around." The sneer turns cruel as he looks back at me. "Did you enjoy my mating present?"

Oh, Luna... a vampire head in my bed was his idea of a mating present?

I gulp, staying silent.

He holds out his hand to me.

"Come over here, Elizabeth. You won't like what I'll do if you don't."

He means it, too. A sadistic bastard with countless challenges under his belt, there are so many ways he can hurt me.

And not just me.

Yup. Definitely still terrified of him.

My wolf rolls over to expose her belly as I take a hesitant step toward Walker. Before my foot can hit the snow again, Aleks lashes out, gripping me gently, keeping me at his side.

"Stay with me, księżyca."

"Elizabeth! Who is this vampire to tell you what to do?"

How many times did the Alpha use that same commanding tone with me? And how many times was I able to ignore it? Too many, and never—but that was before Aleks.

He answers so I don't have to.

"You don't recognize me, wolf?"

"Ah." Walker's lips curl. "It took me a second. You don't look the same without the silver bullets plugging up your chest."

"You dare come here again? After what you did to me? After what you did to Elizabeth? And you think she'll choose you when she could have—"

Aleks stops short before he can say the last word: *me*.

He doesn't have to. Walker's not stupid. He knows exactly what Aleks was about to say—just like he knows how to tuck that knowledge inside and use it at the opportune moment.

"What do I have to lose?" Beneath the moonlight, his honey gold eyes gleam. "Because of you"—he flings his left arm behind him, gesturing at the towering mountain at his back— "because of them, I have nothing. Can you blame me for trying to at least choose a mate?"

Peyton hisses.

Without looking behind him, Walker backhands her with his right arm, sending her flying to the snow-covered ground.

I guess she already had her one warning. She hits the earth hard, her hand flying to her face, but she doesn't question Walker again.

"My pack is gone. My territory is being divided up by scavengers. I have nothing," he repeats, "but if you won't give me my mate, I will have my war."

*No.*

Aleks hunches his body, lowering himself in an offensive crouch. "I won't be responsible for another one."

There's so much emotion in his declaration, I shiver. What… what does that mean?

I don't know, and if Walker does, he refuses to remark on it. Instead, with his jaw tight and his expression stubborn, he says, "I will."

"Not if I kill you first."

When Walker laughs, I have to fight to resist the urge to grab Aleks and run away with him.

"You think your threats will stop me? Give it your best shot. You pull it off, and my line lives on through my daughter. Ruby might deny me, but we're the same. In looks, in power, and in the need to control. We'll win this war, and my daughter will be the queen she was born to be. And all because of me."

Okay. If he wasn't already insane before his defeat, he sure as hell is now.

"There won't be any war," Aleks says firmly.

"Fine. Then give me the girl."

"No."

"No war. No mate."

Walker's voice has developed a teasing edge.

I'm immediately on guard. Something's not right. He's up to something.

"Aleks—"

"I came all this way in the snow. I should get something out of this." His eyes brighten suddenly, turning to molten lava in the moonlight. "I know." His hand slips behind him. When he pulls it back again, he's holding a gun that looks eerily familiar.

"I'm not as good as Christian. Maybe you'll get lucky, you fucking corpse."

Just like that, a bullet explodes out of the gun.

Aleks dodges it easily.

Another shot. Another miss.

My vampire gives him a look that clearly means, "Is that the best you can do?"

And that's when Walker turns the gun on me.

I instinctively know what's going to happen even as he pulls the trigger mercilessly. He was willing to throw two shots away to lull Aleks into a false sense of security because the Wicked Wolf doesn't hesitate to aim for my head.

I throw up my hands uselessly as Aleks jumps right in front of me.

One bullet, then a second punches his upper chest.

Bowing forward as soon as they hit, careful not to fall back against me even after he's been shot, Aleks drops to his knees, clutching his upper chest.

Not just bullets, I realize. Walker shot him with *silver* bullets.

And already they're hard at work, weakening him.

The satisfied look on the Alpha's face proves my suspicions true. He did that on purpose, using Aleks's protective instincts for me against him. He didn't want me dead—he just wanted me to be the reason that Aleks is incapacitated for the moment.

He keeps his gun aimed high with one hand. The other? He flexes it, releasing his deadly claws.

"It took an entire clip to capture him in the district," he says, so conversationally I can barely believe it. "Two already and he's down. I can keep going if you make me, Elizabeth. With enough silver in him, he won't be able to stop me from taking his head, either. I'll kill him."

He will. I know he will.

"Don't!"

It makes it so much worse that Walker derives pleasure from just how panicky my shout was.

He grins, and it's the most genuine smile I've ever seen apart from when he was lording over the deadly challenges in the pit. "See? I knew you wouldn't want that, not after he took those bullets for you. Leave with me and I spare him. Give me what I want or else I..."

Walker doesn't finish his threat. He doesn't have to. We both know exactly what he wants from me. What he's *always* wanted from me.

It's not just being his mate. The Alpha will throw me inside another gilded cage with him, but he won't be satisfied unless I turn the key myself.

What can I do? Peyton is still lying in the snow, and Aleks is on one knee, struggling to rise. Even after he took two bullets so that I didn't, he's doing everything he can to protect me.

He calls out my name—*my* name—but I force myself not to hear it.

*What can I do?*

To save the vampire I was born to love, I'll do *anything*.

I want him, but I can't have him. He'll find another. Julia. Gem. Me... he'll find another.

He always does.

I just wish, this time, it could've been *us*.

*I'm sorry, Aleks.* My apologies aren't as rare, but I can't bring myself to say it out loud as I approach him from behind. *I'm so, so sorry*.

Before he can figure out what I'm about to do, I lay my hand against his cheek.

Tapping into my wolf and the ability given to us by the Luna herself, I try to snap the thread tying us together.

It... it doesn't work.

Aleks's is normally cold to the touch. Not now. My hand is on fire.

No. Not just my hand. It's... every part of me.

I *burn*.

The last time this happened, the blowback was so powerful, a scream ripped out of my throat before my eyes rolled back in my head and I was out for a while. Grabbing Gem, trying to sever an unbreakable bond... I paid for breaking my promise to her.

We're not mated, me and Aleks. Not completely. And while I have my doubts that it could ever work when I'm just another female's replacement, they're not enough to snap our fledgling bond.

My body burns, and I scream. Even as I realize that the tie between us is still there, the pain receding as quickly as it came, once again I pay for going against the Luna's will.

I crumple to the dirt. Still aware, still on fire, but at least I'm vaguely conscious enough to sense what's going on around me.

Aleks's answering bellow hits me like it's part of a dream.

I'll never know exactly what happened. My eyes were open, but unseeing. My wolf yowled in agony as the blowback hit her, burning the both of us, her screams drowning out Aleks's bellow, Peyton's screech, and Walker's excited yell.

My vampire has two bullets in him because of me. He's down one fang because of me. He just launched himself at a fierce enemy because of me.

And he manages to defeat him—because of me?

I don't know. What I *do* know, though?

Gem couldn't kill him. Showing her birth father mercy, she defeated him during their challenge before letting him go.

Aleks doesn't hesitate.

The Wicked Wolf of the West never stood a chance.

---

I'm still battling the aftershocks of my "gift" when it's all over and he's scooping me up in his arms, holding me against his wounded chest.

"Elizabeth? Elizabeth!" He reeks of blood—his own, and the bitter blood of the Alpha—but the cool touch on my cheek banishes the last of the burn. "Answer me, księżyca."

I blink a few times, desperately clearing my vision. When I do, all I see is his blood-stained shirt as he palms my head, keeping me from looking anywhere else. "Aleks?"

He sags to the ground with the both of us when he hears my weak voice. "I thought he'd killed you. I thought I failed you again."

"What? No... no. You didn't. It was me—"

"You tried to break our bond."

I don't deny it. I can't. "I... I had to."

"I lost my beloved once before. I won't lose you again."

"I'm not Julia," I whisper into his chest.

"No," he agrees. "But that doesn't change a thing I said."

I move my head just enough to see the stark look in his scarlet eyes. "Aleks—"

"I couldn't let him take you from me," he says, and I can't tell if he's talking to himself or to me until he his voice roughens. "You're mine, Elizabeth."

I'm not, though. I might not have been able to severe the tentative bond between us because, deep down, neither of are ready to walk away from what we could have, but we don't have forever yet.

But my vampire is suddenly more fierce than I've ever seen him when he wasn't fighting. Red eyes on fire, blood staining the corner of his math, his hands spattered with gore...

The words catch in my throat. He accused me of denying him once before. And now... I just can't.

Aleks runs the back of his knuckles down my cheek. His skin stinks like Walker's blood, but I don't mind it. The Wicked Wolf is dead, and the predator inside of me revels in knowing who is responsible for the kill. My mate protected us, and my wolf whines to get closer to him.

I lean into his touch as I realize something I haven't denied in a while now.

I might not be his, but Aleks is *mine*.

Our bond isn't final—not yet—but it's undeniable. Suddenly, I want to tell him that we might have a shot at this. Peyton might be trouble, and I have my own issues to work out when it comes to being jealous of his past, but Jack Walker is no longer the bogeyman I search shadows for.

And all thanks to my vampire.

"Aleks... about the bond..."

"We'll talk about that later. Let's get you home first, then I must go see Roman and—"

At the mention of the lead vampire, I realize something else.

"Wait a second," I murmur, cutting him off. I thought the buzzing belonged to my skull, but as my regenerative properties continue to kick in, banishing the blowback from my curse, it's only getting more noticeable.

It's not buzzing. It's vibrating.

"Is that your phone?" I ask him.

He doesn't seem surprised at my question. In fact, he looks

annoyed that someone might be trying to interrupt him. "Doesn't matter. They should be messaging me."

Only... it turns out that they have been.

Still holding me to him, Aleks pulls the phone out of his back pocket, jaw clenching as it stops vibrating. He doesn't hide the screen from me and, together, we see that he has six missed calls—and eleven messages—all from Cadre vampires.

I gulp. "Put me down."

"Are you sure?"

"I'm okay." Since he took the two bullets meant for my brain, I'm probably doing much better than he is. "You need to find out what's going on and deal with that."

He hesitates, but slowly shifts me so that I can stand on my own two feet.

"It wasn't pretty," he warns. "Behind me... I don't want you to see what I did."

He's still crouching in the dirt. At this level, I can easily brush one of his curls out of his face. It's sticky—more blood, I see—but that doesn't bother me.

My poor vampire obviously thinks I'm more fragile than I am. I might not be as strong as an alpha, but I'm still a shifter. Not only that, but for two years, I had to watch every challenge that Walker either hosted or took part in. The things I saw then ... I prayed to the Luna that he lost every single one, and when he finally did, Gem spared him.

Maybe I'm as bloodthirsty as Aleks, but I *need* to see that Walker is gone for good.

"I need to," I admit. "I need to see what you did to protect me."

My heart skips a beat as he vows solemnly, "I will always protect you, księżyca."

I press a quick kiss to his temple, then turn to take in the scene as Aleks—with a shaky, unnecessary breath—dials his phone.

He's watching me, searching for my reaction. It takes everything I have to take in the scene stoically, but... he was right. It's not pretty.

And I'm *glad*.

There's blood everywhere. It paints the snow a deep, rich red, turning the dirt a darker shade where their brutal battle reveals the dirt. One lump of mangled flesh has to be Walker's remains. The blond head—forced from his shoulders, killing him—looks like it's been punted fifteen feet away like it was a football.

Peyton is gone, too. Not dead, like I'd secretly hoped, but vanished. Over the blood, I can't even pick up a hint of her scent trail as she bolted.

In the end, she was just as loyal to Walker as he was to her...

Behind me, the phone connects.

"Aleks." Dominic's voice thunders down the line. "They have Roman."

I spin so quickly, I nearly slip in the snow—or maybe that's blood. It doesn't matter.

"Roman?" I echo.

If they weren't before, Aleks's eyes are blazing red with pure bloodlust. "What do you mean? They... who's they—no. It doesn't matter. If they have him, why haven't you gotten him back?"

Any time I met Dominic, he was suave. Put together. The male on the other end of the line is in a full-blown panic.

"We couldn't! None of us could, Aleksander."

"Why the hell not?"

"Because he forbade us from following after him and the wolf! All vampires in Muncie. But Cameron said you were checking the borders for a breach. For god's sake, tell me you're out of bounds."

Walker's remains are. That means that, at some point, Aleks was, too.

Would it work?

Only one way to find out.

I press my hand to his arm. He meets my gaze, nodding just the once.

"I was, but I'm coming back now. And I *will* find Roman."

Dominic said wolf, didn't he?

*My loyal Beta is taking care of one...*

Walker might be finished, but he isn't done.

I tilt my head back, showing him my black eyes. "We both will."

# CHAPTER 18
# DIE FOR LOVE

In the middle of Muncie, there is a three-block square that is abandoned. I don't know why. It has some kind of bad history, and it's basically off-limits.

So of course that's where Walker's Beta dragged Roman off to.

Aleks guessed. Dominic only knew that a grim-faced shifter wearing a fang asked for a meeting with the head of the Cadre. Roman allowed him to come up to his office, and barely twenty minutes later, the wolf marched him out of the building at gunpoint.

Every member of the Cadre that was near obviously wanted to stop the determined wolf, but Roman refused to let them. He gave the orders that his vampires stand down, then left with the gun-toting shifter. Dominic and some others started calling and texting Aleks as soon as our boss was forced into a blacked-out dark red sedan and driven off.

While we were facing off with Walker, his Beta was doing

exactly as the Alpha had boasted: he was being loyal to the end, and getting him his war.

Because even I know that if a wolf shifter harms the head vampire, there will be consequences.

From the second I heard that the Beta carried a gun, I knew who it had to be. It's not usual for a shifter to use human weapons, but Christian Morrissey—Walker's final Beta while he was the Alpha of the Western Pack—was... different. He was a marksman, too, with a skill that impressed even Walker.

The last time he faced off with Aleks, my vampire ended up with a bullet in each limb to incapacitate him. Aleks had been in a killing rage, fresh off of slaughtering his shifter opponent, and Christian hadn't batted an eye when Walker told his Beta to shoot him.

It hadn't killed him then, just like the bullets wouldn't kill Roman now. But with enough silver pumped inside of a vampire, the fanged supes turn docile. Weak.

Easy prey.

The sedan makes tracking Roman down nearly impossible. With the windows rolled up and the doors closed, neither one of them would leave a scent trail for us to follow. I have no tie to Christian, and Aleks has never taken either male's blood, so we can't track them by a bond.

We don't have to.

Aleks knows every inch of Muncie. Since it became a designated Fang City, he's considered it his territory. And though he doesn't spare time to explain why he's so sure that Christian would've driven Roman to the abandoned sector, when we spy the empty red car on the edge of it proving his hunch correct, Aleks doubles his speed. We've been running from the outskirts of Muncie, leaving any unaware humans who witness our flight in shock and awe. This is supernatural speed, and in any other situation, we would have to downplay our strengths when out on the streets.

Not now, though. Not while Roman needs us.

Aleks agrees. His scarlet eyes shining beneath the moonlight like freshly spilled blood, he pushes himself to his limit; even with the silver blazing inside of him, he's faster than me. Tapping into my wolf, I work hard to close the gap between us.

Aleks rasps out another couple of words in Polish—*nie ty*—before gesturing for me to fall back. Shaking my head, I stay right beside him.

I almost lost him once. After our confrontation with Walker, I don't want to let Aleks out of my sight.

He's too focused on our pursuit to argue. I don't blame him. I can't let Christian hurt Roman. The head vampire has been so good to me, allowing me to live here, giving me a job, even subtly nudging me and Aleks together... would Walker and his Beta even have turned their sights on Muncie if it wasn't for me? Maybe, because of Gem's ties here, but he hadn't attacked Accalia, had he? He'd gone after *us*.

As I run, I'm constantly stretching out my senses. Breathing in deep, I finally catch a hint of their scents on the breeze. Roman and, like I thought, *Christian*.

Now, if I can, Aleks probably does, too, but I still grab his arm.

He spares me a quick glance. As beautiful as he is fierce, I swallow a lump in my throat before stammering out, "Up ahead. I can scent them."

A quick nod. "We go to the left then."

I get it. Instead of walking into what might be a trap, we'll circle around and approach them from behind. With my ability to conceal scents from those near me, it'll be a way to catch them off guard. I normally have to focus to use that part of my "gift", but as soon as Walker lured us to the edge of Muncie, I'd triggered it almost subconsciously for both me and Aleks.

For once, my curse can help me instead of hurt me. We know where Christian has Roman, but he won't know we've tracked him down until he sees us.

Hopefully, it'll buy us some time.

The two of us slow down as we take the last corner, only for Aleks to lose control and fly down the street when he finally spies Roman.

The noble vampire has his hands bound behind him. He's still standing, perched on the corner at the other end of the block. Christian is at his back, the mouth of his gun against Roman's head.

Aleks hisses. My wolf reacts by letting out a yip when we realize just how real the danger to Roman is. Being shot in the head probably won't kill him, but it might. And if it didn't? It would definitely put him down long enough for Christian to grab the hilt of the sword he has strapped to his back.

We stop when there's less than a block separating us—and not because we want to.

It's Roman. His aura pulses, a warning to both of us to stay away. It's enough to have my wolf howling, desperate to turn tail and get the hell out of here, but Aleks?

He staggers backward. It's like some invisible hand shoved him away so that he can't get any closer to where Christian has the gun pressed to Roman's temple.

And the only one strong enough to do that? Is the head vampire himself.

Ever since I met Roman Zakharov, I couldn't understand why

everyone in Muncie treated him like a bogeyman. Even Gem did. I knew he was the leader of Muncie's Cadre, so it was a given he had to be powerful. I just had no idea *how* powerful until he unleashed his aura on us.

Suddenly, Dominic's panic makes a lot more sense. Roman had forbidden any of his people from following him. If that wall of power was what they were up against, no way could they disobey him. They physically couldn't go after him.

But Christian is a beta wolf. Strong, but nowhere near strong enough to defeat Roman even if he used his gun. He had Roman trussed up, his hands probably tied with a length of silver chain, but Roman had still been able to use his aura against me and Aleks.

The only reason he's over there is because he's *choosing* to be.

"Aleksander," he calls out, oddly conversational. "I didn't want any of you to witness this."

Understanding hits, slamming into me so hard it's like an anvil's been dropped on my head. Barely an hour ago, I was running with Aleks, heading to the border to face off against the unknown threat breaching our borders. I'd thought then that Roman had orchestrated the meeting; when it was revealed that Walker was waiting for us, I was sure of it. Now? I realize that Roman's moves were even more subtle than I expected.

Not only did he give Aleks his chance at revenge, he also got him out of his hair so that he could do something as ridiculously noble as this.

*I'm glad your wait is over... mine is, too...*

Did he know he would be doing this tonight?

I... I think he did.

Aleks is frantic. Palms outstretched, he tests the barrier that Roman's thrown up, growling under his breath when he can't get past it. He grunts and he shoves and he pushes before he hunches his shoulders, imploring Roman with his gaze.

His soft voice lowers an octave as he calls out, “Drop your shields. Let me get to you.”

“I can not.” When Aleks immediately starts to argue, Roman shakes his head. “No. I *will* not. I gave my word.”

“Your word? Your word about what? Roman, stop this!”

“Didn’t you hear him? He won’t,” Christian cuts in. “And even if he would, *I* can’t let him.”

Before any of us can react, he kicks Roman’s legs out from under him, forcing him to his knees.

Roman’s aura falters. Either that, or the rage pouring off of my vampire is so strong that—even with two bullets inside of him—he can push past it.

“Nyet,” yells Roman sharply. *No*. What comes next is a rattle of Russian that means nothing to me, even as I buckle under the weight of its obvious command. “Odna zhizn' na besschetnoye kolichestvo. Ya delayu eto dlya nashego naroda. Ty dolzhen pozvolit' mne, staryy drug!”

I have no idea what he said, but my vampire?

He goes immovably still. After swallowing roughly, he says, “Wolf. Why do you do this? Roman has only ever sought peace between our kinds.”

“That’s exactly my point,” Christian answers. “He might want peace.” With Roman on his knees, Christian moves the gun to the back of his skull. Using his free hand, he strokes the fang hanging off of his neck. “There are plenty who don’t. Other vampires want his head. I’m more than happy to give it to them.”

“But *why*?”

“Because the rebels have given their word that they will stop rising up against the Cadre with my death," answers Roman. He juts his chin out even as Christian hovers over him. "One for many. I give my life gladly."

"You don't have to do that!"

"Of course he does," Christian tells Aleks. "And it would've been done already if you hadn't interrupted." His dark eyes turn toward me. "Where is he, Elizabeth?"

I don't have to ask who he means. "He's dead."

The Beta doesn't look the least bit surprised to hear that. In fact, he looks... *satisfied?*

But then his brow furrows. "Who killed him? You or—"

"He threatened my beloved."

Aleks hunches slightly as he bites the words out, his hands clenched into fists at his side. His aura is electric against my skin, but it doesn't hurt. It feels familiar to me. Safe. As if he'll do that and more to anyone who dares threaten me.

Instead of realizing that Aleks is already plotting to take him out next, Christian's eyes light up, echoing the insanity I saw in the Wicked Wolf's gaze before he goaded my vampire to attack him. "Then the Alpha got just what he wanted. Dead at the hand of a parasite."

I was right. They planned this. Walker. Christian.

Roman.

This end was inevitable. That doesn't keep me from calling out to the Luna, beseeching my goddess, hoping for Roman's sake—for *Aleks's* sake—that broken, battered, hopeless Elizabeth can do something to stop this.

But I can't. If the Luna hears me, she doesn't answer, and both males on the other side of Roman's barrier are determined.

Reaching behind him, Christian grabs the hilt peeking over his shoulder. In one practiced motion, he unsheathes it.

I stop breathing.

Roman might survive a gunshot to the head. But a blade to the neck?

Never.

Christian's banking on it, too. "Now all I need is the top parasite taken down by one of my kind and he'll have his war." Kneeing Roman in the back, he sneers, "Say your goodbyes."

Roman is regal to the end. "We'll meet again one day, Aleksander. And Elizabeth. It was a pleasure to know you both." I barely stifle my sob as he holds his head high before addressing Aleks again. "Until then, you know what's expected of you."

Aleks doesn't deny it. Though every muscle in his body strains to go to him, he stays where he is, even as he rumbles, "It doesn't have to end like this."

"Enjoy your beloved, sobrat. And don't worry for me. I look forward to seeing my Kira again."

Aleks opens his mouth, but nothing comes out. He just gives Christian a murderous glare. "Don't do this. Please."

"Too late."

Christian swings his sword. Aleks immediately grabs me, tucking me into his side. Burying my head against his chest, I close my eyes so I don't see what happens next.

I hear it, though. The whistle of the blade, the thud as Roman's head is separated from his shoulders, the pained grunt as Aleks stands there, watching as his friend—his brother—sacrifices his life for his people.

Aleks's body bucks, almost as if he physically felt the same blow. Then, suddenly, his arms are clutching my shoulders, whirling me away before shoving me behind him. With my eyes screwed shut, I have no idea what's going on. I let out a cry of surprise as I stumble forward, righting myself at the same time as my eyes spring open again.

I'm facing away from Aleks. Spinning around, I discover exactly why Aleks pushed me away.

Christian dropped his bloody sword, trading it for his gun again. Now that Roman is... is *gone*, he's turned his attention on us. And since Aleks's instincts are to protect me, he's using his body as a shield.

I'm a wolf. My instincts are shouting at me to do the same thing for him.

I reach for him, screaming when the first crack of gunfire explodes through the night.

*Boom.*

*Boom.*

*Boom.*

*Boom.*

*Boom.*

With an impassive expression on his sallow face, Christian doesn't hesitate as he plugs Aleks full of silver. Two bullets dead to the chest, one in each thigh, and a single shot in his right shoulder.

That last one has Aleks bellowing in pain as the force of the hit has him rearing back before dropping to his knees.

He pounds the asphalt with his left fist, hissing out a stream of Polish too fast for me to recognize any of it except for one single word: zabić.

*Kill.*

Christian lowers the gun. "Threaten me all you want. You can't do anything about it now, and I fulfilled my word to your headless leader by letting you live tonight. The next time we meet? You won't be so lucky."

"Me?" Aleks's normally gentle voice is a hoarse rasp. "I'll pluck your spine from you and make you see it before I drain you."

"Big talk for someone full of silver. You can't even get out of the dirt."

He isn't wrong. Though Aleks's aura crackles and pulses with obvious rage, he's still down. He might've been able to push past Walker's two bullets, but five more? Until he expels them from his body, he's no match for another supe and we both know it.

That doesn't mean I'm going to leave my proud vampire on the ground. Throwing Christian a look of tear-filled loathing, I dash toward Aleks, intent on helping him to his feet.

He throws his left arm—the only part of him that's unwounded—behind him. "Stay back, księżyca. Don't come any closer."

What?

Why?

*Oh.*

For the second time tonight, I'm staring down the barrel of a gun. And, just like before, I know that the bullet is aimed right at me.

Christian has strode forward, arm outstretched, hand completely steady. His dark eyes are focused on me, Aleks forgotten as he says in an emotionless tone, "I saved this one for you."

My breath catches in my throat.

He smiles. "I bargained for that parasite's life. But you, Elizabeth… Alpha never would've wanted you to bond with a bloodsucker. This is for him."

"But he's dead!"

"Now it's your turn."

My wolf whimpers, my instincts telling me to move.

I *can't.*

Aleks has seven silver bullets in him. He's on his knees, bowed beneath grief and pain. Even so, as his blood-red eyes lock on Christian's steady hand, he forces himself to get up.

The Beta's head swivels to look at him. His smile thins into a line of grim determination. He's fighting the urge to fire on Aleks again.

He claims there's only one bullet left. Would Aleks survive an eighth hit? Maybe, but he shouldn't have to. He's already taken seven for me.

I'll take this one for him.

*Save him*, commands the Luna. She only echoes my own instincts. *Save your mate.*

One step away from Aleks, another step toward the Beta, purposely drawing his attention back to me. That's all I manage before Christian's finger jerks on the trigger, the bullet exploding out of his gun.

I'm a supe. Silver is excruciatingly painful to all of us, but shifters—especially wolves—have a weakness to the metal. A single bullet isn't enough to kill me; it'll only make me wish it had. If Aleks can still move with *seven* bullets, I can handle one.

And I believe that until Christian's bullet unerringly pierces my heart.

With Aleks's roar of rage blowing out my eardrums, I gasp a single breath as everything around me goes hazy and dim. The pain is indescribable—but it doesn't last. My whole body seizes, and suddenly I'm falling, falling, falling.

My heart stops beating even before I hit the ground.

# EPILOGUE

I thought I was dead. In fact, I was sure of it.

I'm not.

It was a close call, though. Two days later, when I wake up in a hospital bed, a red-eyed Aleks sitting at my bedside, I realize just how close it was. If my vampire hadn't gotten me to the supe hospital in Muncie in time, I would've died on the street.

Just like Roman had.

Christian knew what he was doing. Either he killed me, getting revenge for Walker's death, or he wounded me bad enough that Aleks would be forced to choose between saving me or avenging Roman's murder.

He chose me. When Roman died, his aura died with him, and Aleks could have gone after Christian. Instead, he scooped me up, carrying me out of the abandoned sector where he flagged down the first vampire he met who was in a vehicle. Shuffling me in the backseat with him, he commanded the female to drive us to the hospital—all while Christian took the opportunity to get away.

He hadn't left my side since. When I woke up again, the first thing I did was ask about Roman. With a pained expression, Aleks told me that Dominic is taking care of everything right now, and that all I needed to worry about was recovering from surgery.

That's right. To repair the damage the silver bullet did to my heart, I had to have surgery. A team of humans in the know worked on me, putting my heart back together so that my regenerative properties could heal the near-fatal wound.

I should've been dead. And when I murmur that out loud, Aleks shudders.

He knows I'm right.

I've never seen him like this. So... defeated. Even when he was thrown in the pit, he was defiant and unstoppable. Slumped in the hospital chair, telling me what happened after I went unconscious because I begged him to... this isn't the Aleksander Filan I know.

And my newly repaired heart aches for him.

"It's going to be okay," I lie. Because how can it? Walker is dead, but so is Roman. Christian and Peyton made it out of Muncie, and from the whispers I overheard when I was semiconscious before waking fully earlier, Aleks and Dominic have been discussing the vampires that resist the Cadre's leadership. The rebels Roman mentioned before he—

Before he—

I struggle to bring a weak grin to my face as I echo softly, "It'll be okay."

He nods, a single curl falling forward, brushing against his upper cheek. "Now that you're awake again, it will be."

There's something in the way he says that. Almost like he's been sitting vigil, expecting me to die in front of him.

Just like Julia did.

I should've—and I'm still not so sure why I didn't.

"How... how did I make it? When I fell, I thought that was it for me."

"Tak. And it would've been only... I fed you my blood." He pauses, as if unsure how I'm going to react when he adds, "A lot of my blood. It kept you alive until I could get you to the surgeons. I would've done anything to bring you back."

*Bring you back...*

Panic flares up in me. I tamp it down, even though I can't stop myself from asking, "Am I a vampire now?"

"What? No. You'd have to die to be turned. And it was close, mój księżyca, but you never died." A fierce expression twists his features. "I wouldn't let you."

Okay, then.

In that case, I don't see what the problem is. Aleks is looking at me like I'm already dead, or if he's lost me for good.

But I'm right here.

Most supes can survive being shot. Taking a silver bullet to the heart, though? I should be dead. If it wasn't for Aleks, I would be. He kept me alive, he got me to help, and he stayed right next to me the whole time.

"You saved my life."

Aleks leans forward in his seat, gingerly taking my hand in his. "It's only fair. You *are* my life."

I squeeze. For months, I refused to believe what my instincts were telling me. I stayed away from Aleks, only moving to Muncie when I felt like I had no other choice. Even then I ignored him, then rejected him, before finally allowing myself to think that maybe Fate had gotten it right after all.

I might be Aleks's second chance, but he's my only hope.

Meeting his red eyes, I ask, "What happens now?"

"Nothing. At least, not until you're all better. We'll figure out what comes next later." The unnatural shade of his irises grows impossibly deeper. "Together."

Nodding in agreement when it becomes obvious that he's expecting an answer, I try to hide my sudden discomfort. My stomach tightens and my throat grows dry as I realize something.

When I asked my question, I wasn't only talking to him. I was asking the Luna what Fate has in store for us.

But, for the first time that I can remember, she doesn't answer me.

The goddess who's been my constant companion has gone silent, and I have no idea what that means—only that it can't be good...

CLAWS AND FANGS BOOK FIVE

# TASTE OF HIS SKIN

SARAH SPADE

INTERNATIONAL BESTSELLING AUTHOR

CLAWS AND FANGS BOOK FIVE

Cover by JoY Design Studio

# FOREWORD

Thank you for checking out *Taste of His Skin*!

This book is the second half of Aleks and Elizabeth's story (that began in *Hint of Her Blood*). In case you don't remember what happened in the previous book, it ended with a confrontation between the featured couple and Jack Walker. While the Wicked Wolf is dead, his defeat didn't come without a price. Roman Zakharov, the vampire leader of the Muncie Cadre, sacrificed himself to keep the peace in his Fang City. Elizabeth and Aleks have consummated their mating, but have not performed either the shifter ritual—the Luna Ceremony—or the vampire blood-bonding that makes them forever mates just yet. At least, not as far as Elizabeth knows...

This book is set a couple of months after the events of *Hint of Her Blood*, with Aleks the new leader of the Cadre, and Elizabeth waiting for Christian and Peyton to retaliate against her for her part in Walker's death. She also hasn't heard anything through her link with the Luna, the revered goddess that belongs to all wolf shifters. The only thing she has is her fledgling relationship with Aleks, and even her grip on that feels tenuous at best. She's still worried that he thinks of her as a dead female's replacement, and Aleks... well, he never wanted to be leader. He just wants Elizabeth—and that's where we are now.

Enjoy!

*xoxo,*

*Sarah*

## CHAPTER 1
# KOCHAM CIĘ

Lost in the throes of mind-blowing pleasure as I come down from another climax, I'm not sure what feels better inside of me: Aleksander Filan's cock or his fangs.

Considering he has me on my hands and knees, his body bowed over mine so that he can mate me from behind—my wolf's preference—while still feeding from my neck, I decide the answer is *both*. As a vampire, his bite is often enough to set me off like a rocket, but add that practiced stroke as he goes in and out as if his body was made for mine? Thank the Luna that he's my fated mate so, technically, it *was*.

This is the third orgasm he's given me tonight. One, right after dinner when he decided going down on me was the perfect dessert for my bloodsucker, then two more after we moved from the settee in the living room to the bedroom we share in his apartment. He's single-mindedly devoted to getting me off, as though making up for just how busy he's been this week. Not that he isn't always a generous lover, but lately... it's like he's rarely here. I'll take him while I can.

And, just now, I'm *taking* him.

When Aleks has drunk his fill of my blood, he releases his fangs, then laps at the marks left behind on my throat. He always does that, even though we both know that I'm a shifter and my regenerative properties will heal his bite almost before he finishes. I could keep them if I wanted to, but based on how often I make myself Aleks's favorite meal, I'd look like a pincushion if I did.

No. I'll keep the one that counts, the mark that will create our forever bond—if we ever take that next step in our relationship.

For now, I'm not thinking about tomorrow. I'm thinking about how Aleks has begun to increase his rhythm. Vampires don't have to breathe, but in the two months that we've been living together, I've learned that he does sometimes. When he's angry, when he's emotional... and when he's quickly heading toward his own climax.

He's panting just enough to be noticeable, one hand gripping my naked hip to keep me in place, the other lightly stroking the length of my spine.

"Can you stand another?" he rumbles, his Polish accent becoming thicker with his own lust. "Księżyca." A gentle grunt. "Tell me what you need."

*You*, I think.

"I don't think I can, Aleks." From my earlier shouts, my voice is raspy and raw. "It's too much."

"It's never too much."

He's right about that. Reaching around me, he tweaks my nipple at the same time as he buries himself all the way inside of me. My vampire is forever in control. The only times he isn't—when his supe side comes out full force—are when he *chooses* to let go. He wants to play my body like he owns it, and he pushes our groins together, hitting me in just the right spot to have my arms going weak as another climax slams into me.

Once I start to tighten around him, Aleks squeezes my side with just enough pressure to help me ride out this latest wave right as he empties himself inside of me.

When he's finally done—and I'm *done*—Aleks shifts so that he's laying flat on his back, tugging me so that I'm sprawled over his flawless body. His hand goes right to my sweat-soaked hair, running his fingers through the strands as he hums in proud male contentment beneath me.

I snuggle up against him, reveling in having my mate near.

"I'll give you a small break," he murmurs, "then we start again."

My traitorous body decides it likes that idea. So does my wolf. Greedy bitch is already telling me to shake my ass to entice Aleks to mount me already.

Down girl, I tell her. I'm a shifter, but my human body can only take so much.

"Really? We've been at it for hours." Turning my head, I glance at his bedside table and gape at it. "Shit, Aleks. Literally."

My vampire is more than two hundred years old. When it comes to modern tech, he's managed to keep up with it, albeit begrudgingly. He has a phone—that he barely uses—but there are relics of the past all over his apartment. One of them? An old-fashioned alarm clock with blaring red digits that went out of style before I was born.

Courtesy of that clock, I see that it's two o'clock in the morning. To most of Muncie, that's the middle of their "day"; as a Fang City, a majority of vamps sleep during the day and live it up at night. Since moving me in with him, Aleks has tried to acclimate himself to my sleeping cycle, so he slathers on SPF 500 and does business during the sunlight hours. Not always, considering there are Cadre responsibilities he can only take care of in the AM hours, but usually.

This last week, I barely saw him for a few hours for dinner before he had to leave again. When midnight hit and he was still with me in bed, I could hardly believe it. Almost as much as I can't believe that that was two hours ago.

No wonder I'm exhausted.

He chuckles. I feel the reverberation all the way to my toes. "We could clean up and go to sleep, if you like."

And miss out on this time with him?

"Ten minutes," I offer. "I'll be ready for another round by then."

He presses a kiss to the top of my head. "Tak, Elizabeth. Anything for my beloved."

Too bad we never make it to ten. Barely two minutes later, while I'm dozing softly as he strokes my back with his fingertips, a piercing ring echoes through the quiet of our room.

My eyes shoot open again. I momentarily freeze. Aleks mutters a curse in Polish under his breath.

Ah, well. It was good while it lasted...

With a sigh I can't quite keep back, I'm already starting to climb off of Aleks before he says, "I'm so sorry. I have to get that."

"I know. And don't be sorry. Sometimes Muncie needs you more than I do. You're the leader now. I understand."

"Maybe. But that doesn't mean I don't need you."

I force a smile to my lips. "I'll be here when you get back."

Aleks grips me gently by the chin, angling my head back so that he can take a kiss before he leaves. His lips are warmer than usual courtesy of the blood I'd shared with him. "I'm holding you to it."

He would, and that's exactly why I continue to stay without any bond to keep me tied to him.

Because Luna knows it's Cadre business, Aleks scoots out of the bed. With my shifter's eyes, I watch his ass as he glides across the room, snagging his phone before leaving the room and disappearing down the hall. If I strained my ears, I could hear every word of his conversation, but I don't. Just because I'm a shifter, that doesn't make me entitled to my vampire's private conversations.

It wouldn't matter anyway since I know exactly what he's going to say when he comes back.

By the time he returns to the room, I've already pulled out fresh underwear for Aleks, his favorite tailored slacks, and a sweater; I go with a light brown because it brings out his eyes. I set the clothes out on the edge of the bed before grabbing a nightshirt for myself and climbing under the covers.

His soft green eyes glitter with some unspoken emotion when he sees the clothes. I wait to see if he'll tell me that they're unnecessary, but he just reaches for the sweater and tugs it on over his curls.

"Emergency?" I ask. It's always an emergency.

All Aleks says is, "I'm sorry," again as he finishes getting dressed.

I fake a yawn. "Told you, baby. Don't worry about it. Ten minutes was probably a generous estimate. You wore me out."

His lips quirk just enough to tell me that he isn't buying it, but he'll go along with my lie for my sake. "I'm your mate. That's my job."

He's not my mate. Not yet. At best, he's my intended.

Not like I'm going to point that out. Just like I'm not going to state the obvious: that his real job is as Roman's replacement in the Cadre building.

I've gotten to know him well enough to understand that he doesn't want to leave me alone in our bed, but he has no choice. His duty to the supes and humans in Muncie must come first.

As if he can sense what I'm thinking—and there are times I would almost swear that Aleks can—he strokes the underside of my jaw, then says, "Remember, I'm only a phone call away, mój księżyca. If you decide you do need me more, I'll be back before you know it. Nothing will keep me from you."

Nothing except for his duties as the newest leader of the Muncie Cadre...

I kiss him again, hoping he missed out on that last traitorous thought. "I know. Be safe, okay? Kocham cię."

My Polish accent is atrocious. Between the dictionary Gem gave me and the translation app I installed on my replacement phone, my handle on Aleks's birth language is getting better and better the more I study. But I'm a California she-wolf. No matter how hard I try to get the Eastern European dialect just right, I'm not there yet.

For Aleks, it's the thought that counts—which is exactly why I spend my ample free time distracting myself with learning his native tongue.

His expression softens, and any doubt that he doesn't feel the same fades in the next heartbeat right before he murmurs, "Ah, Elizabeth, my beloved. Ja też cię kocham."

*I love you, too.*

---

Beloved.

Long after Aleks has left the apartment and I toss and turn through a couple of hours of fitful sleep, I'm still remembering the way he looked at me and called me his 'beloved'.

Aside from his pet name for me—księżyca, which means *moon* in Polish—Aleks likes to refer to me as his beloved far more than my given name. It's as if he's reminding both of us who I'm supposed to be to him. A beloved is a vampire's mate, whether fated or chosen, and they develop a bond as strong as that between shifters using blood.

How? I… I don't know. Aleks has never brought it up. When we first got together, I couldn't keep from wondering just how vampires bond their mates to each other. For shifters, it's easy. We have a ritual known as the Luna Ceremony for a very simple reason: it revolves around our goddess. To claim our mates and form a bond, we have to ask for the Luna's blessing, mate under her watchful eye when she's full, and leave a claiming mark on our chosen mates.

Vampires don't have a goddess. No god, either. The way they worship their thirst and their need for blood is the closest thing the fanged supes have to a religion. That, and their fanatical need to form communities where they have easy access to human blood donors. Their bonding relies on blood—I know that much—because blood is everything to a vamp.

At this point, though, I'm afraid to ask my vampire. I don't want to be pushy. With everything that changed after Roman's assassination and my life-saving surgery, Aleks has more than enough on his plate. Relying on him to soothe my insecurities for the countless time just isn't fair.

He's done everything he could, starting with pointing out that the locket with Julia's picture in it is kept in a small wooden box in the top drawer of his bedside table. I didn't ask him to, but I'd be lying if I said that it didn't make me feel a little better that he wasn't walking around with it on his person.

And we all know that I'm a terrible liar.

He loves me. I know he does. Just like I know that, if we were ever fully bonded, it would be an unbreakable tie. It already is. I tried to snap it when Walker threatened to kill Aleks if I didn't leave with him, but though my "gift" hadn't vanished yet when I attempted to break my fledgling bond with Aleks, it didn't work. I still remember how much the blowback hurt.

But does he love *me*? Or is he in love with the idea of having a beloved?

He hasn't called me Julia again since the first night I fed him. He treats me like a queen. It's a huge difference compared to what my life's been like the last decade or so, and I should be thrilled that he loves me.

Just... if he does? Really does? Why aren't we bonded yet? It's almost like one of us has one foot out the door, and I can't tell if it's Aleks—or if it's me.

Ugh.

What makes it worse is that I'm having these thoughts while I'm lying in Aleks's bed, his scent embedded in my skin, surrounded by the musk unique to our mating. There's no reason to believe that he isn't all in, except maybe for the fact that it's been more than two months since he claimed me as his mate in front of the former leader of Muncie and we still don't have any kind of permanent bond.

The Luna Ceremony is out. When I woke up in the hospital after being shot with a silver bullet by the Wicked Wolf's ex-

Beta, I realized that the Luna—the goddess who whispered to me my entire life—had gone silent. Without her blessing, I can't bond Aleks to me. And my vampire doesn't seem too keen on making me his by the vampire rites.

At least I'm here. I'm safe. I'm loved. Sure, I don't have a job —after Roman's death, I couldn't go back to the Cadre building even if Aleks offered me to stay on with him—and I can't help but feel like a giant mooch, but he loves me.

I'll cling to that belief fiercely because, Luna help me, I don't know what I'll do if he doesn't.

# CHAPTER 2
# THE BRUNCH QUEEN

Most people don't believe this, but vampires eat.

Well, obviously. Though they're considered to be undead, they need something to survive on, otherwise they wouldn't exist. For the fanged supes, it's blood. Human or other supes, they're not picky, and a vamp suffering from thirst is almost as dangerous as a feral shifter off of their leash.

But just like how pop culture has it that the bloodsuckers can't stand to be out in the sunlight, it's the same when humans believe that vampires only survive on blood. With the right level of sunblock—Aleks keeps a store of SPF 500 in our bathroom—vampires can face the light of day, and while blood makes up a substantial part of his diet, he does eat real food occasionally.

Younger vamps, like Leigh and the others, eat it more often. That's why I'm not surprised when Gretchen decides we should meet for an early spring brunch at a classy joint closer to the center of Muncie, fittingly called The Brunch Queen.

I only worked alongside Leigh for a couple of weeks in February, but it was enough to form a fast friendship. She was a secretary like me before Roman promoted her to patroller so that she could work alongside her beloved, Tamera. Neither one of us work the front desk at the Cadre building anymore, but I hang out with them and Gretchen pretty often. Because two of the three of them are fully Cadre—with Gretchen refusing to give up her carefree vamp lifestyle even if her mates want to serve their community—Aleks doesn't worry about me going out with them.

And even if he did? All I have to do is remind him that I wear his fang around my neck. In Muncie, that makes me untouchable, and we both know it.

When I still hadn't heard from him around noon, I figured he would be busy until night fell again. Normally I can find ways to occupy myself in the apartment, but every now and then the loneliness gets to me and my wolf. Gem, another recent friend of mine, is the female Alpha of the Mountainside Pack. While she'll always answer the phone for me, she can't just drop what she's doing because I'm bored.

Luckily, the Trio can.

Gem used to call them the Nightmare Trio. Can't really blame her. The first night she arrived in Muncie, Leigh, Tamera, and Gretchen decided she would make an excellent late-night snack. Aleks actually stopped them from attempting to feed on Gem, and that's how she ended up becoming his roommate. Of course, he only did so because he sensed she was an alpha female—like Julia had been—and he thought she was his beloved.

She wasn't, but they're still close friends even now. To Gem's annoyance, the Nightmare Trio became my friends, and though she can't stand them, for my sake she refers to them as the Trio now. It stuck, and so I do, too.

I messaged Leigh earlier to see if she was free, knowing that the message would be passed along to her two beloveds. As the name implies, as sunset spotters, Leigh and Tamera patrol the borders of Muncie during the shift when the sun goes down. I figured they weren't working and I hoped that meant they might want to do something with me today.

That's how I ended up at The Brunch Queen with three gorgeous vampire females. Because Tamera and Leigh are Cadre, we get our pick of a table, and because late April in Muncie can be beautiful, we chose a four-seater outside.

We place our orders with the human server. The Trio, of course, each order a Bloody Mary with their small brunch meal. I go for steak and eggs, and an orange juice.

My drink comes out first. Since a vamp Bloody Mary is literal, their drinks take a little longer to prepare.

While they're waiting, Gretchen—who'd been studying the design on her claw-tipped nails as Tamera and Leigh made small talk about new protective measures the patrollers are putting into place under Aleks—perks up suddenly. I have no idea why. In the time I've known her, she's made it clear she finds that side of her beloveds dreadfully dull, but then she taps her nails against the table.

"Speaking of, can you believe the rebels are still finding a way to be such a massive pain in the neck?"

My stomach tightens. It's suddenly queasy, and without any food to try to settle it, I reach for my glass of orange juice and take a small sip.

I *hate* the vampire rebels in Muncie.

Every time I hear about them, it reminds me of Roman's

noble sacrifice and how it turned out to be in vain. He allowed Christian to behead him because he believed his death would bring peace between the two different vampire factions in Muncie: those who supported Roman as leader, and those who wanted things to go back to how they were when the cruel dictator, Marcel Claret, was the head vampire in Muncie.

Marcel is long dead. Now Roman is, too. If his sacrifice meant anything, the rebels should've stopped their infighting. But then Aleks became the new leader, and the peace lasted a couple of weeks at most before they started testing him.

They're the reason why I barely see my vampire as much these days. In fact, I wouldn't put it past those bloodsuckers being the reason behind the emergency that's kept Aleks away since early this morning.

Tamera's gaze flickers my way. "Gretch, maybe this isn't what we should be discussing over brunch."

"Why not? It's true. At least last night they only drew a little blood." Tossing her long blonde hair over her shoulder, Gretchen snorts. "Not much of an assassination attempt, if you ask me, but they should know better than to test Aleksander. That's one vamp who, if you want him dead, you better not miss. And yet they insist on trying."

*What?*

I blink.

"I'm sorry. What was that?"

"Oh, come on, Elizabeth. Don't play coy with me. I know I'm not Cadre, but I hear things." Right. From her mates. "Everyone's talking about how three rebels jumped Aleksander when he was leaving the Cadre building yesterday evening." She sniffs. "They used silver knives. Who does that? If you're gonna go for a vamp like our fair leader, at least use a sword."

Tamera gives me an apologetic grimace. "It's not as bad as it sounds. Gretch is right. Aleks barely got a scratch before he turned the blade on the rebels. He was fine."

I know he was. I ran my teeth across his throat after that attack and there wasn't a single mark on the ivory column.

Does knowing that help me right now? Not even a little.

My whole life, I've never had the best poker face. Sometimes, when Tarot wasn't bringing in enough money for me to survive on my own as a lone wolf, I got myself involved in other get-rich-quick opportunities. Playing poker against unsuspecting humans was one of them. With my wolf picking up a spiking heartbeat, or sweat eking out of their pores when they were suddenly nervous, I definitely had the advantage. Pity I couldn't bluff worth a damn, and all the supernatural instincts in the world can't help when you're dealt a crap hand and don't know how to fake it.

Maybe if I'd stuck with it and taught myself to become a better liar instead of throwing everything I had into reading my tarot cards, then I could've stopped myself from how I reacted to Gretchen's casual reveal and Tamera's hurried way to cover up for her beloved. But I hadn't, and I didn't, and I was so shocked by what she said that my fingers flexed, the glass pulverizing beneath my shifter strength, orange juice spilling out all over the table.

And off of it. Though it hadn't been my intention, the orange juice follows the path of gravity, flooding directly into Gretchen's lap.

The blonde vampire shrieks, jumping up from her seat. So does Tamera, reaching instantly for a wad of napkins to shove at Gretchen. Leigh stays seated for a moment, her eyes going from pale amber to deep red in a heartbeat as she gasps an unnecessary breath. Her gaze zeroes in on my shaky hand.

Oh. I'm bleeding. I wiggle my hand a few times, knocking away as many of the glass shards as possible, then close my fingers into a loose fist to hide the sight. It's not so bad; I'll be healed in a few minutes. Probably better that I don't flaunt fleshly spilled blood in front of a table of vampires, no matter who they are.

Leigh exhales. The red fades away, her irises returning to their normal pale color. Tossing her box braids behind her, she leans toward me.

That's when I realize that she's staring at my eyes.

It's not something I do consciously. When my emotions flare up and get the better of me—like, oh, maybe hearing that my lover was nearly assassinated multiple times and I had no idea—my Luna-given silver irises turn inky black.

The Luna goes quiet, my ability to sense and snap bonds disappearing with her, but my eyes still do their freaky thing. Because why not?

It's bad enough that I'm the only shifter who lives among the vamps in the Fang City. Letting my friends know just how different I am from other she-wolves? Lovely. Just freaking lovely.

"Elizabeth," Leigh says softly. "Are you all right?"

No. No, I am not.

Aleks didn't tell me. He came home last night, bringing me my favorite sandwich for a snack, then immediately seduced me into bed. I did manage to ask him about his day, and all he said was that it was the same as the day before.

Right. Because, according to Gretchen, that wasn't the first time the rebel vamps tried to kill him—and I had no clue.

"Yeah. Sorry. I just... I remembered something I had to. I can't believe I forgot. You guys enjoy brunch without me. Tell the owner to put in on Aleks's tab if you want, but I... I gotta go. Bye."

And then, before any of the Trio can try to stop me, I scoot around the table and make my escape.

Thank the Luna we were planning on eating outside.

---

IF I WANT TO CONFRONT ALEKS, THERE'S ONLY ONE PLACE TO go. The Cadre building. Since taking over for Roman, he spends nearly every hour of each day in his office on the twentieth floor.

Roman used to keep his office on the twenty-first. Because Aleks is still mourning his old friend in his own way, he refuses to go a single floor higher than where Roman used to lord over the Cadre building. The secretaries at the front desk have the order that I can visit Aleks there whenever I want, but I'm still grieving, too. I haven't been back in months.

I don't go back now.

I'm not ready to confront my vampire just yet. I figure there has to be a reason why he kept the attack from me, and if I ask him about it, he might actually explain why. I don't think I really want to know. If it's because he thinks he needs to coddle and protect me, I might lose it on him.

Even though I'm not an alpha female, I'm still a shifter. Protecting me is one thing. But coddling me? I can't. I just *can't*. What we have will never work if he doesn't realize that I can take care of myself.

It won't work if he's hiding something from me, either. So, yeah... maybe I don't want to know.

That's why, instead of going to see Aleks while he's at work, I decide to do something I've been putting off for weeks now.

Though he tells me repeatedly that, if I want a job, he's happy to put me on the Cadre's payroll—and if I don't, he doesn't mind if his beloved stays at home… in fact, he *prefers* that one—I just can't bring myself to do it. That doesn't mean that I don't have another offer.

When I first moved to Muncie and I needed to make some money to survive, Gem set up an interview for me with her old boss. Charlie is a vampire who runs a supe bar named after himself. It caters to vamps and humans in the know, and months ago he was looking for a bartender to replace Gem when she moved permanently to Accalia.

Gem thought I would be perfect for the job. When Charlie passed on me, she was livid. Of course, it all came out in the end that Aleks used his reputation in Muncie to convince Charlie not to hire me. At that time, he hadn't quite claimed me yet, though he considered me his. He didn't want me working the bar, so he used his influence to get me rejected.

I understood. Supernatural males get a little reckless when they're in the mating dance, and Aleks thought that a delta wolf might be meek enough to let him bulldoze right over her. He learned quickly that wasn't the case, though Gem hammered the message home when she flipped out on him for interfering. And that was nothing compared to how she ripped Charlie a new one for going along with it.

After Gem was done with the two males, I had a job offer from Charlie, plus Aleks's promise that he would support me working at the bar if that's what I wanted to do. Up until now, I've been thinking it over, but after I bolted from The Brunch Queen and purposely headed in the opposite direction of the

Cadre building, I realize I can take a trip down to Charlie's and find out if he still needs help.

It's something I've been meaning to do, and maybe I'm being petty, taking the trip to that part of Muncie without telling Aleks because he conveniently forgot to mention he was attacked by traitors last night, but I figure I might as well.

Besides, it's not like he won't know anyway—and I won't even have to be the one to tell him.

How could I forget? In Muncie, you can't do a damn thing without the Cadre leader knowing about it. That goes double when you're his beloved.

The Fang City is full of vampires. I've grown used to their overlaying scent so the tang doesn't bother my wolf these days as much as it did in the beginning. However, when a familiar aura brushes up against me, it stands out.

Somewhere behind me, within reach of my wolf, is Dominic Le Croix.

When the aura stays at a steady distance for the next six blocks, no matter what direction I take, I have to admit what I suspected from the moment I caught his scent: he's following me.

Now, there are plenty of reasons why he might be doing that. The biggest one might be that he's not at all, that it's a coincidence that we're going in the same direction. Dominic's beloved is a human bartender who works at the bar I was heading toward. Though she's Cadre now, too, Hailey refused to leave her job after she bonded with Dominic. Maybe he's going to visit his mate.

Right. And maybe I'll sprout wings and be the first wolf who can fly.

This isn't the first time I've been walking around Muncie and caught one of Aleks's trusted comrades in the not so far distance. When I called him out on it, my vampire didn't deny it. The Cadre, he explained, protects the whole Fang City. And Aleks? He protects *me*.

If that means he sends some of his patrollers out to watch over me when I leave the apartment? So be it. I wouldn't be surprised if either Tamera or Leigh—probably Tamera, since she's higher up in the Cadre's hierarchy—let him know that I left brunch abruptly. Without their eyes on me, someone else has taken on the job.

For a moment, I pause. Then, glancing over my shoulder, I wave at Dominic so that he knows he's caught. When he doesn't wave back, instead nodding his head solemnly in my direction, I figure I'm right.

I let out a huff. Having a vampire tail usually doesn't rub me the wrong way like this, but I'm still struggling to deal with the idea that Aleks might have died last night and I never would've known. Why should he get to monitor my every step while keeping secrets?

I know the answer to that. Because he's the head vamp, and I'm his beloved.

Supposedly.

Out of the corner of my eye, I peer inside of Charlie's wide window. I could walk in there, take the bar owner up on his offer of a job, and then... what? Have to deal with Aleks's people watching me while I learn how to tend a bar?

Forget it. It was a silly idea anyway.

If I really need money? I don't have to work in a bar.

I have another full-proof way to get some quick cash.

## CHAPTER 3
# BLAME THE TRAY TABLE

Aleks says I don't need money. That, in Muncie, his name—and the fang hanging off the chain around my neck—is as good as gold. So even if he's not there to provide for his beloved, all I have to do is visit a supe establishment and I'll want for nothing.

I wish I could do that. With the exception of the two years I spent in the Wolf District where we bartered for whatever we needed, I've spent my whole adult life finding some way to survive. The habit is ingrained in me. I can't just stop now.

Right after I left my birth pack, I had to do things I'm not proud of for food, shelter, and money. I've scavenged in dumpsters, spent long stretches in my fur, and sold my body when I had no choice but to stay in my skin. I've gone hungry. I've stolen, too. I never relied on anyone else because I've never *had* anyone else.

And then I followed an aching belly and twitchy fingers to a human carnival where I had my fortune told by Madame Zoe, and she gave me the deck of cards that changed my life.

With these cards, some grit, a little determination, and a ton of bravado, I could make money another way. I didn't have to sleep with males for food; I just had to con them. After what happened with Kyle and Peyton, I swore off males entirely—until I met Aleks, and even then I rejected the pull I felt toward him for more than five months.

But as much as I love Aleks—and I do, I really do—I would do anything for my tarot cards. In this world, they're the only thing that's *mine,* and I proved that when I risked returning to Walker's abandoned Alpha cabin after he lost his challenge to his daughter. I couldn't leave the district without them if I could help it, and when I moved into Aleks's apartment, I made sure I threw them in my duffle bag that first night.

I usually keep them stored in the bedside table Aleks bought for me. Lately, though, I've been carrying them around in my back pocket.

It's the tray table's fault.

I'm a shifter. Even if it's safer for me to stay close to the apartment, there are times when my wolf wants out. There's no denying her. I usually shift, then take a run around the park, but even a walk in my skin is enough to placate my other half. More often than not, Aleks joins me, but he's not always home.

He's not happy about it, but he understands that he can't keep me caged inside. I need fresh air, and my wolf also needs to have a sense of her territory. The townhouse used to be mine. Now both halves of me consider the three-block radius around the apartment building as the beginning of a den for me and my mate.

It was during one of my walks around our territory that I

found the table in a pile of trash thrown on the corner at the end of a block. I scavenged it, gave it a good wash, and kept it for one reason only: it was the perfect height and size to serve as a table for me to offer tarot card readings.

When I first moved to Muncie, I wondered if I'd be allowed to read fortunes here. It wasn't long before I gave up on the idea. Fang City vamps make it clear that shifters don't belong, and I didn't want to draw attention to the fact that I was one. I'm not worried about that anymore. These days my every movement draws a vampire's attention, thanks to my relationship with Aleks.

Might as well make it work for me.

It's not about the money. While it's nice to have some in my pocket, I respect Aleks too much to act like my fated mate can't provide for me. Bringing Tarot to Muncie? It's never been about the money. It's about being Elizabeth Howell, honing my skills in case I ever need them again, and finding some way to occupy myself while Aleks is busy with the Cadre.

I've only done it twice since I scavenged the tray table, and both times Aleks mentioned it over dinner; as if I didn't already know he had his patrollers keeping an eye on me, that sealed it. Turns out, he liked that I was doing something that I enjoyed, and as long as I stayed close to the apartment, he didn't try to stop me.

Not like he really would. Even if we're not bonded, I'm his mate, not his subordinate. So what if he's the leader of the Cadre and that makes him the Alpha of Muncie? I'm a shifter. A lone wolf. I'll listen to his suggestions because I care for him, but ultimately I'm going to make my own decisions.

For the most part, I choose to stay inside. But with Gretchen's flippant comment still bouncing around my skull, I don't think I can stand to be surrounded by Aleks's scent without having him home with me. It was bad enough when I returned to grab the tray table, and I don't plan on going back until Aleks is there.

I have hours to kill. Aleks rarely leaves the Cadre building before evening, and that's only because he's making an effort to be the type of male he thinks I deserve. He works during the day, comes home and feeds me, then lays down with me in our bed until I'm curled up, fast asleep. It'll be some time until I expect to see him.

It's the middle of the afternoon when I finish setting up my tray table and the hand-drawn sign I made, advertising my services. In a city as hectic and pedestrian-friendly as Muncie, plenty of lookie-loos gawk at me as they pass, curious to see what I'm doing—or maybe they're trying to figure out what Aleksander Filan's claimed mate is doing, setting up shop on the street corner.

When a few vampires—and a couple of humans—begin to line up in front of my table before I'm completely ready, I figure it has more to do with that than my amazing Tarot skills.

At least I'm entertaining enough to make their patronage worthwhile. After explaining how it works to the striking brunette vampire who's first in line, I get started.

It's not so easy to shove my worry for Aleks to the back of my mind, but I manage. Before long I'm focused on the ever-growing line and the weight of more than a few pale-eyed stares on me. The first half an hour flies by.

Shuffling the cards, I'm just about to lay the spread for the human male up next when a shiver skitters down my spine. Almost instinctively, I take a deep breath, going still when I catch the faintest hint of fennel on the slight breeze. Add that to the whisper of a chill suddenly coming over me and I can tell exactly who is out there watching me this time.

*Aleks.*

I'm so attuned to him, I always seem to know when he is near. I've never tested how far how I can sense him, but it's farther than I've ever been able to pick up on one particular aura, one particular scent. Especially in Muncie, where my delicate shifter's nose is constantly assaulted with the meaty, bloody, icy stink of the countless vampires who live here, I have to be able to pick out the distinct licorice notes that are part of his innate scent to know it's him.

It's more than that, though. The little hairs on the back of my neck stand up when his powerful aura gets close enough, and my heart beats just a little faster. The emptiness that's been inside of me fills a tiny bit more whenever his aura brushes up against mine.

The customer in front of me clears his throat.

I give myself a small shake. I didn't realize that I'd frozen for so long. It was probably only fifteen seconds or so, but I'd stopped shuffling the cards. Standing there like a deer in headlights, even a human would have to wonder what came over me.

"Sorry," I say, murmuring an apology. Aleks is coming closer —no doubt heading for me—but I already accepted this guy's payment. I flip the first card. "The Fool."

His brow furrows. "Okay. That doesn't sound so nice. What does that mean?"

After all these years I know the meanings of every card in my deck, whether they're upright or reversed. Depending on who I'm reading and exactly what they're hoping to get out of it, I sometimes make up my own, but I usually try to stick to the true meanings. I might be a fraud and a charlatan when it comes to

Tarot, but I still respect it. I have to. Without my weathered deck of cards, I never would've survived being a lone wolf for all those years on my own before the Luna blessed me with my vampire.

The human doesn't clear his throat again, though he does shift his balance and that draws my attention back to him. Crap. He's waiting, and I'm still a mile away, thinking of Aleks.

"Oh. Um." Forget about Aleks for the moment, Elizabeth. You have a paying customer. *Focus*. The card is upright. "It's not that bad, actually. This card means you can be a bit of a free spirit. You look on the bright side of life, and you're open to new beginnings."

"Really?" To my surprise, he's listening in rapt attention to my explanation. He grins. "That's cool."

Look at that. I didn't think he really cared about his fortune, and I'm pleased to be wrong. When he first approached my table, I got the feeling that he was more interested in stopping to talk to me than having his fortune told. Lust had seeped into his scent when he paused on the corner, doing a double take before backtracking to get in line behind the two teen girls I was already reading.

Of course, despite being human, his whole demeanor changed when he noticed the fang hanging off of the golden chain around my neck. The lust was still there, but so was the bitter tinge of disappointment, though he didn't leave the line. He must be one of the humans in the know about supes—that, or maybe even a donor—because he is aware exactly what that means.

Sorry, guy. This she-wolf is currently off the market.

But even if I've been claimed by a vampire, that doesn't mean I can't spend the afternoon telling fortunes with my tarot cards.

In fact, now that the whole Fang City knows I'm with Aleks, I can finally get away with it without worrying about being run off from my spot by the local law enforcement—or worse.

I flip the second. It's the Temperance card, upright. "This one tells me that you have a big decision coming up in your personal life. You're going to need patience for it. Don't go for either extreme."

A thoughtful expression flashes across his face. "Yeah... yeah. I guess that makes sense. And I get three right?"

He's supposed to. That's how I run my little hustle. For ten bucks, I'll do a spread of three cards for a customer. It's enough that I can be sure that at least one of them will be a hit, and not so many that I risk going into too much detail and dragging my client out of the haze of belief. Even someone who pays me for shits and giggles will feel cheated if I get it totally wrong.

That's why I rely more on my shifter's instincts than I do any kind of clairvoyance. I might be Luna-touched, but I'm no goddess. I can't tell the future; if anything, I still can't get over my past. Between my eyes, my ears, my nose, I can usually figure out a way to tell my customers just what they want to hear.

I would've for this male, too, only I never get the chance. Before I can flip the third and final card, an icy tendril reaches out at me, stroking my cheek. And maybe I could pretend it was the wind, considering it sends my hair flying around my face in a sudden gust, but I know better.

Since coming to live in Muncie at the beginning of the year, I've run across so many vampires. Only two were powerful enough to wield their auras as a tangible extension of themselves: Roman and Aleks. Roman because he was nine centuries old and the most recent leader of the Muncie Cadre. Aleks because he's taken over for Roman—and because I'm his beloved so I'm exceptionally affected by him. I used to be able to sense Roman's power like a crackle against my skin while Aleks's has always been a gentle caress. Since taking on the mantle of leader, he's only grown stronger.

Or maybe that's because he's bristling with obvious jealousy as he cuts the growing line of customers, stopping right next to the sandy-haired male.

"Hey," the human immediately begins to argue. "It's still my turn. You've got to wait— *oh*."

Oh, indeed.

# CHAPTER 4
# THREE-CARD SPREAD

On the outside, my vampire looks both dashing and contained. His curls are slightly windblown, probably from the speed he used to run from the center of Muncie to the downtown area where I'm set up, and his pale green eyes don't have a single hint of red coloring his irises. At more than two centuries old, he's had a lot of practice controlling his vampire side around humans, regardless of if they know about supes or not.

But I've gotten to know him pretty well over the last two months. Even if I didn't, bonded males give off a dangerous edge when they think someone is poaching on their territory. Aleks thinks of me as his, and though I would never even look twice at another male, it doesn't matter that he trusts me implicitly. The other male is too close to me. He can't stand for that.

Instead of warning my customer back, Aleks smiles at him. He doesn't flash any fang, but he doesn't need to.

The human takes the hint. Muttering something under his breath that sounds like an apology, he steps aside.

Aleks takes his place.

I gather the two cards lying face-up, placing them back in the deck. I refuse to look at him as I do. I don't actually think that, if I ignore him, he'll go away, but I can't help it. I'm torn between wanting to rub my flank against him, transferring my scent to him, marking him as mine, and wanting to slap him for keeping last night's close call from me.

I'm his mate. Maybe we're not bonded yet, but in all the ways that matter, I'm his partner. I should've known.

He'll be able to tell. Already Aleks knows me better than myself. I won't be able to hide my conflicting emotions from him.

So I drop my gaze to the top of my tray table, avoiding his searching stare.

And, Luna, my vampire doesn't like that one bit.

His aura bumps up against mine, insisting I give in to him. He's not angry, not at me—never at me—but he's not happy, either.

"You said you wouldn't do this again," he murmurs softly. "The ignoring me thing."

Damn it. He's right. It really bothers him when I close myself off like I'm doing right now—and I did promise to try not to do that. Just like he tries not to be so demanding and overbearing once I settled in with him. As a shifter, I'm used to listening to a dominant male, but if this mating is going to work, we need to be equals.

For the most part, we are. And I believed that up until Gretchen accidentally let me in on how there's so much that Aleks is keeping from me...

With him, there was never a moment where we decided to be together. It just sort of happened. After Walker targeted Gem's townhouse where I was living, Aleks invited me to spend the night. I just never left, and even if I tried, he would never let me. As far as he was concerned, his beloved belonged with him. In his home, in his bed... that was where he wanted me, and where I wanted to be. So I stayed.

Now, that's pretty common with mates, so I didn't realize how far and how fast I'd fallen until I was in way too deep. We aren't officially bonded, but we live and love and act as if we are.

But if we *were* bonded? I would've known on my side of our tie that he was in danger. I would be able to follow him anywhere, sensing him no matter what, not just when he's near.

If we were forever mates, he'd never keep secrets from me.

Like being attacked by three other vampires at one time...

I jerk my head up. When Aleks's eyes narrow on my face, I know that my emotions have gotten the better of me. Mine must be black.

Hopefully no one else notices. I can explain away my silver eyes to non-supes by claiming I wear colored contacts. Kinda hard to do that when they darken to black without me "changing" them.

Twice in one day. I guess being confronted with the reality of my immortal fated mate almost dying is enough to set off my Luna-touched wolf even when the goddess has gone quiet.

Pretending not to notice, I ask him, "What are you doing here?"

He's supposed to be at the Cadre building. As the new leader, he's never actually off duty, but when he's on his way home to me, he always sends me a message to let me know he'll see me soon. My ancient vampire might not be a big fan of using a phone as an actual *phone*, but he's a whizz at texting.

My phone is in my pocket. It hasn't buzzed once.

"I was looking for you."

"Well," I say, keeping my tone light even as I resist the urge to grind my teeth in frustration, "you found me."

I blame Dominic. What happened? He saw me heading toward Charlie's, then backtracking, and decided to tell Aleks that I was walking around town on my own? I wouldn't put it past him—or for Aleks to track me down to see what I was doing for himself.

He wants to keep me safe. And I appreciate that. I really do. This intense desire of Aleks's to make sure that I'm never in any trouble... for a shifter like me, I feel protected. Loved. Maybe a more dominant she-wolf would have her fur ruffled over it, but all I've ever wanted was to be the most important person in someone else's life.

Does that mean I'm pleased that he scared off my customer like that? Not even a little. Especially since I'm still pissed off about the assassination attempt I didn't know anything about.

I glance up at him again. Though I already knew he was safe and sound and perfectly in one piece since I spent last night with him, I run my gaze over him anyway. Flawless features, carelessly tousled curls, a gentle smile... and a steely look in his pale eyes that tells me that something's on his mind, and it has everything to do with me.

Uh-oh.

"What do you need?"

We're in public. He might be the all-powerful leader of the Cadre, but having sex with me out in the open is still frowned upon. So while the look in his eyes tells me exactly what he needs from me, he settles for saying, "I want you to read the cards for me."

I blink. "Aleks. Are you serious right now?"

"Always, księżyca. Besides, it seems like I'm your only client for the moment."

What?

I glance behind him and frown. He's not wrong. Too distracted by my stunning vampire, I didn't even notice that the few people still waiting in line had scattered after his arrival.

It's good to be the vamp leader. We have privacy without him saying a word.

Dipping his long, slender fingers into his back pocket, Aleks pulls out his wallet. He plucks out a twenty, showing it to me. "I can pay."

"Oh my Luna," I snap, part annoyed, part amused. "Put that away."

He does. "You won't read my fortune, Elizabeth?"

I should know better than to refuse Aleks anything. Even though he's teasing, my wolf whines inside my chest, urging me to give him what he wants.

Ah, well. If it makes both him and my lovesick wolf happy...

I give the cards a cursory shuffle. This isn't the first time I've read Aleks. He finds my affection for my tarot cards charming, and often asks me to tell him his fortune. He knows I'm full of shit, too; that doesn't faze him. Sometimes I think he just likes to listen to my voice.

In fact, the first time he ever brought me food—his homemade white borscht—we played questions for cards. I read him three cards in exchange for asking him three questions.

Remembering that fateful night, I say, "You know I will, but only if you'll answer a question for me."

"And you know that I'm an open book for you always, but if that's what you want, then I agree." Aleks quirks his lips into a sly grin, satisfied he got his way. "Just the one?"

That's all I need. "Yes."

His eyes are sparkling. Now that we're completely alone—even passersby are giving the corner we're on a wide berth—he's in a much better mood than before. He pulled in his jealous nature, content in teasing me like usual.

Let's see if that changes when we're done with our little game.

I have a complete deck of seventy-eight tarot cards, but I usually only deal with the twenty-two that make up the Major Arcana when I'm fleecing tourists. They make a bigger impact, and are the ones most people familiar with Tarot know about.

I don't bother pulling out the rest of the cards. Since I'm only reading Aleks because he asked—and because, twenty-two or seventy-eight, it won't make any difference—I shuffle the deck one last time, then lay out three cards for him.

The Moon. The Lovers. Death.

Aleks chuckles. "Just making sure."

Huffing out a breath, I pick the cards back up, place them at the top of my deck, then shove them in my back pocket. "It doesn't make sense. Every freaking time, it's the same."

"Of course it does. It's Fate," he says, leaving it at that.

It's not Fate. It's a former lone wolf flipping cards at random, and there shouldn't be any reason why The Moon, The Lovers, and Death are the only cards that seem to be in my deck every time I read Aleks.

It all started with that game of ours. I asked Aleks three questions—four, technically—and then laid a three-card spread for him. When I saw that it was The Moon, The Lovers, and

Death, I turned the cards over again before he could see what they were. Since then, they appear every single freaking time.

And despite what meanings they have in Tarot, it's undeniable how they sum up our relationship. The Moon. That's me, and not only because that's the nickname Aleks gave me. The Lovers. Also obvious. And Death. What is a vampire except death personified?

"Whatever. You got your reading. It's my turn now."

Aleks gestures for me to go ahead.

"Why didn't you tell me that there was an assassination attempt on you last night? Or that it wasn't even the first?"

For a second, I expect my vampire to tease and point out that I snuck in a second question.

He doesn't.

The smile slides right off of his handsome face. His pale eyes flash, but they're still green. "Who told you?"

I raise my eyebrows, but I don't say anything.

I don't have to.

Bracing his hands against my tray table, Aleks says, "You had a meal with Gretchen, Leigh, and Tamera this morning. Leigh and Tamera are Cadre. Patrollers. They would know, but also know better than to worry my beloved with Cadre business. But Gretchen... as their third, they might have told her. It was Gretchen." His eyes start to rim with red. "I'll have to remind her that she's not Cadre by her own choice. She should stay out of our affairs."

Crap. I want to hash this out with him, not get Gretchen in trouble. And though he's sounding as cultured and nonplussed as usual, he's not too happy that Gretchen snitched.

And doesn't that rub me the wrong way.

I cross my arms over my chest. "It doesn't matter who told

me. You said I can ask you anything. I'm asking you about last night. Did you get attacked by three vampires who were trying to kill you or not?"

Luna, he's quick. Pushing off of the table, he reaches beneath it. Within seconds, Aleks has my sign tucked under his arm, the tray table folded into its compact form. He carries it easily despite the fact that, as a shifter, its weight is nothing to me.

"Come, księżyca. Why don't we take that question home?"

I already had my answer. But Aleks's reaction just opened up like ten more questions.

"Sure," I tell him. "Let's do that."

# CHAPTER 5
# LAVENDER TEA

Aleks sure loves his tea.

It's one of the first things I learned about him. That he was a vampire, he had two centuries on me, he was Gem's old roommate, and he has this weird thing for tea.

Before we were actually introduced, back when I first started working at the Cadre building, he sent me a package through the mail. It had my name on it, was covered in his scent, and called to me from the bottom of the mail bin. Leigh encouraged me to open it, and I did because I didn't know what else to do.

He'd sent me a box of tea. No note. No reason. Just tea.

Since then, I've discovered that it's one of his pleasures. Like his thriller novels and the old-fashioned murder mystery shows he watched when they were first airing, Aleks might drink blood to survive, but he adores his tea. And because he does? He thinks everyone else should, too.

I drink it because it makes him happy, not because I like it. So when Aleks guides me into the kitchen once we make it back to the apartment, I swallow my huff. Of course he won't want to have this discussion without a cup of tea in front of us.

Pressing a chilled kiss to my forehead, he invites me to take a seat at the cozy kitchen table while he reaches for the tea kettle and one of his canisters of loose tea.

"I'll make us some lavender tea. Then we'll talk."

Lavender tea. Woof. It's pungent, and my wolf already has her belly down, paws covering her snout. I only just keep from doing the same. Once it's brewed, I'll get used to it, and I totally get why he's grabbed that can.

The dark purple herb is supposed to relieve stress and anxiety while also promoting calming. The mood I've been in since brunch, I need it.

I fiddle with the fang on my chain as he moves around the kitchen, filling the tea kettle from the tap, prepping the infuser for the loose tea. He makes chatter, asking me about brunch, checking to see that I ate enough today. When I admit that I left before the meal was served, and that I might've accidentally skipped lunch, I get a stern look from my vampire as he goes into the fridge for a pack of bacon.

To shifters, food is a big part of our love language. Providing a meal for a mate is a shifter's way of saying that they want to take care of you. If you accept it, then eat, you're agreeing with their claim.

From the moment I moved into his apartment, I gave up policing my meals. Aleks is an excellent cook, and he treats cooking for me like he does when we're in bed together: my pleasure is the only thing he's concerned with. He almost takes it as a personal insult when I'm not completely stuffed—with his food or his dick—and I've grown to adore how much he fusses over me.

It's been more than a decade since anyone cared about me. Since anyone wanted to take care of me. I still can't believe that I lucked out to land Aleks as my fated mate, and something as simple as him frying me up a plate full of bacon while the tea steeps is almost enough to make me decide to stop questioning him.

Then again, because I do love him with everything I am, I can't. I need him to know that I care about him just as much, and that I can't even stand the thought of something happening to him.

Still, I'm a shifter. The second the bacon starts to sizzle, the air filling with the scent of it cooking, my wolf lifts her head up. My stomach grumbles. During my lone wolf days, I was hungry more often than not, so to go the whole day without much didn't bother me. Worry for Aleks kept a pit in my stomach that only started to fade when we were back in the apartment. So when he presses a kiss to the top of my head now before placing the plate of bacon down on the table, I thank him, then dig in.

By the time the plate is empty, Aleks has finished with the tea. He takes my plate, placing it into the sink, then comes back with two steaming mugs of tea.

Aleks sets one of them in front of me before taking the seat next to me. I blow on the top, waiting until it's cool enough to sip. Knowing him, he won't say a word about our discussion outside until I start to drink the tea. It's a quirk of his—one that Gem warned me about, just like she told me to shy away from his chamomile tea for some reason—and I've grown used to it.

"How is it?"

Aleks loves tea. I love Aleks. Drinking flower water makes my wolf snuffle and sneeze, but he makes it for me, so I drink it. "It'll be better once you tell me what happened last night."

His jaw clenches. He really, really doesn't want me to know, and though he'll tell me if I push it, that doesn't stop him from trying to brush me off first. "It's nothing to worry about."

"Nothing to worry about? You could've died!"

"It's not that easy to kill a vampire. They'd have to take my head. I assure you, księżyca, they never even got close."

Why doesn't that make me feel any better? I gulp down a mouthful of lavender tea. Luna, let the calming properties kick in before I grab Aleks by the collar and throttle him.

He watches me guzzle the still steaming tea with a bemused expression. He still hasn't touched his, I notice. "Don't burn yourself."

"If I burn the roof of my mouth, I'll heal in a few minutes. What if they got lucky, Aleks? We both know that even the strongest supes don't win every challenge. You're dealing with vamps who want to take down the Cadre. They're targeting you. And you want me to believe it's nothing?"

I think it finally dawns on Aleks that this is really bothering me. This is what he gets for settling down with a maternal delta she-wolf. Luna-touched or not, I'm not an alpha like Gem is and Julia was. I'm more submissive than anything, but I'm also protective and possessive of what's mine like any warm-blooded shifter.

And that's not all.

The idea that Aleks might lose his head the same way that Roman did *terrifies* me.

"Not all of the rebels are martyrs, Elizabeth. They're not willing to die for the cause, even if they're more than happy to end my afterlife. And those who fail earn the same fate as all traitors. If they miss once, I don't give them a second chance to try again."

"Then why?" I don't understand it. Aleks was a respected—and, admittedly, feared—part of the Cadre's leadership even before he took over as the head vampire in Muncie. "Why do they even bother?"

"It happens. Vampires live a long time. It isn't often that there's a power vacuum. It'll settle soon enough. When Roman..." He pauses. I get it, too. It's still so soon, the pain still so raw, and I'd only known Roman Zakharov for a couple of weeks. Aleks had known him for *two centuries*. "When that bękart killed him, it's the first time that there's been an opening in Muncie in a hundred years. Others think they're a better fit to lead than I am. Most keep that thought to themselves, but like those who wanted to remove Roman from the Cadre building, now they come for me."

Knocking his still untouched tea aside with the back of his hand, Aleks reaches across the table, holding his palm out to me. I know exactly what he wants and immediately place mine against his.

"Don't worry for me, księżyca. I didn't tell you because it pains me to see that stark look in your eyes. I have to do this. For Muncie. For *you*. I have to keep the protections in place. Without Roman, it falls to me. Let the assassins try to remove me. Without my patrols, I need something to keep me in shape."

He's teasing. My vampire is doing that for my sake, trying to keep the conversation light. It's a heavy conversation made all the more difficult with the specter of Roman hanging over our heads.

Because Aleks? He doesn't want to be the leader. He's never come out and said so, but it's obvious. A protector through and through, he prefers to be doing his nightly patrols, keeping

Muncie safe from any threats. But, as Roman's second in command, he was hand-picked to succeed him.

*You know what's expected of you...*

It was one of the last things Roman said to Aleks before Christian Morrissey swung his sword. It didn't take a genius to figure out what he meant. With the entire population of Muncie relying on the Cadre's protection, Roman was passing that responsibility onto Aleks.

With a heavy head, Aleks now wears Roman's old crown.

Roman wasn't always the head vampire. About a hundred years ago, when Muncie was a total Fang City, more vampires than humans, the Cadre was led by a vampire named Marcel Claret. He seemed to have been more of a dictator than a ruler, and one day he snapped. He went completely rogue. For the next three nights, he tore through half of the human population of Muncie, plus some of the vamps he lorded over.

Roman Zakharov and a small retinue of vampires—including Aleks—were visiting the United States from an Eastern European Cadre. When one of Claret's victims escaped the borders, they sent a call out for help. Roman answered it, came in with his clan, and executed Claret himself.

Aleks wasn't wrong when he said that vampires are long-lived. There are still pockets of vamps who believe that Claret is the type of leader Muncie should have. Not the brutal rogue, but the cold and calculating vampire who treated humans like chattel. He wanted to fuck them, feed from them, then discard them when he was done. The rebels giving Aleks trouble think that's the right idea.

In Muncie, there are a few blocks in the downtown area that are completely abandoned. The site of the former Cadre headquarters, it stinks of blood to this day, teeming with the ghosts of the humans who didn't deserve to die. It's where Roman confronted Claret, and where Christian brought Roman to be murdered two months ago.

A pang hits me in the chest. "I don't know what I'd do without you."

It's the end of April. I spent more time on the run, rejecting the pull I felt toward Aleks as my fated mate, than living with him as his lover. And yet... I mean it. I love him so Luna damned much that just hearing that he might've been killed—even if, logically, I knew he hadn't been—threw me and my wolf off.

He squeezes my hand. "You'll never have to worry about that. I'm not going anywhere."

I wish I could believe that.

Aleks strokes the top of my hand with his thumb. "Tell me. What can I do to make this easier for you? We're mates, you and I. Compromise. We compromise. I ask you to tell me if you're leaving the apartment and you do." He pauses. "Most of the time."

My cheeks heat up. No denying what that little dig's about. "I can't always stay in the apartment, Aleks."

"I know. I don't expect you to. But like you worry for me, I worry for you. And I know you can take care of yourself. You're my beloved. It gives me pleasure when you let me."

"Like when you have your vamps tailing me?"

"Tak." No shame. My vampire has no shame. "You're the most precious thing in the world to me. I'll do what I must to keep you safe."

See? That's the problem right there. He's protecting me like a good mate should. But what am I doing for him?

I sigh. "I know. I just wish I could do the same."

"You do." At the incredulous look I give him, Aleks's expression turns earnest. "Honestly. Just knowing that I have you to return to every night makes me careful. One traitor, three traitors, five… no one will stop me from getting back to you."

Aleks always knows the right thing to say. And maybe the lavender tea is finally kicking in, but I feel much better now.

Hang on—

"Five?" I squeak. "Have you had to fight *five* rebels all intent on taking your head?"

His pale green eyes glitter. "Not yet. But I promise you, if they try, when I'm triumphant, the first thing I'll do is let my beloved know that her male is safe. How's that for a compromise?"

I nod. Fair enough. "Sounds good to me."

---

Aleks is true to his word. For the next week he keeps me informed on every sneaky move the rebel vamps make. They haven't made an attempt on his life again since, but that doesn't mean that they aren't making life difficult for him.

Based on intel gathered by Cadre patrollers, there are only a handful of true rebels in Muncie. The ones who were bought off by Jack Walker while he was trying to track down Gem first, then me, were sympathetic to the cause, but money was their true motivation. The vamps who attacked Aleks? They're the ones who believe Muncie would be better off with a different leader.

I asked Aleks why he doesn't just have the identified traitors executed. It's basically a challenge, right? In a shifter pack, anyone who challenges the Alpha is disciplined. Depending on the slight, they might lose their place in the hierarchy or even their spot in the pack if they get exiled. If it's a challenge to their death, they could lose their lives.

Way I see it, anyone trying to go for my mate's head deserves to lose their own. My wolf, bloodthirsty when it comes to her mate, is champing at the bit to help.

But that's another difference between shifters and vampires. While Aleks understands where I'm coming from, they do things differently in the Cadre. As head vamp, his word is law, but he's not a dictator like Marcel Claret. Following in Roman's footsteps, he won't just execute a rival for the sake of it. They need to earn their deaths.

As far as I'm concerned, the second they decided Aleks wasn't worthy of leading Muncie, they had.

The upside to that, however, is that far more of his people approve of the job he's doing so far. Though Aleks misses his evening patrols, there are plenty of vamps who volunteer to keep Muncie safe. Roman's death sent a shockwave throughout the entire community, from the vamps to the donors, even to the humans who just thought of him as a prominent Russian businessman. To turn on Aleks was a slap in the face to Roman's memory, and most of the vamps were eager to pledge their loyalty to my vampire.

Then, one day when I'm home alone and desperately bored, I discover just what some of the other Muncie vampires think about Aleks—and me.

# CHAPTER 6
# TWO VAMPIRES AND FIVE UNFAMILIAR WOLVES

The aftermath of the last attack on Aleks is that I spend a lot more of my time inside.

At this point, I've completely given up on my idea to take a job down at Charlie's, and doing Tarot readings lost a lot of its luster when I know that Aleks might just interrupt if he wants to make sure that I'm doing okay. I think he's more worried about someone going after me to get to him than he lets on, and if it's one less worry for my mate, I figure it's for the best that I hang around the apartment until the two of us are a little more settled in our relationship.

Maybe if we were fully bonded things would be different. Sometimes, when Aleks looks at me, I get the idea that he's waiting for me to bolt. And, honestly, sometimes I don't know why I don't. As much as I love him, nothing is tying us together except for the promise of a forever bond. Until it's cemented, though, either one of us could reject it.

I wouldn't. But Aleks... what if he did? He says he loves me.

He calls me his. If that were true, wouldn't he want to bond me to him?

It's only been two months. Humans would think I'm being ridiculous. Only I'm not a human. I'm a shifter. The Luna wanted me to make Aleks my bonded mate last summer. If she was still here, listening to me, offering me advice, she'd be disappointed that I haven't yet.

I think about bringing it up to Aleks, and then I don't. He has so much on his mind right now. As the new leader, his attention is on Muncie. I get that. When he's with me, he's as attentive and loving a male as I could ever want.

I just... I wish he was with me more.

It's the middle of the afternoon. I slept in after Aleks slipped out to head to the Cadre building, and after getting up, preparing something for Aleks to eat for a change, and doing some light straightening up, I borrowed one of his paperbacks and sat down to read.

It couldn't hold my interest. With Aleks's scent filtering through my nose, calling to my wolf, I can't concentrate. Tossing the paperback down on the couch, I decide to head out onto the balcony to get some air.

The balcony outside of Aleks's apartment is technically part of the fire escape. Each floor has a grate landing just outside of the sliding door, plus a flight of iron steps that lead from level to level until it reaches the sidewalk at the back of the building.

It's a lot less crowded down below than it is in the front. Leaning against the railing, I breathe in deep, taking in the peace. It's early spring, and despite Muncie being an urban city, a few stray flowers are blooming somewhere nearby. They smell lovely.

I close my eyes as I lean on the railing. Oh, yes. This is just what I needed...

A door slams, breaking up my reverie. Two icy auras—much weaker than Aleks's, but still obviously vampire—are on the move. I probably wouldn't have even noticed if it wasn't for one obnoxiously calling out to the other, "Be careful, Peter. Watch your step. You know how inconsiderate dogs can be, and I'd hate for you to ruin your shoes stepping in the bitch's shit."

A muffled chuckle, as if whatever it was that the first haughty vampire had said sincerely amused the other, before Peter says, "Keep it down, Gino. You don't want Filan to hear you saying that."

At the sound of Aleks's last name, I freeze. My eyes pop open, but through the iron grate below my feet, all I can make out are two bobbing heads—one a brunet, the other with black hair—as the vampire males are walking casually down the sidewalk.

"What? It's not like he's not aware of it. He's always had this dog fetish. All the vampire females who'd kill to be on his arm, and this is... what? The third one he tossed a fang at?"

"Second," corrects Peter. "Remember? He tried to bag the Alpha's bitch, but even after he moved her into the building, he couldn't seal the deal. Poor guy. The blonde might be a dog, but that was prime pussy he missed out on."

"True. I would've taken her for a ride. Tapped her vein, too, but then I'd have asked Roman to throw her out."

"Shifters, right? Still. Filan seems to enjoy the brunette with the freaky silver eyes. You hear them, right?"

"Oh, yeah. When I can't find a female of my own, I rub one out to her moans and screams." He chuckles. "But if you tell anyone that, Peter, I'll deny it."

Peter laughs. I feel like I'm about to throw up.

I don't know which of my initial reactions is worse: embarrassment that these random vamps are intimately aware of what goes on in our bedroom, shame at just how pleased I am to hear that, according to Peter and Gino, Gem and Aleks never mated while she was his roommate, or disgust that Gino, at least, whacks off to the sounds of Aleks fucking me.

Is it terrible that I feel the most relieved about the shame?

I already knew that. Gem's the type of female who has no problem talking about her sex life, and she's told me on more than one occasion that Ryker's the only male she's ever been with. I don't even think she was trying to reassure me that she and Aleks were just friends. She was only talking about how she waited ten years for Ryker, and how it was worth every minutes to finally have him as her forever mate in the end.

Sometimes I wish I had waited for Aleks. Not that I regret the males I mated with when I was a lusty teenage she-wolf before I discovered the damage a touch of my hand could do, but when I remember Kyle? Yeah... I definitely regret my time with him.

But that's the thing. How can I judge Aleks for his past when I have my own? For a while it bothered me that he believed he was in love with Gem, but that was because she's my friend. They knew each other long before I met either one of them, but still. No one ever said that falling in love made a she-wolf rational.

And I must be out of my Luna-damned mind if I'm jealous of a female who died two centuries before I was born... but I am, and it all comes to a head when I hear one of the vamps—I think it's Peter—mention her name.

I suck in a breath and, cocking my ear, I strain to listen.

They've already gone two blocks away from the apartment building. Other voices are like static around them, but I'm determined. I have to know what they're saying.

And that's when Gino says, "Still. You gotta admit that *is* Julia all over again. Level-headed vamp going nuts for some dime a dozen shifter."

"True. You think he would've learned his lesson last time."

"Right? He's always gotta find these dogs who are trouble. Did you know he added an extra sunset spotter because Hannah swore she found wolf prints on the outskirts of the city? That's what happens when you let a shifter in. They're like roaches. Where there's one, you know there's more."

"It's good to be careful," points out Peter. They're far enough away now that I can barely hear him as he adds, "Don't forget what happened with Julia. When she died and Filan nearly went rogue before waging war on the shifters."

*What?* I grip the balcony railing so tightly, the metal groans. *Why?*

Aleks has never talked about her death, and I never asked. The most I know is that she died tragically before they could be bonded. She was a rare female alpha, so it must have taken a lot to kill her, and Aleks blames himself for not being there when she needed him.

He spent the next two centuries mourning his beloved, hoping he'd find another. He thought Gem might be his second chance because she was another alpha, and then there was me. The spitting image of Julia, only with silver eyes instead of gold.

He swears it isn't just our resemblance that made him realize I was meant to be his; that's just a weird quirk of Fate, though I secretly wonder if he's glad that I look just like her. He told me shortly after he admitted I was his beloved that the blood tells.

A hint of my blood and he'd know for sure that we were meant to be.

When the Luna was still talking to me, she whispered repeatedly that Aleks was mine. From the moment we met, I knew he was my fated mate. It just seemed perfect that I was also his beloved.

But even if I am? Will I ever measure up to the first one he had?

With my head spinning and my heart sinking, I stare unseeingly at the sidewalk below, unwilling to admit that, deep down, I already know the answer to that question.

Even with my impressive hearing, the two vampires are out of earshot now. The only way for me to hear the rest of their conversation is to get down to the ground and chase after them.

For a second, I almost do. It would be so easy to either dash down the fire escape or hop over the side of the balcony. Twelve floors might be too high for me to jump and land comfortably in a crouch, but in a pinch, a shifter should be able to. But then what? Do I honestly want to listen to Aleks's supporters talk about how I'm not worthy of being his mate? About how *amazing* Julia was, and how devoted he was to her?

It's not like I don't already know that.

I just... I didn't know he set off the last Claws and Fangs war because of her.

---

My first instinct is to run.

That's not unusual. I spent so long on the road, running at the first sign of trouble, that my wolf is primed to take off whenever my human half is struggling. As a lone wolf, I had to be careful of other scavengers, predators, even ferals. And those were just shifter threats. Most vampires find community among their own kind in Fang Cities, but not all. Rogues roam the countryside, too, and they could be just as dangerous as feral shifters. And humans... sometimes the non-supes were the biggest threats of all.

Those chatty vampires weren't trying to hurt me. I doubt they had any idea I could overhear their conversation at all. I only just popped out on the balcony to get some fresh air while they were strolling by. Doesn't change the fact that they're gossiping about Aleks and Julia is like a knife carving up my heart.

I don't care that they don't think that, because I'm a shifter, I'm a good enough mate for Aleks. I've thought the same thing myself. But to hear just how much he loved Julia? That he waged a *war* for her? How can I ever fucking compare?

I'm not her. I have her face, but that's it. Aleks says he knows that—he said as much to Roman when he accused Aleks of looking at me and seeing Julia—but I have my doubts. I thought... I thought I'd gotten past my jealousy for a dead female.

I don't think I have.

Sliding the glass door to the balcony closed behind me, I walk back into the apartment. Normally I don't mind the space. Except for Gem's lingering scent in her old bedroom, everything smells like a mixture of Aleks and me. When he's not home, sometimes I shift to my fur and just let it wash over my wolf.

Now, I almost choke on it.

Nothing changed. Not really. I already knew that Aleks had another beloved. Just like I knew that shifters aren't welcome here in Muncie. I got a pass because Gem worked it out with

Roman after she invited me to take over her townhouse; Gem was only allowed to stay in the first place because Aleks vouched for her in front of Roman. Apart from the two of us, shifters rarely come to the Fang City. On the rare occasion that they do, it's never for any good reason.

Take Jack Walker, for example. As powerful an alpha wolf as he was, he only made it past the border because he had a vampire fang around his throat. He was working with the rebel vamps to execute Roman. Though he sacrificed himself to do it—because, in the end, without his pack, all Walker wanted was a war of his own—his right-hand wolf was the one who swung the executioner's sword.

There hasn't been any sign of Christian since. Peyton, either. After I recovered from my surgery, Aleks wanted nothing more than to hunt the shifters down. Someone needed to pay for Roman's murder, and Aleks wanted to be the one to collect the cost. He couldn't leave me, though, and then he took over for Roman in the Cadre building.

Between the increased patrols around Muncie and Ryker sending more of his packmates to watch the edge of the Mountainside Pack's territory, I'd know if either of those two foul wolves were skulking around. After two months, I've convinced myself they got what they wanted when Roman died. Sure, they sacrificed Walker, too, but the war they promised with two prominent supe leaders dead didn't materialize. Peyton's threat to expose me? Nothing came of it. The vampires in Muncie might not want me here, but the majority of them respect Aleks's claim to me. And those that don't? They're too busy trying to lop off his head to pay a submissive she-wolf any attention—

—unless they want to compare her to Aleks's first beloved, I guess.

That's it. I have to get out of here. It's been days since I went further than the balcony, and though taking off, running away and leaving Aleks behind is out of the question, I need to go.

Luckily I have an open invitation to visit Gem in Accalia anytime I want. Apart from loyal Cadre vamps like Tamera, Leigh, and a few others, Gem is the only one he trusts to keep me safe when he can't. Ryker's territory is as protected as Muncie, so as long as I head straight up the mountain, I should be able to go for a run, see my friend, and maybe get my head screwed on straight.

The last time I needed relationship advice, Gem came to visit me down in Charlie's. With things in Muncie changing since then, and Ryker as overprotective of his mate as ever, it's probably not a good time to see if she wants to see me. Besides, I'm the one who needs the fresh air. It can't hurt for me to take the journey up to Accalia.

And I believe that all the way up until I cross out of Muncie and enter the stretch of gravel road broken up by dirt that exists between the vampire and shifter lands...

Before I left the apartment, I sent two texts: one to Aleks, one to Gem. I figured he would know within seconds of me stepping foot outside that I was going out, but I wanted him to hear it from me. See? Compromise. I informed Aleks I was going to visit Gem, but I promised I'd be home before he returned from the Cadre building.

Hopefully, by then, I'll be able to take that conversation I overheard, shove it inside a little box in the corner of my mind, and forget about it completely.

Claws crossed.

To Gem, I just gave her a heads up that I was coming to visit. Unlike Aleks—who can go hours between reading and responding to texts—she answered immediately with a smiley face emoji.

I didn't grab anything to bring with me, not even my deck of cards. My wolf wouldn't let me. Of everything in this world I now own, those cards are priceless to me. Even if I convinced myself that Aleks would be better off without me, I couldn't just run away. I'd have to return for my cards.

Staying in my skin since I don't have a change of clothes, I walk the length of Muncie, purposely ignoring the few vampires I catch watching me go. Aleks's apartment is only about a twenty-minute walk—at a shifter's pace, that is—before I reach the nearest exit to the Fang City.

The Fang City and the outer reaches of the Mountainside Pack just about butt up against each other. In between, there's a twenty-foot-wide stretch of broken road and torn-up dirt patches that separates them. I think of it as a no man's land, and the last time I came this way, Walker was waiting for me and Aleks.

The time before that? Peyton Slade had ambushed me after I visited Gem.

That's the downside to having a pack this close to the Fang City. Without any other shifters living in Muncie, when I scent wolf on the breeze, I immediately think of Mountainside. So far I've been wrong twice, and you think I'd have learned from my mistakes.

Nope.

Halfway across the abandoned, empty stretch, the pungent stink of unfamiliar wolf males slams into me. It's a mixture of musk and piss and dirty fur. That should've been my first clue that they weren't Gem and Ryker's packmates, but instead of turning tail and running back to the safety of the vamp city behind me, I kept jogging forward—

—until a small pack of snarling wolves dart out of the woods that border the road.

Technically, that's still part of the no man's land. Accalia doesn't actually start until you hit the base of the mountain the settlement is built on top of, and the woods are just a few feet outside of Ryker's territory. It's the perfect spot for a group of strange wolves to hide. Far enough that his alpha wolf wouldn't sense them from the mountain's peak, but easy to watch the open space that exists between Muncie and Accalia on the odd chance a lone wolf passes by.

Because I *am* alone. There are five of them, only one of me, and as they fan out, they're blocking my path ahead.

I stop short, hoping that they're just passing through. There's no way they were waiting for me, right? I'm just the unlucky she-wolf who ran into them. This has nothing to do with me being Elizabeth Howell, a Luna-touched female who's been hiding out in Muncie for these last couple of months.

And maybe if I keep telling myself that, I'll believe it. It kind of makes it difficult, though, when the grey wolf in the lead snaps his jaws at me before throwing his head back in a triumphant howl.

The four flanking him join in the howl, all while my wolf begins to tremble. Because that howl? Both of us recognize what it means.

These five were on the hunt and, look at that, they finally found their prey.

Ah, *Luna*.

# CHAPTER 7
# ALEKS TO THE RESCUE

If there was ever a time I wished that my goddess would answer me, it's now. But, just like the last two months, she's silent. I'm completely on my own.

Even worse, with my connection to her severed, I can't tap into her power. Sure, I can still sense bonds—all five of the prowling shifters are fully bonded, though three of the five have shaky mate bonds at best—but I can't do anything about them. My silver eyes have probably bled to black by now, fear overwhelming me. That's probably the most impressive thing about me at the moment. No Luna means I can't use her strength to warn these males back, and without my ability to snap bonds, threatening to take their mates from them won't work.

It would only be a bluff, and despite these five being an obvious mix of delta and gamma wolves who can't sense deception, I'm a terrible liar. They'll be able to tell regardless.

Besides, if they're really here because they've learned I'm

Luna-touched, I don't think admitting that I'm not any longer will work in my favor. It just erases any advantage I might have.

They're here for me. No doubt about that. I just... I don't know why. They're not alphas, so they can't be part of the Alpha collective that makes the laws for the rest of us shifters, and they're not Mountainside wolves. Every one of Ryker's wolves carries a bit of his scent with him, the mark of a pack's Alpha, but I don't recognize any of these guys.

There goes any hope that they're heading down from Accalia for some reason. Whoever they are, they've risked coming this close to both another pack's territory and a Fang City. Considering they're all in their fur, I'm thinking they've traveled a bit, plus it's obvious they've been waiting for an opportunity just like this.

I haven't left Muncie in two months. Until an hour ago, I had no plan to leave today. How long have they been here?

And what are the odds I can cross back into the Fang City before these five wolves are on me?

Someone must have seen me leave. Even if Aleks didn't read my text yet, one of the Cadre patrollers would have to be passing by sooner or later. The wolves can chase me into vamp territory, but they won't get too far.

Right?

I've never been the bravest of females. Given the chance to fight or flee, I'm going to run every single time. That's how I ended up being trapped in the Wolf District for so long. I was too afraid of the Wicked Wolf and what he would do if I attempted to leave that I never tried.

From the moment Roman first gave me a fang to wear, I didn't have anything to be afraid of in Muncie. He might not have marked me as an intended mate, but the fang meant I was under his protection. A vamp had to have a death wish if they tried to go up against the Cadre leader, and that was before Aleks actually started to press his claim that I was his beloved.

Now I have Aleks's. It's as much a mark of possession as it is protection, and though more than a few vampires had targeted my mate since he took over for Roman, I've been safe. The most I've had to deal with are curious looks and catty comments that I unfortunately overhear, just like Peter and Gino's conversation. To supes, mates are sacred. Besides, their issue is with Aleks, not me.

Of course, if they want Aleks to hurt, the easiest way to do that is to go for my throat. I have two knocks against me: I'm the leader's beloved and a shifter. I'd be a naive idiot to believe that they'd never come after me, but with the number of pro-Cadre vamps vastly outweighing the rebels, I've been safe so far.

I should've remembered that, with my "gift", it wasn't just the vampires I had to be afraid of gunning for me.

It's my own kind who are my biggest threat.

---

IT ALL HAPPENS SO FAST.

That's what they say, right? When you're in over your head and you don't know whether to stand your ground and fight or take off like a dog in the night, time seems to slow and then *wham*! It catches up so quickly, you hardly know what's happening.

Only I do. I just can't stop it.

At the last second, I decide to bolt back toward Muncie. With five wolves chasing me, it's better to get lost in the urban city than risk them running me down in the woods surrounding the base of Accalia. Dashing up the mountain is out, too. I'd never make it, and while Ryker would sense unfamiliar shifters once they crossed into his territory, even he wouldn't be able to stop them before they reached me.

The moment I turn on my heel, the shifters react.

I don't see them shift, but they must have because it's a claw-tipped hand that grabs onto my shoulder, trying to stop me from running. The points go from the front of my shoulder to the back, tearing my t-shirt and my skin. I gasp, but the slight pain spurs me to find some way to escape.

It doesn't work. I'd barely taken another step when a pair of human hands grab onto my upper arms, pulling me back until I'm slammed up against a bare chest.

I struggle. He shifts his hold. One hand clutches my throat, his other arm wrapped around my middle. His hold is unbreakable.

I'm caught.

The shifter behind me has a bruising grip. Dragging me like I'm a rag doll, he spins me around so that I'm facing one of his pals.

This male is *huge*. With closely cropped brown hair and a ginormous linebacker-type build, he's also naked. Of course he is. When shifters go from skin to fur, our human clothes don't survive. When we shift back, we're completely nude until we pull clothes on again. In a pack, nudity isn't a big deal for that very reason. Unless sexual attraction is involved, it doesn't mean anything.

Even so, I keep my gaze on his face. Considering his expression is one of disgust, his golden eyes dark with loathing, I probably would've been better off looking at his dick.

"What are you doing?" It comes out like a squeak. "Let me go!"

"No. You're an abomination," he sneers, flexing his fingers so I can see that his nails are pointed claws. "Too dangerous to be allowed to live."

"Why?" It's a gasp. I'm showing weakness in front of these shifters, but I don't care. "I didn't do anything to you."

"Not us, maybe. But we heard what you did at Oak Valley. Got proof. If you broke one bond, you can break a hundred. I worked hard to make my mate choose me. I'm not going to let you take her away. I'll gut you first, then the whole shifter community won't have to worry about a silver-eyed freak ruining our lives."

The shifter at my back tightens his grip on my throat. He's just about choking me, but I manage to focus on the brute in front of me. I search for his bond. It's one of the shaky ones, but now that I'm sensing it, I can tell that he's not the one who has his doubts. The mate he forced into choosing him is.

I've come across that too many times with my abilities. A mate must choose, but sometimes the choice isn't freely made. He forced her to mate him, and he's come all this way to kill me so that I can't break his bond.

I don't know this prick. Never met him before in my life, and odds are that I never would've come across him or his mate. And, yet, he still came here with murder on his mind. Plus, he brought backup.

And there's not a damn thing I can do to stop him.

Worse, he mentioned Oak Valley. He called me a silver-eyed freak.

That means—

"You... you know Peyton."

He doesn't deny it. "You should've kept your hands to yourself. Maybe then I wouldn't have to do this."

*You don't have to do this.*

This time, I can't get out the words. There's no point. He's made up his mind, and just like I've been afraid of my whole life, my "gifts" will be the death of me.

Black spots form at the edge of my vision. The shifter at my back is squeezing me tighter, holding me in the perfect position that the bigger male can gut me like he threatened. I try to suck in my belly when he looms closer, anything to avoid his claws, but it's hopeless.

I'm stuck.

The last thought I have is of Aleks. Of how much I love him, and how much it's going to destroy him when he finds out that I've been slaughtered by my own kind.

As if I conjured him in my final moments, I swear I feel the icy breeze of his powerful aura keeping me company. I revel in it, feeling like I'm not alone even as the big shifter rears back his arm, ready to slash at me with his claws.

He never touches me.

Vampires are fast. So are shifters, but our advantage with speed is when we have four legs. Vamps move so quickly on two legs, it's like they're flying. The icy aura becomes a full-blown gust of wind a split second before a single blur, followed by a pair, comes racing out of Muncie.

The lead blur slams into the shifter, sending him flying through the air. Before he even lands, Aleks materializes, hissing at the shifter behind me at the same time as he lashes his hand around my wrist.

In his surprise, the bastard at my back lets go of me. Aleks yanks me away from him, shoving me behind him, all before a loud thud echoes as the big shifter finally hits the ground a good ten feet away.

At the same time, the other two blurs catch up. Flanking Aleks, I recognize Dominic Le Croix. Next to him is a youngish-looking vamp with dark hair and a fierce expression.

The second the brute slams into the dirt, two of the wolves circling us lose their nerve and simply take off. With a point, Aleks spits an order out in French. Dominic tears off after the two wolves, the dark-haired vampire chasing him.

That leaves me and Aleks facing off against the three remaining.

Before, only two of the shifters had gone from fur to skin. Of the three that stayed shifted, two bolted as soon as the vampires appeared while the third joins his buddies in his two-legged form.

Big mistake, buddy. Freaking *huge*.

Now, I've seen Aleks fight a shifter in his wolf form not too long after he'd been shot. It was a massacre. I've seen what he can do to an Alpha, though my eyes were closed when he destroyed Jack Walker. I heard it, though, and saw the aftermath. There was nothing but bloody hunks of meat left when he was done. A fellow vamp? When pushed, Aleks popped Hector's head off of his neck like it was a dandelion being yanked off a stem.

Three deltas wearing nothing but their skin? Leaving their bellies vulnerable to a raging vampire's teeth and claws?

Three of his own people attacked Aleks and he walked away from it. If I hadn't known about that assassination attempt, I might've been worried. Now? He doesn't need my help, and when Aleks tells me to run back toward Muncie before launching himself at the biggest shifter, I say a wordless prayer to the Luna and watch with wild eyes as he rips them all apart.

They don't just stand there and take it, of course. A few seconds into the fight, the third shifter reverts back to his wolf, using his fangs to take a bite out of Aleks's side. I gasp, but my vampire doesn't falter. Ripping the wolf from his skin, he easily snaps the beast's neck before grabbing another shifter, tearing out his throat.

Blood flies. So does fur and skin and bits of Aleks's clothing. I get slapped in the face by something hot and squishy. Bile rises up in my throat and I force it down, wiping my cheek with the back of my hand.

If Aleks can take out these shifters for threatening me, the least I can do is bear witness to it.

The biggest shifter takes the longest to die, but Aleks is determined. Either that or he left him for last because he was the asshole who was going to be the one who killed me. Whatever his reason, Aleks goes after him only after the other two are dead, but like the others, he's no match for my vampire.

When he's done, he glances up from the mess he made, staring across the open road, eyes searching me out.

I gulp, but don't move an inch otherwise.

Ah, Luna. He is *furious*.

Vampires are the undead. Unless they've recently fed, they're chilled to the touch; even if they're full of blood, their auras are always icy. It's just part of their type of supe. But Aleks? The rage pouring off of his hunched body blasts me with heat even from this distance.

His chest is heaving. Beneath his shredded and claw-torn sweater, I can see the frantic rise and fall as he sucks in an unnecessary breath. His hands are fisted at his side, slick with blood, and his dampened curls are plastered to his forehead. He hasn't retracted his fangs yet, either. He looks every inch the killer that he is, and considering how bad I've fucked up, I shouldn't find that as sexy as I do.

His blood-red eyes are locked on me. He doesn't blink, and I'm helpless to break the stare.

Luna, I love this male. He came for me. He protected me. And, in doing so, probably just declared war.

All I can do is let out the softest, "I'm so sorry," in a shaky voice.

# CHAPTER 8
# BLOOD EXCHANGE

My shaky apology breaks the spell between us.

Punting the nearest shifter body fifteen feet away with the force of his kick, Aleks zooms toward me. He's standing inches away before the thud of the corpse hits the dirt again.

"Sorry?" he rasps out. "What do you have to be sorry for, Elizabeth?"

He can't honestly be asking me that. With three bodies strewn around us, the ground turned muddy with spilled blood, it's pretty obvious why I'm apologizing to him. All of this... and what's going to happen next... it's my fault.

But from the fierce look on his blood-spattered face, I know that Aleks is expecting an explanation. Worse, he's *demanding* one.

"You just had to kill three shifters. You're a vampire, Aleks. It doesn't matter why you did it. What if this starts another Claws and Fangs war?"

For centuries our types of supe have been embroiled in a never-ending war. Skirmishes had started up for less. What if we just inadvertently got Muncie involved in one?

"You think I care about that?" His hands are still fisted as Aleks raises one, pounding on his still heaving chest. "To należy do ciebie. I only care about you. They wanted to hurt you, mój księżyca. If I hadn't gotten to you in time, I might have lost you."

"You didn't," I say soothingly. I lay my hand against his pec. "I'm right here."

I'm not sure he can hear me.

His eyes are red and wild. "I can't lose you. Do you understand me, Elizabeth? Not won't. *Can't*. You're mine."

Aleks grips me by my shoulders. For a split second, I think he's going to shake me, to knock some sense in me, something—but he doesn't. He yanks me into him, holding me against his chest. His hands shift. One goes to the small of my back while Aleks threads the fingers of the other through my hair.

"Potrzebuję cię." His voice is guttural, a demand and a plea at the same time. His accent is even thicker as he translates for me, "I need you."

My vampire exterminated the shifters who attacked me, but not without any damage to himself. His blood perfumes the air with the others. Beneath the gaping tears in his clothes, his skin is working to knit back together. He'll need blood to heal, though. Lots of it.

We have blood bags at home. The Cadre can walk into any blood bank in Muncie and get a fill-up, and that's not counting the donors who would be honored to feed Aleks. Since we got together, he hasn't tasted any living blood but mine. Shifters are notoriously jealous; I hated the idea my mate might stick his fangs in any other female, and Aleks was visibly pleased when I told him I'd prefer he didn't. Feeding was rarely sexual, he explained, but with the right donor it could be. A good bite was the best kind of foreplay, and I've never shied away from feeding him just because.

Right now? He needs my blood more than I do. Aleks saved my life. He protected me. If he wants to drain me to replace what he lost, I'd let him.

But that's not what he does.

I expect him to tilt my head so that he can access my throat. He doesn't. Instead, with just enough pressure that I can't deny what he's doing, Aleks guides my head down, pressing my lips against the column of his pale throat.

"Lick me," he says softly, the rumble of his voice making his throat vibrate against my lips. "Taste me."

This isn't the first time that he's invited me to lap at his skin. Nothing turns him on faster than me suckling near his neck. It's my vampire's biggest erogenous zone, and already I can feel his cock stirring as I begin to nibble.

Anything to prove to Aleks that I'm still here. I'm still with him.

He groans, the ragged sound echoing in my ear. He's panting, too, and though we're surrounded by carnage, he begins to grind himself against my belly.

"Bite me, księżyca. Pierce my skin. Take my blood. Take my love."

I'm not a vampire. And yet... with Aleks, taking his undead blood inside me isn't such an abominable idea. To him, the blood exchange is just a way of showing a connection. Feeding from a donor represents life to him, but feeding from me? It's a way to celebrate our love.

I feed him whenever he needs it. But sometimes... sometimes he needs to feed me, and not just with food. He needs me to take his blood.

So I do.

Tapping into my skittish wolf, I borrow her fangs. My blunt human teeth develop knife-like points as I sink them into the side of his neck. It isn't easy, and I'm probably tearing more of his skin than I should, but Aleks doesn't seem to mind. His groan becomes a throaty moan as he lowers his hand, cupping my neck as he keeps my mouth clamped against him, feeding me his meaty, tangy blood.

Again, I use my wolf. My human side wants to hurl when it thinks about the chilled blood I'm swallowing, but my wolf's stomach can handle it. She knows this is something our mate needs, and if there's one thing she'll always be willing to do, it's satisfy our mate.

My head is angled just enough that I can breathe from my nose otherwise I might've been smothered by Aleks's insistence that I drink from him. Only when the flow starts to become a trickle do I stop sucking.

I have to. If I keep going, he'll be drained and I can't allow that.

Pushing against his chest, he reluctantly releases me. I press a kiss to the hollow of his throat, then straighten up. When I look at his eyes again, I'm so freaking relieved to see that they've mellowed to their familiar sea-foam green color.

As pale as he usually is, though, he's gone as white as a sheet of paper. Purple shadows underline his eyes. His cheeks are sunken in, bones jutting out.

He looks half-starved.

I tug on my shirt. Aleks hisses when he notices that, like his clothes, it's been torn by the shifter's claws. So has my shoulder. My regenerative properties have already kicked in, so the marks are halfway closed over, but they're still there and, oh, my mate doesn't like that.

"Don't worry about them," I say hurriedly, baring my throat toward him. "I took your blood. Take mine. You need it."

"They did hurt you," rumbles Aleks. His eyes are suddenly blazing red again. "If I had the power to, I'd bring them back to life just to have the pleasure of killing them all over again."

Honestly? That is quite possibly the sweetest thing anyone has ever said to me. "Thank you, but I think once is enough. And unless I figure out how to do some necromancy of my own, I might lose you if you run out of blood."

A slight smile tugs on Aleks's lips. "I'm already dead, księżyca. I've risen once before."

"That's my point. Who says you will again? Now get over here. It's your turn to feed."

"I will. But, first, we have to discuss something."

Now? "Can't it wait? You need to feed, Aleks."

"This is important to me. I promise you, I'll be fine. But the next full moon is in eight days."

I knew that. As a shifter, I know the Luna's cycle intimately. But I never thought he paid close enough attention. Then again, I should've known better. When it comes to me, Aleks is aware of *everything*.

But I have no idea where he's going with this right now. "Okay."

"You're mine, Elizabeth," he says again. "Your body. Your heart. I need your soul. I need you to accept me as your forever mate. When your Luna rises again, I'm asking you to make me yours."

I… I don't know what to say. For two months, we've been dancing around the idea of mate bonds. When I finally confessed to him that he was my Luna-given fated mate, he knew that we would only be fully bonded when we performed the Luna Ceremony on the night of the full moon.

Our first full moon, I was in the hospital. The second, Aleks was conveniently occupied at the Cadre building. I just figured he wasn't ready to make this thing between us permanent, especially since he's never brought up making me his blood-bonded mate.

I figured it was a vamp thing. Most shifters are fully mated within the first Luna cycle after meeting their mate; chosen or fated, it didn't matter, the Luna guided us to cement the bond as soon as possible. Immortal vamps have a lot more time—and a lot less of an animalistic nature—so they don't jump right in.

So why is he deciding that this moon is the one where we'll be mated? Because I almost died?

Because he almost lost a second beloved?

Two centuries later and Aleks still harbors guilt over his Julia's death. His biggest regret is that she died before he bonded her to him.

Is that what happened just now? He saw me caught by the big shifter and thought it was happening all over again?

Does it matter?

I don't know. I really, really don't.

In shifter terms, what Aleks just did is the equivalent of him proposing to me. Regardless of his reasons why, I should be giddy that my fated mate is ready to take me from his intended mate to his forever… but I'm not. I can't be.

With the Luna gone quiet for me, how can I get her blessing? Without it, there is no Luna Ceremony.

I want to explain. When I'm not quick to agree to Aleks's offer, he frowns, and I want to tell him that I'm not rejecting him again. I just... I can't. Not right now.

"Elizabeth," he begins, but that's all he says before his whole demeanor changes. The dangerous edge to his aura comes back as he snags me by my upper arm, pulling me into him right as he whirls around.

I sense their approach a moment after Aleks does. Together, we stare down the road, waiting for the two auras to get closer. He relaxes fractionally when it's obvious they belong to vampires instead of shifters, and he nods when Dominic and the dark-haired vamp—looking no worse for the wear—come gliding toward us.

Aleks tucks me even closer against his side, as though he can't stand the idea of letting me go for a second. "Tell me they didn't escape."

Once he reached us, the younger vampire began to gape in ill-disguised interest at the bite mark I left on Aleks. Blood dribbles down his throat, staining the hem of his formerly cream-colored sweater. The bite's not healing just yet, due to how much he already lost, and the white skin around the messy puncture wounds is an angry red.

And I get it. He probably never expected to see a bite mark on his leader. Vampires can only survive on live blood, from either a human or a shifter. None of his people would have any reason to drink his blood, and I'm a shifter and that's not something we do. We bite, yes, claw and mark our mates, but we don't drink their blood.

Unless, I guess, our mate turns out to be a vampire.

Dominic throws him a quelling look. "Everett," he snaps, his French accent obvious in his annoyance. "Answer Aleksander."

Everett flushes. "Sorry. No. They didn't escape. We got them, sir. They won't attack your beloved again."

"Dobrze." Aleks's grin reveals the points of his fangs. "*Good.*"

---

Aleks gives Dominic and Everett orders to clean up the blood and the bodies, then takes my hand in his and walks me back into Muncie without a second look behind us.

We're covered in blood. Aleks more than me, but when I ignored his order to run back into the city, I guess I got caught in the splash zone. That's not counting the... stuff that slapped me in the face, either. We're both a mess.

Luckily, walking around like that doesn't get the same reaction in a Fang City as it would in a human community. Vamps scent that it's shifter blood and are awed at their leader's prowess. Donors are already aware that, despite most vampires appearing gentile and noble unless they're rogues, supes are fierce creatures; it's not unusual for our kinds to fight to the death. And the humans who live in Muncie and still manage not to discover that vampires and shifters are real? They just duck their heads and keep walking, chalking it up to something else weird about their city.

Besides, Aleks is the head of the Cadre. To humans, he's the CEO of the Cadre building, and the most powerful male in Muncie. Rich, powerful people are different than regular folks. They're definitely not about to call the cops on Aleksander Filan, especially since law enforcement in Muncie goes right through the Cadre.

Aleks has his arm slung around me as we walk home. Knowing how uncomfortable I am with the apartment building's elevator, we climb the fire escape together, me in front while Aleks holds tightly to my hand as though afraid to let go.

I remember the discussion between those two vamps down below from a couple of hours ago—hours that seem like years between now and then—and am glad to see that the back entrance to the building is empty when we approach the fire escape. After that, I completely push it out of my mind until Aleks and I have both stripped, and we're standing under the spray of water in the shower together.

He insisted. The blood had dried, sticky on our skin, and the rusty tang was becoming rotten. We needed to be cleaned, but since he was still eager to keep me close, that meant showering at the same time.

Aleks washes my hair, using the tips of his vampire claws to massage my scalp. Grabbing a washcloth, I soap up his body, washing off all the blood from him. I can't help but notice that his cock begins to stir as I make slow swipes over his back, his chest, his ass, but since he's intent on making sure that we're both clean, I purposely avoid reaching for his semi just yet.

Just as I'm reaching up on my tiptoes to wash the blood from Aleks's curls, though, I regret not distracting him by going for his cock when I had the chance. Even as the shower spray runs in pink-tinged rivulets down his sculpted face, his expression is searching as he finally turns the topic of our conversation to what happened earlier.

"Tell me, Elizabeth. Why were you so worried about starting a Claws and Fangs war?"

I nearly slip. Between my shifter reflexes and Aleks's speed and strength, I don't fall, but the way I jumped when he broke the silence with that question? I almost landed on my ass on the shower floor.

His hands are on my elbows, keeping me steady. He frowns. "Are you okay? I know what you saw tonight... it's a lot. I try to keep you away from that side of me, but you're my mate. I'll do anything to keep you safe."

I press my palms against his slick chest. "I love that about you," I tell him honestly. "My wolf... we love that you're a protector. A provider. Never apologize for that, Aleks. I fell for a vampire. If I was put off with a little blood, I never would've come to live in a Fang City."

I meant it as a little tease. Tonight's been so traumatic, and Aleks looks so solemn, I want to show him that I *am* a shifter. I might not be an alpha, but I'm made of sterner stuff than he gives me credit for.

Aleks, though? I should know better. When it comes to me, my safety, and our relationship... he doesn't like to tease.

Bowing his head, he presses his forehead against mine. The water is running clear now, but neither of us makes a move to leave the shower just yet as he murmurs, "It's you. When I thought they might hurt you before I could get to you... it brings out the monster in me. Poczwara. I'll tear a hundred throats before I let anyone harm a hair on your head."

Normally a confession like that would have me melting against him. But after what I overheard earlier... it's not a confession so much as a declaration of war against my enemies.

And since my biggest enemy seems to be shifters, and Claws and Fangs wars always feature vampires and shifters on opposite sides, it sounds to me like Aleks might not mind repeating history for my sake.

I can't let him.

"Don't," I tell him earnestly. "I don't want another war. I don't want you to start another one again. Not for me."

# CHAPTER 9
# THE BEST DISTRACTION BEFORE DESPAIR

He pulls back just enough that he can look into my eyes. "Why would you say that?"

"Because you did it once before," I blurt out. I didn't mean to, but when I meet his gaze, it's like he's pulled the truth right out of me. "For Julia."

That's what makes this whole situation so fucking awful. I already look just like her. I didn't die—only because Aleks saved me in time—but am I doomed to live her life regardless? Same beloved. Same spark for another battle in our ancient war.

His eyes flash, turning red in a heartbeat. It's the only sign that my words got to him since he sounds almost curious, rather than angry, when he asks, "How did you know that?"

I could lie to him, but he'll be able to tell. "I was out on the balcony," I admit. "I didn't mean to eavesdrop, but I heard... enough."

If I thought that would placate my vampire, I was way wrong.

"Tell me. What exactly did you hear?"

To the best of my ability, I play it back for him. In hindsight, I probably should've toned down the "dog" and "bitch" comments, and telling him about the one vampire who masturbates to the sound of our sex might've been a mistake, but Aleks asked and—for better or worse—I answer.

When I'm done, Aleks says in an almost too-conversational tone, "Would you recognize their voices again if you heard them?"

Uh-oh. I know that look. In Aleks's head, he's already plotting to take theirs.

Good thing I pointedly neglected to mention that I remember their names.

"It's fine, Aleks. They didn't know I was listening."

"Księżyca, my love. On more than one occasion when Gem was living with me, I had to hear about how pungent a vampire's scent is to a wolf's nose. And while I adore you and how you smell, there's no way they didn't catch your scent on the breeze if you were outside. There's no way they missed your heartbeat. Vamps recognize shifters because we hear both: you and your wolf's. Believe me when I tell you that they knew very well that you were there." His cultured voice goes hard. "And they will pay for insulting you."

Okay. He's probably right, and I probably was fooling myself when I tried to believe that it was one big coincidence that I overheard that particular chat. Oh, well. It's not like I didn't already know that most vamps don't want me here, even before I moved in with Aleks.

Does that mean I want my vampire going out and avenging me because my feelings got a little hurt? No. I've seen enough bloodshed today. The shifters might've deserved it—they were definitely going to kill me before Aleks returned the favor—but I don't need a pair of catty vampires' death on my head.

Avoiding his steely stare, I glance down. The semi I noticed before is pointing right up at me, giving me the perfect way to change the subject.

I grab it. Aleks sucks in one of his unnecessary breaths, but he immediately stops talking.

Good one, Elizabeth.

I give him a stroke. He murmurs something low in Polish I can't quite catch over the running water.

I squeeze the head. There's no denying the way he grates out, "Księżyca," like that.

That's when I let go. Before he can groan at the loss of my touch, I sink down to my knees and grab him by the base, bringing his cock close to my mouth.

"Oh, I see. This is your way of distracting me," he accuses in a throaty voice. He doesn't seem to mind, though, since he spreads his legs, bracing them against the tile as he gives me access to his erection.

I dart out my tongue, swirling it around the sensitive head of his cock. A drop of pre-cum has already beaded there; sometime during our shower, his semi became a full-blown hard-on, and he's already so turned on I know it won't take much to make my vampire explode.

In between quick licks, I admit impishly, "I am. Is that a problem?"

"Otwórz się dla mnie."

I'm nowhere near fluent in Polish, despite my attempts to learn Aleks's language. Still, he's been my lover for more than two months. I can translate that easily.

*Open up for me.*

Normally he says that when he's getting ready to push this beautiful cock inside of me. Then again, I guess that's what he means now because, as I part my lips, he slowly begins to feed me his hard length.

I lick. I suck. I nibble. He's already called me out on distracting him, but it's more than that. Just like he needed that connection with me—he needed me to taste his blood—I'm dying to have him inside of me no matter what. I want to make him feel good. I want to show him that I might not be able to slaughter his enemies, but as his mate, he can come home and I'll worship his body like the god of a vampire he is to me.

After all, he does the same for me.

His fingers are threaded through my wet hair. The way his body is bowed over me as I encourage him to slowly fuck my mouth shields me from the shower spray. The water is warm on my back, Aleks's icy aura giving me chills as I hollow my cheeks and take him deep.

He groans, and I smile with my mouth full of cock. After a few more sucks, I let the head slip out from between my lips with a barely audible *pop,* taking hold of the base with a tight fist as I continue to stroke him.

"Elizabeth," he murmurs softly. "Mój księżyca."

I want him to finish inside of me, so when he starts bucking his hips into my fist and I know he's close, I start sucking on him again until he shoots into my mouth. His come is chilled, just like my vampire, and that's a sure sign that he needs to drink.

Once I swallow, I wipe the corner of my mouth with the back of my hand, then hold it out to Aleks. Instinctively knowing what I want, he helps me back to my feet, then tugs me against him.

"It's your turn, baby," I murmur, tossing my wet hair away from my neck. It hits my back with a slap, flinging water everywhere, but I could give a shit. Cocking my head, baring my throat to him, I tell him, "Taste me."

I don't have to ask twice. His fangs are buried deep in me before I even finish the last syllable.

Clinging to Aleks, I feed him, and when he gets hard again as my blood fills him, I guide his cock to my entrance so that he can fill *me*.

After that, we stay in the shower until the water runs cold, we're both more than satiated, and Aleks has fucked my insecurities about Julia Złoty away from another night.

---

I've got six missed calls from Gem when I wake up the next morning, plus even more messages asking me about what happened last night.

I'm not surprised she knows. After we got back to the apartment, Aleks sent her a text that I had to postpone my visit to Accalia. Once I was finally asleep, he must've called Ryker to inform the Alpha that five shifters attacked me on the land between our two settlements.

He wouldn't have had a choice. Being leader means taking responsibility for his people, and that goes the same for a pack Alpha. Those wolves weren't from Mountainside, but they were shifters going after one of their own. The nearest pack needed to be informed, especially since an attack on me wasn't just the small group trying to eliminate one Luna-touched female, it was an attempt on the life of the Cadre leader's beloved.

Ryker, of course, would've informed Gem as soon as he had

the chance; she admitted as much in a few of her texts. The latest one came through hours ago, but she was livid. I get the feeling that what Aleks, Dominic, and Everett did to those assholes was a kindness. If Gem had gotten her claws on them first, she would've played around with her prey for a while instead of giving them a quick death.

I've seen her fight, too. And while she can be a little more merciful, her go-to move is sticking her claws inside a chest and tickling a challenger's heart. She's tough, and I'm so glad to have her in my corner.

Of course, it wasn't always like that. The first time she thought I might use my "gifts" against her, she had the points of her claws to my throat before I could blink. Only our mutual hatred for her birth father spared me then. Friendships have been built on less, and even if she wore Aleks's fang around her throat before me, I still adore her.

I adore her even more when I call her back and am treated to a list of all the things she would've done if those shifters had stepped a single paw on Accalia territory before they ambushed me.

There's only one problem. Aleks might have informed Ryker that he had no choice but treat the threat on his beloved as seriously as possible—executing the shifters immediately—but there are packs missing their males right now. Eventually it'll come out that they were killed by vampires. Aleks had every right to fight them; even a shifter will admit that a male has the right to take down any foe threatening his mate, bloodsucker or not. But, she tells me, rumblings are beginning to grow among other packs that can't help but wonder if there was more to Jack Walker's death back in February than Aleks let leave his territory.

The Wicked Wolf was hated by most of our kind, but he was

strong. Powerful. That meant he was also respected. It's a shifter thing. It's how Walker managed to hold onto the Western Pack as long as he did. He killed anyone who threatened his rule, and only lost it because he was too cocky to take a female alpha seriously.

Aleks killed Walker for the same reason as those five shifters: because he was targeting me. The shifter community would understand that—if they knew that the head vamp in Muncie had a she-wolf for a beloved. But, Gem admits, they don't. Somehow that never came up.

I'm glad. The fewer people who know about me, the better. After I get off the phone, promising that I'll come to see her soon, I sink down on Aleks's settee and pray to the quiet Luna that those five dead shifters are the only ones who did.

As if Fate is determined to prove me wrong, though, I have about twenty minutes to hope that maybe everything will be okay again before my world comes to a screeching halt.

---

I'M ALONE WHEN THERE'S A KNOCK AT THE DOOR.

Aleks left the apartment shortly after midnight last night. Once we finished our extended shower, he waited until I had eaten and was lying in our bed before he told me that he was calling an emergency meeting at the Cadre building for every vamp that worked under him. The only exceptions were the increased patrollers he had Dominic set up to make sure that the five shifters didn't have any other buddies sniffing around, but he needed to warn his people what happened just outside of the Fang City.

He swears to me that I don't have to worry about another

Claws and Fangs war, but it seems to me like he's preparing for one anyway. I don't mention it, though, because I finally got his eyes to revert back to their pale green. To keep them from turning red again, I'll go along with it.

He told me he'd be back soon, that I should get some rest. I tried to. The adrenaline from the night before had long worn off, and the endorphins from mating Aleks in the shower had made me dozy. Too bad they disappeared as soon as his icy aura was out of my reach.

For most of the night, I couldn't sleep. And, like always, when I couldn't sleep, I obsessed over my vampire. It got worse when I woke up and saw that he still wasn't back by morning, and I kept Gem on the phone longer than I normally would have to distract myself from how much I miss him.

So when I hear a knock at the door and, reaching out with my wolf, catch the scent of a vampire just on the other side of it, I wonder if it's Aleks. The aura is vaguely familiar, though it lacks the punch of attraction I feel when he's near, but I don't care. I want it to be him so bad, I look past that.

I shouldn't have. When I open the door, I find a freckle-faced vampire with pale skin, a shock of red hair, and soft grey eyes. He's holding a stack of mail in his hand.

"For you, Miss Elizabeth," he says, holding them out to me.

I try to hide my disappointment. Morgan is a freshly turned vamp. A former donor who was given a promotion when the female vamp who favored him offered to make him immortal, he works for the Muncie post office. He also lives on the first floor of Aleks's apartment building, and he takes it upon himself to hand-deliver mail and packages to every tenant in it.

One of the perks of being a lone wolf is the lack of a paper trail. I don't get mail. I have no credit so I never get offers for a loan, a card, or even a bill. No family sending me Christmas cards. I'm as off the grid as it is possible to be, and I have been since I was eighteen.

So why is the handwritten letter on the top addressed to me?

Worse, when I thank Morgan before closing the door again, then lift the letter up to my nose and take a sniff, I notice that it stinks of shifters.

That can't be good.

My stomach sinks. One part of me wants to throw it in the trash. Like, if I don't open it and read it, I don't have to worry about what it says.

Maybe in a fantasy world I could do that. But this is the real world, and it's gritty and bloody and *mean*.

Plopping Aleks's mail on the counter, I tear open the envelope. My breath catches in my throat when I see the block letters on the form, my heart racing when I catch my name, followed by one that's equally as familiar.

And then I read the rest, and my world as I know it comes crashing down.

**ACCUSED:** ELIZABETH HOWELL
**ACCUSER:** PEYTON SLADE

**ATTENTION:** ELIZABETH HOWELL

**YOU ARE HEREBY SUMMONED TO MEET WITH THE ALPHA COLLECTIVE OF THE UNITED STATES OF AMERICA. YOU MUST TRAVEL TO THE NORTHERN WINDS PACK WITHIN 24 HOURS OF RECEIPT OF THIS MISSIVE. THAT ALPHA WILL ACCOMPANY YOU TO THE GATHERING WHERE YOU WILL BE PUT ON TRIAL TO ANSWER TO THE ACCUSATIONS MADE AGAINST YOU.**

**SIGNED,**
THE ALPHAS OF THE U.S.A

# CHAPTER 10
# LET ME IN

Two minutes ago, I was wondering how much longer it would be until Aleks returned from the Cadre building. I wanted to feed him again—both the meal I prepped, and a little blood for sustenance—and show him just how much my wolf appreciates him as our protector and mate.

But this letter…

All I can think about now is getting the heck out of Dodge. Or, in this case, *Muncie*.

I can't stay here. That much is obvious. For a couple of hours, I might've convinced myself that the five shifters who ambushed me last night were a fluke. With them dead, no one had to know what happened. There'd be no war, and so long as Peyton kept her mouth shut, I wouldn't have to worry about the Alpha collective discovering what I used to be able to do.

Glancing down at the letter in my hand, I almost want to cry.

Because now? I *do* have to worry about it.

I can almost guess what happened. Peyton didn't just tell

those five that I had the ability to break mate bonds with the touch of my hand. She must have gone through with her threat to inform the Alpha collective. Somehow the small shifter group was the advance guard. Whether they knew the collective would summon me to one of their gatherings or they wanted to get to me before I could have a chance to plead my case—and tell them that that part of my "gift" was gone—it doesn't matter. They came, and my vampire slaughtered them for it.

And now I have an official summons telling me that I have twenty-four hours to present myself to the Alpha of the Northern Winds Pack.

I'm familiar with him. Of course. Lone wolves need to have a handle on shifter politics to survive, and I'm no exception. I fell out of touch during the two years I was trapped in the Wolf District, but my five months on the run updated the dossier I kept in my panicked mind. Dash Harrigan has a reputation for being a tough yet fair Alpha. If he's the one chosen to be responsible for making sure I get to the Alpha gathering, I at least am looking at a fair trial.

The Northern Winds Pack is about three hours away from Muncie by car, a little longer if I'm in my fur. I can easily make it by the twenty-four-hour deadline.

Too bad I have no intention of going.

Why should I? If I tell them that the Luna has gone silent and my "gifts" are gone, will that save me? Or will they decide I'm still too much of a threat and put me down because there's a chance that they might return? Either way, I can't risk it. I managed to avoid being outed to the collective for almost twelve years. If I go on the run again, I can't see why I wouldn't be able to stay one step ahead of them.

The problem is that Peyton knows where I am. The Alphas,

too, obviously. How else could they have sent a letter to Aleks's apartment for me? If I stay, I'm only putting my vampire in danger.

Crumpling the letter in a shaky hand, I think about what Gem said. It isn't just vampires as a whole that are putting shifters' backs up against the wall. They mentioned Muncie specifically. And, sure, she might try to convince me that they're just grumbling because word got out that it was a Muncie vamp who finally ended the Wicked Wolf's reign of terror, but we both know why Aleks killed Walker.

As much as he wanted revenge for what Walker put him through, Aleks challenged the former Alpha over me. He slaughtered three of the five shifters—leaving the other two to his vampires—for me. And if I tell him I'm terrified because the Alpha collective is coming after me now, he'll do anything he can to protect me from the other shifters.

I don't doubt that. From the moment Aleks claimed me as his beloved, he's put me above anyone else. He'd fight the whole Luna-damned world for me, but even Aleks has his limits. He can't stop every Alpha in the United States, and I would lose him if he tried.

*I'll tear a hundred throats before I let anyone harm a hair on your head...*

He won't forgive me for running without telling him. I understand that. He'll think we can figure this out together—but I know better. I'm a lone wolf. I always have been. I've been fooling myself all along that I could have Aleks, but I have to admit, while I'm his, he's never really been mine.

If I'm going to lose him anyway, I have to at least know that he made it. That he survived.

It's my turn to protect him. And if that means running and leaving him behind, that's what I'm going to have to do.

I don't second-guess my decision; running away from a problem has always been my first instinct, and this time is no different. Instead, shoving the sweaty, crumpled letter into my back pocket, I race for the bedroom I share with Aleks. My wolf lets out a mournful whine when the scent of our mating hits me, but she doesn't fight me. We both know this is for the best.

Grabbing the duffel I've kept stowed in the closet, I stuff it full of as many clothes as I can fit. My deck of tarot cards go in the front pocket. Hurrying to the kitchen, I grab some non-perishables in case food is hard to find, and though I think about taking one or two trinkets that I can flip for cash, I don't. I have my cards. If I need money, I'll earn it.

I'm already going to hurt Aleks enough by leaving without a word. I won't steal from him before I go.

My nerves are ratcheted as high as they can go. As I glance around, taking in the apartment for one final time, my wolf is up, pacing around inside of me. At least while I'm in Muncie, I'm going to have to be in my skin, but once I break out of the Fang City, I'll have to go fur, lugging my duffel behind me.

I don't leave a note. What can I say? That I love him, and I'm only leaving to save him? Maybe it's a good thing we didn't make it to the next Luna. I would've only had to reject him anyway when I couldn't ask and receive her blessing to make him my mate, and if I had? He never would let me go.

When he gets word that I snuck out of the city without telling him, I highly doubt he will.

Unless...

I don't want to do it. It's leaving me unprotected from those who might jump at the chance to do Aleks harm, and even if that's the more practical reason to leave the fang necklace in place, my heart aches at the idea of taking it off. It's a sign of Aleks's love and affection for me. Since I accepted my place at his side, I haven't removed it.

If I take it off now, my heart might ache. But Aleks? I think it'll break his.

I don't have any other choice. There's magic in a vampire's fang. I wouldn't be surprised if he could use that to follow me since, when it's on, my scent takes on some of his licorice notes. He'd find me, and I would be helpless to reject him again.

The only reason I can right now is because I'm more afraid of losing Aleks permanently than I am him casting me aside as his beloved. I've had months to get used to the idea of never truly claiming my vampire. But the idea of him dying? Of him losing a challenge and just being gone from this world?

I can't live in one that doesn't have Aleksander Filan in it. It's as simple as that.

Even if I'm not his bonded mate. Even if he finds another shifter female to pamper and flatter and protect… I don't care. If only for a little while, he was mine, and it's my turn to take care of him.

With shaky fingers, I reach behind me and unclasp the gold chain. Once it's off, I place it gently on the glass table in the living room so that he won't be able to miss it—and that's if he didn't instinctively sense that I took it off.

After that, I heft up my duffel, slide open the glass door to the balcony, and start down the fire escape.

The clock's started. Aleks and the rest of the Cadre are probably still occupied. I've got to be quick, but this might be the only chance I'll have to leave before I bring more trouble to Muncie.

So I do.

---

I NEVER EXPECTED IT TO BE SO EASY TO LEAVE.

With most of the Cadre vamps off the streets, the ones who pass me by might not recognize me without Aleks's fangs. I have to ignore a few prejudiced comments about me being a shifter, and a couple of come-ons from vamps and humans who don't know or care that I can go furry—and, Luna, did I not miss *that* —but other than that, they leave me alone for the most part.

It helps that my duffel is specifically designed for shifters. Instead of looking like an oversized gym bag, it's charmed so I can carry it when I'm in my two-legged form and my four-legged shape and it appears almost like a big purse. Though my anxiety is spiking and it takes everything I have not to just bolt, I take a leisurely stroll around Muncie, going a roundabout way to the borders. I specifically avoid the section of no man's land from last night for a hundred different reasons, least of all because I'm terrified that there might've been more than five shifters hunting me.

I have every reason to be frightened, and I prove that almost immediately after I leave the sanctuary of the Fang City.

The second I left, my stroll became a sprint. I don't bother stripping off my clothes before I give control over to my wolf; I put on a cheap outfit on purpose so I could afford to lose it. I run faster as a wolf, and no matter how Aleks reacts, I need to put as much space between me and Muncie as soon as possible.

That's not the only reason I pour on the speed. I've barely made it the first ten miles before I realize that someone is following me.

Vampires have a notable base scent. So do shifters. My kind of supe carries an earthy smell, something unique to each of us, and, yes, just a hint of wet dog for some reason. No self-respecting wolf will admit it, but it's true, and I almost stumble as I get a snout full of the shifter chasing me.

One of my "gifts" that I actually didn't mind was an ability to shield my scent and the scents of those near me. I don't know why, when the Luna went silent, she didn't take that gift away. So frantic to escape Muncie, it never even occurred to me to cover up my scent until I realize that there's a shifter on my tail.

I don't know who it is. They're not familiar to me, but it doesn't matter. Any shifter chasing me is someone I want to dodge.

Here's hoping that I can.

---

I DON'T KNOW WHERE I AM, ONLY THAT I'VE MANAGED TO avoid both humans and supes—including the shifter who trailed me across at least two state lines.

I didn't know where I was going. The only important thing was going in any direction but north so that I could bypass the Northern Winds Pack. Considering I'm on the East Coast, I ran west and hoped for the best.

My pads are bloody. I've lost clumps and clumps of white fur because I've purposely kept my path to any densely wooded areas when possible. I tore through the food I carried with me that first night when I pushed my wolf to exhaustion after I caught the hint of the shifter on the breeze behind me. I've gotten maybe six hours down total for sleep, and I ate whatever small prey animals my wolf was quicker than.

It's been three full days. The first night, I expected Aleks to appear behind me. Vamps are fast, so I had to be faster if I wanted to outrun him. The longer I went without sensing his icy aura there, the more I had to admit I was right. Leaving Aleks's fang behind, running out on him without a word, no sign of him near... he was letting me go.

I expected that. So tell me why it hurts so Luna-damned much to know I was right?

Those twenty-four hours have come and gone. Once their imposed deadlines passed, I worry about running into any shifters. I don't know how far rumors about my abilities have gotten, but it's a safe bet to believe that, since the Alphas all know, so do their packmates. Any shifter I meet could sell me out to the collective.

No, thanks.

I can't go on like this, though. By the third evening, my wolf is getting ready to collapse. I need food. Safe shelter. *Sleep*. I need somewhere to hide because constantly running isn't sustainable. If I can find a cave or someplace to cover me, I might be able to hunker down again and plan my next move.

For once I think the Luna has truly blessed me; it's about freaking time, considering how much I've gone through these last few years. Following my instincts, I push my wolf deeper into the dark woods. The air is clean, the land unpolluted. There's no sign of humans on this land, or anyone really. Perfect for a lone wolf.

It's even better when I stumble upon an abandoned one-room shack that has all the markings of a feral's den.

Ferals are the most dangerous of my kind. As shifters, we are an equal mix of our human halves and our beast. Ferals are more wolf than man, with very little impulse control. They're wild.

Unpredictable. They do what they want, when they want, and there's nothing to temper their mood or their violence. Pushed too far, they might turn completely wolf—but only if they're not put down for being too much of a threat to other shifters first.

Now, while lone wolves are shifters that reject being part of a pack, a feral is completely on its own. They still crave territory, though. They can't help it. So long as they're still partly human, a feral will make itself a house-like den in the middle of the most inaccessible parts of nature.

Bones litter the outside. There's no denying the old stink of blood and fur and rot that clings to the wood. Gashes from claws mark nearly every surface on the outside, and when desperation leads me to shift to my skin and use my opposable thumb to turn the doorknob, I see it's even worse inside. My nose tells me it's been abandoned for a couple of years at least, though there's still a pallet of torn fabric—probably the remains of clothes that ripped to shreds during a hasty shift—mixed with fur and something that looks like hay.

A scuffed-up wooden table is on the edge. Two homemade chairs sit on opposite sides, facing each other. One has a gouge taken out of the wooden back, with dried blood splashing the whole thing, turning the pale wood brown with its color.

So, yeah. Definitely a feral's den.

I don't care. It has a roof, a door, and a window in case I need to make a quick escape. In a pinch, I can use one of the chairs as a weapon. Surprisingly, the tap has running water, and the solar panels that are out of place on the shabby roof give me enough electric light from the single hanging fixture that I don't need to mess around with candles.

Which is good because I don't have any.

All I want to do is collapse on top of the pallet and knock

out. My wolf assures me that there isn't a threat around for as far as she can sense, but just in case someone somehow finds this shack with me in it, I pull one of my simple shift dresses out of my duffel bag and shrug it on over my shoulders. I could sleep as my wolf, but I haven't been back in my skin for days. I really should give her time to rest her paws.

Besides, even in my skin, I've slept in worse places than a pile of musty hay and some unknown shifter's clothes.

Keeping my duffel bag within reach, I plop down in the nest on the ground. It's not the most comfortable thing in the world, but it's better than laying on the hard floor. My wolf agrees with me. Or maybe she just is desperate to rest because I can already feel her curling up, her muzzle on her front paws. Following her lead, I fall fast asleep.

I didn't plan on waking up until at least morning. It was around evening when I passed out, and when I jerk awake, I can see through the window that it's pitch dark outside. The only light comes from the moon, a few days out from being full, and she shines down on the midnight black forest.

At first I don't know what made me wake up. I'm drowsy and stiff, and I just want to close my eyes again... until I realize that my wolf is up, her ears cocked, a soft whine coming from her throat.

Or maybe that's mine.

Am I imagining it? Despite the electricity and the running water, the shack doesn't have any heat, and the woods can get cold at night in April. I don't have a blanket, and while shifters run hot, goosebumps cover my bare arms as if I'm freezing.

Ice. It smells like ice, mixed with fresh meat, blood, and...

Licorice.

*Aleks.*

I hop to my feet, my wolf snapping her fangs at me to hurry. Peeking out of the only window in the room, I don't see anyone out there. I step back, then eye the door. There are no windows built into the slab of wood. No peephole, either. If I want to see if my suspicions are right, I have to open the door.

Do I want to? Inside of me, my wolf is singing a song to her mate. She knows exactly who is approaching the cabin.

And when I throw open the door and see the Luna's light reflecting off of Aleks's pale skin in the distance, I do, too.

He doesn't say anything. Neither do I. The silence of the woods seems to echo as my pulse pounds, my heart thumping wildly. I make no move toward him, and for a few deafening beats of my heart, Aleks stays where he is, silhouetted by the moonlight.

I blink. Silly, Elizabeth. You know how fast vampires are.

I blink again, and suddenly he's only a few feet away.

"Księżyca," he rasps out. "Won't you let me in?"

# CHAPTER 11
# TASTE OF HIS SKIN

I take a couple of steps back inside the shack.

It's a retreat. I know it is, just like I know that I'm not moving away from him out of fear. This is Aleks, and despite the red rimming his pale eyes, I'm not afraid of him. He'd never hurt me.

No. I'm backing up because, if I don't, I'm about to fling myself into his arms. Based on the emotionless expression on his sculpted features in spite of his almost pleading tone, I'm not so sure he'd welcome me. He's pulled in his vampiric aura so I can't even get a read on his emotions through that. All I have to go on is the red in his gaze, and the undeniable knowledge that I left him three days ago without a word.

Yeah. I don't think Aleks is very happy with me.

But he's here—and I have no idea how. Since throwing him to the ground and mounting him like my wolf wants me to do is currently out of the question, I settle on hugging my mid-section and asking in a quiet voice, "How did you find me?"

In Muncie, I never doubted that he knew where I was at any given moment. Between his patrollers keeping an eye on me, and his supe senses allowing him to track me down anywhere in his territory, no matter where I was, Aleks could find me.

But I've spent three nights running. Not once did I catch his aura closing in on me until he appeared in the woods surrounding the abandoned shack mere hours after I did, but he hunted me down so unerringly, it's almost like he has a tracker on me.

I don't have a phone. I ditched mine in Muncie so that I wouldn't be tempted to get into contact with him or Gem or Leigh and her mates; I could always find a way to call them later, but it wouldn't be that easy. Even if I suspected that my vampire would use human tech to track me—and I never would, not in a million years—he couldn't because all I have are the clothes in my duffel bag, my deck of cards, a little bit of cash, and that's all.

I even left my fang behind... so how did he find me?

My tone does something to him. I'm not afraid, but even I'll be the first to admit that I sounded like it. His expression softens and, before I know it, he's closed the gap between us entirely. He glides right into the cabin, kicking the door closed behind him with a graceful move before he takes my chin in his hands.

I gasp. Up close, I notice the purple circles underlining his eyes. His fingers feel like icicles against my skin, but that's not why I gasped. The only time I've ever seen Aleks this disheveled was a few days after he'd been the Wicked Wolf's captive and he was thrown in the pit, half-starved and full of bullet holes, to fight a shifted wolf.

He looks like he ran just as long as I did, chasing me without feeding, though the blood that spatters the hem of his dirt-covered sweater tells me it wasn't without some kind of fight. There's even a healing burn down one side of his face from where his super-strength sunscreen must have worn off.

And he went through all that to get to me.

"Oh, Aleks..." I whisper.

He strokes the height of my cheek with the side of his silky thumb, cutting me off. "Through our bond. I'll always be able to find you, and I promise you this: I will always look."

My heart skips a beat in my chest, but then I realize what he said: *through our bond.* Laying my hands over his, I gently push him away from me. I can't deny that we have a bond between us, but without it being finalized, there's no way he should be able to use it to follow after me.

So why did he say that?

He lets me put space between us again, though I can tell by the way he sucks in an unnecessary breath that it's the last thing he wants to do.

I glance up at him. "We don't have a bond that works like that."

"Of course we do—"

"We never performed the Luna Ceremony," I remind him. "So how could we?"

His cheeks go hollow, his eyes more red than green all of a sudden, as he says, "With a blood bond, that's how."

"What? We don't have one of those, either!"

"Oh?" He arches an eyebrow. "And you're sure of that?"

"Well, yes—"

"When you never even bothered to ask how it's done?" Aleks says over me. Anger seeps into his accented voice, though he's doing everything to keep from raising it. "When I discovered that my beloved was a shifter, I made it my mission to learn just how your kind form their bonds. But you didn't."

He's not wrong. I never brought it up, but neither did he. I just assumed that, when he decided to bond me to him, he'd tell me how.

And now he wants me to believe he already has? *When*?

Something else ruffles my fur. Instead of admitting that he's right, I go from hugging my middle to crossing my arms over my chest. "Which one? Which beloved?"

His expression goes guarded. "Wybaczcie?"

*Excuse me*?

Only with Aleks could I tilt my chin up at him, daring a visibly upset vampire to answer me. "Which one?

I hit a nerve there. Immediately his expression goes from guarded to closed-off. "So that's what this is all about. Julia again? I thought we put her behind us."

He did?

A lump lodges in my throat. I can't help it. Despite wondering what he was doing here, I was so fucking happy to see him standing out there—and now it's all gone to hell. I can't even blame him. It's me. The problem has always been me.

I sigh.

He stiffens, but stays a couple of feet away from me.

"No, Aleks," I tell him, "I don't think either one of us has."

He purses his lips. I see the tips of his fangs peeking out from beneath the upper one. Avoiding my stare now, his gaze glances around the one-room cabin. He takes in the scratched wooden table, the pallet in one corner, and my duffel thrown next to it.

"You deserve better than this, Elizabeth," he murmurs, his

voice gone gentle. "Let me take you away from this place. Then we can talk."

I shake my head. "I don't think that's a good idea."

"Then we'll talk here. "

I think I said everything I had to when I left his fang behind on the glass coffee table.

Still, I can't help but ask, "Talk about what?"

"Julia."

My stomach goes tight. "That's definitely not a good idea."

Moving slowly toward me, careful in case I bolt, Aleks waits until there are only a few inches between us before he takes my hand, weaving his fingers with mine. "Ah, księżyca. If a ghost of a female is keeping you from me, then I think it's the best idea. I need you to understand. Please... let me do this. And if you still want to run when I'm done, you can. I'll chase you, of course, but at least you'll have all the facts."

I shudder out a breath. Aleks... he's offered to tell me about Julia before. Gem, too. Shortly after I moved in with him, he pulled out the locket with Julia's portrait in it from his bedside table and told me that I could ask him anything. He's an open book, right? Whatever I wanted to know, he'd answer me truthfully.

I couldn't bring myself to do it. I'd been afraid that he carried her around in his pocket wherever he went, and it was a relief to know he kept it in his bedside table instead. That's all I cared about. What happened with Julia... if I asked about her, I had to brace myself to hear about how amazing she was, how he wished he'd bonded her to him before she died, and then deal with another round of wondering if he only settled for me because I could be her physical twin.

I told him the barest details of my past. I thought I was okay with him doing the same. Sometimes I still got jealous when I thought of him loving Julia and pining over Gem, but I would remind myself that I was in his bed. I was the one who fed him. He chose me, even if we weren't bonded.

But if Julia Złoty hadn't died two hundred years ago, he never would've been able to...

When I can't find the words to answer him, Aleks uses our joined hands to lead me over to the table. He waits until I'm seated, then kneels next to me. Aleksander Filan, the leader of the Muncie Cadre, goes to his knees by my side, laying his hand on my thigh as if genuflecting to me.

Oh my Luna.

"Aleks—"

I want to tell him to get up. That he's too good to be on his knees like that, and if there was only one seat, I could sit on his lap. But I never get the chance.

"I'd only known Julia for two weeks before she died," he begins, tilting his head back so that he's looking right into my eyes. "I never made it to the full moon with her, and though she recognized me as her fated mate, she refused to give me blood. When I offered her mine, she was revolted. I couldn't bond her to me, and I had to wait until the full moon to let her claim me. That's how a blood-bonding works," he tells me. "A vampire shares his blood with his beloved and takes hers inside of him. Just like your Luna Ceremony, the mate has to choose. I asked you if you were my beloved, księżyca. The first night we made love... I asked you. You told me you were. You chose me as your male."

I... I did.

Gem was the one who told me I should "take him for a ride". I never thought he really wanted to be tied to me for life—especially when a vampire can survive everything except decapitation—but I wanted him so bad, I gave in to mine and my wolf's need to fuck him out in the woods.

I remember every second of that night. The tang of an oncoming snowstorm hovering in the crisp air, the crunch of the iced-over accumulation beneath us, and how amazing it felt to have his chilled cock working its way inside of my overheated body.

But before he ever put the tip in, Aleks made me look at him. *Are you my beloved*, he asked. *Do you accept me as yours?* Only after I told him I was did mating become inevitable.

He stalked toward me. He said, *You're mine. Forever.* Then, while our bodies were connected, I invited him to feed from me while we fucked me. He did, and then he begged me to do the same.

"We've been blood-bonded since then?" I whisper.

He nods, not even a lick of shame on his handsome face. "I bonded you to me, and I was hoping you would bond yourself to me during the next full moon. But then—"

Then the Wicked Wolf came and challenged Aleks for me. While Walker acted as a distraction, his cruel Beta took Roman as his political prisoner. Roman sacrificed himself for his people, and then Christian shot both me and Aleks.

The silver bullet had pierced my heart. I nearly died. I spent the first full moon in the hospital, and when Aleks avoided me for the second, I figured he didn't want to even attempt the Luna Ceremony. I mean, I couldn't—not with the Luna gone quiet from my life—but it hurt that he never offered to make our relationship permanent in any way.

I had no idea that he already had.

"Those shifters who nearly breached Muncie were a wake-up

call. I could lose you. I told you already. I *can't*. I needed to make you mine in all ways as soon as I could, but then you ran." His eyes have never left my face, but I notice that they're suddenly glinting in the weak electric light. Holy shit. Those are *tears*. "Was it me? What could I have done to keep you, księżyca? Tell me. I'll do it. I never had the chance to love Julia. And Gem... she was safe because I always knew her heart belonged to Wolfson. But you... you were mine from the moment I laid eyes on you in California."

His tears do something to the pit of my stomach. I was lost at his confession, but those tears... I need a distraction before I crawl onto Aleks's lap, beg forgiveness, and never leave.

So I point out, "That was almost a year ago, Aleks. After the Western Pack disbanded, I didn't see you again for more than five months until I finally moved into Gem's townhouse."

"You didn't see me, but that didn't mean I wasn't there. Watching you. Guarding you. Making sure no one ever hurt you again."

From the moment I took over Gem's house, I woke up to Aleks's scent and his boot prints out in the snow. But there was still a five-month gap, unless—

"That... that was you." When I could've sworn I recognized the icy aura during those lonely nights on my own and I convinced myself that I missed my fate mate so much I began hallucinating he was near. Only I'm beginning to think they weren't hallucinations after all... "Wasn't it?"

His eyes are still glinting, but his lips curve ever so. "I told you, my beloved. I will always follow you."

We move at the same time, Aleks rising up from the floor while I hop off of the chair, throwing my arms around his neck. Over the last few months I've kissed him countless times, but there's an urgency and an emotion to this one that zips straight to my soul. Our teeth clash, his fang nipping my bottom lip, blood mingling as I stroke his tongue with mine.

The ferocity of the kiss gentles after a few seconds, but it becomes something stronger. Something deeper. I tug Aleks's curls, pushing against his hard chest, eager to hold him tight as if afraid he'll change his mind.

I'm clinging to him, so it's Aleks who is the one to pull back first. My wolf yips—and, okay, maybe I do, too—but he doesn't go anywhere. On a sigh, he tucks my head under his chin, wrapping his arms around me, simply holding me close. Because I need his touch almost as much as he obviously needs mine, I circle his waist while laying my cheek against his shoulder.

We stay like that for a few moments, just reveling in each other's presence. I breathe in his scent, my wolf eager to take in the licorice-like notes and bask in them. I don't know how I thought I could leave him. Even though my intentions were good, they were a mistake.

Aleks is mine. Now, forever, and always. I'm his, too.

Whatever happens next, we'll handle it together. Whether it's the rebels in Muncie or the Alpha collective who are probably ticked off I ignored their summons, as long as I'm with him, it'll be okay.

My vampire obviously feels the same way. Once he finally lets go again, Aleks immediately reaches into his pocket. He pulls out a fist. Slowly, he unfolds his fingers until he's showing me the golden chain with the white fang nestled in his palm.

"You're my beloved, mój księżyca. My moon. The other half of my soul. I gave you my heart even before I gave you my fang. You're everything to me, Elizabeth. Won't you take this back?"

How can I say no?

If I take that fang back, I'm accepting everything Aleks told me. That we both have our baggage, just like we both have our pasts, but so long as we have a future to look forward to together, everything is going to be all right.

Swooping my hair over my shoulder, I give my back to Aleks so that he can loop the fang around my neck and clasp it.

"Elizabeth?"

"Put it on me," I tell him. "I never should've taken it off."

Because I *am* his beloved. His blood-bonded mate. Deep down, I think I knew that all along. I just couldn't admit it because my insecurities and my trauma made it so that I couldn't believe that an amazing male like Aleks would willingly want to tie himself to me. It was easier for me to throw up a shield, loving him from behind it. I've been hurt so much before. If Aleks rejected me, I don't think I'd ever recover.

But he didn't reject me. Long before I even went all in with him myself, he took me as his mate.

And as soon as the Luna listens to my prayers again, when I can ask my goddess for her blessing to make Aleks my forever mate, I'm going to do the same for him.

*Finally*, murmurs the Luna.

## CHAPTER 12
# RUN OR YOU'RE DEAD

I jump at the sound of her voice inside my head right as Aleks finishes clasping his fang around my neck.

"I'm sorry. Did I pinch you?"

I whirl on him, excitement leading me to grab him by the sleeve. "I heard her. The Luna. I *heard* her."

"You did? What did she say?"

What I've known all along. "That I'm yours."

Aleks grins. "She isn't wrong."

*I'm not*, says the Luna. *And I'm glad to see that you're finally accepting that yourself, Elizabeth.*

"Is she saying something else?" Aleks asks. "Your eyes... they're shining so brightly, it's like they're a mirror. You look beautiful, Elizabeth. You look happy."

I am. I can't believe it. I thought... I thought that I'd never hear from her again. I'm so stinking pleased to have her voice in my head again that I don't even doubt the way my eyes must be flickering and shining. When my negative emotions get to be too much, they darken to black. During mating, Aleks sometimes mentions that my eyes seem more silvery and bright than usual. Is that why?

Makes sense. If there's anyone in the world who makes me happy, it's my vampire.

"She said that she's glad I finally accepted myself. And I did," I confess, "when I finally accepted that you love me for who I am."

"Oh, księżyca. I don't just love you. I *adore* you."

*And that is why I chose you for him, my daughter.*

I'm still clutching Aleks's sleeve. With his other hand, he takes mine, giving my fingers a quick squeeze. "Your eyes just flickered again. Take your time, my beloved. Talk with your Luna."

I want to. I have so many questions I want to ask her, especially since I'm not sure if this is a one-time thing or if she'll be my conscience and my guide once more, but I hate the idea of letting Aleks out of my sight. Not because I'm afraid he's going to leave me, too, but because... I don't know. I have this weird feeling in the pit of my stomach all of a sudden.

Call it intuition, but I think Aleks should stay with me inside the feral's den.

"I don't know..."

He bows his head, meeting my gaze pointedly as he looks down his patrician nose at me. His pale eyes don't have a lick of red in them, but I've seen determination before—and Aleks is determined. "I'm going to take a patrol around the woods. Make sure they're as abandoned as they seem. I'll be right back."

I let out a small laugh. That male and his patrols. Lifting our intertwined hands up to my mouth, I press a kiss against his chilled skin. "Don't be gone long."

"I won't," he vows.

He closes the door behind him when he leaves. I take a moment to just revel in the way his scent has already filled the small room before I sink down on the non-bloodstained seat and close my eyes, reaching for the Luna again.

Since I was a young pup and I realized that, like others in my line, I was Luna-touched and could speak with her if I concentrated enough, I found that sitting somewhere peacefully with my eyes shut made it easier to understand her. The Luna is a goddess, the most powerful shifter who ever lived, and over centuries she's become the moon personified.

Her voice has always been so soft and gentle. She was a female alpha when she was alive, but there's something so maternal about her, I've never once been afraid to contact her.

Like now.

*Why did you go*, I ask. I probably sound more accusing than I should, but she's never left me before. Even during those awkward teen years when I tried out as many males in my birth pack as would have me, she never judged, only made sure I knew that I wouldn't find my fated mate among them. Because, well, yeah. Mine turned out to be a vampire.

Looking back, I probably should've figured that one out a long time ago...

I shake my head. Focus, Elizabeth. The Luna is listening. *I needed you and you were gone.*

*You had to figure it out on your own, my daughter. I could help you. Guide you. But, in the end, your life is yours. The bonds you make are yours.*

*But Aleks is mine, right? And I'm supposed to be his...*

*You are his. Just like Julia was once. But that only proves my point,*

*Elizabeth. She made her choice. She didn't accept her bond. She didn't accept her mate.*

What? *I don't understand.*

*Do you know what spurred the last war between my wolves and the vampires?*

*Well, yeah.* At least, I thought I did. *It was Aleks's love for Julia.*

*No. It was his despair at losing his beloved to her Alpha. That's what happened. When Julia forsook her bond with Aleksander, she went to her Alpha for protection. She was one of my chosen. A rare female alpha. He saw her as a threat to his power and was angered that she might take a vampire as a mate instead of his successor. He killed her. He killed her, and blamed her bond with the vampire as the reason why she had to die. Aleksander was only avenging her death when he challenged the Alpha and won.*

That sounds like Aleks.

I'm not sure what shocks me more: that Walker wasn't the first Alpha that Aleks challenged and defeated, or that the grand love story I built up in my head about Julia and Aleks is... not what I thought it was.

*Why didn't he tell me?* I don't know why I'm asking the Luna. I should be asking Aleks. I just... I don't understand. *She never really was his beloved, was she?*

*Not like you are. She might've been, had she chosen differently. The promise of a bond was there. That's what makes a true mate, Elizabeth. The choice. And that's why I had to step back and allow you to make yours. And you have.*

I did, didn't I? When I offered my throat to Aleks and took back his fang, I didn't even hesitate. It had nothing to do with his past with Julia or Gem, or even my instinct to run away if only because I thought I was somehow saving him. I took it because I love him, and even if our story won't have a happy ending, either, I'm done fooling myself that I don't.

*So what happens now?*

*That depends on you. Your mate has already bonded you to him in the ways of his people. I'm nearly at my power. If you want to make him yours, the only one stopping you is yourself.*

She's not wrong, is she?

*Of course not. I'm your goddess. I might not get it right every time, but I'm never wrong.*

I grin. With my eyes closed, sitting alone in the empty shack, I grin like a fool.

Too bad the contentment doesn't last...

Now that I know the truth about Aleks bonding me to him through my blood, I realize just how sensitive I've become to his aura. When I first met him, back when I was in denial that he could ever be my fated mate, his scent was more powerful than his vampire power. Over time, I thought I was just growing used to the pungent, meaty notes that marked Aleks as a vampire... but I wasn't, was I? I was feeling my mate through a supe bond I didn't know anything about.

How else can I explain the sudden sense of foreboding mingling with a territorial need to protect what's mine that floods through me? Because those emotions don't belong to me. I'm just sensing them through the bond I have with Aleks.

And that means—

"Aleks!"

My eyes shoot open. It doesn't make any logical sense to me, but I don't care. Aleks is in trouble, and though the emotions reverberating down our bond tell me that he's only concerned with keeping me safe, those actually could be mine since all I want to do is protect my vampire.

I dash to the front door and throw it open. From where I stand, there's no one there. Aleks said he was going for a patrol so I'm not surprised he isn't in my line of vision, but I can't shake the feeling that something's wrong.

*Focus,* whispers the Luna. *Feel him.* Find *him.*

Right. Aleks admitted that he can always find me through our bond because he's drunk my blood. Well, I've probably had a good cup of his since we became mates. It should work for me.

Taking a deep breath, trying to steady my racing nerves, I search inside of myself for my side of our bond. My wolf is sitting up, ears flat against her skull as she whines, but I delve deeper, deeper, deeper… *there*.

How did I never notice it before? Now that I'm searching for it, it's a scarlet ribbon stretching between us, different from a shifter bond and not quite what a vampire tie looks like, but that makes sense, doesn't it? We're two different supes, so our bonds are as unique as our mating.

Giving my head a clearing shake, I decide I can marvel over that later. For now, I'm convinced Aleks needs me. No point in wasting time when I have to get to my mate.

Turns out, I don't need the bond to find him. Not when a shot rings out in the air, drawing my attention to it unerringly.

*No. No*!

Whether I'm jumping to conclusions or not, the crack of a gunshot means one thing to me and my reconstructed heart: Christian Morrissey has finally returned for his revenge.

It has to be. I don't know why I don't scent him out here—I'm definitely not covering his scent for him, though I've heard enough wolfsbane might disguise an innate scent to a degree—but, unless hunters are out there, shooting into the darkness, there's only one supe male I know who brings a gun to a challenge.

I hope I'm wrong. In case I'm not, I decide I won't give him the chance to go for my heart again. Shifting in a flurry of torn material, my clothes toast, I dash off in the direction of the gunshot.

Claws crossed he's not so good at finding the heart on a wolf.

I'm not that worried about Aleks yet. Well, no. I *am*, but if Christian only shot him once, that's nothing. I've seen Aleks take multiple silver bullets and keep moving, and as quick as he is, he won't let Christian get him in the heart like I did.

It's tricky, running through the unfamiliar trees at a fast enough clip to reach him without my thundering paws giving my location away. I trade a little speed for stealth, and am rewarded when I come upon Aleks facing off against a shifter with a gun.

Only... that's not Christian.

What?

He's a young delta shifter. Barely twenty. In the darkness, his hair looks black, but it's probably a rich brown. The hand gripping the gun is shaky. Even from this distance, I can hear the thudding of his heart, smell the sweat pouring off of him. I wouldn't be surprised if he pisses himself, he's so scared.

Then again, he's staring up at a vampire whose eyes are the color of blood, his fangs long enough to reach his bottom lip.

A long ago rhyme from my childhood suddenly pops into my brain.

*When a vamp's eyes go red, run or you're dead...*

I'm not afraid of Aleks because I know he'll never hurt me. This poor kid? He doesn't have a prayer.

I sniff. The sweat is overwhelming, the scent of terror

clinging to him just as bad, but the most notable sulfurous stink belongs to the gunpowder.

Aleks shakes his head. I'm not sure what the conversation was before I arrived, but I must have walked into the middle of it because all Aleks says is, "I didn't want you to bother my mate and you shot the gun anyway—and, worse, you *missed*," before he takes a step closer to the kid.

To my shock, the delta turns the gun on himself. No hesitation. No fear. A little piss, to be honest, but I guess he decided it was better to shoot himself in the temple than deal with a vampire stalking toward him.

The gun fires. Blood flies. The kid drops down dead, the gun landing at his side.

"Pity," Aleks mutters under his breath, crouching down to check that the shifter truly is dead. When he sees that he is, he straightens. "What a waste."

Seriously. I... I can't believe that just happened. I'm still gaping in surprise at the huddled body crumpled on the forest floor when, out of the corner of my eye, the shadows behind Aleks move.

Wait. That's not a shadow.

That *is* Christian.

The gaunt Beta from California, with the dark grey eyes, deep black hair, skeletal build, and an affinity for always wearing a black suit that helped blend in with the shadows.

He's also holding a gun, but there's no shake there. He knows exactly how to use it.

I can attest to that.

A trap, I think. They laid a trap. I don't know which one of us it's for—most likely me, since it finally hits me that beneath the suicidal delta's fear is the same shifter scent that followed after me when I first left Muncie—but it doesn't matter. With Aleks looking a little disappointed that the young delta killed himself, and Christian somehow cloaking his scent, the former Beta of the Western Pack is stalking my mate, hunting him, and Aleks... Aleks is letting him.

He's a vampire. A trained killer. I asked him once how he does it so easily, not because I was judging him, but because I'm a she-wolf and the most I've hunted is a deer. He had to explain to me in gentle terms that, long before Fang Cities, vampires thought of humans as their deer. He had to hunt to feed, and though he never drained a human before, supes live dangerous lives.

I'm proof of that, even if I've never killed another person myself.

He has skills that he learned only after being turned. He also has his vampire abilities. One of them is knowing when prey is near by their panicked heartbeat.

Then again, this is Christian. He doesn't panic. Like a rattlesnake, he's calm, cool, and collected—and then he strikes.

Which is why I'm not so surprised when Aleks straightens up, listening for a moment before he chuckles.

"Elizabeth?" His back to me, Aleks sounds vaguely amused. "I hear your heartbeat. I tried not to let our young visitor disturb you, but he obviously had other plans. You might as well come out now."

To my horror, Christian steps forward right as Aleks turns. "What? Was I gone too long— ah, you're not my beloved."

"No," Christian says, raising his gun. "Elizabeth's not here. But I'll make sure you tell her to meet you in hell when I see her next."

Wrong on both counts, asshole.

What happened? Did Christian dupe that poor kid into being his pawn? Or did he sell him on the same martyrdom that Jack Walker believed in? Either way, watching as Christian prepares to pull the trigger on the gun, something snaps inside of me.

For the first time in my life, I see fucking *red*. I don't think. I don't hesitate.

I attack.

I'm not sure if Christian even had the chance to fire off a shot; if so, he also missed. Rearing back on my hind legs, I pounced on him. So consumed with staring down Aleks, he never saw me coming until I got my first bite in.

I went for his gun hand. I bit the whole fucking thing off. With a sickening crunch and a thud, both the hand and the gun go flying.

Christian howls, and maybe if he'd taken a second to shift at the beginning of the brutal fight, he might've won. He was a Beta, after all, and an experienced pit fighter. His weapon of choice might've been the gun, but he had claws and fangs and knew how to use them.

But I had the desperate need to protect my mate on my side, and years of pent-up frustration at males like Christian controlling me to fuel my rage.

He never stood a chance.

I don't know how long I continued to rend and chew and slash after he was dead. Enough that Aleks finally dared approach me. I don't think I've ever been so close to going feral in my entire life, and if he hadn't been there to whisper my name, I'm not so sure I would've come back at all.

But he is, and he does, and I do.

"Elizabeth? Elizabeth? Księżyca? Can you hear me?"

*Mate*. That's my wolf trying to poke my human consciousness. *Maaaate*.

Mate.

I shift. As soon as I'm in my skin again, my legs buckle.

Aleks is right there, catching me before I hit the bloody earth.

My eyelids flutter. "Aleks? What... what happened?"

"We were ambushed, my beloved. Roman's murderer... the skurwysyn who nearly stole you from me with his silver bullet... it seems he came to finish the job. Only my fierce she-wolf stopped him before he had the chance."

I follow the direction of his stare. When I see the bloody clumps everywhere, my stomach rebels.

"Oh my Luna." I peer down in horror. "I killed him!"

Like I said, I've never killed another being before. I've fantasized about it when it came to Kyle and Peyton, and even Jack Walker, but I didn't think I had it in me.

Aleks cups my face with his hands, forcing me to look at him instead of the mess I made of Christian. "No," he says gently yet firmly, "you saved me. Oh, my beloved księżyca, you saved yourself."

I... I guess I did, didn't I?

# CHAPTER 13
# THE VAMPIRE'S BRIDE

At my urging, Aleks buries Christian and the delta kid behind the shack.

I have to explain that I could care less if the crows and vultures peck Christian's corpse; the kid I feel kind of bad about, but he threw his lot in with the disgraced Beta, so maybe not *too* bad. However, one look at Christian and it's obvious that another shifter tore him to shreds. I don't know if those two were working on their own—or if other wolves sympathetic to Walker and Christian's cause might be looking for him. Then there's also the little matter that I'm technically a fugitive of the Alpha collective. My scent and blood are all over him.

That's all I have to say. Trembling in my bare skin, Christian's blood painting me red where my own gashes and quickly closing wounds aren't already lending it color, I explain it to him. I'm barely done before he swoops in, gives me a quick kiss, then starts to gather up the pieces of the wolf I left behind in my rage.

Once he's done, he leads me back into the shack. I'm still a little shell-shocked, though I feel a lot better once I know Christian is buried. With gentle hands, Aleks uses the shred of my blouse as a washcloth to wipe away the blood. He hisses when he sees how deep some of Christian's defensive bites go into my midsection, but I assure him that I'll be okay.

Probably would be a lot more convincing if I wasn't still shaking like a leaf.

I lie and tell him it's because I'm cold. He doesn't call me out on it. He just reaches for my duffel, pulls out the first dress he finds, and pulls it on over my head like I'm a child who needs to be taken care of.

That has me snapping out of it. I'm a shifter. A she-wolf. To protect my mate, I just chewed up a Beta and spat him back out again. I can dress myself.

That doesn't mean I'm not appreciative of his care. I am. At that moment, I don't regret jumping in front of Aleks like that. It doesn't matter that Christian could've shot me like he did only a few months ago. I love Aleks. I'd gladly die for him if I had to.

But I didn't. I'm still alive. So is he. Behind his careful facade, I see a male that's barely holding it together. I know what he went through when Christian's silver bullet nearly killed me the first time. I can only imagine what he's going through now that he almost lost me again...

He took care of me. It's my turn now.

Once I'm dressed, I turn to him. I wash my vampire up at the sink, getting rid of the blood, the gore, and the dirt that stained his hands. Once that's done, I make him take his clothes off so that I can do my best to get the bloodstains out with what I have. Unlike me, Aleks didn't stop to pack before he came after me, and he didn't think to remove his shirt and pants before he carried Christian's remains out back with his bare hands.

He lets me wash the sweater, but folds up his pants and puts them out of my reach when I ask for them. I don't question it. They're black so they hide any stains that might be on them; it's his sweater that looks like it's been through hell.

With as much devotion and care as he showed me, I take care of him. Then, once the rush and the fear and the adrenaline of the fight wear off, replaced by love and the realization that either one of us could've just *died*, I take one look at Aleks's nearly naked body and decide that I need to prove to myself that we're both alive.

He's more than willing to let me. Against the wall of a rundown shack in the middle of an abandoned forest, I fuck Aleksander Filan until I no longer feel the urgency that comes with remembering once again that neither of us is truly immortal.

As soon as we're done, we both wordlessly curl up on the nest on the floor. I doubt there's a single soul in the world that would've ever guessed that a vampire like Aleks would willingly lie in a feral's nest, but he does. For me—*with me*—he does.

I don't know how long we lie there together. One thing for sure, it isn't long enough before Aleks is easing me gently to the side.

My eyes were closed, halfway dozing in the safety of Aleks's embrace. I quirk one open. "Mm. Where are you going?"

"I promised myself that, if I found you, I would be honest and tell you about the blood bond. But that's not all. I need to make you understand just how serious I am about you."

"Aleks? What are you—"

"Shh," he says softly, hushing me. "Let me show you and, hopefully, you will understand."

Thanks to the solar panels, there's still a little light from the single bulb hanging over our heads. My shifter's sight is strong enough that I could see what he's doing regardless, but with the light, there's no denying it when he pulls a small black box out of his pants pocket.

Coming back to me, he flips the top of the lid open, plucking out a simple golden band.

"Is that a..." I can't even say it.

So he does. "A ring? Yes. Gold, because I know shifters prefer it, but also because it's tradition. I'm an old man. For two hundred years I waited for the one woman who could make me whole, and supe or not, I'm a product of my times. I believe in tradition, and it's traditional to give your bride a golden wedding band."

Now I don't know *what* to say to that.

Shifters don't have weddings, not like humans do. We have a Luna Ceremony, which is kind of like the vow, and some couples throw a party when they're done. Alphas usually do, to give the pack a chance to welcome the new mate into the community, but most deltas just keep it to themselves. There's definitely no ring involved.

Vampires have their blood bondings. That's what they do as a supernatural race, but not all vamps are born. Some, like Morgan and Aleks, are turned into what they are. Two hundred and twenty-four years ago, Aleksander Filan was born in a small Polish village. And now, all these years later, he's holding out a golden ring for me.

"You, Elizabeth Howell, are my beloved. You're my mate. And, if you'll accept me, you'll be my bride."

Because old habits die hard, when I finally find my voice, I can't keep myself from asking, "Have you had one of those before?"

Aleks doesn't even hesitate. "A bride?" At my reluctant nod, he says, "No. No mate, either. But, księżyca, I *have* had a beloved. I can't change that, just like I can't change what my life was like before you came into it."

"I don't expect you to." To my surprise, I actually mean that. "You lived for more than two hundred years without me. There's still so much about you I don't know." The Luna proved that when, even after two months of living with Aleks, she revealed how much about Julia he kept concealed. "I want to know everything. That's why I asked."

And, okay, because I'm a jealous she-wolf. But I'm working on it.

Honest.

Aleks's lips quirk. "Then say 'yes'. When you become a vampire's bride, forever takes on a different meaning. We have forever to learn everything about each other. If only you'll say 'yes'."

I watch how the faint electrical light plays off of the golden band.

*He's yours*, murmurs the Luna.

*I know*, I murmur back.

I hold out my hand. "Of course I will. I'm yours."

He slips the ring on my finger, then kisses the knuckle in front of it. "And once we make it to the full moon, you'll make me yours for life."

I grin down at the ring nestled perfectly on my finger. "Yeah, I will."

---

The Luna won't be up for a couple of more days. Aleks has his phone with him, but shocker: there's no service in the shack or the woods surrounding it. I kind of want to hide out with my vampire for as long as he'll let me, and based on how he doesn't seem to be in any rush to go, it would be easy to convince him.

It's not fair, though. He's done so much for me, sacrificed even more, all while taking on the mantle of being Muncie's head vamp shortly after losing Roman. In so many ways I've been selfish. It's about time I start thinking about what's good for Aleks, and not just me.

He didn't come out and say it, but I'm pretty sure that he didn't sleep a wink since he found out I left him. Based on my head start and how little rest I got, to catch up to me as quickly as he did, he couldn't have.

Vampires don't need as much sleep as humans and shifters do. Three straight days of running while worrying about his beloved? He was probably pushing exhaustion when he found me, then he had to deal with Christian. Shortly after he slid that ring on my finger, he curls up around me and knocks the hell out.

He's sleeping so deeply, the only sign that he's even aware that I've left the straw nest is when his fingers flex, clasping the air where I'd been a few seconds ago. His flawless brow furrows, drawing attention to just how peaceful he was. I barely resist the urge to kneel next to him, caressing his porcelain cheek with my fingers.

He almost looks like a statue laying there. But even the

masters weren't imaginative enough to come up with a male as shockingly beautiful as my Aleks.

I glance down at the ring on my finger. My vampire husband.

He wants to have a wedding. He murmured that last night right before he fell asleep. A big wedding where we can invite every Cadre vamp in Muncie to witness him making me his wife. Instead of keeping me as his dirty little secret—like Kyle did, and like how I feared for so long that Aleks was doing the same thing—he has this fierce need to show me off.

I'm not saying no. I mean, I'm wearing his ring, aren't I? I just think we need to wait until things settle down to talk about that. At the very least, let's focus on our upcoming Luna Ceremony first.

I'm a simple she-wolf. I don't need much in life. As long as I've had the basics to survive, I've been satisfied. Even so, I think being Aleks's beloved has spoiled me a little. As much as I don't want to return to real life, I'd rather not bond Aleks to me in a feral's shack.

I let him sleep, though, because he needs it. By the time he's finally stirring, it's almost noon. I've packed up everything I brought with me, and as soon as Aleks notices that I was just waiting for him to wake up, I tell him I'm ready to go.

When he doesn't argue, I know I was right to prepare to leave the shack. He has his responsibilities to the vamps and people of Muncie. I've kept their leader from them for too long. It's time we head back.

---

Aleks is everything I ever hoped to find in my mate. Gorgeous. Kind. Strong. A protector.

He's also a stubborn bastard sometimes, a fact he proved when he immediately led me to the first supe-friendly airport he could find to charter a flight back to Muncie. Turns out that, after zig-zagging over the place, I ended up somewhere that was a two-day drive from our Fang City. By plane? We were landing in a small town about a half an hour outside of Muncie before sundown.

I hate planes. I'd never been on one before, but now that I have, it's safe to say that it's going to take a lot of convincing by Aleks to ever get me to go on one of those enclosed metal contraptions again. Talk about a cage. The entire flight my wolf was torn between whining in discomfort and not understanding why I wouldn't stick my head out of the closed window so she can sample the air up so high.

To make up for it, he doesn't order a car to take us the rest of the way into Muncie. Jogging alongside me in my two-legged form, we take a leisurely run from the airport to the borders of the Fang City.

In retrospect, I probably should've gone in the car. Maybe if I had, we might have avoided running into the two shifters waiting for us in the empty stretch between Accalia and Muncie.

It's been months since I've seen her, but her sickly-sweet maple syrup scent lives rent-free in my mind. One sniff and I know exactly who it's going to be before I actually sight her.

I catch another—unfamiliar—shifter's scent on the air with enough time to detour and enter Muncie at another point. It's habit to go this way, since it's the nearest path to the apartment without going by the haunted couple of blocks that everyone in Muncie avoids, but I didn't have to.

I do anyway, because I can't resist confronting her after everything she's put me through.

I'm not surprised when Aleks tries to steer me away from taking that road. With his supernatural senses, he knows there are two shifters lying in wait for us. As my mate, he wants to shield me from them. As the head vamp of Muncie? He *can't*.

Vampires and shifters are ancient enemies. Me being fated to end up with Aleks doesn't change that. Though every instinct inside of me tells me that they're here for me, there's still a chance that they could represent a threat to the people in Aleks's territory.

"This way," I tell him, taking the lead.

Aleks curses under his breath, but he doesn't try to change our trajectory again.

And there she is. A smirking Peyton Slade, standing next to a tall, burly blond-haired Alpha with a flat expression and shrewd gold eyes.

She must've sensed us coming, too.

I stop when there are about fifteen feet between us and them. Calling out to her, I ask, "What are you doing here?"

As if I didn't know. The Alpha's scent wasn't familiar, but I've seen his picture before. If you know the right sites, lone wolves form their own communities online. We warn each other about what packs to avoid, what territory we can squat on, and who might be willing to turn the other way if we need to spend a little time with one of our kind before moving on.

I haven't checked in on my old contacts since I came to stay in Muncie. They were a godsend when I was avoiding Aleks all last year, but I've gone underground a bit since then. I still know who that male is—which means my question is redundant.

I'm pretty sure I know why they're here.

Her cackle of glee has a pit forming in my stomach even before she gestures at the male nearby. "This is Dash Harrigan.

Alpha of the Northern Winds Pack. You missed your trial date. We've come to correct that little oversight."

"Trial?" echoes Aleks. He lays his hand on my shoulder. "What do you mean?"

He knows. I explained it to him at the shack, and he brushed it off, assuring me that I was Cadre now. The Alpha's laws don't apply to me.

I knew better. I just... I guess I hoped I could avoid this, almost as much as I knew from the moment I caught the unfamiliar scent that I was probably running into a situation exactly like this one.

The Alpha clears his throat. "She's been summoned by the Alpha collective to discuss her unique... abilities. She's been accused of using them cruelly. We're offering her the chance to explain."

Oh, Aleks doesn't like that at all. His fingers bite into my shoulder, though he keeps his tone neutral. "She has to decline."

If only it was that easy. "Aleks—"

"You don't get to decline a summons from the Alphas, you bloodsucking parasite. The alternative is being put down. At least, this way, I get to watch Howell suffer a bit before they decide she's too big of a freak to be allowed around normal shifters."

Before, when I first saw Peyton, I was torn between wanting to walk up to her and slap that smug look off of her face and clutching Aleks to me so that she can't get her claws in him. I haven't forgotten how she vowed to take my mate from me the same way I "stole" hers, and even though she fucked Jack Walker thinking he was mine, I wouldn't put it past her to get her revenge by setting her sights on Aleks.

I should've known better. There are some prejudices not

even a twisted shifter like Peyton can get past. And then there's Aleks. My gentle, cultured vampire has a switch that turns him from bloodsucker nobility to a vicious killer in seconds: *me*.

"I won't let you touch her. None of you."

During the whole exchange, even when he was speaking, the Alpha had hung back. Once Aleks hunches his shoulders, coiling his body as though he's prepared to fight them both, Dash's eyes go from a soft gold to a molten lava. He must've been keeping his level of dominance contained because, with a steady snarl, he releases it.

Woah. My wolf immediately whines, eager to submit to the much stronger beast.

Unfortunately, my human half agrees. Aleks could probably take him. As strong as Dash's dominance is, the Wicked Wolf had an edge. Aleks was able to take him on, though I think both of us accept that Walker's death came as easy as it did because Aleks was particularly determined and Walker was prepared to play the role of the martyr to get his war.

I turn around, clutching Aleks's sweater with my fists. I have to yank to get him to break the stare which is probably a good thing; Alphas take prolonged eye contact as a challenge, and my attempt to stop Aleks from attacking might be in vain if Dash accepts.

"Aleks, baby, listen to me. Are you listening to me?"

I kept my voice low enough that it's clear I'm only talking to him. After a moment when the red in his irises gleams, he blinks, and my vampire is back. "Elizabeth..."

"Listen. I have to go. I know you don't like it. Believe me, I don't like it, either. But I have to. Please don't make it harder than it is."

"I won't," he assures me, voice thrumming with emotion as

he tucks a strand of hair behind my ear. "But I'm coming with you."

My voice was low, but they still heard both of us easily.

"Your mate can't come with you," the Alpha interjects. "I'm sorry."

Surprisingly, I think he actually means it.

I also think the only reason why Aleks pulls back the last of his own ferocity isn't because he's intimidated by Dash or because he's affected by his dominance. Nope. He's slightly mollified by the way the Alpha refers to him as my mate.

I take the opportunity to throw my arms around him. One part of me needs the contact, while the other knows it's the only way to keep him from losing his temper again. And considering I have no choice but to leave him so soon after he found me, I have to.

"He's right, baby. You have to stay. Muncie needs you." I do, too, but this is shifter business. Just like how there are things that have to do with the Cadre that I'll never fully understand, this is what he has to expect when he has a she-wolf as his beloved. "I have to go with them, but I'm coming back."

"Make it before your Luna's full, księżyca. I gave you the last one to decide if you want to be bonded to me or not. I can't make it through another without you."

Me, neither.

"I will. I swear it."

If the Alpha collective doesn't decide I'm too dangerous a threat to shifter stability to be allowed to leave, that is.

# CHAPTER 14
# UNEXPECTED VISITORS

I don't know what's worse: being a pet or being a curiosity.

In the Wolf District, I was definitely both, but that was only because the Wicked Wolf made me his pet after I convinced him that I could never be his mate. At the Northern Winds Pack? I'm definitely a curiosity.

We arrive late at night. It was a three-hour run from Muncie to Chione, the wooded settlement where the Northern Winds Pack make their home. At the Alpha's urging, we shifted from skin to fur before we left.

Aleks patted my flank and looped my duffel bag over my head, then stood on the empty stretch of land. Through our bond, I could sense him watching me until I was out of sight. I felt a pang when he could no longer see me, but now that I'm aware of my bond with Aleks, I sent a pulse of pure love down it.

He returns it, and I know that, even if he's not *with* me, I carry his love with me wherever I go. And I will see him again.

After the plane ride, I actually don't mind the run. With us in our skin I don't have to listen to whatever nastiness Peyton is spewing at me, though she does get a kick out of snapping her jaws at my tail and trying to trip me up. Eventually Dash jumps in front of her and gives her an Alpha stare. Peyton falls in line after that, but she did cause the three-hour run to creep up to almost four.

It's past ten o'clock when we arrive at Chione. The Alpha grunts at me and Peyton before padding off to his cabin and his waiting mate, leaving us in the care of his Beta. Because I'm the accused and she's the accuser, we both have to stay until the Alphas have gathered to listen to our explanations. Because I missed my first summons and Dash had to come to Muncie, the collective decides to host the meet in Chione.

Luckily for me, being on opposite sides of this shifter battle means that we have to be kept separated. The Beta, Freddy, brings me to an empty cabin that—not so surprisingly—is located near enough to the impressive one belonging to Dash and his mate. The meaning isn't lost on me. Dash was forced to track me down, and now he's got his eye on me. There's no use in trying to escape.

I don't bother. I actually try to hole up in my borrowed cabin until it's time to meet the Alpha collective. It's certainly nicer than the feral's shack, but, yeah... that was a lost cause. I guess it's been too long since I've been in a shifter pack because I forgot how any change to the pack's routine gets the rumor mill running like nothing else.

The whole morning countless packmates stop by to "introduce" themselves to me. I know what that means. It's an excuse for them to come and gawk at the Luna-touched female. I lost count of how many shifters *ooh*-ed and *ahh*-ed over my silver eyes while notably keeping their distance as if afraid I'll rush them and go on a bond-snapping spree or something.

Like in the Wolf District, this pack has a communal dining area. My options—put plainly yet, somehow, still friendly-like by Freddy—are eat with the pack or go hungry. Since the food smells amazing, despite my uneasy belly, I eat.

Dash joins me, alongside his pretty mate, Emily. At first I think it's because I'm a visitor to the pack and, regardless of what happens at the trial, shifter etiquette usually reigns supreme, but I'm quickly corrected.

This isn't lunch. It's an interrogation.

I guess that makes sense. As the host Alpha, Dash is responsible for making the initial assessment. He's already decided that it'll be a full trial—with a total of twelve Alphas acting as both judge and jury. That, he explains in a gruff tone, is due to the severity of the accusations against me. Since Peyton claims that I have this sick urge to break bonds, the Alphas are worried that I could upset the balance of shifter society.

My goal is to prove them wrong. So when Dash starts asking me questions about my abilities, I answer him honestly. I can't get a read on whether he believes I'm harmless or not, but I can say one thing: the mating between Dash and Emily is solid as a rock.

She smiles when I tell them so, and Dash—seeing his mate's smile—starts to look at me with a lot less distrust than before.

I'm allowed back to my cabin after that, though either Dash or Freddy comes to get me every time a new Alpha arrives at Chione. Of the twelve, four make it by dinner, and I sat down and was interrogated by all of them one-on-one to give them my side of the story.

I know they're listening to Peyton, too, and I'll have to go through it all over again when the twelve actually run the trial, but I leave each session feeling a little more worried about my prospects.

And, okay, that's putting it mildly. By the time night begins to creep in and I sense the Beta at my door *again,* I'm a bundle of fucking nerves.

But I answer his knock because what else am I going to do?

"Sorry to disturb you so late, Elizabeth, but you have a visitor."

For a split second, I wonder if Aleks somehow decided to follow me up north after all. Stepping out onto the porch, I look for my vampire. Disappointment floods through me when I don't find him, though I do perk up a second later when I see who *is* there.

"Gem! And... Ryker? What are you doing here?"

Gem is standing a few feet away from my cabin, wearing her trademark tank top, her thumbs tucked through the belt loops on a pair of dark denim jeans. Her long blonde hair is cascading in waves down her back, and I see that she's still wearing the golden fang nestled between her boobs.

Ryker is hovering right behind, as always. He's gotten a haircut since I've seen him last, his dark hair closely cropped to his skull. It makes the Alpha seem impossibly more dangerous—or maybe that's just the look in his dark gold eyes.

She breaks for me. Ryker is right on her heels.

"Elizabeth!" She grabs my hand. "I'm so glad to see you."

"How did you..." I exhale roughly. As much as I wanted him here, I never thought he'd send babysitters after me. "Aleks. He sent you."

Gem squeezes my fingers while Ryker's jaw tightens at just

the mention of Aleks's name. Close to a year after he made Gem his forever mate and he still can't keep himself from reacting. I get it, too. If I wasn't comparing myself to the feisty alpha female in front of me, that's only because I was competing with a ghost.

"He didn't," Gem says. Her nostrils flare enough that I know she's sampling the scents clinging to me. Her golden eyes flash, her dominant aura flaring around her as her claws prick the underside of my fingers. "But he should have. He should be here, too."

She's not hurting me. If she wanted to, I have no doubt that she would. Same thing with her dominance. As an alpha, if she really turned on the power, Gem could have me baring my throat to her. This is just a small preview of what she can do.

Ryker picks up on it. Laying his hand on Gem's shoulder, the simple act of contact has her reining in her aura. Then he says, "You know he can't. Not without an invitation from the collective," and she has to reluctantly agree with him.

"Thanks, babe. Sometimes I forget that Aleks is a vamp."

Ryker rubs her shoulder. "Lucky you. I never do."

"Wait." I'm confused. "So he didn't tell you I got a summons?"

"No," Gem retorts, "and when I get back to Accalia, I'm going to ask him why. I get why he couldn't come, but he shouldn't have let you go alone."

Actually, I'm glad he did. As much as I enjoy having a protector, after what happened with Christian... it's nice that my mate believes I can take care of myself.

He's so getting lucky for having faith in me.

"If it wasn't Aleks," I ask, "then who told you?"

"Look over there."

I glance where Gem is pointing. Dash is standing by two other Alphas. One of them I talked to earlier this afternoon. The other, a big, bulky bearded male, must be a new arrival.

She points out the Alpha with the beard. "See him?"

I nod.

"That's Bishop Dupuis. He's Alpha of the Sylvan Pack out of the Southwest. I think they're based around Louisiana or something."

She looks at Ryker for confirmation. He gives it with a jerk of his chin.

"Thought so. Anyway, Bishop mated this delta she-wolf that used to belong to the River Run Pack. Sofia." Again, Ryker nods. "Sofia still has family in River Run. When Bishop was put on trial duty, all he was told was that it had to do with the fabled Luna-touched female." Gem pauses, tugging on my hand. "Hear that? You're fabled."

"Gemma..."

"I'm getting there, Ryker. Cool your jets. Anyway, Sofia was talking to her sister about Bishop meeting the Luna-touched female and how they're not sure you should be able to be on your own. Then, supposedly, you missed your deadline, they had to drag you here, and Bishop started for Chione. Sofia told her sister, it got around the pack until it eventually reached Kendall. River Run's our ally. Kendall told Ryker, Ryker told me, and here we are."

"But... why?"

Ryker snorts. Obviously he took the trip because Gem made him, but I wasn't asking him. I was asking Gem.

"Because I'm still part of the Muncie Pack," she says. "Pack sticks together, even if one of them is a stubborn lone wolf. I couldn't leave you to face them alone. That reminds me..." Letting go of my hand, Gem turns to Ryker. She flutters her lashes at him. "Babe?"

"Yeah, sweetheart?"

"Can you go over there and make nice with the other Alphas? My dad got us a ticket onto Dash's territory, but I don't want to leave just yet. Why don't you see if you can figure out a way to get us to stay for the trial."

There's something about Ryker Wolfson. To anyone else he's a vicious Alpha who has a quick temper and sharp claws. But when Gem looks at him... he just turns into a puppy dog, doesn't he?

Not like I'll ever admit to having that thought. Still. It's true.

"Of course." Ryker swoops down, giving Gem a quick kiss. "You can count on me."

"I know." She darts out her tongue, swiping it along her bottom lip. "I've got total faith in you."

Ryker snorts. "These days maybe."

Gem shoots her middle finger up at him. She does that a lot, I notice, but that's probably because she loves the reaction she gets from her mate.

"Don't tempt me," he retorts, throwing open his arms. "I thought you wanted me to talk to the other Alphas?"

Gem rolls her eyes. "I do. Go."

Chuckling under his breath, Ryker listens to her, but not before shooting her a look filled with heat and promise.

For a moment, Gem looks like she's going to swoon. Instead, she fans herself. "God, that male is so fucking sexy." She glances over at me, then starts, as though she'd forgotten what she was doing while ogling her own mate. "Sorry about that, Elizabeth. What was I saying?"

"About your dad—?"

"Right. We only got in to see you because I asked my dad to put in a good word with Dash. Dash idolizes him because my dad chose to mate my mom instead of relying on the Luna to name him a fated mate. Dash did the same thing, going against fate to pick his. After we discovered the trial would be held here, Dash said we can come see you before they start this stupid trial bullshit. Be moral support, you know?"

Actually, I do. And I'm so fucking grateful that she did that for me. "Thank you, Gem. You don't know how much that means to me."

"I had to. Not just for you, either. Aleks is my best friend. All I wanted was for him to find someone who made him as happy as Ryker makes me. He never thought he would, but I told him to have faith. Then he met you, and I got to hear my four favorite words in that sexy accent of his." She pauses for a moment, then adds in a horrible imitation of Aleks's voice: "'Gem, you were right.' Ah. Music to my ears."

A lump lodges in my throat. I decide to look past Gem calling Aleks's accent sexy—because, well, it is—in favor of what she just told me. "Aleks said that?"

"Many, many times," Gem confirms. "If I didn't know it wasn't possible, I'd think he might love you more than I love my mate. And, trust me, that's a *lot*."

I don't know how to respond to that. The sound I make is one part laugh, one part sob, and it seems entirely appropriate for the moment.

"See? Keep your spirits up, okay? It's going to be fine," she says. "I promise."

"I'm scared," I admit. "Some kind of she-wolf I am, but, Gem... I'm terrified they're gonna blame me for something out of my control. I just want to live my life. No Alphas ordering me around. No jealous females stalking me. I just... I just want Aleks, but I'm so scared that I'm going to lose him right after I *got* him."

Gem reaches out, tapping my ring finger. "Speaking of... don't think I didn't notice that ring you got there. You get married and forget to invite your best friend?"

Ah, Luna. Aleks is her best friend, but she's *mine*, isn't she? She has to be. Only a friend as good as Gem would listen to me confess that I'm a lousy she-wolf, brush it off, and point out the ring Aleks only just slipped on my finger.

"No. This is... a placeholder, I guess. From Aleks. If I make it out of this alive, he wants to have a real wedding. You can come to that one."

"I'll be your maid of honor." She pauses. "Matron? I'm mated, does that count?" She waves her hand in front of her. "Whatever. I'm going to be there because, I promise you, nothing's gonna happen to you. I'll make sure of it."

That's an alpha female for you. She's convinced she can take care of anything.

"Besides," she adds, a more serious note finding its way to her tone, "it's good to be afraid every now and then. Keeps you sharp."

"Are you telling me that *you* get scared sometimes?"

"Oh, yeah. We all do. Way I see it, that's our human brain's talking. If we never got afraid, we'd go feral. None of us want that."

I think of the sad, abandoned shack with the musty nest and the bones outside and have to admit that Gem has a point.

"You're right."

She grins at me. "Of course I am. And you'll see. I'll be right about the trial, too."

Luna, I hope so.

# CHAPTER 15
## A LITTLE DEMONSTRATION (A WHOLE LOT OF PAIN)

The trial is set for noon the next day. By then, the last of the twelve Alphas should be ready to meet with me. Ryker offered to stand in for one if they needed him to, and though I doubt they will, Dash agreed. That allowed Gem and Ryker to stay.

Thank the Luna. At least, if this all goes sideways, I won't be alone.

To be honest, I'm hoping this all works out. The three Alphas I already met with yesterday didn't seem too disturbed by my abilities, though that could be because they only heard what I could do and saw examples of me reading other supes' bonds. If I walked up to somebody and snapped their mate bond for shits and giggles, I doubt that they'd be as unconcerned.

Not that I would. I never have. The only times I broke bonds were when unhappily mated pairs asked me to, or when my former Alpha forced me. He used me as another tool, a way to keep the Western Pack and its enemies in line, and he turned me into a broken, shattered mess of a she-wolf the entire time I was trapped in the district.

I'm better now. Stronger. I'm not completely whole, but I think I've become something different. Forged in the fire of Aleks's love, I've remade myself into an Elizabeth that's a whole lot more unbreakable than she was a few short years ago.

The Luna helped, too; more accurately, not having her there to rely on for the last two and a half months did. I had to deal with my own thoughts, my own insecurities, and figure my own shit out by myself for the first time in my life. Even now that she's back, her presence isn't as noticeable as it used to be. In fact, I think I filled the spot she occupied with my feelings for my vampire.

If only he was here with me…

When Dash and Bishop walk me into the den where the trial will be held that day at noon, I gulp. Maybe it's a good thing that I convinced Aleks to stay behind. If he saw the set-up, he'd know that this is a lot more serious than I let on.

I certainly do.

Every pack has an Alpha cabin. It belongs to the leader of the pack, and is his personal home on pack land. Since most Alphas take a mate shortly after they perform their Alpha Ceremony, their mate lives with them. Any pups they have will, too. Other than that, no one else is allowed in the Alpha cabin—except for the den.

Because packs are so community-driven, there needs to be a place where packmates can go to talk with the Alpha without encroaching on his personal territory. That's how dens were formed. In each Alpha cabin, there's a room designated as the den. So long as the Alpha is in residence, any and all packmates can go to the den and be sure that their Alpha will see them.

In the Northern Winds Pack, the den is attached to the back of the cabin. In a suburban human home, it would be the garage; in a shifter pack, it's the den. The inside is carpeted, the walls paneled with wood made from the trees that surround Dash's land, and I can see tracks in the carpet from where furniture usually stands.

Today, anything that might have usually been in the den was removed. In its place, there are two cafeteria-style tables placed back to back, plus enough chairs for the twelve Alphas preceding over this trial. Ten are lined up, each one more dominant and imposing as the last. Two chairs are vacant: one at the end and one in the center. After pointing me toward the spot where I'm expected to sit, Bishop plunks down in the chair on the end. Dash takes the center seat.

Across the tables, there are two stools. One is set on the right side of the room, one on the left, with a good twelve feet separating them. I sit on the one to the right. The left one is empty.

Behind me, there are four folding chairs for some reason. A little overkill, since Ryker and Gem are the only ones sitting back there, but I disregard it. Maybe they expected a bigger turnout or something, I don't know. I'm just glad that Gem and Ryker are close enough to lend me their support.

Once I sit down, the door flings open again. Peyton comes stalking in.

She glances at the back, scowling when she sees the two empty chairs. Mumbling under her breath, she says, "Fucking Kyle," then angrily drops down on her stool.

The trial begins just the way I expect it to. As the host Alpha, Dash runs the show. He explains what we're doing here, and has Peyton repeat her accusations. Then, when Peyton's done, it's my turn to refute them.

Too bad I can't.

For about an hour, I have to explain what I can do. From the way my eyes change colors, to how I can conceal a shifter's scent, and my family's long relationship with the Luna... they want to hear about it all. One suggests we might be descendants of the first female alpha, but since I don't know why my maternal line has always been gifted, I just shrug.

And that's when they ask me about my skill with sensing and breaking bonds.

I tell them everything. These are all Alphas here so, even if I was a good liar, they'd know. It's not worth risking pissing them off by lying.

Finally, Peyton has had enough. When the Alphas aren't quick to condemn me, her silent fuming becomes a sudden explosion.

"Is that all we're going to do? Listen to her run her mouth? She's admitted that she can do just what I said she could. So let's get on with it. No more questions. Sentence her!"

Okay. Now, Peyton had made a bunch of comments while I was talking. I ignored her. The Alphas asking for clarification in regards to what I was saying ignored her, too.

But Gem... I think she's hit her limit.

She rises from her seat in the back. Her dominance is just as powerful as the other alphas in the room, but she has one thing on her side that they don't: she's not an Alpha of a pack. In Mountainside, Ryker is the Alpha, while she's his female. It's a shifter thing. If she left and formed a pack of her own, she could've made any male her alpha, regardless of his rank. It's the same for the male Alphas. Their mates become the female alpha of the pack, with the Alpha—the pack's leader—at the tippy-top of the hierarchy. Most Alpha couples are equals, but the biggest difference comes down to something as simple as this. Ryker is an Alpha, Gem isn't, and because she isn't, she's the only dominant one in the room who could shut down Peyton Slade without bringing pack politics into it.

And that's exactly what Gem does.

"Put up or shut up, Peyton. You have such a problem with Elizabeth, fine. None of us are universally liked. But since you want to blame her when your mate fucked around on you and she broke your bond, I've gotta tell you that you're picking on the innocent one here. Maybe your mate should've kept it in his pants."

Is she trying to help me? I'm not so sure how she thinks reminding everyone in the room that I did exactly what Peyton's accusing me of is going to work in my favor, but the dare on Gem's face makes me think *she* thinks she is.

Next to her, Ryker Wolfson's eyes are burning bright like lava as his lips curve in a proud smirk that says, *That's* my *mate.*

It's a low blow. Everyone here knows it. When shifters mate for life, none of us want to admit that there are a few rotten apples in every bunch. Our kind of supe might be hard-wired to be loyal to our bonded mates, but males like Jack Walker and Kyle prove that it's not the case for all of us.

Kyle cheated. You can blame me for falling head over heels for a male I knew nothing about, but I didn't know he had a bonded mate back at Oak Valley. If I snapped their bond so easily that I didn't even know it was there, it was a whisper of a thread to begin with.

And she's been blaming me for her failed mating for seven years because of it.

I don't know what she's hoping to accomplish here. Gunning for my head all because I fucked her mate... it's not fair. It's not right. He manipulated me as much as he betrayed Peyton, yet it's the two of us sitting on opposite sides of the Northern Winds Pack den, spilling our guts out for all of these strangers.

I get that. But Peyton... her face twists into a nasty look as she glares at me. Because of course she does. "You stole him from me!"

Gem scoffs. "Please. I met the Oak Valley Beta. My dad's the Alpha of Lakeview, and he was at one of the gatherings I want to with my dad. I was barely nineteen and that prick tried to stick his tongue down my throat."

Ryker's head shoots toward Gem. "He did what?"

Gem shushes her mate. "The only difference is that Elizabeth made it so you weren't stuck with a male who was the pack peen. You're free to choose a male who loves you. Fated mates are great, but we all know the Luna doesn't get it right all of the time. She obviously didn't with you and Kyle."

"I don't care," snaps Peyton. Jumping to her feet, she jabs a finger in my direction. "She ruined my life. I have to ruin hers!"

Yeah... that's exactly what she's hoping to accomplish here after this is all done, isn't it? Ruining my life—or ending it.

Gem arches an eyebrow. Tilting her head just so, her long blonde ponytail falls over her shoulder, nestling next to the golden fang—one of Ryker's—hanging off of a chain that she wears around her throat. "And how do you plan on doing that?"

"Jack said they'd kill her. That she was an abomination and... and a *freak*. That she shouldn't be able to play around with mate bonds like that. He said, if you all"—she waves a wild hand in the direction of the twelve Alphas in front of us—"knew the truth, you'd execute her so that her line ends with her. He *said*—"

"My sperm donor said a lot of shit, and none of it was good. You know where it got him? Dead. And the whole world is better for it."

"Jack was a good male! He should still be here, and Howell should be nothing but maggot food."

Wow. Tell me how you really feel.

I'm used to Peyton talking about me like that. But Gem? She's *not*.

"Okay. You've just touched my last fucking nerve, Peyton." She gestures with her fingers, giving her a "bring it" wave. "You and me. Heads will roll in this den, but it won't be Elizabeth's."

Peyton goes still. "Are you challenging me?"

"Luna damn right I am. What do you say? You accept?"

Shifter tradition says that the challenge should come from the lower-ranked wolf. Technically, Peyton should be the one to throw down the gauntlet, but her issue isn't with Gemma Swann. It's with me. But Gem? She thinks of me as one of her own and, alpha wolf to her core, she's going to stand up for the more submissive wolf.

And, Luna, I love to see it. Peyton might have just admitted she wants the Alpha collective to sentence me to death, but it's still nice to see Gem tossing the challenge out like that. She's a hothead, but she's in my corner, and I love her for it.

The only thing is, because Gem's the more dominant wolf, Peyton gets to decide if she wants to risk fighting her. It's an imbalance of power for someone of Gem's ranking to target a delta like Peyton, so no one will think any less of her for refusing to face off against an alpha.

Well, I will, but I probably don't count.

Peyton opens her mouth. Closes it. Shakes her head and,

purposely avoiding the murder written in every line of Gem's deceptively innocent face, she takes her seat again.

Dash clears his throat. "That's enough of that. There will be no more challenging today. We are here to discuss what Elizabeth's Luna-given gifts mean for the rest of shifter society."

Gem's golden eyes flare, locking on a new target. "It only works against shaky bonds to begin with, and only if she tries on purpose to break the bond. This is ridiculous. Elizabeth is a delta for Luna's sake and we're treating her worse than the Wicked Wolf of the West ever was! And, know what else? The Luna blessed her to be able to do this. You think of that? You think our goddess didn't do it on purpose?"

"Gemma, sweetheart," murmurs Ryker, patting the seat next to him. "Let's not do this today."

"Fine." With a huff, Gem plops down next to him. "But I mean all of it."

"That's a good point," says a dark-haired, Latino Alpha a couple of seats down from Dash. I don't know him, but he reminds me of Luis Cruces, the Alpha of the Gravetail Pack. Maybe it's his son? "About the blessed Luna. Now, I'm a new Alpha, only just performed the ceremony a few months ago. Correct me if I'm wrong, but you... you're the female alpha, right?"

Ryker is the one who answers him. "Who's asking?"

"Sorry. Rafael Cruces. Gravetail Pack." Ha! I was right! "I missed the last Alpha gathering in July and was hoping to introduce myself to the infamous Ruby Walker."

"She's taken," Ryker says flatly. "And her name is Gemma Swann Wolfson, not Ruby Walker."

"My apologies about the name mix-up," Rafael says, punctuating his apology with a chuckle that tells us he meant no harm.

He has a gentle laugh at odds with the sad look in his dark gold eyes. "That's not what I meant. She's lovely, yes, but it's more about her rank. She's an alpha, as you are, Wolfson. And, again, correct me if I'm wrong, but your pack butts up against the vamp settlement where Elizabeth lives with her mate."

Gem lays her hand on Ryker's thigh. "Yeah. So?"

"And you're not worried? That she might turn against you, use your Luna-given powers on your bond?"

"What? Of course not. I just told you all. It doesn't work like that."

"You're sure?"

"No," cuts in Peyton. "She can steal any shifter's mate bond! You have to punish her!"

Rafael ignores her. Instead, he focuses on Gem. "If you're sure, you wouldn't mind... proving it, would you?"

Oh, no. He's not suggesting that I try to break Gem's bond in front of the collective, is he?

I gulp. Now that the Luna is back, so are all of my "gifts". And while the Alphas know that—I proved it when I told Dash and Emily about their bond—none of them have seen me attempt to break a bond except for Gem and her mate.

It wasn't pretty then, either.

Her gaze flickers my way. She frowns. "You don't know what you're asking us to do. She won't break my bond. She can't. But if she tries... you're asking me to hurt my friend. That's fucked up, Rafael."

"It's okay." If this is what I have to do to prove it... I get off my stool, walk over to her. "If you don't mind, I'll do it."

Gem glances at Ryker next. With a sigh, she says, "You know I love you, babe."

He nods. "And you know that there's no getting rid of me,

Gemma. It's for life, you and me. So go on. Show him how unbreakable our bond is."

Straight-backed and proud as ever, Gem thrusts her hand out. I grit my teeth and brace my legs, knowing what's going to happen, but no matter how many times I experience the painful blowback of an unbroken bond, it never gets easier.

I'm not really sure what happens next. The second I touch Gem, the bond holds just like we knew it would. Pain racks my entire body, and I'm pretty sure I just collapse into a pile on the carpet because, when I come to again, I'm curled up on my side. Gem's crouching next to me, guarding my vulnerable body from the others. Ryker is standing at her side.

To my surprise, so is Rafael.

Gem hears me stirring. Looking over her shoulder, she says, "You good?"

"Been better," I say weakly. "And your bond?"

"Strong like titanium," she confirms.

Oh. Good.

The two males back up to give me space as I pull myself up and off of the floor. Gem offers her hand to help me up. I wait a second to make sure that I've gotten my abilities under control, then take it.

I know what she's doing. By offering me her hand, she's not proving how weak I am. She's letting the other Alphas see that it takes more than an accidental brush for me to try to break a bond otherwise I'd be flat on my ass again.

Instead, I'm on my feet. Shaky, but fine.

Rafael is giving me a scrutinizing look. I don't know what they all discussed while I was out, but no one seems surprised when he waits until I'm seated again, then approaches me.

I flinch.

"I want you to touch my hand." He gentles his voice for my benefit. He must've noticed the flinch. "You've given us an example of what happens to a mated pair who don't want to lose their bond. Here." Rafael holds his hand out in front of me. "Let's show the Alphas gathered here what happens when a supe does."

Ah. I peer closer at the handsome shifter with the sad eyes. Too distracted with everything else, I didn't really pay attention to his bond. Every Alpha had one, so I ignored them all. But Rafael... I understand now. He has a fated mate, but not only has he not bonded her to him, she has a bond with someone else.

She chose another male, but she didn't release Rafael.

How can that be, I wonder. I look a little closer and then I see what makes Rafael's bond incomplete. Poor guy. His fated mate is an omega wolf. No wonder he's holding on to it subconsciously. Omegas are the glue of any pack, making it whole. Any shifter lucky enough to bond to an omega would never willingly let them go.

But Rafael's fated omega chose to bond to another male. Until he does the same, he'll have an echo of their intended tie—unless I take it from him.

So I do. Tapping him on the top of his hand, I instinctively erase the featherlight tie still connecting him to another female.

He gasps. I take a few steps back, hoping that I made the right choice to agree to break his bond for him.

Luna, this wasn't a trap, was it?

"Rafael?" rumbles Bishop. "Did it work? Do you still sense my sister?"

Oof. I didn't know that the omega on the other end of Rafael's bond was another Alpha's *sister*.

Rafael nods. "I— *yes*," he breathes out. "I've finally set her free."

Bishop nods. It's hard to tell with such a stone-faced male, but I think he actually looks relieved.

Maybe… maybe this is going to work out in the end.

Rafael moves back to the table with the other Alphas. Dash announces that they're going to take an anonymous vote, using a piece of paper. My heartbeat ramps up when he says that each Alpha must decide my fate.

A 'yes' vote means that they believe I'm no danger and I'm free to go.

A 'no' vote means that I'm too big of a risk to shifter society and… He doesn't finish his sentence, but he doesn't have to. If the Alphas vote 'no', Peyton's probably going to get her wish.

He also offers the Alphas the chance to abstain. If they're not persuaded by either display, or they're not sure, they can leave their papers blank. Once they're done, the eleven other Alphas pass their papers facedown to Dash. He shuffles them, then reads them out loud.

With a vote of ten to zero, with two members of the collective abstaining from voting, the Alphas conclude that my gifts are mine to do with as I please—but if someone challenges me over them, I'm on my own.

"That's it?" shrieks Peyton. "That's all?"

I wait to see if there's anything else. As the Alphas begin to get up, talking amongst themselves, and Rafael gives me a curious look as he rubs the heel of his hand over his chest, I wait to see if Peyton is going to challenge me.

I'd fight her. If I had to, I would. Drawing on my fight to the death with Christian, I… I think I would win, too.

But Peyton doesn't say a word to me. Whether it's because

she's terrified of Gem, or she doesn't want to go against Dash's earlier decree that there would be no more challenging today, or, Luna forbid, she was afraid of what I could do... Peyton Slade surprisingly keeps her mouth shut. And, with a flounce, she disappears out of the den.

I let out a shaky exhale of relief.

Do I think that I've seen the back of her?

Not even a little.

Am I glad this whole ordeal is over?

More than you would ever know.

Am I dying to get back home to mate?

Luna fucking *yes.*

# CHAPTER 16
# TAKE THE LEAD

Gem and Ryker keep me company all the way back home.

Home… I still have a hard time believing that I have one. Not just a place I return to to go to sleep, or a place where I keep my stuff before I hit the road again, but a spot where I'm wanted. Where I'm loved.

Where I belong.

I'm so eager to get back that I actually spur the two alphas to go faster. Like me, they ran the distance from Accalia to the Northern Winds Pack. They could've driven—there were some roads accessible to the forested pack land—but Ryker isn't the biggest fan of being in a car. To shifters, closed-in vehicles are like elevators. They remind our beastly halves of cages and most of us avoid them if we can. Gem gets around it by driving a Jeep, but with the Northern Winds Pack only about three hours away by paw, they didn't bother.

Sometimes even an alpha wolf wants to shake off their

responsibility and just run wild in the woods. And I wouldn't have minded if their running turned into foreplay like Ryker was obviously attempting, but I had a mate of my own to get back to. I kept running ahead, Gem catching up if only because she's just as protective of me as Aleks is, with her mate bringing up the rear.

Poor Ryker. I didn't mean to cockblock him, but it's been days since I touched my mate. He had Gem last night. He could make it a couple of hours longer until he gets to mount her again.

Then again, maybe not.

The second the three of us reach the neutral zone between Muncie and Accalia, the big wolf snaps his jaws playfully at Gem's tail, guiding her up toward the mountain's path. She yips, whirling on her mate, forcing him to stumble at her speed, but she doesn't seem to mind his urgency. In fact, taking advantage of his stumble, she breaks for the trees, knowing that her mate will always chase her.

Just like mine.

As Ryker disappears into the woods behind Gem, I give them a full-throated howl. It's both a 'thank you' and a 'goodbye'. My tongue lolls a bit, my wolf doing a chuffing sort of laugh as Ryker's return howl sounds impatient, Gem's teasing. I gotta say, it's amazing how a shifter's howl can be so many things, *mean* so many things, and it makes me realize how grateful I am to have friends like them so near.

I might always be a lone wolf. I might never join another shifter pack. At least I know that, when I need them, I always have two strong alphas close by to remind me that I'm still a she-wolf. I'm part of an amazing supe community. Most importantly, I don't have to be lonely.

And I'm not. How can I be? Because, standing just a foot or two past the border of the Fang City, his pale eyes gleaming in the afternoon sunlight, his arms crossed over his delicious chest… his aura reaching out toward me, wrapping me up in his essence though he hasn't moved an inch… is my mate.

Luna, he's fucking *gorgeous*. I should be used to it by now, but after the time away, I'm struck all over again by him. This beautiful male is *mine*.

It's not just his outer beauty that has me slowly padding toward him, stunned to see him waiting for me. Sure, the caramel-colored curls and sculpted features don't hurt, but it's who he is that makes him irresistible. He's thoughtful. Caring. Protective. Wildly jealous and a brutal killer; both things that are a plus to a shifter. Devoted. And maybe he's also secretive and haughty, and he always thinks he knows what's best, but no one's perfect. Aleks isn't.

But he's perfect for me.

Once I start toward him, he uncrosses his arms. Dropping his knee to the dirt, he throws them wide open. Pure joy fills my chest like an overinflated balloon. My padding becomes a sprint as my wolf races to get within his arms.

He closes them around me, running his chilled fingers through my fur, nuzzling the top of my head with his chin. He rubs his cheek against the side of my muzzle. As if he's been holding his breath the entire time I was gone, he exhales roughly, fluttering the fur near my neck as he holds onto my wolf tightly.

"Ah, księżyca." He presses a kiss to the space between my ears. "Welcome home, my beloved."

My wolf preens under his loving attention.

Look at that. I guess I'm perfect for him, too.

It takes a little convincing for my wolf to let me give control back to my human side. Both of us recognize that Aleks is our mate, but because he's a vampire who doesn't have a four-legged form, I definitely spend more time with him with two legs. Now that she's getting all of his attention, she's hesitant to give it up. She has to, though. Aleks might be the head vamp in Muncie, but I don't want to cause him any trouble when locals start to wonder why a white wolf is strolling around the city.

Promising her that she'll get another chance to snuggle with our vampire soon, my wolf steps back. Once I'm sure no one is around except my mate, I shift, then grab a dress from my duffel bag. From the charge in his aura when Aleks gets a look at my naked body, I almost expect him to forget that we're just outside of the safety of his territory.

He has better control than I do. I was about to offer to take him in the woods for a quick and frantic mating when Aleks snags my hand, pulling me into him as he whispers in a ragged voice, "My God, księżyca. I can't fucking wait to get you back home."

Me, neither.

Once I'm dressed, Aleks grabs my duffel, still holding tightly to my hand. On the walk back to the apartment, he grills me on every detail about the meeting with the Alphas. Relief flashes across his face as soon as he hears that they won't be bothering me again. I know then that Aleks's boast—that he would tear out a thousand throats to keep me safe—was no idle one. My fierce protector really would've gone up against the Alpha collective for me.

Luna, that's so fucking sexy.

Because I want to jump him myself for that, I pick up the pace. Aleks matches it easily, a low seductive chuckle sending shivers down my spine. He probably can scent my body getting ready for him and knows exactly what my plans for our reunion are.

To distract myself, I ask Aleks about Muncie. We only have a couple of blocks to go at that point, so he gives me a quick rundown of anything important that happened while I was gone. My mate has finally figured out that, anything that involves him, it's something I want to know about. Whether it's ridiculous—like one of his vampires getting caught feeding off of another vamps' preferred donor—or serious—like the next rebel trying to be the one to take Aleks down—I want to know.

Thank the Luna, but it seems as if the attempts on his life have slowed down. There hasn't been one since the night three vamp males tried to cut him with a silver knife, and it seems as if Aleks's prediction that it was just the change in leadership bringing out the zealots might have proven true.

And I get to believe that for about two minutes more before Aleks's phone rings.

Damn it. We were so close to reaching the apartment. Like, I see it. It's right there.

But Aleks is the head vamp. To love and accept him, I have to accept that. He has to answer the phone, and he does.

It's a quick exchange. The male vamp on the other line says that there's been a report of a possible rebel stalking the apartment building where we live. Another vamp called it in, letting the Cadre know that the vamp is one of those who wants to see Aleks replaced, and if he has to eliminate Aleks himself, he plans on it.

Oh, great. They're not just ambushing my mate now. They're

turning his possible assassination into a community affair. I mean, who does that? Who runs his mouth about targeting the most powerful vampire in Muncie?

An idiot, that's who. And if this is what he has to deal with as leader? No wonder he thinks it's nothing.

Especially when he rolls his eyes and asks, "What level threat is he?"

The Cadre vamp scoffs. "A two. Maybe. The intel was shoddy, and the vamp might even be a fan of yours, Aleksander. Personally, I think it's a bottomfeeder looking to make a name for himself. I know you expect these threats funneled to you personally, but Cynthia is patrolling nearby. I can reroute her and have her do something about it."

"Don't be ridiculous, Samson. I'm actually right there," Aleks says. "I was heading home when you called. I'll take care of it myself."

I wait for him to hang up his phone and slip it back into his pocket before I announce, "If you're going, I want to go with you."

Aleks pauses. I can tell his instinct is to immediately refuse, but the last few weeks have taught him that that's not the right approach when you're dealing with a shifter, especially when she's your mate.

He thinks about it for a moment, then says, "You do? Why?"

Good question.

I have one for him. "I heard the vamp on the line," I say, no ounce of shame. Not when it's this important. "They told you there was a possible traitor sniffing around our building. They could've sent that other patroller to handle it and find out if he's on your side or against you. You offered to do it yourself. Why?"

I think I surprised him. Usually when he gets these calls, I purposely don't listen in. I also don't offer to go, or question why he is.

But things are different now. I'm his blood-bonded mate. His beloved. He wants to follow me across the country? Well, it's my turn to stay by him. I know he's going to go. That's the kind of male he is and he proves it by saying, "Because I'm head vamp now and it's my responsibility."

I get that. I still want to go with him.

"Listen. Do you remember when I found out that some of your vampires were turning on you? Trying to hurt you? Kill you?" When he nods, I tell him, "You said it was nothing. It's not nothing to me. It never is."

"Mój księżyca."

*My moon…*

"Wait. Please. I know you have to go, but… just give me a second to make my point. It's taken me a while to figure out why I got so upset. I know how good you are. I know what you're capable of and, Luna, I love you for it. But…"

Aleks takes my chin in his hands. "But what?"

I take a deep breath. I had a lot of time to think, both when I was running from him, then when I was separated from him during my short trial. I didn't expect to have this conversation so soon, but if not now, when?

"Do you know how many challenges Walker forced me to sit through? Back at the district, when he made me be his pet… can you even guess?"

Almost a year since the last one and I still have nightmares about the reckless loss of life and the Wicked Wolf's cruelty. Like he was the emperor ruling over a gladiator's match, the only one in the pack with the power to decide who lived and died, he wielded it with a smile.

Bastard.

"Oh, Elizabeth," he says softly. "Too many. It was too many."

One was too many. "You're right. Sometimes he fought, sometimes he made others fight to the death for his own sick amusement. It broke me. You helped put a lot of the pieces back together, but it's going to take longer than a couple of months. I saw you fight," I remind him. "I know how well you can. But I can't help it, Aleks. Walker's proof that you can win a hundred challenges. You only have to lose *one*. And when I think of you fighting all those rebels on your own for a position you never even wanted... I can't stand the not knowing. I'd rather be there. Let me come."

"I never wanted you to see how cruel I can be," he whispers.

Laying my hands over his, I shake my head. "You're not cruel. You're a protector. For me. For Muncie. But who protects you?" I wait a beat to see if he'll answer before I add, "Me. I will."

Aleks kisses me, then lowers his hands. Mine fall to my side.

He grins. "Well, what are you waiting for? Let's go."

---

If I was trying to make a move against an Alpha way more powerful than me, I'd at least be stealthy. The dark-haired, narrow-eyed vampire stalking the walkway behind our apartment isn't. He has that eerie vampire glide, so he's quick, but he's glaring up at the twelfth floor as though working up the nerve to fly up the fire escape and attack Aleks at home.

That's the part that gets me. Later, I realize I might've taken his possible bad intentions a little bit personally—but what should I have done? He brought his aggressions to our home. It was one thing for them to go down to the Cadre building to confront Aleks, but *our home*?

Barely tempered rage comes off of Aleks in an icy blast. Seems like he's not too happy about that, either.

His back was to us when we moved around the corner to meet him. As if Aleks's aura knocked him off his stride, he stumbles, then whirls around on us.

"You," he says, his voice lyrical though his beautiful face is twisted in an ugly look. "It's about time you show up, Filan. You think you're so untouchable. You think you deserve to fuck up our city. I'm here to prove you wrong."

He has red eyes. That's not too unusual. Just like how my eyes go black with emotion, the same can be said of vampires. True, it's also a sign of bloodlust, but maybe he really isn't here to try and hurt my mate.

And that's when I see the silver knife he's clutching in his hand.

Tapping into the rage I feel at the thought of anything happening to my mate, my eyes go black as I jump in front of Aleks and bare my teeth at the other vampire. It would probably be a lot more impressive if I was in my fur, but I don't shift just yet. I want him to understand me.

"If you want to get to Aleks," I snarl, "you have to go through me first."

"You might be a dog, but that just means I can put you down without any trouble."

Aleks stays behind me. Not because he needs me to stand in front of him against any threat, but because I think *he* thinks it's adorable that I am. Either way, we're a bonded couple. We're just beginning to learn that we have to face the world as a team.

This is our chance to prove it. So, in that conversational tone of his that is anything but, Aleks tuts, then says, "Don't call my beloved a dog, if you please."

The red-eye vamp scoffs. "Poor Filan. Can't run a Cadre and has to settle for mating a dog. And we thought it was bad under Zakharov. At least he didn't embarrass the rest of us by sticking his cock in one of her kind. I knew you were desperate with the Alpha's bitch, but really? You couldn't find someone to make the Cadre stronger?" He spits on the ground. "Pitiful."

"Again," says Aleks, "I'd ask you to stop insulting my beloved."

Reaching behind me, I pat my mate on his chest. He might've said that I could help him handle this latest threat, but if this idiot keeps running his mouth, Aleks is going to go for his throat before I get a chance to make my position clear.

"It's fine, baby," I tell him. "He doesn't know that I'm stronger than I look."

"Right." The mocking tone is a little grating, but I expected it. "Because all wolves think they're stronger than vampires, is that it?"

"No." Unlike the rebel vamp, my tone isn't mocking. It's actually quite pleasant as I tap my temple, drawing attention to my black eyes. "Because I'm not like regular wolves. How's your beloved, by the way? It was a fated match. I get the sense you love her very much, which is a shame."

He looks a little rattled at that. "I guess that's because you think Filan is going to kill me? Well, surprise." He shows off his silver knife. "Only one of us is armed. I think the odds are in my favor even if there are two of you."

As the Luna flashes against the blade, I'm reminded of that day at brunch when Gretchen made fun of the three vampires who went after Aleks with a knife. She'd said something about how they should've brought a sword, but even that wouldn't be enough to take down my mate.

I know that. Does that mean I like the idea that every bravado-filled vamp is going to try?

Nope. And that's why I'm still holding Aleks back, standing between him and the knife-wielding vamp who is the latest to challenge him.

Good thing my mate is a vampire. If this was a shifter challenge, I'd have to stand back and not interfere. But as a vampire, all bets are off. If this idiot thinks I'm going to stand here and let him try to hack off Aleks's head without stopping him, he has another think coming.

But I also meant it when I said that he loves his mate. I can sense it, and though he'll have to pay for betraying Aleks, I'm going to give him a choice. He might be willing to lose his life by going after my mate. On the odd chance he survives challenging Aleks, is he willing to lose *her*?

"Funny that you mention being armed." I hold up mine, twisting my hand on my wrist like a princess wave. "All I have is this hand. You know what it does, though?" Before he can spit out some answer that I probably won't care for, I tell him. "One touch of my hand and I'll snap your bond in two. Don't believe me? Ask Dominic and Felicity. I broke theirs. I'll break yours, too."

I'm bluffing. His bond seems strong enough that I might not actually be able to—but he doesn't know that.

"You're lying."

I smile. "Am I?"

The vampire looks over my head, locking eyes with Aleks. "I only wanted what was good for Muncie. They said she was your weakness. I... I didn't know."

I'm not surprised. I've spent my whole adult life keeping my abilities a secret from the shifter world. Even after I came to live in Muncie, I did everything I could to keep them under wraps. Roman knew, thanks to Gem, but that was all.

Things are different now. With the Alpha collective on my side, I don't have to hide them anymore. Might as well use them to support my mate instead.

Just like he'll do anything to support me.

"She might be my weakness, but that doesn't make her weak," Aleks tells him. "Who said that?"

The vampire's expression becomes bewildered. His eyes fade from red to a light hazel color. "I… just *they*, I guess."

Ah, Luna. Really?

Aleks moves into me, laying his hand over my shoulder. "Then you better do yourself a favor, Justin, and stop listening to *they*, yes? Believe me, I also want what's best for Muncie. That could be you if you get rid of that knife."

With a clatter, the silver knife hits the sidewalk.

Smart vamp. Each one of us knows that, while I might've been bluffing, Aleks wasn't. He gave Justin the chance to rethink what he was doing. If he insisted on challenging Aleks anyway, I might have been able to snap his bond. No doubt in my mind that Aleks would've fought him and won.

He nods his head, giving my shoulder a squeeze. "Tak. Now go home, kiss your beloved, and hope that if our paths cross again, I don't remember how much you insulted mine."

Justin mutters something under his breath that might possibly be an apology. I don't know. Don't really care, either. He didn't try to attack Aleks; that's all that matters to me. And when he bows his head deeply in Aleks's direction before disappearing into the shadows of the night, I'm pretty sure he'll never try pulling that stunt again.

Glancing over my shoulder and up at my mate, seeing the pleased look on his aristocratic features, I know he thinks the same thing.

I laugh.

He furrows his brow. "What?"

"Nothing."

"Oh? Is that so?"

I shrug. "I was just thinking that, if all those threats were like that, I might have worried for no reason." It's a tease, and we both know it. "Also, it's nice to see that not everyone who pisses you off ends up without a head. I was starting to get a little worried there, Aleks."

He throws his arm over my shoulder, tucking me into his side. "If I killed every vampire who disagreed with me, I wouldn't have any to lead." He makes a thoughtful sound in the back of his throat. "Actually, that might not be so bad of an idea."

Snorting under my breath, I bump my hip against him. As if I believe that. He might not want to be the leader, but there's no one better in Muncie to look out for the Cadre, and we both know *that*. "Come on, baby. Take me home."

He presses a kiss to my temple. "As you wish."

# CHAPTER 17
# FOREVER MATES

At the time, I thought it was a little weird that the Alpha collective went to the trouble of gathering twelve Alphas together for my trial, interrogated me, interrogated Peyton, and then had a decision made in barely forty-eight hours. It was like, if they weren't going to punish me for something completely out of my control, what was the point?

Now, I understood why I had to be called against them. If I didn't know me, I'd be spooked at the prospect that there was a shifter who could go around and break bonds when it suited them to. It didn't matter that I'm not like that. That I never meant to hurt others and ruin their lives. My track record speaks for itself. I was obviously a threat to all shifter kind, and it was right that the collective had something to say about that.

On the plus side, I don't have to worry about the threat of them hanging over my head. The matter's been settled, and if I decide to use my Luna-given "gifts" against those who don't deserve it, whatever happens is my problem to deal with. But did

I really need to be dragged in front of the twelve like that if the whole thing was going to be settled so quickly?

I realize something the morning after I return to Muncie. Despite Aleks and I mating into the early morning hours after we made it to the apartment, I wake up with my skin itchy, my pussy soaked, and my tits heavy and aching. I've never been so fucking horny, and that feeling only grows to pure sexual frustration when I roll over and see that Aleks is missing.

He left a note for me on the kitchen table, next to a breakfast frittata he must've whipped up before he left. It's still fairly hot, so he couldn't have been gone long, and I'm not surprised when his note says that he had to head to the Cadre building to take care of some things, but he'd be back before nightfall.

In his elegant script, he adds one line to the bottom of the page: *I look forward to tonight's full moon.*

I almost slap myself on the forehead. How could I have forgotten? I guess, in the back of my mind, I knew that tonight was when the Luna would be at her peak, but I was so stinking happy to just be with Aleks again, I didn't even think past last night.

No wonder the Alpha collective finished my trial as quickly as they had. Even though the need can be terrible before a bond is complete—and it is, last month was awful, even if Aleks only stayed away so that he didn't take advantage of my need while I was struggling with the Luna being gone—it's still pretty much all-consuming once you find your mate. No bonded shifter will be away from their mate on the night of the full moon. Of course they had to finish up my trial yesterday so they could all be with their mates tonight.

Just like I'm going to be with mine.

I have to admit, it's the most heavenly form of torture,

waiting for Aleks. The later it gets, the lustier I get. I refuse to give myself a hand, though. This is it. My mating night. A few quick orgasms might take the edge off, but I kind of don't want it gone. I think it'll make tonight more memorable, even if I can't help but check to make sure I'm not leaving a sopping wet spot on the settee as I wait impatiently for Aleks to get home.

Never let it be said that my vampire doesn't have perfect timing. Right as the sun goes down, the Luna beginning her ascent over Muncie, I feel his icy aura through the door a split second before it eases open.

He steps in. Proving he knows me as well enough as he does, his arms open wide a split second before I fling myself at him.

Now, I'm not a shy female. I never have been. Sure, I'm not a dominant she-wolf, but when it comes to my pleasure, I know what I want. I know how to ask for it, and when a male is willing, I know how to take it.

So when Aleks gives me one of those low, sexy chuckles and asks if I prefer to have dinner first or if we should get right to it, my response is to crook one arm around his neck, tugging him down to me so that I can kiss him right as I shove my hand down his pants.

Questing fingers find a cock that's already hard and heavy against my palm. It's an awkward angle, and our kiss is messy and frantic and like nothing a stranger might expect from the aristocratic Aleksander Filan, but I manage to take a firm hold of it. Aleks groans in my mouth at my first squeeze. His hands go straight to my hair, threading his fingers through the length, kissing me until I'm almost light-headed from the lack of air.

He can tell. Breaking the kiss, he holds me tight even as I continue to fondle his erection. "I guess I have my answer."

Yes. He certainly does.

Doesn't hurt that I'm already naked. To me, nudity is no big deal. I've eaten countless meals in my skin after a shift just because I either didn't have a change of clothes or I didn't want to bother pulling them on only to have to shift again. Of course, that changes when there's sexual attraction and need involved—like now—but I didn't see the purpose in waiting around in clothes that were only chafing my over-sensitized skin.

Gesturing at my body with my free hand, I cock an eyebrow at him. "I'm ready when you are."

Reaching for the hem of his sweater while bracing his legs so that I can still have easy access to him, Aleks yanks it over his head.

With a small sound of regret, I let go of him and slip my hand out of his pants. I could play with him all night long, but if I want to bond him to me, I need to do more than give him a hand job. He pauses when I release him, his sweater still hanging off of one arm.

I reach for the button on his pants. His eyes flash from green to red as he yanks the sleeve off of his arm.

Oh, Aleks. You didn't think I was changing my mind now, did you? Oh, no, no. I was just helping him remove his pants.

Maybe he did. I'll never know. Instead of second-guessing me, instead of asking if I'm sure, my vampire assumes that this—that tonight—is a done deal as he kicks off his shoes. "How do we do this?" he asks, his voice gone low as I slowly, slowly pull down his zipper for him. "I know I'll mark you with my bite. Of course. But the actually claiming sex... does it have to be under the moon?"

You know, I love him even more for never doubting that I want him to be my bonded mate. We might've had some communicative snags between us, and I'll never get over how I let my own insecurities lead me to run from the best thing I've ever had, but this is now.

This is *forever*.

"Not always. It being the night of the full moon is enough, but most shifters prefer to do it somewhere that she can see us." It's a superstition—I know that better than anyone since the Luna has already blessed my mating... she has from the moment she first whispered, "Mine," to me in regards to Aleks —but also tradition. "I was thinking maybe the park, but that was before I knew I couldn't wait to get you inside of me. Here's fine."

If it means that the cock I just freed from his underwear is going to be mine now instead of later, I could care less where we mate.

I go to reach for it again. Before I can, Aleks closes his hand gently around mine. "I have a better idea."

I glance up at him. He's looking over my shoulder at the glass sliding door that leads to the balcony and the fire escape.

Blinking in surprise, I say, "What? Really? Are you serious?"

He firms his jaw. Oh, yeah. He's serious. "It's our balcony. Our territory. If you don't mind that anyone passing by might see, we would definitely be beneath your Luna."

Right. And Aleks would make it perfectly clear who he's chosen to be his bonded mate.

I bite down on my bottom lip. Mating with an audience doesn't bother me. The stretch behind the apartment building is usually empty anyway, and it's not like our supe neighbors don't know that Aleks fucks me. Part of my shifter nature almost insists that I do it. Mating should be spontaneous and wild, no matter where or when it takes place.

Another glance at Aleks assures me that he really wants to

claim me on the balcony. Does it matter why? Not really. As long as he claims me—and *now*—I could care less where.

"Okay." Taking my hands from his, swiveling my hips just enough to entice my mate, I head for the door.

When I don't hear footsteps behind me, I glance over my shoulder. Aleks—suave, gentile Aleksander Filan—is still standing there, pants and underwear around his ankles, blood-red eyes gazing ravenously at my ass.

I smile at him. "What? Aren't you coming?"

Probably not the best choice of words since he already has a bead of pre-cum on the head of his cock. Not only did he really want me to say *yes*, but now that I have, he looks like he's seconds away from nutting.

I crook my finger at him. Better hurry because I don't want to waste a single drop. It all belongs to me, and by the end of tonight, the whole world will know it.

He kicks off his clothes so that he's as naked as I am. Taking a tentative step toward me, as though he's the predator and I'm the prey he's worried about scaring off, he gives his cock a quick stroke to tame the beast. "And you're sure, księżyca? You said it yourself. We can bond me to you anywhere."

Am I sure?

"What do you think?" I ask.

Then, before he can answer, I slide open the door and pad out onto the balcony in my bare feet. The iron railing is a perfect height for me to lean my elbows up against it, arch out my back, and present my ass to Aleks.

Within seconds, the chill of his body replaces the late April breeze against my bare skin. He bows his over mine, covering me completely. With a quick yet gentle shove, he swoops my hair over my shoulder, baring my neck to him.

I know why, too. As soon as the mating begins, it won't be complete until he's marked me.

"Come on, Aleks," I whisper, my voice carrying over the still night air. "Don't make me wait any longer."

That whisper is the last time I'm quiet during our mating. With a gentle kiss pressed to the side of my throat, Aleks shifts his weight behind me, then begins to guide his cock inside of me.

I don't know how many times we've mated since we got together. As a shifter, I prefer it to be hard and fast, though everything Aleks does feels amazing. There's something different about the way he's entering me tonight, though. Like it's the first time all over again, and he wants to make it magical.

Screw that.

Keeping one arm braced against the railing so that I don't lose this position, I reach behind me. Borrowing my wolf's claws for a second, I jab Aleks in the ass. My vampire growls—actually *growls*—and slams the rest of the way home.

Ah. *Finally*.

After that, it's just what I dreamed my mating night would be. It's a frenzy of lust and need, love and promise, with my blood and Aleks's blood mingling with the sweat and fluids of our mating. The railing trembles as he pistons into me from behind, but I have no worry that our vigorous fucking is going to take the whole balcony down. Even if it did? My mate would find a way to shield me.

He always has. And, now that we're about to be fully bonded, I know he always will.

That's why I'm not surprised when he changes our positions. He has his back against the railing, putting himself between me and any possible drop, as he hefts me up, encouraging me to wrap my legs around his waist as he slams his cock back inside of me again.

We're face to face now, staring into each other's eyes as we work toward our forever. And if that makes it easier for Aleks to take a few sips from me before he pushes my head toward his throat, begging me to bite him back, that's one big coincidence, I'm sure.

The whole time I can't help but think about how... how *right* this is. Aleks is mating me with the moon up above, Muncie down below. Though it's an urban city and it's never really quiet —especially in this part of the downtown area—it's almost like we're the only two souls around. All I can hear is the slapping sounds of our bodies meeting, my shouts of pleasure as I get closer and closer, and Aleks murmuring my name over and over again. Not even my pet name, either. My given name.

*Elizabeth, take me. Just like that. Yes, always like that...*

*You'll always be mine, Elizabeth...*

*Bite me, Elizabeth. Taste me. Take my blood...*

*I could live off of yours forever, Elizabeth...*

*I love you, Elizabeth...*

It's as though he wants to hammer home the point that he knows exactly who he's with, and exactly who his beloved is.

And that's Elizabeth Howell, and I thank the Luna every fucking day that she gave this male to me.

He's already brought me to come twice, between penetrating me and reaching between our bodies, stroking my clit as he increases his pace to match the way he's circling my little nub. He lasted longer than I thought he would, considering how turned on he was when he got home—as if the Luna was affecting him as much as she was me—so I'm not surprised when he follows close on the heels of my second climax.

My pleasure cranks up to an eleven, knowing he's about to come. Not because I was waiting for him to finish, but because this is it. The moment I've been waiting for my whole Luna-damned life.

I'll finally have an unbreakable bond of my own.

As Aleks begins to grunt his release, he presses a quick kiss to my neck, then strikes with his fangs. This isn't the nibbles from before when he needed a sip of my blood to keep our connection. This is a supe male marking his female with all the determination built up inside of him. I explode again with the pleasure of his bite, but it's more than that.

Our bond has snapped into place. Aleksander Filan is truly my Luna-blessed forever mate.

---

WE MOVE INSIDE AFTER THAT. ALEKS ACCOMPLISHED WHAT HE wanted to do. If there was any doubt that I was his and he was mine, he settled that matter pretty obviously by claiming me where every single vamp in a five-block radius would hear us, scent us, and know exactly who their leader's forever mate was.

If there's one thing I learned since falling for Aleks, my male is insatiable. So long as he's full of my blood, his recovery time is even more impressive than a shifter male. Within minutes of him coming out on the balcony, he's already hard as a rock again.

I'm hungry for him, too. Moon Fever is *real*. My wolf aches for her mate, and any second he's not filling me, stretching me, fucking me is a moment of agony. I need his cock more than I need my next breath, and considering I'm not one of the undead like he is, that's saying something.

Aleks is more than happy to oblige. It doesn't matter that

our bond can't be any more complete than it is at this moment. He fucks me like he's going for extra credit, and I absolutely adore it.

Not surprisingly, I'm the one who flags first. When my wolf is finally satiated, and the moon starts to trade places with the sun so her control on me fades, I hang onto my mate as he finishes one final time, then push him away playfully.

Aleks immediately responds by switching his hold on me so that I'm huddled up against his warm chest. I'd been riding him, stealing kisses as I bobbed up and down on him, eager to lay my claim on every bit of him. He has bloody marks on his throat from where he invited me to taste him repeatedly; now that I know every exchange strengthens our blood bond, I do it eagerly. I fed him as much blood as I could spare, too—leading to his body temperature almost matching mine—with Aleks constantly returning to the same spot where he bit me during our balcony mating.

It's easy for him to. After all, I have two silver-white marks to act like a guide.

The Luna Ceremony is done. My goddess has given my mating her blessing, Aleks both marked and mated me beneath her watchful gaze, and now I wear his bite on my throat like a badge of our eternal love.

Right now he's lapping at it. My arms wrap snugly around his waist, my cheek resting on his shoulder. I specifically cocked my head so that he could reach his mark, and he laves at it as though expecting it'll disappear. That I'll heal it, and it'll be gone.

Nope. For as long as I live—and now that we're forever mates, that will be as long as Aleks does and not a second longer since I *won't* live without him—I'll wear that mark on my skin, just like I'll wear his fang over my heart. He's my mate. I'm proud to let the whole world know that.

Just like how Aleks is more than pleased to show off my messy bites on the pale column of his throat while he has them. He might not be able to keep the scars the way a shifter can, but that's okay. I'll bite him whenever he wants.

Because, Luna help me, I love the taste of his skin.

# CHAPTER 18
# I FINALLY HAVE A PURPOSE

The Alpha collective made it clear: if I want to use my Luna-given gift, I can, but I have to be responsible for any fall-out that might happen when I do.

I thought that was fair enough, and honestly more than I'd been led to expect from them for so many years. Even before I found an unbreakable bond with my beloved mate, I respected them in others. The first time I accidentally snapped a shaky bond, I had ignorance on my side. I paid the price anyway, making myself an outcast from my birth pack. After that, I was careful. I liked to believe I wasn't responsible for whatever the Wicked Wolf made me do while I was kept as his pet, and I sold my services to Roman because the vampire leader rarely used them.

And then, of course, I lost them. It took me finally understanding that my abilities were gifts from the Luna, that they'd been a blessing instead of a curse all along, for them to return. I have them back, and considering they saved my fur when I thought it was all over for me, I'll treasure my tie to our goddess for the rest of my long life.

Not only that but, for the first time in years, I'm my own boss now. I'm a liaison between the two races of supes these days. As the mate to a Cadre leader, I have a really solid in with the vamps; between Gem standing up for me, and the Alpha collective saying I'm not a threat to anyone else, I'm as good as untouchable to other shifters. No one's better for my new job than me.

In fact, you could say that, thanks to being blessed by the Luna the way I was, I'm perfectly suited to be the current acting liaison.

Honestly, I'd do anything to keep another Claws and Fangs war from brewing. For Aleks's sake, for my new friends, and for the family I hope to continue building here in the Fang City.

It took a little... convincing to get him to agree. My mate is still traumatized by Julia's death, and after he spent the last few months waiting on tenterhooks for something to happen to me, his worst fears came true when those shifters attacked me, then I ran from him. Between me rejecting our bond, then leaving him behind to face the Alphas on my own, I pushed my overprotective vampire to his limits. He wouldn't cage me—not the way that Walker did back in the Wolf District—but if he could keep me safe and sound, either in the Cadre building or our apartment, he wanted to.

I was the one who pushed back, and not just because I wanted to be the liaison. I had other ambitions.

Now, I'm not an alpha. I'm not like Gem or Julia. I'm *other*. When it comes to shifters, I exist outside of the hierarchy. In the Fang City, my status only has to do with who my bonded mate is. I wanted to prove that I had a purpose, too, and if it's being a bond sensate, then that's what I was going to be.

Because Muncie is a Fang City, I obviously specialize in reading vampire bonds; because I'm Aleks's bonded mate, I'm part of the Cadre. An office on the nineteenth floor of the Cadre building—one below Aleks's, so that I'm near enough to soothe him while having territory of my own—was a belated mating gift from my vampire. Knowing I'd have to return to the building eventually, I graciously accepted.

For all the times I thought of the leader of the Cadre as the Alpha of Muncie, I'm only proven more right when I discover that part of Aleks's duties is to bless finalized blood bondings after they're complete. Like how Dominic and Felicity went to Roman to request his permission to consider their bond dissolved, Aleks is the first to congratulate a newly mated pair.

Of course, before they request a meeting with Aleks, they come to see me.

I don't break bonds anymore; at least, not unless a couple wants an Elizabeth-aided supe divorce. I've found my purpose as a vampire matchmaker, instead. Not what I had ever expected would be my fate during those long years as a lone wolf—and even longer time as the Wicked Wolf's pet—but I should have trusted in my goddess. After all, she made my fated mate the most amazing vampire ever. Why wouldn't I eventually use my gifts to help his race of supernatural?

I let them know if I sense a prospective bond between two—or, like Leigh, Tamera, and Gretchen, more than two—souls. Vamps and shifters have their own way of recognizing their beloveds and their fated mates, but it's a little trickier for a chosen mate. I use my abilities to tell them whether it's a good match or not and leave them to proceed from there.

Helping other supes find their forever instead of constantly worrying that I'll snatch it away from them... this is it. This is my calling. This is what the Luna always meant for me to do, and when I admit that to both Aleks and myself, my goddess whispers, *You finally understand, my daughter*.

This time, when she goes silent again, I don't feel her absence like an ache deep in my gut. I'm following the path she set out for me. I don't need her to guide me anymore mainly because I've finally stopped running from my fate.

I have my mate at my side, with a bond so unbreakable, not even death will separate us. I'm embracing what I can do. When I'm not reading bonds, I have Cadre members visiting me to entertain them with my tarot cards.

I... I'm happy.

Somehow this lone wolf found community among her ancient enemies, love with a male two centuries her senior, and her place in a pack made up of bloodsuckers, all while using her Luna-given gifts—no longer a curse—to serve her new packmates. And I mean it, too. I'm deliriously happy.

With the vampire rebels quiet—*for now*—there haven't been any attempts on Aleks's life in weeks; he was right, and the grumblings about a new leader have finally seemed to die down after the two of us faced off against Justin. The Wicked Wolf is dead. Christian is dead. After being punished by the Alpha collective, I heard that Peyton slunk her way back to her ex-mate and the Oak Valley Pack with her tail between her legs. Ryker has assured me that she'll stay there, and Aleks vowed to get revenge on her if she so much as comes within a hundred miles of Muncie.

I've seen him fight. Despite being gentle and caring with me, my sexy vampire is also a vicious killer when he's pushed to it.

Then again, so am I. Christian was a revelation. To protect my mate, I'll do anything.

To keep me safe, so will Aleks.

Patting my chest, I run my pointer finger along the curve of his fang. Other shifters see the twin silvery-white points on my neck and know that I've been marked by a vampire. Vamps know one of their kind has claimed me by the magic in the fang hanging over my heart. A symbol of protection and ownership, I don't need it to show all of Muncie that I belong to Aleks. Our mating is evident from how deep his scent is embedded in my skin, our blood mingling, our lives forever entwined. Still, you can't blame a girl for showing off. Now that Aleks is *mine*, I'm even happier to let the rest of the supe world know.

And if it has my mate reverting to Polish, his pale eyes bright with love and emotion and desire when he sees how proud I am to wear both his bite *and* his fang? Well, I'm happy. I want him to be, too.

He is. Even if he wasn't as open and honest with his love for me as he is, I'd know. As the weeks pass, our bond is only growing stronger, and I can't imagine what my life would've been like if I continued to reject the pull I felt toward him like I tried so desperately to do in the beginning.

That's why, about a month after I left the meeting with the Alpha collective and ran straight into Aleks's arms, I made a decision. As Muncie's very own matchmaker, I have no problem sensing bonds and giving advice about if they're shaky, solid, or even fated. But breaking them? I'd rather not get involved.

I never want to be blamed again for coming between a pair of mates. It might've been an accident, like what happened with the Alpha couple of my birth pack, or I was manipulated, just as Kyle manipulated me to break his fated bond with Peyton, but I don't care. I'm going to leave all that to the Luna. I'm out of the bond-breaking business, for the most part.

Especially since the one downside to Peyton outing me to the Alphas is that my abilities are common knowledge in the shifter world now.

I'm too well-protected to have to worry about a shifter like Walker coming after me to get control of my gifts. But ever since news broke, Aleks has had more than a few reports of shifters approaching the borders to Muncie, eager to meet with the Luna-touched female.

Whether they come to gawk at me or because they want to see me perform like some kind of circus monkey, I don't know. My mate immediately increased the Cadre patrols around the Fang City after the close call with those five shifter males. No shifter is getting into Muncie on his watch, and eventually that becomes common knowledge, too.

Elizabeth Howell Filan is off-limits.

Except, it seems, for when a friend calls in a favor...

Gem's smart. Before she got in touch with Aleks, she called me first. She might be an alpha female, but I'm basically the co-Alpha of Muncie these days. Though it was Aleks's permission she needed to get a free pass for one of her packmates, she needed *mine* to talk to Aleks.

It's a mated shifter thing. Add in the fact that I still have to grapple with how she used to wear Aleks's fang around her throat, and Gem's making it clear that she's no threat to my mating. If I say 'no', she'll respect that.

Of course, this is Gem. Even though her dominance doesn't translate over the phone, she's done so much for me, I'd give her anything she asks for. She wants to send one of her packmates down from Accalia to meet with me? I clear my afternoon, then give her the go-ahead to speak with Aleks.

My mate immediately comes down to see me after she called him. Like Gem, he needs to make sure I'm okay with it before he agrees to let another shifter pass our borders. He'll refuse her if that's what I want, even if it reignites the animosity between him and Ryker. And I love him all the more for giving me the choice anyway.

After kissing him senseless, I tell him it's fine.

And it might've been, if it wasn't for what Gem's packmate came to see me about.

# EPILOGUE

I recognize the big, brawny male the moment Everett escorts him to my floor. The young vampire leaves us alone when I make it clear that I don't want—or need—someone watching over me. Despite the shifter's size, he'd never hurt a female.

Big guy goes by Duke, though that's not his real name. Before Gem moved to Accalia, he was another Jack—like Jack Walker—and she hated the reminder of her birth father so much, she decided to call him Duke instead. Though Duke's a member of Ryker's inner circle, his rank is a delta. He had no chance against Gem, and the name stuck.

He's Duke, and before the trip he took across the country to California, he used to be one of Gem's personal guards. I never really got the details from her, but four packmates pledged themselves to her right before she performed the Luna Ceremony with Ryker. She's been trying to get rid of them since, and only managed to off-load one of them.

As Duke gingerly sits down on the seat across from my desk, I know I'm looking at him.

"Hello, Duke," I say warmly. "How are you?"

His brow is furrowed, his golden eyes bleak as he nods back in greeting. "Been better," he says, his voice rough and scratchy. He lifts a hand, rubbing the side of his throat, drawing my attention to the thin silver lines that travel the length of it.

Claw marks.

*Mate marks.*

I open up my senses. There's a twisted bond wrapped around the male, but despite the marks on his throat, it's not complete.

Suddenly, I'm pretty sure I understand why Gem insisted that I meet with her packmate in Muncie, instead of me taking the trip up to Accalia. For Duke's sake—and probably mine, too —I think this might be a conversation that needs to be had away from pack land.

I just hope I'm wrong.

"Gem told me you needed to speak to me. That it couldn't wait." She said it wasn't her story to tell, but I was the only one who could make him see sense. Let's find out if she's right. "What can I do for you?"

"It's about Trish."

Patricia Danvers is a delta she-wolf, another member of the Mountainside Pack. Though I only met her once, when the Wicked Wolf sent Aidan Barrow—a Mountainside traitor—to bring her back to the Wolf District to force Gem and Ryker's hand, she'd been unconscious at the time. Pumped full of quicksilver, Walker wanted her docile. He quickly realized that she wasn't going to be as easy to control when she wasn't drugged, and when Trish refused to shift back to her skin after regaining consciousness, he had her locked up in the district's cells.

I heard about her captivity through the rumor mills that always ran rampant back then. I'm ashamed to say that, on one hand, I envied her for being able to refuse Walker in ways that I couldn't; on the other, I wished someone would come for me the way that Gem and her two guards came for Trish.

So much was going on when they were in the district. Walker had me moved so that I was kept near him at all times, and then Aleks was another casualty of his cruelty, so I was dealing with the realization that I found my fated mate. I barely had time to notice the bond that might belong to a pair of strangers.

Now, though, sitting across the space from Duke, hearing the pain in his voice as he simply says her name... I know exactly who is on the other end of Duke's jagged bond.

"Your mate?" I ask softly.

"The female that should've been my mate," he answers, "but who can't be. That's why I came here. That's what I have to ask you... you can snap bonds. Break them. Yeah? She has too much to worry about right now. I... this tie between us isn't helping her. It's *hurting* her. It needs to go. Can you do that?"

Can I? Usually, when one mate wants to separate from another, all it takes is a brush of my hand and a little concentration. But even though his bond isn't straight or whole, and he's verbally asking for it to be snapped, that's only when the mate *wants* to separate.

And Duke? He doesn't. I can sense his desperation to keep the tie fighting against his instinct to sacrifice *anything* for his female's happiness.

Poor guy. He's holding his breath, waiting for my answer, though I'm not sure if it's the one he's expecting or even hoping for. It doesn't matter. It's the only one he's going to get.

"Not all bonds can be broken—or should be," I tell him after a moment's thought. "Bless the Luna, but even fate doesn't get it right all of the time. But even when she does, it's not always easy. That doesn't mean you should give up on it."

Look at Gem and Ryker, for one. From what I've heard from her, he rejected her for his very own "reasons", and she ran before he could explain just how ridiculous they were. The couple stayed apart for a whole year before they found their way back to each other, and now their bond is unbreakable.

Then there's me and Aleks. I ignored the Luna's constant whispers for five months, and even when Aleks was showing me how much he loved me, how much he cared, I still couldn't find it in me to believe him until it was almost too late. Our mating wasn't easy, but it was worth it.

If Duke could figure out a way to straighten the bond he shares with his female, it would be worth it for them, too. I know it, even if it's hard to explain to someone without my abilities.

I don't have to. Leaning forward in the seat, Duke asks, "So you won't break the bond? You won't even try?"

I honestly don't believe it would do anything except cause me a painful blowback when my gift inevitably fails, but I don't bother telling him that, either.

I just say, "I'm sorry, but no. I won't."

He sighs, hanging his head. "I was afraid you'd say that." Duke shoves his fingers through his thick, dark hair before straightening in the seat, meeting my gaze with a shadowed expression. "Probably more afraid that you'd agree."

Just as I thought. "Because you didn't really want me to, did you?"

"No. But it doesn't matter what I want. It only matters what's good for Trish."

I give him a gentle smile. "And that right there is exactly why I can't do it."

"What should I do then?" asks Duke. I get the idea that he isn't really asking *me*, but simply throwing the question out to the universe in an act of desperation.

I answer him anyway.

"Just love her." I think of Aleks, and how everything changed once I allowed myself to love him—and to believe that he actually loves me in return. "Love her, and it'll all work out somehow."

After all, it did for us.

CLAWS AND FANGS BOOK SIX

# STAY WITH ME

SARAH SPADE

INTERNATIONAL BESTSELLING AUTHOR

CLAWS AND FANGS BOOK SIX

# STAY WITH ME

SARAH SPADE

INTERNATIONAL BESTSELLING AUTHOR

Cover by JoY Design Studio

# FOREWORD

Thank you for checking out *Stay With Me*!

This is a novella (~30,000 words) that brings the **Claws and Fangs** series to a close for now. I love this world, and I visit it in the **Stolen Mates** series, so I can't imagine leaving it for long.

With this book, though, I bring it full circle by featuring Trish Danvers and the Mountainside Pack. The "other female" from the first book, Trish went through a lot over the course of Gem and Ryker's story. By the end of *Forever Mates*, I knew I wanted to give her her own happily-ever-after. And no one is better for her than Duke, the gentle giant delta who has loved her from afar for years… she just didn't know it yet.

She doesn't when this novella begins, either—but she will, and I'm so glad that these two characters find their forever with each other. He's so good for her, and even though Trish might still be the selfish female who once schemed to come between Gem and Ryker, once she sets her sights on Duke, the big guy doesn't stand a chance.

I hope you enjoy!

*xoxo,*
*Sarah*

# CHAPTER 1
# NIGHTMARES

He's chasing me.

It's the same dream I've had for more than seven months now. I'm in my fur, dashing through a crowded woods, my ears flat against my skull, my white tail streaming behind me. As a she-wolf, I'm usually the predator; with the dark gold wolf dogging my every step, I'm the most enticing of prey. He snaps his jaws, almost closing on me before I swerve, barely avoiding his fangs.

There's laughter in his honey-gold eyes, a humor that is somehow also cruel and calculating. He has plans for me for when he finally runs me down. And while he uses his dominance against me, trying to get me to submit to his alpha nature, I'm so damn scared that my self-preservation wins out. I run because there's no alternative.

I can't let him catch me.

When I'm awake my human brain reminds me that this is nothing but a nightmare. In reality, Jack "Wicked Wolf" Walker never chased me, though the few times he lowered himself to gloat about taking me captive, the dark humor was written on his deceptively handsome face. If he decided to hunt me, I have no doubt it would play out just like it does in my dreams—but he didn't, because while I was prey, I wasn't his target.

I was his *bait*.

I also know that he can't chase me now anyway. The former Alpha of the Western Pack is dead, murdered by a pretty boy vampire who wanted to save his lone wolf mate from Walker's clutches.

Lucky her. When I was in a cage in the Wolf District, I knew no one was coming for me. I'd burned too many bridges with my Alpha and his mate to think they cared, and though I have friends and family among my packmates, I'm not the *one* to anybody. I don't have a mate, and I never thought a single soul would risk their hide for me.

But they did. Gemma—the female Alpha of our pack, and the last shifter I expected to come to my rescue—took the trip from Accalia to the Wolf District, bringing two of her personal guards with her while Ryker, Mountainside's Alpha, stayed behind with the rest of the pack. And I know it wasn't just because I was trapped in a cage across the country from my home. Gem was actually the Wicked Wolf's biological daughter, and she had her own score to settle with him.

She's not in my dreams. When her father chases me, it's just the two of us until my wolf collapses from exhaustion, Walker howling in triumph as he grips the scruff of my fur with his fangs, preparing to mount me.

That's how I know for sure it's not real. While shifters are part human, part beast, our human side rebels at the idea of mating while we're in our fur. It's just... it's not done. Even a sadistic bastard like Walker wouldn't try to mate me when I wasn't wearing my skin—which was exactly why I stayed in my fur nearly the entire time I was his prisoner.

Tonight's dream is different, though. Just when the ghost of Walker is stalking toward me, the air splits with a menacing growl of a bark. His ears twitch, one paw paused as he searches for the source of the sound, while I crawl a few paces away on my belly.

The wind whips by, the leaves over my head rustling. As the echo of the howl dies down, I don't hear anything else, which makes me wonder if I imagined it. Out of the corner of my eye, I see the dark gold wolf flick his ears again before padding forward. He's panting, but it's not because he just tore through the trees that surround his hidden territory in California.

He's panting because he's excited from the hunt, and I have no escape.

I whine, the sound pulling from my throat. In response, another howl breaks through the night before thunderous paws pound against the ground. Seconds later, it becomes clear that they're heading straight for the clearing I collapsed in.

I find the strength to lift my head off of the dirt right as a moving shadow leaps out the darkness, landing beneath a stray moonbeam. The Luna bounces off of his sleek fur, flashing against his golden shifter's eyes.

It's a grey wolf, I see. Bigger than the Alpha, though his dominance is nowhere as strong, the grey wolf doesn't need to be a higher rank to get his point across. His size does it for him, as does the warning he puts into his rolling growl.

He's come for me—and he's not about to let Walker get in his way.

Instead of being frightened, I feel an inexplicable pull toward him. I don't know this wolf—at least, in my dreams, I don't—but there's something about him. He makes me feel safe, and if there's one thing I've craved more than having someone pick me for me, it's knowing that I'm protected.

The giant grey wolf... he'll protect me. It's just instinct. I have to get to him.

I yip. Too weak to do anything but move my muzzle, I gaze up at him. If I can get to him, everything will be okay. *I* will be okay.

If I just—

My eyes spring open. I'm laying on my naked belly, just like I was in my dream, only I'm in my two-legged, human form. Not surprising—I've maybe shifted a handful of times since I was rescued—but I'm completely bare in case I lose control while I'm asleep. I've sacrificed too many pairs of good pajamas to sleep-shifting, and it's my habit to strip down before climbing into bed.

Why not? It's not like I'm sharing it with anyone else...

Now that I'm awake, I give my head a clearing shake and shove my blanket away from my lower half. The thin covering is wrapped around my legs, another casualty of my recurring nightmare. I must've been "running" in my sleep and now my blanket is twisted all around me. Frustrated and still confused as to what woke me up so suddenly, I kick until I'm free.

Then—another habit—I take a deep breath, sampling the scents in the air.

It's the first week of May. Shifters of all types run hot, and though it's still chilly up on our mountaintop settlement this time of year, most of my packmates keep their windows open to the breeze. Not me. It would be easier to protect my territory—my cabin—if I could use my wolf's nose to scent any threats creeping up on me... but I can't. I need to know no one can sneak in through my window, even if it's harder to catch nearby scents through the glass windows and two wooden doors.

As a delta, my senses aren't as strong as other wolves, but I can still pick up the enticing aroma of bacon nearby regardless. That must be what woke me up. No self-respecting she-wolf can ignore the enticing scent of cooked meat when it's so close. Bacon especially is powerful enough to reach me inside of my sanctuary.

Climbing out of the bed, I pad over to my dresser. Nudity might not be a big deal to my kind of supe, but I already have a reputation in Accalia. For the most part, I've earned it. Doesn't mean that I'm going to prance around naked. The catty gossips —ironic since every Mountainside packmate is wolf—would love to have more ammunition to toss my way.

I can just hear them now.

*Did you see the Danvers girl?*

*Still so desperate to attract a mate, she's walking around in her skin.*

*Make sure she doesn't set her eyes on your male because Luna knows that, if she made a play for the Alpha even after he had his intended, none of the rest of our mates are safe...*

Because that's me. Trish Danvers, home-wrecker. Not even a home-wrecker, really. *Attempted* home-wrecker because, no matter how hard I tried to convince Ryker Wolfson that he should choose me over his fated mate, I never stood a chance.

I tried, though. Can't deny that. For most of my mature years —since I was about twenty and I decided my best chance at forever was with the future Alpha of the pack—I was fixated on making Ryker mine. It's all I wanted. The security of being the female Alpha of the pack, and the protection of the most powerful wolf around. Plus, Ryker is gorgeous, and I honestly believed that I loved him.

Just like I believed that I would be a better mate for him than his own...

Since he was our Alpha's son, I always knew that I had until Henry passed and Ryker succeeded him to convince Ryker to choose me. It's how it's done. Alphas rarely take mates until they're installed as leader of the pack, and once they are, their Luna Ceremony follows closely on the heels of the one that makes them Alpha. I thought I had time—and then Henry died in an accident, and Ryker became Alpha when I was barely twenty-four.

And that's when all of Accalia discovered that the Luna whispered that his fated mate was the daughter of the Lakeview Pack's Alpha, an innocent-appearing omega who was only a year older than I was.

At first I thought I was doing them both a favor. A formidable alpha wolf, Ryker would've eaten an omega she-wolf alive. Especially blonde-haired, golden-eyed Gemma, with her big smile and her bouncy curls. But then... Ryker never wanted me. Despite all of my efforts, I knew it. His attention was always elsewhere, and the first time I saw his dark gold eyes land on Gem when she wasn't watching, I knew.

She wasn't only his fated mate. She was his chosen mate. I'd lost him before I ever had him—and I was heartbroken.

Does that excuse what happened after? How I listened to our traitorous Beta's whispers when Shane Loup told me that Gem wasn't really an omega, but a rare alpha instead? Or how I blackmailed Ryker into choosing me otherwise I would tell the whole shifter world about her? Not to mention the countless ways I bullied our Alpha's intended, telling her that *I* was Ryker's chosen mate when he made it obvious time and time again that he only had eyes for her?

No. No, it doesn't. And while all of that happened two years ago, when I yank open the second drawer of my dresser and see the folded piles of sundresses packed inside, my stomach goes tight. I'd gone through a phase where I thought, if I styled my light brown hair in curls, and I pulled girly sundresses on that looked like Gem's when she was still passing as an omega, maybe Ryker would see what he was missing. It wasn't that unusual. A lot of she-wolves stick to simple dresses because they're easy to remove when we're getting ready to shift. But me... I preferred blouses and jeans until I made the change to attract Ryker.

I was wearing a pale pink sundress the day that Aidan Barrow asked me if I would meet him down at the garage where the pack vehicles are stored. It was destroyed, slashed up and covered in blood after he attacked me, and when I panicked and shifted after he tried to maneuver me into one of the open trunks, the dress was nothing but bloody tatters beneath me. I got a few swipes in with my claws and fangs before he shot me full of quicksilver—something he did repeatedly to ensure I was sedated for the whole trip to the West Coast—but that was the last time I wore one of my dresses.

While I was kept in a cage, I stayed in my fur. Only once did I shift to skin, and that's because the Wicked Wolf hit me with the full weight of his alpha stare. I couldn't refuse him, though I threatened to hurt myself if he tried to keep me from shifting back to my wolf. He had no reason to refuse. I was a pawn, a bargaining chip, a way to lure Ryker and Gem into the trap he'd set for them. I might not be able to talk while I'm a wolf, but I can hear, and I know that he only took me on the odd chance that Ryker developed some feelings for me.

After all, I spent years telling anyone who would listen that, one day, we'd be mates. I never thought it would put a target on my back, though. I just thought, if I was persistent, I could make my own happily-ever-after.

I was wrong.

I haven't thrown the sundresses away. I keep meaning to, but whenever I pull open this drawer, after my stomach tightens, my immediate reaction is to shove it closed. That's what I do now, wishing I could just remember that my blouses and t-shirts are in the next drawer down, with my jeans hanging up in my closet.

Grabbing some fresh clothes, I hurriedly get dressed. Only the promise of a breakfast I didn't have to make would get me moving this quickly, and minutes after I woke up, I'm shuffling in my bare feet toward the back door of my cabin.

I inch it open, pushing it the rest of the way when I see the covered plate sitting on my back porch. Closing my eyes, I breathe in deep. I smell bacon, yes, but that's not all.

Something musky, something woodsy, with a hint of sharp pine. Like Christmas in May, my heart skips a beat.

I know exactly who left this plate for me. And because it's from him, I can accept it without any hesitation.

So I do.

Food has a special meaning to shifters. In most packs, it's the Alpha that provides for his community. In individual families, it's the parents' responsibility to feed their pups. That's just accepted. But when a male or a female of mating age offers food to a prospective partner, it says: I will protect you, I will feed you, and you'll want for nothing if I'm around.

Not me. I'm pretty sure I'm the only exception to that in all of Accalia.

I know the meal is from Duke. If anyone else left me a plate of—I peek under the foil—bacon and scrambled eggs, eating it is the same as signaling that I'm interested in pursuing a mating with them. It's letting another wolf take care of me. But Duke... he's been taking care of me for months now, and not because he has any kind of sexual interest in me. He treats me more like a pup that needs to be guarded and guided, and he has since the moment he found me savage and terrified in that cage in California.

Well, now I know why I woke up. It wasn't the food, was it? It was him bringing it to me. He must've just dropped it off, too, because if he'd been around longer? I never would've had the nightmare to begin with—even if it does explain why I dreamed that a massive grey wolf was rescuing me.

When Duke is near, I sleep peacefully. And when he isn't... I wish he was.

Because the big delta wolf is the only thing that keeps the bad dreams away, even if I have no idea why.

# CHAPTER 2
# DUKE CONLON

Duke Conlon.

As I dig into the still-warm breakfast, I sigh as I think of him.

Duke... that's not his real name. His real name is Jack, but last year when Gem came back to Accalia to finalize her mate bond with Ryker, she started calling him Duke for some reason. Well, no. I know why she couldn't call him Jack. That's the Wicked Wolf's first name, and I still get a shiver when I think it, too. But Duke? When I asked him after we returned home, he just shrugged and said it's what she called him and he didn't argue so it stuck.

I'm not surprised. The big delta is no match for the dominant she-wolf. It's like if Ryker told me that, instead of going by the shortened version of my name, he wanted me to only be known as Patricia. I'd be Patricia Danvers, instead of Trish, and that would be that. So Duke's Duke now, even though I used to know him as Jack.

Well, kinda.

Unlike me, Duke isn't from Accalia. While my family being part of the Mountainside Pack goes back for generations, Duke comes from a pack of traveling wolves. Most shifter communities stay in one place, keeping their distance from humans and other supes, but there are a few packs that are nomadic. They get permission to visit other, more stable territories because they're also traders. For shifters who don't want to leave pack land, we can barter or buy from these travelers.

I never really paid attention since my parents made sure I had everything I wanted, but our old Alpha, Henry, was more than willing to up our numbers anytime he had the chance. When Duke petitioned to join the Mountainside Pack, Henry allowed it, and Duke became fast friends with Ryker and his circle.

Now he's part of the pack council, with Ryker as Alpha and Jace Burke as Beta.

He also used to be part of the foursome that serves as Gem's personal guard. After a year's absence—that still makes me feel guilty when I remember that I caused it—she returned to Accalia last summer. Right before she completed the Luna Ceremony that made her and Ryker forever mates, four wolves pledged their loyalty to her. Duke and Jace were two of them, my cousin Bobby another, and Dorian Howard was the fourth. While Ryker is responsible for the safety of the entire pack, these four wanted to make sure that his mate was protected.

Lucky Gem. An alpha female who doesn't even *need* protection, and she had four of the most strongest deltas in Accalia lining up to have her back. At the time, I was working hard to get past my jealousy. She was good enough to give permission for me to return to Accalia after Ryker banished me, and I resolved to start over. I needed to be better.

And I was... until Barrow tricked me and I ended up the political prisoner of the most feared shifter in our world.

Something happened while I was trapped in the Wolf District, though. Something changed. When Gem showed up with Jace and Duke, the big shifter voluntarily gave up his freedom so that he could be locked in the cell next to mine. I went from only knowing him as Bobby's pal, Jack, to falling asleep to his rumbled promises that he was going to make sure nothing happened to me.

He was going to keep me safe, and nothing was going to stop him from bringing me back to Accalia in one piece.

It's been seven months since he held up his end of that harshly whispered vow, and that's not all he's done, either. As if he can sense that I'm home, but I'm nowhere near whole, he's stepped back from being one of Gem's guards. Instead, he spends most of his time watching out for *me*.

I'll be the first to admit it. I'm broken. Weeks in a cage, curled up as my wolf... I didn't go completely feral, but it was close. I relied on my other half too much, and now there's this almost... disconnect between us. My wolf is there, I can sense her, but it's like I've been blocked from her. The idea of shifting has sweat forming at the base of my spine, a mournful howl building in the back of my throat. I just... I can't.

Does that mean I need a personal guard? Of course not. Trusting Barrow taught me a lesson I'll never forget, and these days I prefer to stay around my cabin. My mother makes sure my kitchen is stocked full of food so it's not like I have to leave if I don't want to. Watching me has got to be the most boring job in Accalia, but when I began to sense Duke close by my cabin more than could be explained, I finally went to the Alphas' den and met with Ryker and Gem to ask them about it.

My Alpha and his mate exchanged a look, with Gem teasing that she's grateful to have the number of her guard whittled down to three. Ryker just told me that, if I wanted him to order Duke to stay away, he would, but I didn't want that. I only wanted to understand *why* he was out there.

And, sure, I could've gone and asked him. Our time together in the cells of the Wolf District forged a bond that I don't think will ever be broken. It's not a mate bond, of course—I doubt I'll ever have one of those—but Duke kept me sane while I was on the edge of turning feral. I might be broken, but he stopped me from shattering. That's not really that surprising. Male shifters are protective of those weaker than them. He obviously thinks I need him and, well, I think I do, too.

We're friends. I guess that's what you can call us. I've never asked him why he watches me as if expecting I'll break, and we don't discuss what happened in California, but we're friends now. He brings me food when he has extra, and when he doesn't have pack duties busying him, he curls up in his wolf form outside of my cabin, keeping the nightmares at bay.

I've found him there before. I'm not sure he knows that I do—I've never mentioned it—but, sometimes when I can't sleep, I find peace watching the big grey wolf slumber on my back porch as if he doesn't have a cabin of his own. And maybe I "accidentally" left a blanket out there to make it more comfortable for him, but at least he always folds it up before he goes. The gentle giant is a man of few words, but we don't talk about his sleeping habits, either. We... we kinda don't really talk that much at all. We don't need to. It's enough just knowing he's close.

And if I wonder what it would be like to invite him to spend the night inside of my cabin with me? I quickly shove that idea out of my head. He worries for me. He feels bad that I was betrayed by my packmate, and caged by a cruel Alpha. I'm not a possible mate to him. I'm nobody.

I look down at my plate, half-empty despite my nightmare leaving me queasy.

I'm nobody—except, maybe, to Duke Conlon.

---

In Accalia, I'm a fixture. A pretty fixture, sure, but a fixture nonetheless.

That's... actually not new. For longer than I want to admit, that's been my life. The pretty almost-mate to Ryker, the head bitch in the group of she-wolves around my age, and one of the long-established Danvers clan. If anything, I was known for my looks and my attitude. Kind of pathetic when I look back on it now, but until the moment I was banished, I liked my life.

I had it all mapped out. I'd be the Alpha female, living in the Alpha cabin with Ryker, absolutely untouchable. Only... turns out, I became *very* touchable and for one reason only: my imagined tie to a male I never stood a chance with.

Once I was home again, I vowed that I would prove I was more than that. That was seven months ago and I'm still trying.

It's hard. Barrow's betrayal didn't just piss off the whole pack. I fell for his lies and ended up beaten, drugged, and captured because one wolf was nice to me following my banishment. You think I would've learned my lesson after Shane Loup used me to drive a wedge between Ryker and his mate. Nope. Barrow flattered me, I believed him, and in the end I returned to Accalia with my claws and fangs blunted, my tail tucked between my legs.

My parents worry over me. I don't have any siblings, but my cousins, aunts, and uncles tried to close ranks around me before I put a stop to that. My packmates whisper. The older gammas think I had it coming, while my old friends... well, let's just say they stopped coming to see if I wanted to go for a dish and run sesh anytime soon.

Kind of hard to join a pack run when my wolf prefers to stay right where she is: far away from anyone else.

Life moves on. At least, for most of us, it does. I'm still struggling, but I'm not the only one.

And that's why, when I do want to see any of my old friends, I know there's someone in Accalia who will always welcome me.

Audrey Carter is about twelve years older than I am. Before last year we didn't really run in the same circle. She was happily mated to Grant when I was still a young pup, though her younger brother, Shane, was in the same age group as me and Ryker and a bunch of other packmates. That's how I first knew her, through Shane, and her tie to her brother is the reason why we've become so close since last summer.

In all of the pack, Audrey is the only one who understands what it's like to be an outcast. Not because of anything she did—unlike me—but because she was Shane's big sister and the only family he had when he turned on Mountainside. She blames herself for not noticing how dark he went, and when Ryker was forced to put him down, she was the only one to visibly mourn our former Beta's death.

She loved her brother, but she's as loyal to Accalia as I am. No one doubts that. Her place as one of the maternal deltas is solid. Her mate is a member of Ryker's pack circle. There's not a single shifter who blames her for what her brother did.

Except for Audrey herself, of course.

When it first came out that Shane betrayed Ryker by working with the Wicked Wolf and targeting Ryker's mate, Audrey came to visit me. Like the rest of the pack, she knew that I was helping him try to drive Gem and Ryker apart. At least, I *thought* I was helping him to keep the pack strong while also getting the male I wanted. Turns out he was manipulating me, turning me into another pawn in a convoluted plan I still don't fully understand. Either way, I was the only one who had any insight into Shane's motives.

I told her as much as I could which, admittedly, wasn't really a lot. I was too consumed with getting my own happily-ever-after to second guess why Shane thought I'd be a better mate for the Alpha than Gem to care *why* he was helping me. Looking back, I realize just how flighty and ridiculous I was. Still, making amends for my actions didn't just stop with the Alpha couple. I tried my best to support Audrey, and now she's my best friend.

She's a sweetheart. There's not an ounce of darkness in her which makes you wonder how Shane became so twisted. Just born that way, I figure. A gentle she-wolf, Audrey honestly does whatever she can to keep the morale in the pack up. Once upon a time that was going along with the pack council's plan to throw an unprepared Gem at a feral Ryker during the full moon. Nowadays, she works as the pack seamstress when she isn't doing everything she can to help out the rest of our packmates.

Including inviting me for weekly sewing lessons that couple as unofficial therapy sessions for the both of us.

I usually visit her for a lesson and lunch every Monday. Since the new year, I've learned how to darn socks, sew up any holes in a packmate's clothes that come from partial shifts, and I've even started a quilt that I'm planning on adding to my back porch. At my pace, it probably won't be done until next winter, but I think Duke would like it.

If he's still watching over me, of course.

Today's Thursday. I don't know if Audrey is busy, but after last night's bad dream, I don't want to be alone. With Duke obviously too occupied to be my babysitter today, that leaves me with only a handful of choices: visiting my parents on the northern side of Accalia, visiting Bobby or Nina, my younger cousins, or seeing if Audrey is willing to keep me company until I shake off last night's shivers.

Bobby is one of Gem's trio of guards. With Jace our new Beta, and Duke… Duke, Bobby and Dorian Howard spend most of their time making sure our female Alpha doesn't do anything she isn't supposed to. Only when Ryker is with her do they back off, something I just don't understand. When I asked Bobby, he said it was a rare female alpha thing, and I decided I didn't want to know any more about it so I dropped the subject.

Ryker's not in Accalia today. Ever since rumors got out about the Luna-touched female who lives in the Fang City at the foot of our mountain, he's been spending a lot of his time going back and forth between our territory and the nearest shifter pack in River Run. Walker was killed in Muncie, and there are rumors that some of his former packmates are looking for retaliation. Add that to the group of marauding shifters who attempted to kill her, and the way she was summoned to meet with the Alpha collective—including Ryker and Gem who left Jace in charge for a couple of days—and tensions are higher than they have been lately. The vamps say they're prepared for any scuffle between supes, but the two Alphas are working to keep another Claws and Fangs war from breaking out so close to their land.

As our Alpha, the whole pack senses it when he's gone. It's easier to tolerate because Gem's still here. That's why shifter tradition has it so that a new Alpha almost always takes a mate shortly after he takes over the pack. We need balance, and an Alpha's mate provides it.

Would I have been able to? I… I thought I would. Now it doesn't matter.

On the plus side, I don't have two determined wolves dogging my every step. Just one who is conspicuously absent today.

And, no, I'm not annoyed that there's no sign of Duke at all as I get ready to leave, then take the walk over to Audrey's cabin… uh-uh. Not even a little.

Nope.

---

When I visit Audrey, we have an unspoken agreement. I don't mention Shane anymore, and she doesn't bring up this weird… thing I have going on with Duke Conlon.

She did in the beginning. She implored me to open up to her when I felt ready to, to tell her about what happened after I went missing. Because her mate is high up in the pack's hierarchy, she knew all about how Duke is the reason I made it out of the Wolf District at all. Not as if his need to watch me is a secret. In Accalia, there aren't any, and everyone knows that I somehow triggered his protective instincts.

Too bad I didn't trigger his mating ones…

Audrey was working on hemming a dress for Flora, a newly

mature she-wolf who is getting ready for her Luna Ceremony next week. Flora is a delta, and so is her intended, a shy male called Mack. To become bonded mates, they have to wait until the Luna is completely full, mate beneath her to ask for her blessing, then mark each other to prove that they choose to be bonded together forever. Unlike an Alpha's mating, there's no real ceremony. The pack congratulates every newly mated pair, but it's a private ceremony.

Still, a young female wants to look her best for her mate, and the dress Audrey is working on is perfect for the occasion.

"The soft pink will really bring out the golden notes in her eyes," I tell Audrey. "It's beautiful."

"I gave her the choice of pink or white," Audrey confides, "but after... well, most girls are going with color this season."

Right. Because Gem wore a white dress for her Luna Ceremony with Ryker, and it ended up stained in blood after the challenge from Shane that interrupted the pack-wide affair. Perfect for an alpha female, not so much for the more delicate shifters in our pack.

When I was a pup dreaming of my mating night, I imagined a mellow yellow shift dress that would complement my tanned skin, my hazel eyes, and my light brown hair. I still wear that color—most of my t-shirts and blouses are a shade of yellow—but a fancy dress... maybe not anytime soon.

Then again, it's not like I have a prospective mate, either.

I'm only twenty-seven. Shifters that grow up in the same pack as their mate usually find each other young. I didn't, which is probably another reason why I fixated on Ryker Wolfson the way I did. The whole pack knew that Ryker's mate would be from out of Accalia, just like mine would have to be. If we chose each other first, it wouldn't matter.

And then, of course, the Luna whispered that Gemma Swann was his, and I screwed up by not respecting that. Now they're mated, I'm not, and if I want to find a male to accept me, I'm going have to leave Accalia.

No, thanks.

Glancing up from her hemming, Audrey gives me a curious look. I don't know if the topic we were discussing put the idea in her head, or she just knows me pretty damn well by now, but I'm almost expecting it when she asks, "What about you, Trish? Still going lone wolf?"

I shrug. "Unless the Luna drops a male shifter in my lap who doesn't mind hooking up with Trish Danvers, it seems like that's my fate."

"That's an... interesting way of looking at it."

It's the only way I have. "It's fine. I've got time." We may not lives as long as vamps, but shifters can reach a century, easy. "If it happens, it happens. I promise I'm okay."

Audrey's a delta. An Alpha might be able to tell when their packmate is lying to them. Luckily for me, she can't.

It's my turn to change the subject. "Now, about my quilt. I've already started attaching squares to it, but how do I finish off the ends? I was thinking—"

My words are cut short. Two familiar scents filter in through the open window of Audrey's personal den, followed by the auras belonging to a pair of delta wolves.

One is Grant Carter, Audrey's mate.

But the other...

I can't help it. Like a moth drawn to a flame, my head swivels toward the front side of her cabin.

"Aud? Audrey, honey, I stopped by to grab some lunch. Got Duke with me, too. Hope you don't mind."

I don't see Grant. Considering he mentioned lunch, he probably headed straight for the kitchen. Or maybe he's behind Duke. Luna knows even a male of Grant's build could hide easily behind Duke's bulk.

He's huge. I've never seen him naked, but I doubt there's a spare ounce of fat on him. He's got this boxer's shape and size, bulky and brawny on the top, with legs as thick as tree trunks. It's amazing how gentle and kind he can be considering he looks like he could snap even a raging, bloodthirsty vamp in half. I know firsthand that his catcher-sized mitts stroke a trembling wolf with reverence, and his eyes...

Shifters' eyes can come in all shades of browns, hazels, and golds. His are a darker hazel than mine, but there are times when the color shifts to a bright gold.

Like right now.

He's the epitome of tall, dark, and handsome. He wears his dark hair short, showing off his strong features, and I've come to realize that—now that I'm no longer obsessing over Ryker—Duke is one of the most attractive males I've ever seen before in my life.

His name is a sigh. "Hi, Duke."

"Trish? What are you..." His brow furrows. "It's not Monday."

Why am I not surprised that Duke knows that I spend my Monday afternoons at Audrey's?

Probably for the same reason that he looks confused that I'm here on a Thursday.

He's my guard. I'm the she-wolf he's been watching. Of course he knows where I am at all times.

I guess I'm predictable in that way.

Then again, I don't think he expected me to find the excuse

to leave as soon as he entered the room where I was sharing a Coke and a conversation with Audrey.

"You're right. I just stopped by for a visit. I should probably be heading back to my cabin, though."

"You're leaving now?"

It seems like the best idea. It's one thing for Duke to keep an eye on me from a distance. I don't understand it, but I don't mind. Having him right there, fighting the pull between us that I noticed after our time in the cages? I wish I was a stronger female than I am. He's my friend, and that's all he can be.

Which is why I don't even bat an eye when he offers to walk me back to my cabin instead of joining Grant and Audrey for lunch.

I'd expect no less from such an honorable male.

"Sure. That would be nice of you."

Out of the corner of my eye, I see that Audrey is frowning. "Nice? Trish, sweetie—"

"Thanks for the drink." I stand up. "The chat, too. I'll see you on Monday."

"Um. Yeah. Okay. Take good care of her Duke."

His gaze never leaves my face as he answers in that solemn, deep voice of his, "I always will."

# CHAPTER 3
# SHADOW

Once we're outside of the Carters' cabin, I expect my shadow to quietly escort me back to mine.

That's what Duke is, I've long decided. My shadow. A big one, sure, since he's a giant of a male, but he doesn't often walk at my side. In fact, he usually keeps his distance, watching over me from afar.

He's done that since we returned to Accalia. As though he's expecting me to have a mental breakdown at any minute, it seems like he's always *there*. Not that it bothers me. It doesn't. My time away from the pack changed me. I'm not the she-wolf I used to be. Instead of expecting males to sniff at my tail—which I gladly rejected them because I only wanted Ryker—I'd rather they leave me alone... except for Duke.

We don't often have conversations. It's hard to do so when your shadow prefers to stay a good couple of feet behind me, forever silent. A few stand out in my mind—nearly all of them revolving around how I'm feeling these days—but I asked him once if I should call him by his real name or his nickname. After how he took care of me, I didn't want to think of him as just another packmate. He was my friend, and I respected him.

He'd looked at me, surprise written on his ruggedly handsome face, before he rumbled out a quick, "Call me whatever ya like. But what about you? Is it Patricia, or Trish?"

I'll always be Trish. But when he said *Patricia* in that bass voice of his, I couldn't help but remember the way he called my wolf the same while I was spiraling back in the cells. She had responded as if she'd been waiting for him her entire life, and though I told him, "Trish," when he asked, I admitted to myself that what he said went double. He could call me whatever he liked.

I'm the type of she-wolf who used to adore being the center of attention. Not anymore. I've had my fair share of it. In my foolish youth, I was the talk of the pack because I told anyone who would listen that I aimed to make Ryker mine, no matter what. Even after Gem left, and Ryker spent a year searching for her, I persisted even when I knew I shouldn't have. Looking back, I admit that I deserved to be banished from the pack. I got lucky to be reinstated, and luckier still that my Alpha didn't leave me to rot in California.

Rumors swirl. I know better than most that shifter packs gossip worse than little old ladies. I went from being the assumed mate for the Alpha heir to Trish Danvers, homewrecker, in a year. Since then, I'm now damaged goods. But I'm trying to be better.

Nothing made that more clear than when Duke gave me the opportunity to call him whatever I wanted. The old Trish would've felt the need to one-up Gem, maybe give him a nickname just from me. Or I could've been contrary, referring to him as Jack since that's his name.

But I don't. I can't call him Jack—for the same reasons the Alpha female doesn't—and when it comes to Duke... it seems as if he likes the nickname; it definitely suits him. Over the last year or so, every packmate refers to the big male as Duke.

So I do, too.

I'm actually kind of surprised when he doesn't fall back as soon as Audrey's front door is closed. That's usually what he does, almost as if he's eager to keep some space between us, but not today. His big hand hovering an inch or so at the small of my back, he shortens his stride so that we're walking side-by-side.

He's still quiet, though, and as we start for the path that will lead us toward my cabin, I decide to break the silence for no other reason than that I like to hear his voice.

It... it does something to me. When the bad memories start to rise, or I feel the walls closing in around me like I'm still in that tiny room in California, his gentle rumble is enough to help me get past it. Not that I can admit that to him. For some reason, he already thinks he has to watch over me, even though there hasn't been any more trouble in Accalia since Walker's death. If he—or anyone—found out just how much I rely on Duke... it's not fair. It's not fair to make him responsible for a broken she-wolf he has no tie to.

If only he did...

Giving my head a small shake, I glance up at him. His expression is careful, kind of like he doesn't want to spook me.

He doesn't have to worry about that. I might have come out of my abduction a lot more aware of what dangers this world can hold, but I'll never be scared of Duke. As big as he is, as fierce as I know any wolf shifter can be, if there's one thing I'm absolutely certain of, it's that I have nothing to fear from Duke Conlon.

I give him an encouraging smile, a little surprised when his cheeks immediately go pink. "You know, you don't have to do this. I'm not too far from Audrey's."

He nods. "I know. But I'm a protector. It's my job."

Right. As one of the pack enforcers, Duke takes on the role of protector for the rest of us. The deltas and gammas who don't want to have anything to do with pack politics or supe concerns. We live our lives in a secluded community, but we can do that because we have a powerful Alpha to lead us, and the more dominant wolves to keep us safe. Between prowling the mountain and patrolling the borders of our territory, anyone who wants to cause trouble has to go through them first.

Unless, of course, they're a pack traitor. Someone like Shane Loup or Aidan Barrow... those who smiled to your face while they were trying to figure out where the best place was to stick the silver knife in your back.

They didn't have to sneak onto the mountain. They were already here.

Another shake. Duke's brow furrows, but I change the subject quickly before he gets concerned with just how dark my thoughts are these days.

"Is that where you were last night? Pack duty?" I ask casually.

Probably a bit *too* casually.

Most decent Alphas take the safety of the pack seriously, and Ryker is no exception. There's never a moment that there aren't at least three wolves on duty, checking the border. That means overnight, too. Since Duke wasn't outside of my cabin, I just assume that he must have been on.

And doesn't that just prove that I'm still as selfish as ever?

Duke could have been anywhere. He has a small single-room cabin set on the eastern side of the mountain, and he's a high-ranking pack member. I know he's not mated, but he could still have a female he meets with in his free time.

I'm out of the loop. Before California, I never paid that much attention to any other male than the Alpha. After, whenever I thought of Duke mounting one of the unmated females in Accalia, I had a hard time controlling my claws. It got to the point that I ruined my manicure enough times when they would unsheathe without any warning that I stopped polishing my human nails.

I still have a hard time getting the image of Duke—big, brawny, handsome Duke—in bed with someone else.

Now, I've never mated myself. I had waited for Ryker to take me as his mate, and when he refused, I still held out hope he might grow desperate one full moon and settle for me anyway. The last Luna before his mating ceremony with Gem, I even followed Shane's assurance that, if I threw myself at him when the moon fever was high, he might fuck me just because I was willing.

Of course, I didn't know then that Shane was manipulating me the same way he was screwing over the pack and our Alpha. He wanted Gem for himself, and he arranged it so that I was at the Alpha cabin when she came looking for Ryker while the Luna was at her peak. But Ryker wasn't there—he was locked in the basement of his personal cabin, shifter chains restraining him from going after his mate—and that was the last chance I had before he banished me for trying to come between him and Gem.

I was only gone for about six weeks before I begged to be allowed back home. The next full moon after that, the Alphas were joined, and I was abducted a few days later. After how long I spent terrified that my first mating would be a forced one, I still haven't found a male to attempt since I've been back.

I'd never tell another soul, but last month? That was the first time I wondered if maybe... maybe Duke would be interested. He's unmated. I'm unmated. Shifters go wild when they feel the pull of the full moon, and sex is nothing if not a biological urge. Growing up, I'd heard whispers about how powerful the need could be, and I finally felt my first hint of it then.

As if I needed another reminder that I was never meant for Ryker. Pride and envy had me sure that I'd be a good match for him, and Luna knows he's a gorgeous male, but I never felt like I'd go to my hands and knees for him willingly.

But when I look at Duke—

Whoa. I'm looking at him now.

More importantly, he's looking at *me*.

"Yeah, actually. I wasn't supposed to do the overnight, but Benjy's pup had her first shift. He was celebrating with his mate, so I took over for him." He pauses, his forehead furrowed. "Why did you ask?"

"Uh." Crap. How am I supposed to answer?

"Are you... did you need me?"

Double crap. I don't want Duke to think that he *has* to take care of me. That's something I'd only ever expect from a mate, and I've given up hope that there's some male in Accalia who wants to put up with what it means to choose Trish Danvers as his.

So I shrug. "Sometimes you're there. Sometimes you're not. I just noticed you weren't, that's all."

It's not all. See? This is why I go along with his choosing to stay quiet. I open my mouth, I say something that would have been better left unsaid.

"Oh, Trish... you had another nightmare, didn't you?"

And I just did it again, didn't I?

Good thing that being a she-wolf means that I'm quick on my feet. When Duke's soft murmur reaches me, I stumble over my feet, but I regain my balance before I land on my butt.

Duke's quick, too. Though I sense his hand moving to steady me, he pulls back before his skin makes contact with mine. That's a surefire way to insult a supe, and unless I give him permission to touch me, I could lash out at him if he catches me off guard.

Would I? I... I don't know. Not on purpose. Not to Duke.

But I might. Especially now that he's mentioned my nightmare.

How does he know? We can pretend that he doesn't spend most nights sleeping outside on my porch and that I have no clue he's out there. His lingering scent and the blanket I leave for him make it obvious that's bullshit. I feel safer having him close, and he's right. He's a protector to his core.

I never told him about my nightmares, though. So how does he know?

"Duke—"

"It's okay. It won't happen again. I'll ask Ryker to keep me off of the overnights."

"What? No. I don't... you don't have to do that."

"And like I told you before, I know. But unless you ask me not to, I'm going to do it anyway." He waits a beat, before rumbling, "So? Are you going to ask me?"

I'm not, and we both know it. If I wanted him to leave me alone, I would've marked my immediate territory last September, made it clear that he wasn't welcome so close. No male shifter could sleep on a she-wolf's porch without her permission, express or otherwise. I want him there. I just wish he had a different reason to stay with me than the one he has.

*Pity.*

As if I could pretend otherwise. Nope, especially when he clears his throat and says, "Have you shifted recently? Let your wolf out for a run?"

When my gaze drops to the dirt, he makes a sympathetic sound in the back of his throat. "It'll do you good, Trish. If you get in touch with your wolf, it might stop the nightmares."

Right. The nightmares where I'm trapped in my fur again, with the Wicked Wolf chasing me.

"I never said I had any nightmares," I tell him. "Besides, I'm fine. I'm home. I'm safe."

And Walker's dead. He can never hurt me again.

"You are," he says, a finality to the two words that chases the dread settling in my gut away... for the moment, at least. "But... I've been thinking. Maybe you should visit Dahlia. She might be able to help you more than I can."

I dare a glance up at him. Instead of the pity I expect, his expression has turned earnest.

That's the only reason why I decide to be honest and admit, "I have. And you're right. She helps a lot, but I'm not the only shifter in Accalia. I can't monopolize all of her time."

Dahlia is our Omega. Her rank of wolf is the glue that holds a pack together. Like a therapist in the human world, just talking to the spiky-haired, blonde wolf leaves you feeling a bit more at peace than you did before. She's also a schoolteacher for the young pups, so there are a lot of calls on her time. She's kind enough to see me when she can—and, I admit, it's probably more due to her good-hearted, omega nature than because any of my packmates think Trish Danvers is worthy of their sympathy—and, like Duke, Dahlia helps keep the nightmares away for a while.

When Gem first came to join our pack, everyone believed she was another omega. She'd been pretending to be one her entire life, and because her dominance was so different than any other rank-and-file she-wolf, it made sense she was an omega. The only other female alpha in shifter tradition was our revered goddess, the Luna herself. No one ever guessed she could be the second—but Shane knew. He knew, and he told me, and I used Gem's hidden secret to blackmail Ryker into rejecting her.

I can't change what I've done; I can only admit that I was wrong, and try to be better in the future. Dahlia is our only Omega. With Gem, we thought we'd have a second, but we don't. I'm not the only one who needs Dahlia's wolf to deal with my own demons.

That's why, when Duke says, "You need her. It's not monopolizing anything if you need her more," I shake my head.

"Why not?"

My knee-jerk reaction is to tell the truth. "Because I'm not important enough."

"Of course you are."

"That's sweet, Duke, but I know what I am. Who I am."

"So do I."

That has me finally looking up again. As we continued to walk, I'd avoided meeting his eyes as we drew up to my cabin, but when Duke's voice goes impossibly deep, I have to see if I imagined what I heard.

I… I don't think I did.

His eyes have melted to a soft golden shade. His jaw is chiseled, his features hard, but there's a sudden gentleness to them as he tucks his chin into his chest, making it easier for him to stare directly into my face.

He lifts his hand. I can feel the heat pouring off of his fingers as he ghosts his thumb over my cheek. He never makes contact, but he doesn't have to. I shiver anyway.

"What?" I ask.

It's a squeak. The word slips out, but I couldn't keep it back. It was impossible. There's promise written in every line of his face, a promise that reminds me of the fierce Duke who reached past the silver bars, burning his human arm raw just to stroke my fur, reminding me that he was there—and that he would do anything to bring me home again.

My cabin is behind me. Somehow, Duke is closer than we've been in months. My heart is racing, my wolf up and keening as she recognizes something in his golden gaze that my human half just can't understand.

And then he murmurs, "You're important to me."

I blink. My lips part, but I don't have any idea what to say to that.

Later on, I still won't be sure if the emotions of the moment made me read more into his intentions than were truly there. His eyes drop from mine down to my lips, his chin jerking forward. I get the sudden feeling that he's about to kiss me, and I freeze like a deer in front of a predatory shifter.

Maybe he was. Then again, maybe he finally noticed how close we were all of a sudden and he was about to back away. I'll never know because, like that very same deer confronted with a hungry wolf, I choose to flee.

Duke doesn't chase. When I take a few hurried steps back, then bolt for my door, he stays exactly where I left him.

About ten feet separate us. As I try to slow my racing heart, I lift up a hand. "Good night."

He does the same. "Sweet dreams."

Right now, I'd rather not have any at all.

With a quick wave, I let myself into my cabin. And though I can still sense his bold, comforting aura just outside of my territory, I turn the lock on the door and let out the breath I hadn't even realized I was holding.

# CHAPTER 4
# LOCKS

The locks should've been my first clue that I'm not okay.

We don't lock our cabins in Accalia. There's no reason to. You should be able to trust your packmates or the whole idea of living in a shifter community, sharing goods and wealth, providing for the next generation of pups... it's bullshit. Shifters are hard-wired to live together and support each other. Those that aren't either choose to be a lone wolf or go feral.

And then there are the bad seeds like Shane Loup. A beta who wanted nothing more than to be an alpha, he acted the role of the perfect packmate all while working behind our backs. Worse, I *helped* him.

I want to think I'm not like him. Hurting my pack was never part of my plan. I honestly believed that, as Ryker's mate, I'd make it better. We didn't need an outsider she-wolf coming in to join with him, especially when I believed she was an omega. Having a rare female alpha take the top spot would be a coup for any shifter pack, but she came with baggage. The Wicked Wolf wanted her, and so did Shane. If I got Ryker out of the deal, I didn't care—so long as Mountainside was safe.

But it wasn't. At least, not for me. Because of everything I've done, I put a target on my back. It might be gone now, but the illusion of safety that hung over my cabin, the trees, and the mountains I've lived on my whole life... it's gone, and I don't know if I'll ever get it back.

Logically, I know that the locks won't do shit. A shifter's brute strength would snap the doorknob right off if they really wanted to get to me. Still, for the same reason I keep my windows closed, I lock the doors behind me anytime I return to my cabin. It's something small that makes me feel better, and anyone with good intentions would respect my need for security these days.

I just wish I could go back to the way I used to be. Carefree and flippant, a quick tongue and a satisfied smile... that's the old Trish. The new Trish takes a deep breath before checking the door one final time, then retreating to the kitchen for a small snack to settle her nervous stomach.

Maybe Duke's right. In the first few weeks after I returned from California, I saw Dahlia every couple of days. Both my Alpha and my parents insisted on it, and I was so screwed up that I snarled at them to leave me alone. I was like a wounded animal backed into a corner, even in my skin, and I almost attempted to challenge the three shifters who had any authority over me and my wolf.

Luckily, they didn't take me up on it. My parents never would, no matter how much I snapped my fangs at them, and Ryker... he's a good male, and a better Alpha. He arrived in the Wolf District shortly before the whole Western Pack imploded, so he was there to see what the quicksilver sedative and the silver cell did to me. Duke, too. I'll never forget how he actually stood between me and Ryker, daring to meet our Alpha's eyes, warning him that he wouldn't be ordered to stand down until *I* gave the command for him to.

That's how I ended up riding in the backseat of the rented car with Duke while Gem drove and Ryker sat shotgun. Halfway home, I finally felt secure enough to shift back. Forever the gentleman, Duke immediately closed his eyes. Gem barked at Ryker to do the same, which I get. Nudity isn't a big deal in a pack, but I had made a move on her male before. I couldn't expect her to forget that. As for Duke... he's just a good guy. Of course he wouldn't peek, even if it didn't mean anything to him.

He did, however, offer me a shift dress he grabbed with him before we left the Wolf District. Simpler than the sundresses I used to wear, it covered me up until we made our way back home.

I thought that would be the last time he took care of me. Nope. Seven months later, he still is. I don't know how to tell him that, while Dahlia's wolf has soothed some of the jagged edges inside of me, it's a delta who's done the most work putting me back together.

So maybe I should visit her again. It's been a couple of weeks since I have, but when Duke's wolf does even more to stop the nightmares and the bad memories and the countless what-ifs from racing through my mind... I'd rather rely on him.

It isn't fair. I know that. I'm putting too much pressure on a male who I'd talked to maybe twice before he saved me from the lowest point in my life. The way I see it, though, he doesn't have to. He says it's his job. He's a protector for the Mountainside Pack.

And, well, I'm a packmate, aren't I?

It's a flimsy justification at best. I don't care. For as long as he wants to be my shadow, I'll let him. It's the closest I've ever had to anyone being mine.

If only he was for real.

---

WHEN I FINALLY FALL ASLEEP MUCH LATER THAT NIGHT, I expect the nightmares to follow me. Most days I can shove my past behind me. It's something I've always been good at. I used to be able to shake off the day, no matter what, and still have a pleasant night's sleep.

Not anymore.

It's probably not the healthiest coping mechanism, but I still try. If I don't think about what happened after Barrow first turned on me, or when Walker's dark, menacing aura would visit me in the cells, threatening me more effectively than the words the cruel Alpha tossed my way, then I can pretend I'm the old Trish again. It never lasts for long, but it's worse when I fall back into the spiral of reliving those awful moments.

Barrow was a kid, barely twenty, and he sliced me to ribbons before injecting me with enough quicksilver that my hold on my wolf has never been the same. Walker told me that I'd be another one of his personal bitches, a willing pussy whenever he wanted it, because my Alpha all but threw me away. If Ryker didn't come, I'd be passed along to any male who wanted me, and maybe then I could see how long I'd stay so pretty...

Even dead, his threats still haunt me the same way his golden wolf chases me into my dreams. I can never escape him—except for when I sense the comforting energy of a protective wolf who will never, ever harm me.

I sleep dreamlessly for a few hours before I wake up suddenly. It's pitch dark in my cabin, and I reach out instinctively. It's such a subconscious act, one I do without even really meaning to, and when my wolf follows an invisible thread and finds Duke's waiting at the end of it, I sit up.

I don't know why I'm so surprised that he's out there. Sure, I left him standing off the edge of my porch after that strangely charged moment between us, but he's the one who mentioned my nightmares. If he somehow figured out that I suffer from them when he's out patrolling Accalia at night, if he wasn't on duty now, of course he'd stick around.

That's what a decent protector like Duke Conlon does.

I don't know why I start to climb out of bed. Or maybe I do, but I want to blame my sleepy state for what happens next. It doesn't matter either way. My wolf whines, imploring me to go to his, and after I snag my blanket off of my rumpled sheets and shrug on a nightgown, that's exactly what I do.

Tip-toeing on my bare feet, I know instinctively that he's still out back. I push open the door and immediately find him.

In his human form, Duke stands above a crowd. He's no different when he's shifted to his fur. Dark grey and massive, he sprawls out over nearly the entire length of the blanket I leave outside for nights like these. He's on his side, legs stretched out in front of him, belly falling and rising in time to his chuffing breaths.

He's dead asleep. Knocked out to the world. I have no doubt in my mind that, if a threat approached, he'd flip like a switch, waking up to confront it with barely a missed step. But since it's just me and him and the trees that surround the back of my cabin, he sleeps on while I look my fill.

I should go back inside. He's here, and that means that the nightmares won't find me tonight. But then I remember the look in his eyes I swore I saw before I bolted. His gentle rumble, the way he told me I was important to him… and I close the door behind me before stepping lightly over to him.

Duke snuffles, but his wolf doesn't stir. Not even when I drop to my knees, then cozy up against him. I prop my back up against his bulk, turning my face into his sleek fur. This close, the pine scent is stronger than ever. I breathe in deep, letting it settle over me.

In the Wolf District, we had bars between us. Walker's people allowed Duke to stay with me, just not in my personal cell. That didn't stop him from trying any way to make some physical contact between us, even if the silver burned him over and over again. He wanted me to know I wasn't alone.

As I drift off to sleep, soothed by the sounds of his wolf deep in slumber, I do the same for the big delta.

No matter what happens, at least one good thing came out of my captivity.

We have each other.

---

I'M UP BEFORE DUKE. GOOD THING, TOO, BECAUSE I'M BARE-assed naked.

It's the whisper of the breeze against my overheated skin that tickles me awake. I stretch, and it takes me a second to realize that his fur is cradling my bare back, and my nightgown is gone.

Not only that, but my muscles don't feel tight anymore. The slight headache—a rarity for a supe—I'd been battling for days has disappeared. In fact, I feel better than I have in a while.

And that's because I… I shifted.

It's obvious. When a shifter goes too long between changing forms, we pay for it. In a world full of humans who have no idea that supes exist, it's a given that we spend more time in our skin. Throw in the fact that we communicate better with words than howls, and shifters don't fuck in the fur, and our two-legged shape is the default.

But we're shifters. We need to shift. If our wolf doesn't get their fair share of being in control, we get antsy. Our skin itches, then our muscles clench. We get stomachaches. Headaches. Fatigue. All signs that our body needs to change shapes, but ones I purposely ignored for way too long.

A laugh bubbles up inside of me, one that I swallow as I scoot to my knees, looking at the disturbed grass beneath my legs. The grass is torn up, my feet muddy. I must've shifted, then dug in the dirt with my paws before circling around and falling back asleep with Duke. At some point, I shifted back to human —obviously—but that doesn't change the fact that I did it. I shifted.

Now that I've gone wolf again, I can admit my deepest, darkest shame: I was afraid that I'd never be able to let her out again without it being a struggle on my human side.

It's the quicksilver that fucked me up. I don't know if my reaction is usual. Though Audrey's not proud of what she did, she only served a couple of drops to Gem in a doctored glass of Coke. Enough to sedate the powerful alpha female, but there was no harm done. Within a couple of hours it wore off, and that gave the pack council time to escort her to Ryker's cabin.

They didn't shoot her up with it like Barrow did me. She got a couple of drops. I got two or three doses a day during travel so that I was a groggy, frightened mess when I woke up in the Wolf District, completely naked and cut off from my wolf.

Walker's people gave me a shift dress when they brought me to the cell that would be my home for the next few weeks, but the second I could finally tap into my other half again, I shredded that thing before shifting to my fur.

I refused to shift back. Let them think I was an animal. During my stay, I *was*—

—until Duke found me. Until a piece of home chose to sit at my side, soothing me with his bass voice, promising me everything and nothing if I could maintain my tenuous grip on my sanity. I did. Barely, but I did.

The quicksilver has been out of my system for a long, long time. I sense my wolf in every breath, every sigh, every beat of my Luna-damned heart. Still, she didn't want to come out. It wasn't just me. It was both of us. She needed the time to heal, to lick her wounds, and I needed to prove that I was me again. Trish.

Now, though? With the proof of my latest shift around me—literally, as my nightgown is scattered pieces of fabric dusted over our blankets—I finally feel whole.

And I have Duke to thank for that.

I doubt he'd see it that way. All he did was play the role of my guard, sleeping on my back porch so that my wolf sensed his and knew she was safe. I might have taken advantage of his kindness to curl up next to him, but I was in my skin when I did that. I haven't sleep-shifted in years, but wrapped up in Duke's aura, I did.

I'm still broken... just not beyond repair. I can shift again.

I'm whole.

Another laugh escapes me. For the first time in forever, I feel light. Free. It's like a weight I hadn't even realized I'd been carrying was lifted from my shoulder. I want to bounce. I want to run. I want to drop to all fours, give control over to my other side, throw back my head, and howl in shuddering relief.

I don't, though, if only because Duke is still slumbering where I left him. I can care less if I wake up all of Accalia... just not him. He sleeps like a hibernating bear, rumbling and snorting, but I know it's because he spends more hours a day protecting our pack—protecting *me*—than he can even make up in a couple of short naps. If he's resting, sleeping through me joining him outside *and* sleep-shifting... well, I'm not going to disturb him.

But I will do something.

I wait until I've put enough distance between us by crawling to hop to my feet and hurry for my porch. So giddy, I don't even stop to lock the door. I just race for my room, grabbing the first change of clothing that I find, all while my brain is whirling.

He does so much for me. I don't care if it's because of his role as protector. So many of my packmates gave up on me after the trouble I caused. I don't blame them, but the truth is what it is. Duke could've abandoned me, too. He didn't, though, and it's about time I show him how much I appreciate it—and how much I've grown to care about him.

I'm a shifter. There's only one way I can do that and make sure he gets my meaning.

With food.

## CHAPTER 5
## CUPCAKES

My mother is giddy when I ask her to get me all of the ingredients I need to make cupcakes.

I'll be the first to admit I was a late bloomer. It's part of the reason why I didn't even think about who I would take as a mate until I was twenty. I was too distracted when I was young, no one really caught my attention as a "practice" mate, and I had a hobby that I preferred when I wasn't hanging around with the other she-wolves.

As a pup, I spent a lot of time in the kitchen because my beloved grandmother used to bake breads and pastries for the pack. For a while, I entertained the idea of taking over for her when she retired. It wasn't long before I realized I couldn't bake bread for shit, and I didn't have the patience for fiddly pastries like choux and puff.

But, Luna, could I make a mean cupcake.

When you're a pup, you can feed anyone and there is no hidden meaning to it. As I got older, I couldn't just bake cupcakes for fun, only if I was serving them to family and my girlfriends; no innuendo there. Males would think differently unless I was the pack baker.

However, before I could decide if that's what I wanted to do, I fell for Ryker. Hard. I should've known then that, if my cupcakes couldn't sway him, *I* never could, but from twenty on, I only baked for him. When he refused to take them, I stopped baking at all.

Mom tried to see if I wanted to start up again after my banishment was lifted. Same story when I came back from the Wolf District. She remembered how happy I was when I was creating recipes for the tiny cakes and decorating them with frosting and fondant designs. In her kind way, she thought she could bring the old Trish—the good Trish—back with some flour, sugar, and butter.

It didn't work. I can't tell you the last time I pulled my mixer out of storage. It wasn't something that interested me—until I have the impulse to bake a dozen for Duke Conlon.

I don't tell her who I'm making them for, of course. Knowing my parents as I do, they'll get it in their heads that, this time, Duke might be the one for me. They've been pushing me to search out a chosen mate these last couple of years, and I'm sure they'd be ecstatic if it was a respected council member strong enough to protect their only pup.

Or, Luna help me, they might get the idea in their skulls that Duke might even be the *one*. My fated mate.

Yeah, right.

He can't be. I would know. Even if I'm too screwed up to recognize my forever standing there in front of me, he'd have some kind of clue. It's instinct.

Not that it matters. Even if we're not fated, we could be

mates, and I don't want to give my poor parents the impression when that's not how Duke sees me at all. Because, while an alpha wolf is usually blessed with the identity of his mate, regular deltas aren't. We either luck out on finding our fated mate or we don't. But since we're also not solitary creatures, we make the best of it and choose a mate instead.

He could have anyone.

Though, as I start setting the ingredients out, muscle memory taking over as the familiar scents of vanilla and sugar, baking powder and butter fill my cozy kitchen... I have to ask myself: why not me?

Now, he's not my fated mate. I'm fairly sure of that. I've known of him for years, and have gotten closer and closer in the last seven months. If he was, there should've been some sign that we were meant for each other. Some kind of bond building between us.

Sorry, I don't count the trauma bond, or his need to protect me even now that we're home. So, no. He's not my fated mate.

Duke's never made any move like I could be his, either. I'm probably being ridiculous, mistaking my gratitude and affection for something else... but all the way up until I'm standing outside of Duke's cabin, a dozen cupcakes in my trembling grasp, I can't help but wonder: what if?

I know he's home. I can sense his comforting aura like a warm blanket on a chilly mountain night even from twenty yards away. I'd taken a chance, hoping he'd be at his cabin instead of on patrol—and that he'd be alone—but I've always been impulsive.

It took everything I had to wait until the cupcakes were cool enough to decorate them, and even longer for the frosting to set before I could transport them through the woods. By the time

Duke opens the door, my wolf is almost whining, looking for some sign that he is pleased by my token.

One thing for sure, the puzzled look on Duke's face when he sees me standing there definitely isn't one.

"Trish? What are you doing here?"

He sounds guarded. Wary. Makes sense. He must've figured out that I'd snuck out to sleep by his wolf last night, but it was equally obvious that I left him before he woke up. So focused on planning what kind of cupcakes I was going to make, I didn't even think to offer him some breakfast. As if nothing was different, I walked away, and he did the same when he got up.

But something *was* different. I felt it when my wolf shifted for the first time in ages, and it only became undeniable as I was baking. Whatever relationship we have, I don't want Duke to go back to being the silent shadow in the distance. For good or for bad, we have a tie forged in silver, and I need to respect that.

Starting with making him an offering of his own.

"I made you something." Holding the cupcake platter out to Duke, I say, "Here. These are for you."

At first, he doesn't take it. My heart sinks all the way down to my feet when all Duke does is stare at the twelve frosted cupcakes as if he can't believe what he's seeing.

"What's this?"

"You're always bringing me food. I thought it was about time I did the same."

Everyone knows what it means when a shifter provides food for another. For so long, I've accepted that I was the only exception... but I don't want Duke to be. I want him to take these cupcakes from me and know that I'm saying: I will feed you, I will love you, and you'll want for nothing while I'm around.

I wait on a bated breath to see if he will, swallowing the

sound of relief when he does with a solemn, "That was nice of you."

Screw nice. "If you say so."

Him accepting them isn't enough. For my wolf to be satisfied, he has to actually take a bite.

"Go on." I use my chin to gesture at the tray. "Aren't you going to eat them? Have a bite?"

"I will. Later. Thank you. I… thanks."

Standing there, Duke awkwardly holding onto the platter, I realize that there was nothing else to do. Unless I decide to climb him like a tree and shove one of my cupcakes into his mouth, I can't force him to eat them if he doesn't want to. I just have to hope he does.

I smile, though my heart's not quite in it. For a female who spent years being endlessly rejected by the male she chased, you'd think I'd be used to it. I'm not. And, Luna, it's especially worse when I thought I might… I might have found someone else who would accept me for me.

I guess I was the one reading way too much into it.

---

I SHOULDN'T BE DISAPPOINTED. TELL THAT TO MY WOLF.

The whole way back to my cabin she was laying flat on her belly, paws forward, muzzle resting on her legs. I almost want to mimic her pose. The high from shifting last night has come crashing down on me, all because I saw something that wasn't there and made a foolish, rash decision to act on it.

Like I said. I should've known better.

After I enter my cabin, locking the door behind me like usual, I do the routine check to make sure no one came inside while I was gone; without a key, I can't lock up when I go, though even pouting, my wolf is strong enough to sense any intruder upon my return. I frown when I see the mess I left behind in the kitchen. So excited to bring my cupcakes to Duke, I left the bowls and dishes and half-filled piping bag where they were.

I don't have the energy to clean up yet. Like my wolf, I'd rather throw myself a pity party I don't deserve. So, retreating to my bedroom, I do exactly that. Kicking off my shoes, I plop down on my bed and rest my eyes.

Claws crossed that I don't fall asleep. Mood I'm in following Duke's rejection, I wouldn't be surprised if I have a doozy of a nightmare.

Luckily, I don't, even if I do knock out. I nap for the next few hours, finding solace in my loneliness and dreamless sleep. I might even have gone without dinner and slept right through the night if it wasn't for the fact that, shortly before dark, there comes a banging at my front door.

I hear it first, heart leaping into my throat as my eyes spring wide open. The rest of my senses come online seconds later. Once I catch the scent of the delta male outside, I understand why my wolf didn't warn me of his approach. That's family out there, and no matter how messed up I am, I'm not afraid of family.

*Bang.*

*Bang.*

"Trish? I know you're in there!"

*Bang.*

Rolling my eyes, I glance down to make sure that I didn't sleep-shift again. Nope. I'm still wearing the same blouse and jeans from earlier today so I don't have to worry about hearing

Bobby complain that I've scarred him for life by prancing around naked in front of my cousin.

"Trish!"

"Hold on," I holler back. "I'm coming!"

To my reply, the idiot bangs on my door again.

I swear, there better be an emergency in Accalia for all the racket he's making. Like, honestly, I need him to warn me that we're under attack, or one of Walker's not-dead Betas found us, or Aleksander Filan decided to wage war on the Mountainside Pack. Something like that.

I definitely don't expect him to march into my cabin once I unlock the door and wave an empty cupcake wrapper in front of my face.

"I can't believe you did this to me! I stood up for you. When Walker had Barrows grab you, I pleaded with the Alpha to find some way to bring you home safe. And how do you repay me? With betrayal!"

You know, everyone else in Accalia handles me with kid gloves. My parents. Duke. Even Audrey.

Not Bobby Danvers.

I roll my eyes. "What are you talking about?"

"Duke's my pal. You're family. I didn't get involved because you two have got to work this out yourself, but that's before you brought cupcakes into it."

"Again, I ask: what are you talking about?"

This time, I'm referring to the first part of what he said—you two have got to work this out yourselves—but Bobby is still only irrationally focused on the last bit.

"Cupcakes!" The youngest Danvers of this generation, he's always been the one closest to his wolf. As he snaps out the word, I see his canine teeth have become fangs. "I stopped by

Duke's and smelled the buttercream. And do you know what I found?"

I'm pretty sure he's going to tell me.

He waves the wrapper again. "This! This was all that was left!"

What?

"One wrapper? But I made him a whole dozen."

"Yeah. I *know*. I saw all of the wrappers, but this is the only one I got before he ran me out of his cabin. He ate them all and got snappish when I asked for a wrapper to lick the icing. Can you believe it?"

Um. No, actually. I can't.

I go warm. My whole body... it heats up with pleasure.

Because Duke? He ate the cupcakes. He ate all twelve.

He ate my food.

I don't care what the big delta thinks it means. To me, it means something particular.

It means... it means I might have a chance. A small one, sure, but a chance is a chance—and I've done way more with less.

Bobby is still ranting and raving. My toes are just about curling against the wooden floor of my cabin, and he's still complaining about selfish enforcers and betraying relatives.

"If you're baking again, you can make me some, too," he says. "I'm your cousin. Family. Until the two of you get your act together, I should come first."

Maybe. Maybe he's right. Maybe Duke and I do need to get our act together.

And maybe I should thank Bobby for coming here to tell me because, Luna knows, I'm not so sure Duke ever would... well, not yet, at least.

I hold up my hand.

Pack council or not. Protector of the alpha female or not. Dominant shifter or not... Bobby is my younger cousin. I have some sway. He clicks his fangs together, waiting for me to say something.

That's why, feeling generous, I wave toward my kitchen. "If you stop talking right now, you can lick the beaters. There's still some batter in the bowl from this morning, and the piping bag of buttercream should still be fresh. Knock yourself out."

Bobby yips, then lunges for me, smacking a kiss on my cheek. "Thanks, Trish. You're the best!"

I'm not. But I'm trying my hardest to be.

---

If my way to even out some of the power imbalance between us is by baking Duke a dozen cupcakes every day, then that's what I'm going to do. It might not be much—especially since he continues to sleep outside of my cabin, with or without me—but it feels like something to me.

We do this for about three days before he finally eats one in my company. I don't leave until he tells me what he thinks about them, and after he says it was the best cupcake he's ever had, I can't help myself. I throw my arms around his side and squeeze as much of him as I can.

Hugging Duke Conlon is like hugging a tree, only softer and infinitely hotter.

Speaking of heat...

This afternoon, I used my baking session as a way to distract myself more than anything. The warmth I felt a couple of days ago hasn't faded yet. In fact, it's only grown stronger. Heat pouring off of the oven has me exchanging my normal clothes for a simple shift dress. Nothing as extravagant as my old collection of sundresses, the shift dress is more like a slip than anything else. No underwear, either, since it's chafing my skin.

I'm not just overheated. I'm overstimulated.

While the cupcakes are baking, I take a cold shower and bring myself to come twice before the timer goes off. It doesn't help. In fact, it just makes me realize how... how *empty* I feel.

Like everything would be okay if I found something hard and thick and sturdy to shove up inside of my aching pussy.

My freshly washed hands are shaking as I'm icing the cupcakes. Sweat builds at the base of my neck. I scoop my shower-damp hair over my shoulder, wiping it away with my wrist. It doesn't help, though the contact makes me realize that I don't just feel hot on the inside.

I'm really burning up.

Talk about denial. It isn't until I step out onto my porch, clutching my platter of cupcakes like a lifeline as I notice that tonight is the night of the Luna, that I realize what's wrong with me.

This is moon fever, and I'm already lost to it.

I guess it makes sense. Mature shifters feel the need to mate —and Luna knows I have—but they can... handle it on their own if there's no partner for them to choose. If there is, if there's someone our wolf will accept, the Luna's pull makes it so that it's harder to refuse.

And when you go against the Luna's wishes... she makes you pay with the fever.

There's only one way I can treat it. Find the male my wolf would welcome and entice him to mate.

Too bad I don't have any idea how to do that.

It's supposed to be instinct. Like so much of being a shifter, we do what we feel is right—but that got me in trouble before. Relying on my own wants and desires ruined my life. I'm not about to ruin an innocent male's, too.

Of course, if I bring these cupcakes to Duke's on the night of the full moon and one thing leads to another... well, you can't blame a she-wolf for that, can you?

Apparently, I discover, you can. At least, your cousin can.

I don't know if he guessed I would make a move on his friend or not, but Bobby waylays me just outside of Duke's cabin. For a moment, I think about accusing him of cock-blocking me—or maybe bribing him with Duke's cupcakes—and that's when I notice the grim expression on his usually easygoing face.

"Let me stop you right here, Trish. Go home. Wait out the full moon where it's safe. And, Luna help me, keep your doors locked."

Right. Because with my newly developed paranoias, the last thing I need is for my protector cousin to tell me it's a good idea to lock my doors.

"Okay. I will," I tell him, if only because he looks like he won't take no for an answer, "but I just want to drop these cupcakes off to Duke first."

"You can't."

"Bobby—"

"You don't want to see him. Not tonight. Trust me."

He's a Danvers. Of course I do.

That doesn't stop me. "I'll leave them on his porch. I won't even see him."

But if Duke sees me...

Bobby shakes his head. "You'd be wasting your time. He's not even there."

"How do you know that?"

Bobby runs his fingers through his hair, claws leaving track marks in their wake. I can tell he doesn't want to answer me—but after a few moments, he does.

Probably because I threatened to never make him another cupcake again as long as he lived. Oh, well. It does the job.

"Ah, Luna, Trish. It's 'cause he went off to borrow the Alpha's chains."

# CHAPTER 6
# CHAINS

Chains.

Every pack has a pair. Forged from silver, they're absolutely unbreakable. All supes react to silver, and shifters are no exception. It weakens us—a fact I know all too well after my time in a cage lined with silver bars—and it burns our skin raw if we touch it.

No shifter will choose to put on a pair of chains unless there is no other option. They're for ferals, mainly, or those who aren't too sure of their control.

Everyone in Accalia knows the rumors about Ryker and the chains. I hate to admit that I know for sure that they're not rumors, and our Alpha spent every night of the full moon chained in his cabin's basement because he was a danger to the rest of us.

He was a shifter without his true mate, and for a whole year, he didn't know where Gem was hiding out. Their bond was strained, magic covering up her scent, and he had no way to track her since it seemed as if she'd just disappeared. No one knew she was insane enough to risk death by fang in Muncie—or that she survived, the only shifter living in the Fang City. Ryker's wolf still wanted his mate, though, and he would've burned the whole world down to get to her if he could.

The chains were essential. When the moon fever hit him, not even an alpha wolf could break through the mystically forged silver chains. His pack council set him free the next morning, and we all agreed to pretend that it wasn't happening. Alphas need complete faith and loyalty to lead their pack, and none of Mountainside wanted their pity for Ryker's unfortunate situation to get in the way of that.

If he felt anything like I have tonight, I put him through torture. Tomorrow, when the fever breaks, I'll experience guilt for my actions all over again. But tonight? All I can think about is how my wolf picked one male for me to entice—and he needs the Alpha's chains.

There's only one reason why he would: Duke is a shifter without his mate.

I've known him for seven months. More, really, but our friendship only began those awful days in California. He's never once mentioned that he has a mate. No one in Accalia has. As far as I know, he's unmated, just like me. No female would stand by and allow their mate to protect another she-wolf, no matter what his position in the pack is.

So maybe he doesn't have a mate—but he has an intended. A female his body and wolf believe is his, and who he'd be with if he could. Since he can't, he's choosing chains and a night of agony in Ryker's old basement.

Makes sense. Only a handful of cabins have the underground rooms to begin with. From the rumors that have whispered through the pack's gossip mill, Ryker's chains were big and heavy, but also screwed into the cinder block wall in his basement. They're not something that Duke could bring to his single-room cabin. He has to be there.

When I walk away from my cousin, my thoughts spinning like a top, I'm sure he expects me to return to my cabin. I make sure to head in that direction until I'm out of sight, then quickly start sprinting through the trees. Good thing I left the cupcakes with Bobby so that my arms are free to pump as I run.

Before he was the Alpha, Ryker was the Alpha heir. He was still high up in the pack that the cabin he took after he became a mature male was on the outskirts of Accalia, on the opposite side of where his parents' cabin stood. If I take the right path, I can make it there without any of my packmates figuring out where I've gone.

Only Bobby knows that I was looking for Duke tonight. So many other of my fellow shifters will be with their own mates. What do they care if I follow through with my plan to see if he'd be interested in having sex with me?

I'm sure his intended mate would care. But, see, that just proves that old, selfish Trish will never be gone and buried, no matter how hard I try. I want Duke. Forever would be nice, but I'll take just tonight if I can. He doesn't have to agree. He can stay true to his intended if he wants, but I wouldn't be Trish Danvers if I didn't at least give him the option to choose me.

---

No one in Accalia locks the doors, except for me. Even on the night of the full moon, with the Luna running him ragged and leading him to reach for Ryker's chains, Duke leaves the front door unlocked.

The basement door, too.

I let myself in quickly. Because I'm me, I do lock the door, and because I don't want anyone distracting us, I drag a chair in front of it, too. A determined shifter could still get inside, but at least I made it a little harder for them.

A howl erupts from below my feet. I can't tell if Duke knows I'm the one moving back and forth over his head or not, but the pain in the howl is enough for me to give up on barricading the door further. That's the keening cry of a wolf in need, and mine is here to answer the call.

Hurrying for the basement door, I take a deep breath on the first stair, then step lightly down the entire flight.

"Oh, Duke..."

If I had any reservations about my selfish plan, they're shot to hell when I see big, strong Duke Conlon crumpled on the floor.

No shirt. No shoes. His jeans are torn in a couple of places from where his body started a partial shift before the silver in the chains affected him, and his head is hanging on his neck. He's breathing hard, and when his head jerks up, as though he's just caught my scent, he looks at me like he can hardly believe what he's seeing.

"Now I know I'm hallucinating," he mumbles. "Damn moon fever."

I hurry over to him. His brow is slick with sweat. So is his muscular chest. Padding wraps around his wrists, keeping the silver cuffs from burning his skin, while the length of chain is snaked around him.

Cinder block dust is in a pile beneath the points where the chains are screwed into the wall. They've held tight, though not for a lack of trying.

When the worst of the fever hits him, he must put everything he has into breaking free of the chain and going to his mate.

Dropping to my knees, I lay the back of my hand against his forehead. Burning up, just like I thought.

Because I'm not his mate, I expected him to jerk away from my touch. He doesn't. He leans in, gasping as if he's drowning in the ocean and he's just sighted land.

Just sighted his salvation.

"Trish..." he whispers.

"That's right. It's me. No hallucination, either."

"Why? It's not safe... you shouldn't be here."

I ruffle his sweat-soaked hair. "There's nowhere safer for me in all of the world than right beside you, Duke."

"No. You don't know... not tonight. Not the Luna..." His eyes go from gold to hazel, then back to gold again. "I can't fight her. I'd fight anything for you, baby, but not the Luna."

My heart skips a beat when he calls me 'baby'. He's never done that before. I've been Trish, and I've been Patricia, but... I want to be Duke's 'baby'.

That seals it. I don't know what tomorrow will bring. Tonight, though, I'm going to be his 'baby'.

"You don't have to fight anything," I tell him. "Not tonight. But... you've got moon fever, don't you?"

"It's so hot," he murmurs. "Why is it so hot?"

He isn't wrong. I was burning up myself already, but once I

got my first eye full of a near-naked Duke? I'm about to combust.

"It is hot," I agree. "I'm hot, too. You... you wouldn't mind if I took my dress off, would you?"

His eyes flash. "Don't tease the beast, baby. Please... you don't know what you're doing."

I know exactly what I'm doing. "It's the moon fever," I explain. "I'm hurting, Duke. I'm burning up. You said you'd take care of me—"

He snaps his teeth. They're not fangs. The silver keeps his wolf contained, so they're not fangs. That doesn't change the meaning of the gesture. "I will *always* take care of you."

"You asked me why I'm here. It's because I know you will. And, right now, what I need is something only you can give me."

"Oh?" He blinks rapidly, as if trying to focus. As if trying to understand that I'm really here. "What's that?"

I move into him. Then, before I can think better of what I'm about to do, I grab the erection straining against his worn jeans. "This."

He could've told me to back off. He could've shoved me away. He could've even hoisted his hips, pressing his hard-on against my palm.

He doesn't do any of that.

Instead, he crosses his arms behind me. Duke's not quite touching me—he's holding his arms out so that the chains can't reach me—but I'm all but trapped in his arms.

"I've got you," he rumbles.

"No," I say, reaching down to unbutton his jeans. "I've got you."

Duke goes immovable still the second it registers what exactly I've done. I maneuvered myself within his arms, and now

I've got one button done. Two buttons done. With a quick tug, his zipper is down and his cock...

Oh, Luna.

He's a big male. I already knew that. Of course his dick would be proportional to his height and his bulk. However, when I see the monstrous crown winking up at me, followed by the length that springs out now that his jeans aren't confining him... yeah. Only my unswerving resolve and absolute belief that this male will never hurt me

"Whoa." That's all I can say. Except for, maybe, "Luna, Duke. This is going to feel amazing inside of me. I mean, if you're willing."

A rumble rises up from his chest. "Trish Danvers is offering to let me stick my cock inside of her. I'd have to be a fucking idiot to refuse." His laugh is low and has my stomach clenching.

Or maybe that's my empty pussy.

"Just further prove this is a fever-filled dream. No way this is real life."

I run my finger around the head of his cock. When he sucks in a breath, I smile up at him. "Tell me. That feel real?"

"That feels like I'm about to come in my jeans."

"Uh uh." I waggle my finger at him. He groans at the loss. "No coming until I've got you where I want you. Deal?"

"I should be the bigger male—" he begins.

"Believe me. You are."

His eyes glimmer. "I should tell you to go. Even if you're just a dream, I shouldn't take advantage of you—"

I jab him in the chest. "I think I'm the one taking advantage of you."

"You're not. Because I want this. I want *you*. So I'm not going to tell you to go again. You're here, you're hot, and I've never felt anything better on my cock than your dainty hand. You need me to take care of you. I'll do that and more. You got a deal."

I chuckle, pleased that this seduction went a whole lot easier than I expected. "You could've just said 'yes'. But I guess I can accept that, too."

In answer, he snaps his teeth again.

"One thing, though. Don't bite me." I don't know why I say that. It's not like he can—not with his fangs, at least. Then again, maybe I *do* know. Every young she-wolf is warned never to let their partner mark them on the full moon unless they want a mate bond. That's how the Luna Ceremony is performed, after all. And while I'm willing to take Duke away from his intended for just one night, I refuse to steal another female's happily-ever-after.

"If that's what you want, I vow to the Luna I won't. I won't hurt you at all, baby. If this is what you want, I'll make you feel good."

In answer, I glance at his arm. "Drop them."

He does.

Climbing out of his embrace, I quickly reach for the hem of my dress, discarding it in one frantic motion. I toss it away, knowing I'll need it to cover me up in the morning, but for now...

"Get on your knees, Duke." As soon as he does, I point at the ground. "Sit back on your heels."

My need cranks up to eleven when I see how submissive this normally dominant male is.

Whether he realizes it or not, I've just gotten him in the perfect position for me to mount him. I figure, when this is all said and done, he can justify saying 'yes' to mating me because I did the actual work. Especially since he's chained to the wall, there isn't much of a choice unless I want to risk getting burned. Even if I did, no way will Duke allow it.

No. The only way to get this started is for me to climb up on him.

Just in case, I check with him as soon as it's obvious what my intentions are. Looping one arm around his neck, I straddle his thighs, spreading my legs so that his bobbing cock is prodding my inner thigh.

"Is this alright?" I ask. "Do you mind if we do it like this?"

"You can do whatever you want to me. As far as I'm concerned, I'm still hallucinating. This can't be real."

It is, Duke. It is.

I grip his cock so that I can aim. It's a little unnerving when I can't close my fist around his girth, and if it wasn't for the moon fever spurring me to do this, I think I would've wimped out entirely.

The second I work his head inside of my pussy, I almost do.

His eyes, a glazed-over gold, narrow on me when I stiffen. "Trish, baby... you don't have to do this. If the moon fever's got its claws in you, I can make you feel good without mating. I can lick you and touch you until you're ready to take this step."

I'm ready now. I have to be. This is my only chance.

I push, and the head goes in. So does the first inch or two of his cock.

"No. I want this. It's just... oh." I knew there would be a little discomfort, a little resistance, but the pressure... it's a lot. My body is primed to mate, both me and my wolf willing. That doesn't change the reality that Duke is huge and I'm not. It'll fit... I just need a second. "I'm okay." Leaning forward a bit, I don't feel as stuffed as before. I wiggle, and the slight panic ebbs as I sink further down on him. "It's not as easy as I thought, but I'm okay."

He brushes my hair out of my face. Duke's watching me closely now, and there must be something he notices in the grimace I'm trying to hide that has his whole body going taut.

"Trish, baby... is this your first time?"

I don't answer him. I'm afraid if I tell him that it is, he'll stop me. Of course, if he changes his mind, I would climb off of him —but I've come this far. My wolf is telling me that is right. This moment with Duke, with the Luna out and the moon fever raging through me... it's *right.*

I just need him to agree with me.

In my feverish brain, I decide that, if I can get seated, then start the actual mating, I'll distract Duke from his question. Why I thought so, when Duke's proven to be immovably stubborn in his own way, I have no idea, but that's my plan.

I take another inch of his impressive cock inside of me before he shakes out the length of chain, getting it as far away as possible from me before he lays his hands on my hips. He doesn't squeeze, but his gentle grip is enough to keep me exactly where I am. Half-pinned on his length with no relief in sight, he tilts his head back so that he's staring at my eyes instead of my bare breasts.

"Trish... am I the first male you've ever mated?"

It's a ragged whisper, his wolf finding his way out in his tone. There's possessiveness there, undeniable need, too, and something I can't quite put my claws on.

Whatever it is, it's obvious that he won't let either of us move a centimeter until I answer his question.

My hands are still on his shoulders. Taking care not to prick him with the claws I can't retract, I knead the tense muscles. "Does it matter?"

Duke shudders. "It shouldn't. Luna knows it shouldn't. But I'd be a fucking liar if I said that it doesn't make me feel some kind of way that you chose me for your first. I'll take you any way I can have you, Trish, but I've gotta know. If it's your first time, I gotta do right by you. I gotta be careful."

That's exactly what I don't want.

# CHAPTER 7
# SCARRED

I don't know what comes over me. It's like I have some desire to show Duke that, sure, he might've seen me at my lowest, but I'm made of stronger stuff than that. That doesn't excuse the fact that, my wolf in control, I lash out with my hand.

My claws rip down his throat, leaving four thin bloody tracks in its wake.

"You slashed me," he says in awe.

I swallow the apology that rises up. If he looked angry, I might've, but he looks... amazed? "Hey. It got your attention, didn't it?"

"It most certainly did."

His blood is trickling down his throat. I have this urge to lick it up, so I do.

"Oh, Luna." I don't know what I did, but his grip on my waist loosens. Wiggling just enough, I sink a little further down. He groans. "Trish, you're fucking killing me."

"I'm not," I promise. "I'm just fucking you. Listen... I... I don't want careful. I know you're gentle, but I don't want that tonight, either. I just want you. Is that okay?"

"You want me? Then take me."

He jerks up. A sharp pain, almost like a pinch has me gasping, but even before he's checking to make sure I'm okay, it's fading away into something blissful. Duke's seated himself entirely inside of me, and I've never felt more whole in my life.

"Yes," I breathe out. "Yes... this is exactly what I wanted."

"How is it? Are you okay?" he asks again. "Did I hurt you?"

"No. But if you don't do that again, I'm going to hurt you some more."

He chuckles. It's a strained sound, yet somehow relieved. "Mark me all you want. I won't bite you... I swore I wouldn't... but my body. It's yours, Trish. Use it however you want."

That's all I needed to hear.

I move slowly at first, then pick up the pace when the pressure becomes a consuming pleasure. He reaches parts inside of me that I didn't think could be touched, all without doing a damn thing but perching on the floor, hands behind him as I hold on tight and ride.

After a minute or so, I start to whimper. I need something else. I... I don't know *what* exactly, just that I'm racing toward a pinnacle that won't be reached without a little help. I've come before. In the quiet of my bedroom, rubbing myself to thoughts of what it would be like with a strong male... I've come. Always a tiny pop of pleasure, then a relaxation that almost has me humming before I fell asleep.

This is so much more. The friction of my pussy slamming down on him is a feeling I've never known before, my clit bumping with every pass. I reach between us, rubbing it frantically. That helps, but not enough.

And that's when Duke lifts his hand—claws sheathed—and grabs my boob. He tugs the nipple, flicking it with his blunt fingertip, always angling his hand so that the chains are away from us. My whimpers become pants, and my pants become a shout of triumph when he takes my nipple between his teeth, laving it with his tongue, just as I begin to climax.

He waits until I'm finally coming down from it before he trades sucking on my tit for nuzzling it, a hoarse shout vibrating against my clammy chest as he follows after me with his own orgasm.

I grab his head, clinging to him, as he comes inside of me. I'm not sure if I'm suffocating him, keeping his face pressed against my books, but he doesn't push away. In fact, he shoves himself closer, slamming into me so that we're completely one.

Finally, he finishes, and he starts to let his head fall back on his shoulder. Since I don't want him to pass out on me now, I tug his hair, then allow him to breathe again.

"Is that it?" It feels like I've taken the tiniest edge off of my lust, but Duke just came inside of me. That doesn't mean anything since we're bonded mates—I've only heard of one incomplete mating that led to a pup, and she ended up being the second female alpha in our history so I'm not worried about it happening to me—except he finished. "Are we done?"

Duke's husky chuckle sends a shiver down my spine. With a quick twist of his hips, I realize something. He's still hard. I feel fuller than before, almost as if something is keeping us connected.

"I never thought I'd have you like this," he rumbles, his hips jerking upward, ripping a moan from my throat at just how fucking *amazing* that felt. "Now that I do, I'm not going to let you get away that easily. Why? Do you want to go?"

There's something in his throaty tone. I know without a doubt that, if I told him I did, he'd found a way to separate us, then take care of his erection on his own, chains and all. I come first. He made sure I was with him all the way even though *I* seduced *him*. Even after he spent inside of me and obviously wants to again, that hasn't changed.

Ghosting my fingers over the first marks I left on his throat, I wrap my other arm around the back of his neck, tugging his mouth up to mine.

I kiss Duke with all of the pent-up need and passion I've been denying for months now, then nip his bottom lip with my fangs as soon as I'm forced to pull away. I've gone light-headed from lack of breath, but the heavy-lidded gaze he gives me, blood beading on the lushest part of his lip, has me eager to see what else my male can teach me.

"I want you to fuck me, Duke," I tell him boldly. Because that's what this is. It's mating, yes, and casual sex between two friends. But nothing about his Luna-given body is all that casual, and the rawness of the act is nothing less than fucking. "Until I don't know who I am or what I've done, I want you to take care of me like you said you always would."

"Like I always will," he vows darkly.

I gasp at how fierce he sounds, giving him the perfect opportunity to kiss me now.

I taste his blood and nearly come again at how sweet it is against my tongue. Lapping at his lip, I start to grind my pussy against his groin.

He rips his lips away from mine, eyes a blazing gold as he drops his palms to the concrete, lifting me off the ground with nothing more than the strength of his pelvis as he thrusts impossibly deeper inside of me.

"Ah, Trish, baby. You said you wanted me to take care of you. To fuck you. Stick your claws in me and hold on tight, because, tonight, your male is going to do all that and more."

*Your male…*

I know he doesn't mean it. He can't. He's meant for someone else. Then again, maybe he's right. Tonight he is my male, isn't he?

And when he uses his strength to shift our positions, spreading me out on the cool basement floor while pounding away inside of me, I don't know what's fucking hotter about this side of Duke I've discovered.

The way he finally treats me like a she-wolf instead of a pack princess that needs to be coddled—or the way the silver chains rattle as he fucks me again.

---

HOURS LATER, WHEN THE MOON FINALLY BEGINS TO SET, trading places with the sun in the sky, I climb off of Duke for the last time. He's impressively strong, but the silver will drain even the most powerful supe. His cock was willing, though the rest of him was fading, so that latest round ended with me the way we began: with me perched on his thick thighs, sinking down on his cock over and over again while he buried his face between my breasts.

I still have some energy. Just enough to separate our slick bodies and flop down near him, but it's gotta be more than Duke has.

And I believe that until I see his cock is still semi-hard, and his eyes are glazed with both exhaustion and lust as he watches every single move I make.

"Don't tell me you're leaving so soon?"

His voice is a rasp. Probably from all of the times he shouted as he came, or the ragged ways he called my name as I learned every inch of his sculpted body. I left my mark on his shoulders and his throat, and some on his thighs from when I reversed my position and rode him wildly while he kneaded away at my breasts. Tapping into my wolf since the silver kept Duke from using his, I shredded his jeans off of him and kind of, sort of clawed him up, too.

He didn't mind. In fact, he moaned any time his blood perfumed his air. He cut off my first apology with a kiss so deep, I realized that he... he *really* didn't mind. Duke actually started to piston his hips, reaching up to meet me on every bounce even though the concrete floor of the basement had to have chafed his poor ass raw.

He'd be completely healed by morning. The twinges in my pussy, battered ever so deliciously by his cock, would be a memory I treasured and nothing more. That's the best thing about being a shifter. No matter how wild we get, there's no injury during a mating we can't heal.

The aches are already fading as the moon loses some of her hold on me. It won't be morning for a few hours more, and there might be time for another mating after we rest for a while.

So, no. I'm not going anywhere.

He grins when I tell him so, leaning forward to nuzzle my nearest boob. I scoot closer so that I'm within his reach, and to the sounds of his content rumbling, I fall asleep.

I don't know how long he stays away while I slumber, curled at his side. His body warmth made it so that I didn't miss the dress I wore when I came to see him. In fact, sticky with sweat and overheated myself, I could've used a fan down here.

Figuring that's the last lingering effects of moon fever, I decide to see if I can wake Duke up. My internal clock says it's early, but not so early that I can't take the chance to mate him one more time before I leave and have to put the most memorable night behind me.

He has an intended. A mate that he hasn't claimed yet. Just because he was available for me to fuck his brains out this full moon doesn't mean that he will be next month.

I have to take him while I can.

Rising up on my knees, I think about grabbing his cock to wake him up. The monster between his legs is already hard again so I'm pretty sure he'll welcome the interruption to his well-earned rest. Maybe if he *was* my mate, I would... but even I think that's probably too familiar for what we are.

So, instead, I reach out my finger, ready to nudge his shoulder.

I never make it.

Before I do, I reluctantly pull my gaze from his dick, glancing up at his slumbering face. That's when I see it. For a heartbeat, one terrible moment in time, I wait for it to be a mistake. To be my imagination.

It isn't.

Last night, when I begged him to take care of me, his throat was a thick column of unbroken skin.

That was last night.

This morning? It's not unbroken any longer.

It's *scarred.*

And I'm the one who gave him the marks he now has permanently etched on the side of his neck.

# CHAPTER 8
# RIVER RUN

I've never been so Luna-damned grateful that Duke can sleep like the dead before now. He was so careful not to let the silver chains brush me, even after we collapsed in a heap of sweaty, sated limbs together, he angled his gorgeous body away so that I didn't accidentally get burned.

That makes it easy for me to untangle myself from him. And I have to. Someone will be coming by to let Duke out of the chains soon, whether it's Bobby or Grant or any of the other pack council members, and I have to be long gone before they do.

I'm glad I came to him. I'm glad that Duke and I mated. We went into the act knowing that it was just sex. Just a way to work out the need that was riding us both. If he said 'yes' to me, it didn't matter that his erection was meant for anyone else. In that moment, it was mine.

Duke was mine.

But I wasn't supposed to *mark* him.

I… can't believe I did that.

Standing over him, I stare at the thin white lines that travel the length of his throat, horror building. No denying that the bloody marks from last night have faded to a stark scar. I don't understand. They should be gone. Like, I know that I was out of my head with lust when I clawed him, but *they should be gone*. There's no good reason why the cuts have turned into a set of scars instead of healing. Enough time has passed that, with his regenerative properties, Duke should have healed completely while we curled up against each other, sleeping off the rest of the fever.

Should be gone.

Should have healed.

*Isn't*.

Am I seeing things? I know I'm not, but I have to double-check anyway. It just doesn't make any sense. Shifters don't scar. Unless we use a silver compound to create a shifter tattoo, or we purposely keep the mark, it'll disappear shortly after we've been injured. For those lines to linger on his thick throat, Duke must have wanted them to stay.

Why? I… I have no idea. I thought I made it very clear last night that this was just another way for him to take care of me. I needed him, and once he understood how desperate I was, he was more than willing to give me what I needed. And, sure, I told him he could do whatever he wanted to me as long as he didn't mark me, I made no promises.

But that was because I was sure that he'd erase any marks I gave him. He'd have to. If he had a mate out there that he was drawn to but, for some reason, couldn't have, then he wouldn't want to wear evidence of our mating on his skin… right?

That's what I thought. That's what I expected.

So why are they still there? Because they are. They totally are. Four thin lines run jagged down the side of his neck. Duke is a big guy. A strong male. Anyone who sees those scars will know exactly how he got them. It wasn't a challenge that left him marked, it was a female.

It was me.

Worse, I marked a male with an *intended* mate.

That's the reality come crashing down on me as I crawl away from him. Last night, I was so desperate, I didn't care that the chains were evidence that he was meant for someone else. I might have decided that Duke was the perfect male to mate the first time, but that just meant we were two adults sharing one night together. He was suffering from the moon fever as much as I was, so it couldn't be helped. He wasn't a bonded male, and until I saw those chains, I didn't think he had a mate of his own in mind.

He agreed, I tell myself. This isn't Gem and Ryker all over again. He could've said no... but would I have pushed it if he did? I want to believe that I wouldn't have, but when you take a look at my track record... I'm not so sure I would have.

It doesn't matter that I was responding to the Luna's pull on me. Every shifter knows that moon fever is real. For unmated shifters, it's a nuisance more than anything. I've known packmates who get through it by exploring each others' bodies, and those like me who just grin and bear it. It's no picnic, I promise you, but it was manageable.

Last night was... not. I always heard that the needs get harder and harder to resist as soon as there's some kind of bond between two shifters. Whether it was fated or chosen, it didn't matter. He had a bond, I propositioned him anyway, and when he said 'yes', what did I do? I clawed him—

—but he kept them.

He called himself my male.

It was only supposed to be for one night… I wasn't supposed to steal someone else's forever!

Last night, I didn't really care about tomorrow—but now it's tomorrow, and that was precisely the attitude that got me banished from Accalia last summer. I committed the most cardinal sin among our kind: I tried to worm my way between a pair of fated mates. Ryker rejected Gem because of me, and he spent the next twelve full moons in a pair of chains because of me.

I found Duke in chains, suffering the madness that goes along with the moon fever. I knew what that meant. From the moment I saw him like that, it was obvious that he was restraining himself to keep from going after his female.

And what did I do? I went after *him*.

He thought I was a hallucination. He knew I was Trish, but he didn't think I was real.

Well, when he wakes up and discovers that I'm gone, maybe he'll think it really was a dream.

Too bad the scars on his neck will tell a totally different story…

---

River Run is the nearest shifter territory to Accalia.

I always knew that. Growing up, they weren't our allies per se, but we could rely on them in a pinch. That's why, when I got banished from Accalia, the obvious thing to do was hope Kendall Rivers—the Alpha of River Run—would take me in.

I'm not made to be a lone wolf. I'm a pack shifter through

and through, and if I couldn't stay on the mountains, I at least wanted to be around my own kind.

Kendall was willing. I'll give him that much. But the price to gain entrance to his pack was one I couldn't pay, even after being banished. I had to forsake my family, forsake my friends, and give up any chance of ever returning home. If I didn't, if I betrayed River Run after pledging my loyalty to Kendall, he told me he would take it as a challenge and hunt me down.

I respected him being upfront with my choice. Knowing I could never give up hope on returning home, I had to decline, and I was scavenging on the land between his territory and Ryker's when Gem's vamp friend, Aleksander, found me and told me what to do and say to earn my ticket back to the Mountainside Pack.

Did I know he was using me? Of course. After Shane, I was beginning to be a pro at recognizing the signs when a male was manipulating me. He wanted Gem, he thought I still wanted Ryker, and he thought putting me back on the mountains would get us both what we wanted.

He was wrong. I gave up on Ryker even before I was banished, and all I wanted to do was rejoin my pack and make amends for my behavior. And I did—until Barrow slipped under my guard and tricked me...

When I left Ryker's old cabin earlier this morning, I didn't go home. Duke would know to look for me there, and I needed some time to figure out how I was going to deal with my reckless behavior. There was no taking back what I did. I marked him under the full moon, and I only hoped the fact that he didn't mark me means that I can salvage our friendship.

His mate might never forgive me for leaving those scars on his throat. I still can't understand why he wouldn't heal him, though I guess the moon does strange things to us all. Before yesterday morning, I didn't think I'd jump a chained-up Duke Conlon, either, so here we are.

On my run out, I realized that there probably wasn't anywhere in Accalia I could hide from him. He'd find me, if only to apologize, and that... I didn't like the idea of that, either.

So I kept on running.

I stayed in my skin for no other reason than my wolf was pissed at me. She didn't want to come out and aid in my escape, not when she thought I should've stayed behind with Duke. I can still run pretty quickly in bare feet, so I do, and before I know it, I'm edging up to the south side of River Run territory.

Because he's as anal and protective of an Alpha as Ryker, I'm not surprised to see Kendall pacing the lengths of the border as I approach.

I could avoid him. Technically, I haven't breached his territory yet. I was just heading for a place that I knew well enough that allowed me to put some distance between me and my mistakes. No surprise, then, that I took the same path I did right after I was banished.

I could avoid him. I don't.

I jog over to where he's standing, making sure to keep a good amount of distance between us as I wave over at the Alpha.

"Hey, Trish. Long time, no see."

"You, too, Kendall. Looking good."

"Always." That's an Alpha for you. I might be vain, but there's no shifter vainer than an alpha wolf. "What are you doing around here?"

If it was anyone else, I might have gotten out of having to answer that. I'm too ashamed to admit the truth, but this is Kendall Rivers. He's an Alpha whose only loyalty is to his people. And while I tried to petition to join his pack last year when I was banished, he knew all along that *my* loyalty was to Mountainside. If he thinks I present any threat to his people, he's not going to let me walk away without telling him why I'm here.

He sniffs. Before I can say a word, he nods. "Look at that. I guess congratulations are in order."

"Congratulations?"

Kendall nods. "On your new mate. You locked the big guy down. He used to be part of the traders, but he's Ryker's now. What's his name?" He snaps his finger. "Jack Conlon."

A lump lodges in my throat. I'm not sure if it's hearing Duke's old name—or just my reaction when Kendall's meaning finally hits home. I swallow roughly, then tell him, "He goes by Duke now. And he's not my mate."

Even if I wished he was.

With a snort, Kendall says, "Does he know that? His scent is all over. You don't have an alpha's nose, Trish. If you did, you'd know he left a musk that tells all other males to back the fuck off. You're taken."

What?

I shake my head. "No. It's not like that. It was the full moon. That's all."

He gives me a look of such disbelief, I begin to wonder if he's right. I know I smell like Duke and sex. But a warning? I don't get it.

He doesn't explain any further.

Instead, he says, "So why the run by? You thinking about petitioning to join River Run again? Because, I told you last time, I demand loyalty. You'd have to give up on Mountainside."

I could never do that.

With a half-grin of my own, I shake my head. "Thanks, but that's okay.

"That's fine." He jerks his chin. "So long as you stay on your side of the territorial line."

I make sure I do the rest of the time I spend away from Accalia. When the sun starts to set, the moon rising high again, I realize that I've probably been away too long. Following her glow as a beacon home, I chase the moon until I've slunk back onto Mountainside land.

For once, things go my way. No one stops me as I purposely make my way toward my cabin, ignoring my wolf's urging that I search out Duke. I'm in complete control tonight. No blaming moon fever when the Luna's pull on us both is far weaker tonight than yesterday. Tracking him down would be a mistake, and I tell my stubborn wolf that when she starts pacing around inside of me.

Or maybe she's only riled up because she can scent Duke all around my personal territory.

It's fresh. Even if I wanted to pretend that it was from any other night, I can't. Especially when I notice there's a foil-covered plate with a white square resting on top of it on my front porch.

He would've guessed I'd come in this way. He's gone—his scent at least an hour older—but he was here.

And he left me a note.

Crouching down, I pick it up. It's folded in four. My hands are trembling as I unfold it.

One line in a heavy block print stares up at me from the center:

**We need to talk.**

Folding the note up again, I crouch down and slip it under the plate.

I leave them both there. Before, I could fool myself and believe that he only left me food because he was treating me like a pup.

That all changed with the scars.

I know better now. Some way, somehow, a bond formed between us, one I neglected to see until it was too late. No denying that. Today, while I curled up beneath an oak, I finally listened to what my wolf was telling me. There's a shadow of a jagged bond inside of me, barely there but nowhere whole... and I know exactly who is on the other side. It's a bond, but it's twisted, broken just like me, and it's all my fault. I didn't mean to, but I marked him beneath the Luna. I took him from the female he was meant for, and I can only imagine how confused he must be right now. Especially since he would've woken up to me gone like that.

*We need to talk...*

He's right. But I can't.

Not now.

I just... I can't.

Locking the cabin door, I lean up against it with my back, staring up at my ceiling as I try to make sense of everything that happened since last night.

Too bad I can't do that, either.

---

THREE DAYS PASS AND I REFUSE TO ANSWER THE DOOR.

The first night, I caught a whiff of pine and I panicked. I'm not proud of it, but I bolted from my living room couch to my bedroom and slammed the door shut, putting some space between me and the front porch. Duke would know I was still inside my cabin, but I hoped he got the hint and backed off.

Based on the nightmares that haunted me each one of those nights, he did.

I can't sleep. I'm barely eating. My wolf is still angry at me, and I don't know what I'm supposed to do.

Then, to top it all off, four days after I slipped out of Duke's arms and left him on his own, Gemma Swann shows up at my cabin.

These days, she doesn't look like the pretty, porcelain doll she was when she first arrived in Accalia. Her blonde curls are usually slicked back in a long ponytail, her sundresses traded for a tank that shows off her muscular arms, and a pair of black jeans that match her alpha aura. Her honey-gold eyes are clever and shrewd, and the gleam brighter than the golden fang she wears on a chain nestled between her boobs when she glares over at me from her place on my front porch.

"Alpha?" I blink over at her. When I caught the dominant aura approaching my door, it never occurred to me to keep it closed. In the back of my mind, though, I guess I thought it would be Ryker out there because I'm shocked to discover the blonde alpha female standing on my porch. "What are you... I mean, can I help you?"

"Actually," Gem says, "I'm here to help you. Can I come in?"

She doesn't have to ask. She's the Alpha female. While I'm at the bottom of the pack's hierarchy with the rest of the deltas, she's at the tippy-top with Ryker. Even with her containing her dominant aura, I could never refuse.

"Of course. What's this about?"

"About you being Duke's fated mate."

# CHAPTER 9
# FOREVER

Gem takes advantage of my stunned silence to march right inside, kicking the door closed behind her as she says, "Figure you want privacy for this chat."

She isn't wrong.

It takes a second before I'm able to come out of it. "Duke's fated mate?" I echo. "I'm not his fated mate."

"Sure you are. Just because you don't feel the same way and you rejected the mate bond, that doesn't mean it didn't exist."

I don't... I don't understand. "I didn't reject him. I..." This is your female Alpha, Trish. She won't think any less of you, and to be honest, she probably already has an idea—if she doesn't already know. "I fucked him. How do you reject a mate after you fuck him?"

"Easy. By making it a point to tell him not to mark you, then avoiding him while you stew away in your cabin, bringing down the rest of the pack."

Ouch. I'm not supposed to admit that I preferred Gem when

she was a sweet and innocent-acting omega, but I was able to walk all over her back then. Not only is her dominance off the charts, but she's not holding back on me now.

What makes it worse is that... everything she just said is true. I did tell him not to bite me. I did mark him, though I never, ever expected he would take my claw marks and turn them into scars on his body on purpose. When I went to him on the night of the full moon, I'd hoped that maybe he might choose me. Even if only for that one time, I needed someone to choose *me*. I was willing to let him go to his intended when I was done—

—but, if what Gem is saying is true, *I*'m supposed to be his intended.

"I wasn't avoiding him," I lie. "I just... I had to figure out some stuff."

Gem snorts. "For future reference, babe? It's true that an alpha can sniff out a fibber. And you are a big honking liar. The only reason I came all the way down here to talk some sense is to you because no one else dared to bother precious Trish Danvers while she was moping. Not me. It's time everyone stopped protecting you."

"No one's protecting me!"

"And that's two. You want to lie to me again? Just because my mate let you back in the pack, it doesn't mean I forget what you put me through. I can forgive, Trish, but forgetting isn't something I'm too good at. Ryker made me promise I wouldn't challenge you or anything because he knows how much you still get under my skin. I want to prove to my mate that I'm better than that. Like it or not, we're both Mountainside. You and me... we're packmates. Fucking sisters, alright? So stop lying, and start listening."

I am. I heard every word of what Gem said—and, again, she isn't wrong.

"I'm sorry," I begin. What else can I say? "I'm so sorry."

"Forget it. We still got time to hash out our issues later. But that... that's me and you. I'm here about you and Duke."

It hurts to admit it, but... "There is no me and Duke."

"You're right about that. At least, if he goes through with this nonsense, there won't be."

I don't know what she means. "There never was to begin with."

"And who's fault is that? You were too busy mooning over *my* mate to notice when a big hunk of male arrived in Accalia and couldn't stop staring at you. You know why Duke asked Ryker's dad if he could stay? Because of you! He knew you were his mate, and when you didn't react to the bond the same way he did, he thought he already lost you to another male. And instead of leaving, that bonehead spent the next four years worshiping you from the distance—"

I can't stop myself from interrupting. "Me? He never said one word to me until he felt bad I got caught by *your* dad. Before that, I never noticed him. In fact, after you came along, he signed up to be your personal guard. He only started watching my back after."

To my surprise, Gem doesn't take my tone of voice as a challenge. She could, but she doesn't. In fact, she looks kind of impressed that I fired back. "He did. You can't blame Duke for that, though, any more than you can me changing his name. It's... it's an alpha thing. Just know that he didn't mean to pledge himself to me, and the moment he found out you were in danger, his feelings for you broke any hold I had on him. He loves you, Trish. So much that he set aside his own mate bond so that you'd be happy, no matter what. You rejected him four years ago when you barely noticed him, and you rejected him again this last Luna. And you're surprised he never told you that you were meant for him?"

"Meant for him? Really? Then where is he? He tried real hard to talk to me, right? But I haven't seen him in days!"

She raises her eyebrow. Scowling, fierce Gemma is gone. In a heartbeat, the suspiciously curious Alpha is in her place. "What? Are you telling me you don't know?"

If I did, I wouldn't have asked. I shake my head.

"Fucking males. I told him he could go talk to Elizabeth only *after* you agreed. Not to be all noble and go on his own."

Elizabeth. I know that name. She's the Luna-touched wolf who mated the head vampire in Muncie. The one who—

*breaks mate bonds.*

"Wait. I haven't sensed Duke in a while... are you telling me that he went to see her?"

Duke. The male who Gem just told me is my fated mate, who I marked during the night of the full moon, and who I've avoided ever since.

He's not my fated mate. He can't be. I would've known, right? Even if I didn't, he would've told me. For Gem to know everything she did—most of which happened before she even came to live with us—someone told her.

Why would he tell the female Alpha and not *me*?

That doesn't matter. None of that matters. Not if he really did what Gem said.

She nods. "He's there right now."

I dash for the door.

Smart Alpha. Fast, too. Gem beats me to it.

Blocking it with her body, she says, "You can't go."

"Move, Gem. I don't know what's going to happen between Duke and me, but I can't let him do this. If we have a bond, I don't want him to throw it away without me getting a chance to explore what it means."

"He said you weren't happy. He thought, if he did this, you would be."

My laugh is hollow as I purposely meet her stare. "You should know better. I'm not the type of she-wolf who will ever be happy. Now move."

She puts her alpha voice into it. Her eyes glisten, a deeper shade of gold than I've ever seen hers turn. "You can't go, Patricia."

If her dominance hadn't made me give up my idiotic challenge, her use of my full name would have.

She gentles her tone. "We have an agreement. Mountainside shifters can't just walk into Muncie."

I did. After Aleksander Filan found me outside of Kendall's territory and brought me to meet the former head vamp so that I could get permission to enter Muncie and confront Gem... I walked around the Fang City without even a fang to shield me.

As though she's remembering that day last August when she found me pleading my case to Ryker, she shakes her head.

"Roman is gone," Gem reminds me. "Any pass he gave you died with him."

Aleksander is in charge now. The pretty vampire with the dreamy accent. "Ask your friend to let me in."

"I already called in the favor to get Duke in to see Elizabeth. I can't burn another. I'm sorry, Trish. He said he would run this by you first. Elizabeth only needs one mate to want to sacrifice the bond, but I said he needed your permission, too."

Would I have given it? Selfish Trish Danvers?

No way in hell.

I already knew I wanted him. Am I in love with Duke? I... I think so. I never really allowed myself to think about that.

Do I want him to take away my chance to find out if this bond between us is real?

Nope.

"Gem—"

"You can't go," she says one more time, "but you can wait for his return. And you'll know, one way or another, if you still have a shot at your forever."

I guess that's as much as I deserve.

---

There have been too many incidents in the stretch of "no man's land" between Muncie and Accalia lately for me to feel comfortable waiting for Duke there. Instead, I find a spot about a hundred yards into the woods on shifter land, park my ass on a boulder, and wait for some sign that Duke is heading home.

It seems like hours, but it's probably only about one before his pine scent reaches me. All at once, the thoughts and questions and declarations I had ready to throw at him once I saw him again fly out of my head. Instead, when Duke comes within my line of vision, I do the most reckless thing ever.

I throw *myself* at him.

Good reflexes. My male—if he's still mine—has good reflexes. A split second before I reach him, he throws open his arms, welcoming me into his embrace with a tight squeeze as I try my very best to wrap myself around him like a fucking pretzel.

"I marked you." I sound as spoiled and as petulant as a four-year-old child who used marker to claim a toy as theirs. I don't care. "You're mine."

He folds me into his arms. "Oh, Trish. I always was."

"And it's not because of a bond," I rattle on. "One we had, one we don't, one we could've... When Gem told me before I never felt it... she was right. I didn't, but that's not your fault. It's mine."

His hand goes to my hair, stroking it reverentially. He probably has no idea what I'm talking about, what I'm doing here, why I've attached myself to him. I mean, I can sense his confusion—

*I can sense his confusion.*

It's not very strong, but it's there.

A bond.

Tears spring to my eyes. Before I know it, I'm a blubbering mess, smearing tears and—oh, Luna—snot on his shirt. All I get out is, "Don't leave me, I can be better," before dissolving into sobs.

I didn't cry the entire time I was in the Wolf District. Not one tear during banishment. But the relief I feel when I sense Duke on the other side of our twisted bond... forget being four. I'm a damn newborn.

"Shh... Trish, baby. It's okay."

I shake my head.

He continues to coo. "You didn't do anything wrong—"

Yes. I did. "I ignored the magnificent male standing in front of me for *four* years. I couldn't make it through one Luna once I realized how strong my feelings are for you."

Duke tightens his hold for a moment, taking in a sharp breath. When he exhales, he holds me at arms-length so that he can look down at my face. "Four years of full moons without you were worth it for the one we shared. But while I wanted you desperately, the moon fever didn't hit me until the last one. I wasn't sure how I would survive it and then... there you were, like an angel."

I give him a watery smile, tears still leaking down the corner of my eyes. I'm not sobbing anymore, but the relief is still overwhelming. "You said you were hallucinating."

"I thought I was. How else could a bumbling idiot like me lands the most gorgeous female in all of Accalia? It had to be a dream. But if it was, then I'm dreaming again."

"Why? Because I'm holding you tightly? That's because I'm not letting you go. I said don't leave me. It's more than that. Stay with me, Duke. I need you to stay with me. And I need you to understand that I mean it. I was the idiot before. Not anymore."

Because he doesn't stay with me, I'm going with him. He can try to shake me off. I was willing to take on the female Alpha to fight my way to him. I would've lost terribly, for sure, but Gem has a bit of a merciful streak. If she didn't put down her father after she challenged him and won, she'd probably just kick my ass and let me limp my way after Duke.

And I would. Bond or no bond, fate or not, this male is mine. If the Luna thinks so, that's just—pardon the expression—icing on the cupcake.

"I'm not going anywhere, baby." Ducking his chin, he presses a fierce kiss to my lips. "But that's not what I meant. I must be dreaming because I thought I heard you say you have feelings for me. Since they set off the fever and heat inside of you, they must be good ones."

Oh, Luna. Selfish Trish strikes again. Here I am, clinging to him like a barnacle, telling him he has to stay with me, listening to Duke tell me that he will, and I've let him think that I only want him around because of what happened on the full moon.

Yeah, right. Looking back, we both should've known I was a goner when I sleep-shifted next to him. Nothing like falling asleep in your pajamas, then waking up naked next to your male to say: I want you. Even if my wolf wasn't giving me a nudge that I stubbornly resisted for too long, the cupcakes should've sealed the deal.

"They're the best," I promise. "Because I'm in love with you, Duke Conlon. And I dare any female to come between us."

Duke, my gentle giant, my silent shadow, the male I can't believe I didn't notice for so long... he throws back his head and lets out a howl that has my wolf jumping to her paws, my pussy growing wickedly damp in preparation for him to mount us.

That's a claiming howl and we both know it.

But first—

Slipping my hand between us, I tap him in the middle of his broad chest. "Well? Aren't you supposed to say something to me?"

Reaching around me, he places his hands beneath my butt. Without any effort at all, he lifts me up, urging me to wrap my legs around his waist. If we were naked, we could start mating right here, but luckily our clothes protect our modesty.

Even in a shifter pack, some things just aren't done—except on the night of the full moon, of course.

He kisses me again, almost as if he can't help himself, then buries his head in the crook of my shoulder. If he bit me now, it wouldn't matter—I could keep it as a scar, but it wouldn't become my mate mark until he fucked me again under another Luna—and I find that I'm becoming even hotter at the idea that I'll wear his marks the same way he wears mine.

As that thought rushes through my head, I dart out my tongue. I run the length of it over the thin white lines traveling down his throat. I made these marks. They're mine, just like Duke is.

And if I had any doubt that he feels the same way, they're immediately quashed when his deep voice begins to rumble against my skin, sending shivers skittering down my spine.

"I love you, Trish. I always have. I love the female you are, how you're loyal and determined and no one can tell you anything. From the moment I first saw you, I knew that there would never be anyone else. But you... you were looking at the Alpha while I was staring at you. And that was fine with me. I just wanted you to be happy. I'm only happy when you are."

Gem said that he went to break the bond because he didn't think I was happy. I threw in her face that I never was.

But when I cling to him, holding him tight, I realize something.

Duke makes me happy. Baking cupcakes makes me happy. Teasing Bobby, having sewing lessons with Audrey, taking odds on how much longer before Ryker and Gem start popping out pups... that makes me happy.

Hooking my hand around his thick neck, I pull back enough to meet his gaze again. "Look at me." He does. Duke doesn't even blink. "I'm happy. Fucking deliriously happy. But if you think you'll find some way out of this bond we have between us... like, say, asking a Luna-touched female to snap it? You'll see just how quickly you can piss a she-wolf off. You know your scars? I did that when I liked you. You don't want to see what happens when I don't."

I meant it as a tease. I'm so Luna-damned relieved he didn't throw away our shot at forever before I knew about it, I try to make light of the whole situation.

I should know better. That's not the kind of male Duke is—and I love him even more when he reveals another facet of his personality when his gleaming gold eyes turn almost defiant.

"I couldn't go through with it," he confesses. "I wanted to, for your sake, because I loved you too much to hold onto a bond that was making you miserable. But… in the end? I wanted you even more than that."

As if I didn't already know that. The moment I sensed him lumbering up the mountain in his skin instead of his fur, I knew… I just *knew* that his human side had taken the lead on the discussion with Elizabeth. His wolf wanted me, but it would release a mate who didn't recognize that they belonged together.

But his human side? It wouldn't—and I'm glad that it didn't.

I grin over at him. "Look at that. I guess we're both selfish, huh?"

And doesn't that make Duke Conlon the perfect mate for me?

# EPILOGUE

## A MONTH LATER

My head's cocked to the side, hair cascading over my shoulder as I sit at my kitchen table, waiting. I've got a loose curl wrapped around the pointer finger of my right hand. With the left, I'm running my fingertips over the thin white scars that pepper my collarbone.

That's not the only place I have marks. There's a noticeable bite on the side of my throat, a couple of slivers that trail the rounded curve of my boob from where Duke used one of his fangs. At my urging, he marked one of my butt cheeks, and that's not counting all of the tiny scars I have from when he gets too excited and his claws come out during mating.

I'm a shifter. If I wanted to, I could heal each and every one of those injuries without leaving even the hint of a scar. But that's the thing. I don't want to. I spent my whole life being the empty-headed pretty girl with a bad attitude and a selfish streak.

For so long, I believed the only thing I had going for me was my looks. I used to think I was perfect.

Ha.

A human might look at the white marks that cover me and wonder if I'm some kind of walking pincushion. A supe would wonder why my intended—because we're not fully bonded just yet—felt the need to scratch me up like that. But a she-wolf... she would know that I kept my marks because I treasure the physical proof that I'm wanted.

That I'm *loved*.

The first time we mated, I marked Duke. I know now that that was my wolf finding a way to send us both a message. Even if I was stubbornly oblivious to my feelings for him, my wolf, at least, recognized who he was to us. She was laying claim to him the only way she could.

Every time after that, I implored him to take his turn. My big mate was hesitant at first... until he woke up next to me the next morning and saw that the bite on my throat was still there. It nearly broke my heart when I realized he expected me to have healed it after he finished. As if. This male is mine, and he has been since I scratched his neck. It was only fair that I showed all of Accalia that I was his, too.

As if the rest of the pack didn't know. Audrey admitted that Grant was running a small pool, taking bets on how long it would take before Duke got up the nerve to tell me that we were mates. Seems as if *everyone* knew except for me, but because of his standing as one of Ryker's top enforcers, they didn't want to interfere in case I rejected him.

I can't even say that they're wrong. Duke knew for four years that I was his, but he watched as I did everything I could to get Ryker to choose me as his mate. He believed—like I did—that I was in love with the Alpha. That's why I never recognized the promise of a mate bond with Duke. He purposely shielded me from it so that I could shoot my shot with Ryker. And when he thought that I would be better off without him, he tried to leave.

Good thing I didn't let him go. I begged him to stay with me, and he has.

I wish I could say that, if he'd told me back then, everything would be different. I don't know if that's the case. That Trish might've done just what my packmates feared and thrown away a good male for one she could never have. No, Duke needed the Trish that went through hell and came out on the other side of it a better match for him.

Do I think I deserve him? Not even a little. He's too good for me, though he begs to differ; that's why he tried to leave me, because he thought I'd be happy without him. Doesn't matter that he's wrong and I'm right. Selfish Trish marked him, she's mated him, and when he returns from tonight's council meeting, I'm going to make him my forever mate so that he can never try to leave me behind again.

Maybe then he'll finally get it through his thick skull that's the best thing that's ever happened to me...

I just... I can't imagine what's so important that Ryker needed to call his entire pack council to the den earlier this afternoon. Every single mature shifter in Accalia knows that tonight is the night of the full moon. Unmated shifters will be looking for some way to scratch the itch, bonded mates know better than to be separated when the Luna is at her peak, and an intended pair won't want to miss the one night of the month that their bond can be blessed and made whole.

The Wicked Wolf is no longer a threat to our pack. His Beta

and the few sycophants he still maintained after the Western Pack disbanded are either dead or underground. The upheaval that happened in the Fang City on the edge of pack land when the old head vamp was murdered back in February has finally settled down.

For once, there's no hint of a Claws and Fangs war on the horizon. The vampires are keeping to their own business, and the shifter world seems to be calm again after the Alpha collective decided that the Luna-touched female with the gift to break bonds isn't a concern to the rest of us.

Any traitors in Accalia have been sussed out. Aidan Barrow —may the Luna curse his soul—was the last one, and though I know Audrey will never get over her brother's betrayal, it's been almost a year since Shane disrupted Ryker and Gem's Luna Ceremony. We have an Alpha couple that has brought stability back to the pack after the loss of our last one, and I finally have my future to look forward to.

Claws crossed.

As long as my future includes Duke, I can handle anything life throws at me. I proved it already, and though I had to rely on the strength of my mate to get this far, isn't that what a mate is for? A partner in life, someone who can hold me up when I'm too tired, too weak, too frightened to stand? Someone that I can be possessive over, and claim as mine, whether by the marks on his throat or how deeply my scent gets embedded in his skin.

Duke smells like something musky. Something woodsy. A hint of pine, of course, but also cinnamon. He smells like me.

Over the scent of the roast I have resting on top of my stove, sides prepared for a pre-mating dinner I made specifically for Duke, I search for some hint of him. Though he didn't know why the meeting was being called, either, he promised he'd be back before it got too late.

That was three hours ago, and I'm still waiting.

It's fine. I'm not worried that he's not coming back. I'm not afraid that he's realized what he's getting into, or that he's rejecting me. I know Duke now. In some ways, I've always known him. He'll be here.

He has to be.

Through the whisper of a bond that stretches between us, I sense him before I catch his scent. Jumping up, I make sure that I look okay. Because we both know exactly how tonight's going to end, I changed into one of my old shift dresses while I was waiting for him to come back to me. No bra, no panties, just a simple dress that will make it easier to get naked once I have my male where I want him.

Running my fingers through my curls, I pronounce myself as ready as I'm going to get. I have to remind myself that, while performing the Luna Ceremony is a much bigger affair for the Alpha couple, tonight is just for me and Duke. He loves me no matter what I look like, and even if I didn't do my hair and put on some make-up, he wouldn't care.

Still, it's definitely a boost to my confidence when I throw open the door for Duke a second before he reaches for the knob and my male's jaw drops when he gets a good look at me.

He breaks the trance after a moment, hustling me inside and closing the door behind us. The first thing he does after that is swing me up in his brawny arms, giving me one hell of a kiss 'hello' before setting me back on my bare feet.

I grin up at him. "Well, that's definitely a way to greet your female, isn't it?"

His cheeks turn a little ruddy as a hint of a blush colors them. "Sorry. I guess I just missed you more than I thought."

Wrapping my arms around his middle, giving Duke a greeting of my own, I tell him, "Never apologize for missing me. Especially since I probably missed you more." I lay my head against his chest, squeezing him in a hug, then ask, "What happened at the meeting? Is everything okay?"

Duke's hand is laying on the back of my head. With a gentle stroke, he runs his fingers through my styled curls. "You wouldn't believe me if I told you."

"I might. Try me."

His hand lands on the small of my back. It's so nice to stay in this embrace, but that doesn't mean I'm going to let him get out of answering my question. He's got me curious now, and though this position makes it obvious that he's as ready to mate as I am, I waited three hours for him. I can wait three minutes more to find out what was so important.

Tapping him on his back—and, okay, putting a little pressure on his hard-on to catch his attention, I say, "Well?"

Duke sucked in a breath when I first made purposeful contact with his cock. Since he can tell that that's all the action he's going to get for now, he caves. Of course he does. This male will never me anything. "Okay. I'll tell you, but don't get mad."

My brow furrows. "Why would I get mad?"

"Because I spent the last hour listening to the other guys complain that their mates were going to go for their aching balls when we finally left. Turns out, the Alpha can be a bit of a prick. Gemma had to head into Muncie to take care of something, and since his mate wasn't going to be back until dark, he decided to distract himself by hosting a pack council meeting."

I shouldn't laugh. I was rubbing my pussy against the edge of my kitchen chair, I needed some kind of stimulation so badly, so Duke's right. I should be mad at Ryker for keeping my intended mate away from me for such a ridiculous reason. He had to wait to fuck his mate, so he made his right-hand wolves suffer, too.

I shouldn't laugh, but I can't help it. "Oh, Luna. I guess she made it back since you're here now?"

"Yup. As soon as he caught scent of her approaching Accalia, he kicked us all out." Duke finally joins me and chuckles, a husky sound that ruffles the top of my hair. "Good thing, too, because he was about to have a mutiny on his claws. Chains were the least of some of the suggestions the other guys were coming up with."

Yeah, right. I don't believe that for a second. Moon fever or not, Every shifter on the council is one hundred percent devoted to the Alpha. There might've been eight cases of blue balls going on in the den, but I don't doubt that the seven males on the council would cut off their own dicks before they challenged Ryker. He's earned their loyalty. Mine, too. If I had to spend my night crossing my legs tightly, trying to ignore my own need, I would've.

I'm just glad I don't have to.

With my hands pressed against his chest, I push far enough away from him that I can tilt my head back and meet his gaze without leaving the warm embrace of his arms. "You were that desperate to get to me?"

He presses a kiss to my lips. "Nothing will ever stop me from getting to you," he vows solemnly.

I believe him, too. Even when he was still part of Gem's guard, a trusted enforcer for the pack, he found his way to me in California. Following the side of a bond I never even knew existed, Duke tracked me to the cage they kept me in, then insisted on staying with me. He's been by my side ever since, and almost nine months from that moment, we're about to make it so that he'll never have to leave it again.

Luna willing, of course.

Standing up on my tippy-toes, I nip at his strong jaw, then dance out of his hold. Not because I want to put any distance between us. The opposite, actually. There's just something I want to see first, and I start for the other side of the room.

He can't help himself. Like a puppy on a leash, Duke is inches behind me, trotting after me as I dash over to the window. I swallow my laugh of delight. When the only thing I've ever really wanted was to be the *one* to someone else, it still amazes me that—after all I've done—the Luna gave this male to me.

Or, I think as he settles his big paws on my hips, she will.

His warmth makes me shiver. His innate scent, swirling with notes of mine, has me almost whining with desire. My wolf is happy for me to take the lead in this, but she's growing impatient. She wants her mate, and she wants him now.

So do I, girl. So do I.

Duke bows his head, trailing his nose along the column of my throat. I'm not even a little surprised when he stops at the white bite mark that stands out against my tanned skin. Since the night he gave it to me, he seems drawn to it. Nibbling that spot, lapping at it with his tongue... it's all the proof he needs that I'm proud to be his.

After he presses an open-mouthed kiss to that very spot, he nuzzles his cheek against my hair while I angle my head up, glancing up at the night's sky.

There. Completely round and glowing brightly on Accalia down below, I see the moon in all her glory.

It's time. I knew it; as a shifter, I can sense the Luna all the way down to my bones. Still, with my entire forever on the line, it doesn't hurt to double-check.

"You see that?" I whisper. "Isn't she beautiful?"

"I'm looking at the most beautiful creature I've ever seen."

There's something about the way Duke says that. Almost reverential, as if he's worshiping our goddess, but with a promise that reminds me of the vows he made when we were locked together in Walker's cells. Laying my hands over his, I twist my head just enough to get a good look at his face.

He's not looking at the Luna. His hazel eyes gone a soft gold, my male is staring unblinkingly at me.

Oh.

Heat rushes to my face. I shouldn't be embarrassed. Since the night I seduced him during the last full moon, we've been together countless times. The half-bond that formed when I inadvertently marked him without asking for his—or the Luna's —blessing has only become stronger; tonight, it'll be whole. He's told me that he's loved me before. His actions over the last nine months made his feelings for me even clearer.

But the way he's looking at me right now... for the first time in my life, I really feel as if another soul *sees* me.

And, thank the Luna, it's Duke Conlon.

"Dinner's ready," I tell him. "I made pot roast, potatoes, and carrots. And some cupcakes for dessert."

His lips quirk in a small smile. "My favorites."

It's amazing how a tiny little grin can turn this male from handsome to heart-stopping, but it does. Ah, Luna... I'm not so sure I can wait until dinner.

I swallow. "I know. That's why I did it."

We're shifters. We can say 'I love you' with a meal, and that's what I tried to do today. The roast and sides aren't probably as good as the cupcakes will be, but I don't think Duke cares. It could be burnt and he'd gobble it gladly because I made it for him, and we both know it.

When he lets go of my waist, lifting his hands to my cheeks, angling my head so that he can take my mouth, I think he got the message.

By the time he pulls away, we're both out of breath. Not from the kiss, though. This is need, pure and simple, the Luna's power rushing through us. I'm panting, and Duke's expression has become inexplicably hungry.

I don't think it's for food. Just in case, I check.

"Did you want me to set the table, or—"

Before I can finish, Duke swoops me up in his arms. He has one hand wrapped around my back, the other cradling my butt, and he has me in a bridal carry as he starts to stalk away from the window, toward my bedroom door.

As he arrives at the entrance to the kitchen, he pauses.

"Will it keep?" rumbles Duke. He's asking me about the dinner I prepared.

I nod. "It might be a little cold, though, if we get... distracted."

His eyes brighten. It seems as if "distracting" me is exactly what he has in mind. "I don't mind if it gets cold. Besides, that's what they invented microwaves for. So, if you're okay—"

That's my male. Always worrying about what I think.

Luna, I love him.

I throw my arms around his neck. "Dinner can wait. I can't. It's time, Duke. Make me yours."

He crosses the threshold into my bedroom. "You always have been. Even when you didn't know it... you were always mine."

Maybe that's true. If Duke believes it, I'm not going to argue. But when he lays me down on my bed, stripping off my shift dress and his own clothes before settling himself between my legs, I realize something. It doesn't matter. The past doesn't matter. The way he loved me from afar without saying a word to me, and how much time I wasted chasing a fantasy when I had my forever right there... none of that matters.

All that matters is that, after tonight, all of my white scars will turn silvery, our bond will be whole, and Duke will be mine until the end of time.

I might not deserve him, but that's not going to stop me.

After all, it never has before.

# AUTHOR'S NOTE

Thanks for reading *Bound by the Moon*!

That closes out the **Claws and Fangs** series — but not the universe! I have two other series set in the same world, including a rejected mates duet that features the Alpha, Bishop, and the story behind the broken mating between Raphael and Helene, Bishop's sister. Those books are *The Feral's Captive* and *The Beta's Bride*, where the fated mates split up and find forever with their chosen mates :)

I also have a new supernatural series with wolf shifters and witches! Prey, the first book in the **Wolves of Winter Creek** series is out now, and you can get a sneak peek of if you keep reading/scrolling/clicking.

*xoxo,*

*Sarah*

# SNEAK PEEK OF PREY

## THE FIRST BOOK IN THE WOLVES OF WINTER CREEK SERIES

You think that I would've gotten used to being bombarded by good-looking guys since I've been in Winter Creek—and then there's this guy.

When I first met Tristan, I thought of him as beautiful. Remy was striking.

My savior is just my type.

I didn't think I had one until now. None of my boyfriends had anything in common except a tendency to use me for sex and fun before moving on. I've been attracted to all kinds—and some women, too, not gonna lie—but I've never understood the phrase "love at first sight" until right this very second.

*It's just because he saved you, Fallon,* I tell myself. That gut punch of attraction is gratitude. The sudden possessiveness I feel for a man I just met is simply ridiculous.

Right?

I mean, I can't even pinpoint what exactly it is about him that has my palms going sweaty. About five years or so older than me, he has a sharp jaw and high cheekbones that are contradicted by a lush mouth and dark eyelashes that almost look like he's had them done. They frame a pair of amber-colored eyes, too orange to be hazel. Unlike the other two guys I've met in town, he's not clean-shaven. He has a five o'clock shadow that develops into a closely-cropped beard that covers the knife's edge of that masculine jaw. It suits the slight scowl on his handsome features.

Because he's totally scowling now that I can see his face.

That doesn't bother me. More than that, I get the feeling that I *know* him and the scowl is pretty much his default expression. That we're not just strangers who met in the weirdest of circumstances… and it hits me why I feel like this: I've seen him before. Only just a flash, and Tristan distracted me from staring then, but—

"I know you."

He straightens in his chair. "You do?"

"I, uh, yeah. I think I saw you in the town square a couple of days ago."

On the edge of the square, when I shivered because I felt like someone was watching me only to see a guy standing there on his own, nodding at Tristan.

"Possibly." He returns to his slouch, glancing at a point over my head instead of meeting my eyes. "I was there."

*Translation*: I don't remember seeing you—and if I do, it doesn't matter regardless.

Fair enough. I'd gotten so used to Tristan's flirting and Remy's not-so-subtle interest—that I will never return now, thank you very much—that I think it went to my head. Just because those two were interested in the new girl, it didn't mean every guy in Winter Creek was.

Maybe it's better that the man who saved me doesn't seem to know what to do with me.

Yeah, well, I don't, either.

"Anyway, I guess I should thank you." Obviously. "For the woods. And, um, bring me to—"

"My hunting cabin," he supplies.

I take the excuse to tear my gaze away from him, glancing around the room instead. Hunting cabin, he calls it. He isn't wrong. Opposite the chocolate-brown couch I'm perched on, there's a fireplace just behind his seat. There's a single wooden table next to him, a door to my right, and light brown walls covered with stuffed animal heads and weapons.

I notice a mounted stag's head—which, while creepy, is at least understandable—and an honest-to-God's wolf mounted opposite of the stag that has me doing a double-take. An ax is resting on pegs over the fireplace, a crossbow is pinned next to the stag head like it's part of the trophy, and he has lines of arrows posted on the other side of the bow.

Okay, then.

I feel a little bit better now that I notice them. I've got no shot when it comes to using a bow and arrow, but if I can wrangle that ax down, I have some way to protect myself if I have to.

"Anyway, you don't have to thank me," he adds, dragging my attention away from the sharp, silver edge of the ax back to him. "Anyone else would have done the same."

His matter-of-the-fact attitude has me momentarily forgetting about the weapons.

Anyone else would've helped me? Considering it was my grandmother and a dude who made it obvious he wanted in my pants who trussed me up in the first place, I doubt that.

I shrug, leaving it at that.

My savior allows it. Nodding at me, he says, "Besides, I'm more interested in hearing how you ended up tied to a tree in the first place."

I should've been expecting this. Of course he'd ask.

"What?" I offer him a crooked grin. "That sort of thing doesn't happen in Winter Creek often?"

## AVAILABLE NOW

PREY

### WOLVES AND WITCHES AND CURSES, OH MY...

I never believed in the paranormal mainly because I never had any reason to—at least, not until I received a telegram from a grandmother I didn't know existed, inviting me to a small town that was nearly impossible to find, full of shifters and witches that shouldn't be real.

Of course, I didn't know that until *after* I agreed to visit her in her secluded home.

When I pull into town, I almost regret my impulsive decision to take this trip. Bordered on all sides by rivers and mountains and dense forests, Winter Creek is a trap. Once you get in, it's just as difficult to leave. No one has cars here or internet service, and my own phone is a glorified paperweight as soon as I step off the train.

Speaking of the train... I discover too late that it arrives on its rickety tracks once a week if you're lucky. And, of course, there's the small matter of the curse.

Turns out there's a reason why my grandmother finally got in touch with me for the first time in twenty-five years. In Winter's Creek, there's a curse involving a coven of witches, the feral wolf who haunts the dark forest, and a woman from seventy years ago who looks enough like me to convince my grandmother that I'm the only one who can break it at last.

When I refuse, I discover that my grandmother isn't just the head witch of Winter Creek—she's the one responsible for the curse that's kept the town in stasis for the last seventy years. To break it, she's willing to do whatever she has to, including sacrificing me to the big, black wolf that's been lurking in the shadows, watching me since my arrival.

Because the beast in the woods is hungry, and I'm the perfect prey...

---

***_Prey_** is the first in a new rejected mates/fated mates series featuring Fallon Witt, a human woman who doesn't know anything about the paranormal—until she's thrown headfirst into it. While partly inspired by Beauty and the Beast, it also has elements of Little Red Riding Hood—though, in this series, the big bad wolf is the hero, and the grandmother is the true danger in the woods of Winter Creek...

# KEEP IN TOUCH

Stay tuned for what's coming up next! Follow me at any of these places — or sign up for my newsletter — for news, promotions, upcoming releases, and more!

Website
Newsletter

# ALSO BY SARAH SPADE

**Holiday Hunk**

Halloween Boo

This Christmas

Auld Lang Mine

I'm With Cupid

Getting Lucky

When Sparks Fly

Holiday Hunk: the Complete Series

**Claws and Fangs**

Leave Janelle

Never His Mate

Always Her Mate

Forever Mates

Hint of Her Blood

Taste of His Skin

Stay With Me

Never Say Never

Bound by the Moon

**Sombra Demons**

Drawn to the Demon Duke*

Mated to the Monster

Stolen by the Shadows

Santa Claws

Bonded to the Beast

Fated to the Phantom

**Stolen Mates**

The Feral's Captive

Chase and the Chains

The Beta's Bride

**Wolves of Winter Creek**

Prey

Pack

Predator

**Claws Clause**

(written as Jessica Lynch)

Mates **free*

Hungry Like a Wolf

Of Mistletoe and Mating

No Way

Season of the Witch

Rogue

Sunglasses at Night

Ain't No Angel

True Angel

Ghost of Jealousy

Night Angel

Broken Wings

Of Santa and Slaying

Lost Angel

Born to Run

Uptown Girl

A Pack of Lies

Here Kitty, Kitty

Ordinance 7304: the Bond Laws (Claws Clause Collection #1)

Living on a Prayer (Claws Clause Collection #2)

www.ingramcontent.com/pod-product-compliance
Lightning Source LLC
Chambersburg PA
CBHW020532310726
48979CB00014B/2307/J
*9781961594234*